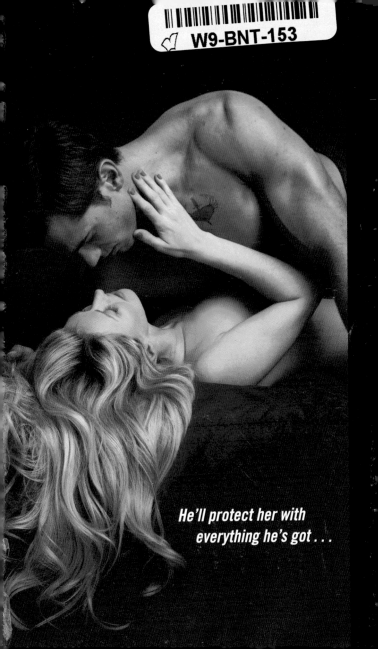

*He'll protect her with
everything he's got . . .*

SWEETNESS.

She'd heard everything he'd said. The passion with which he'd said it. The sincerity that burned from his gaze as the words had poured from his lips. But it was the term of endearment that reached into her chest and gripped her heart. For a long moment, they stood there, bodies touching, faces inches apart, his hands holding her in that firm but gentle way he had.

Thunder rumbled again, closer this time, and her heart was a drum beat double-timing inside her chest. If his hands didn't feel it racing, he'd have to hear it, because the sound was a loud *rush rush* in her ears. Beneath the sports bra and tank, her nipples went hard. If his gaze dropped, she knew he'd see, but she couldn't bring herself to feel self-conscious about it. Not when he was looking at her like he wanted to devour her.

His gaze dropped to her lips.

She shuddered, everything inside her but the smallest voice of reason crying out for him to do it. Just once.

"Tell me not to," he said, his voice a raw scrape.

By Laura Kaye

HARD AS YOU CAN
HARD AS IT GETS

LAURA KAYE

HARD AS YOU CAN

YOU CAN

A Hard Ink Novel

AVON

An Imprint of HarperCollinsPublishers

AVON BOOKS
An Imprint of HarperCollins*Publishers*
10 East 53rd Street
New York, New York 10022-5299

Copyright © 2014 by Laura Kaye
ISBN 978-0-06-226790-0
www.avonromance.com

First Avon Books mass market printing: March 2014

Avon Trademark Reg. U.S. Pat. Off. and in Other Countries, Marca Registrada, Hecho en U.S.A.
HarperCollins® is a registered trademark of HarperCollins Publishers.

Printed in the U.S.A.

10 9 8 7 6 5 4 3 2 1

Chapter 1

Crystal Dean hurried out of the private party room and let the fake smile drop off her face. Damn bachelor party. A lot of times, the groom-to-be was totally embarrassed by his buddies' surprise strip-club party, so things stayed low-key. No such luck tonight. Instead, her guest of honor was so rowdy, handsy, and intent on sampling the wares that she wished she could warn this slimeball's fiancée to run fast and hard in the other direction.

Not that Crystal was an authority on making good choices. Or else she wouldn't be working at Confessions, the strip club where her sorry excuse for a life had landed her as a waitress. Although, it wasn't like she'd had much of a choice. At least her wares weren't up for sampling . . . anymore. And she didn't strip or give "private shows" in the back rooms.

No, Crystal's boyfriend had shielded her from all that.

And, anyway, Bruno was too possessive to share her with anyone else. At least there was some benefit to his control-freak tendencies.

Hurrying down the dim, private hallway that threaded between the party rooms, Crystal ran through a mental checklist of what she needed to do. Another round of drinks for this party. Deliver the appetizers for her other party. Check in with Bruno to see if he was ready for dinner—

The door to the back parking lot wrenched open and a group of men—some who worked for her boss, Jimmy Church, the head of Baltimore's most notorious gang, and a few she hadn't seen before—poured into the narrow space. Crystal stepped back into the shadows, hoping to avoid their notice.

Decked out in a suit and tie that must've strained the resources of even a men's big and tall shop, Armand Lewis, or Big Al, guided the men down the other end of the hall toward Mr. Church's private lounge. The big guy was an Apostle, a senior gang member who had paid his dues, earned the operation some serious money, and proven his loyalty in a whole host of ways you just didn't want to know about.

With their dark slacks and jackets, nothing about the newcomers' appearance was particularly noteworthy, but they exuded an air of authority and self-assurance Crystal recognized. And the unusually subdued demeanor of Al's men proved she wasn't the only one.

She'd place good money she didn't have that these were the "guests" everyone had been preparing for and whispering about the past few days. Tensions had been tight as a rip cord around here. Crystal didn't know who they were or what their business with Church might be, and she didn't want to know. Ignorance—real or feigned—was a survival skill she'd honed early.

Thank God they hadn't seen her. She didn't want any part of whatever they were about.

Crystal was mid-sigh-of-relief when more men pushed through the door. Two of Church's goons struggled to get a barely conscious—and badly injured—man through the opening and into the hall right in front of her. Each of the guys held one of the man's arms over his shoulders, while the man's feet attempted to keep up but mostly couldn't. The poor man's head rolled on his shoulders, revealing bruised, delirious eyes and a busted lip. Dried blood left a trail all down the front of his dingy T-shirt, probably from that lip, or maybe his nose. And she really didn't want to know what the bundle of bloody gauze around his hand hid.

Goon Number One looked her way and did a double take when he noticed her standing there. "Bring some food. Room at the bottom of the stairs." Without another word, they dragged the guy down the steps into the basement, cursing and complaining and puffing as they went.

What the hell had the injured man gotten himself into? Because people only ended up in one of the basement rooms when they were being held against their will. She would know.

It was better all the way around to remain ignorant of the goings-on downstairs. Crystal hated herself a little for thinking that way, but it wasn't like she could do anything about it.

Snapping out of her thoughts, Crystal took off down the hall. Part of not being noticed around here was doing your job, doing it right, and doing it fast. It was a small price to pay for being left alone. Her rush toward the kitchen was why she didn't notice that a man had stepped through the curtained doorway that led into the main part of the club. She walked right into him, her body feeling the hard muscle of his chest at the same time her nose registered his scent—something crisp and clean, like he'd recently showered.

"Whoa," the man said, catching her in his arms.

Oh, crap. I can't believe I just did that. Guys around here never tolerated anything that might embarrass or annoy them, and they always enjoyed the opportunity to put someone in their place. The apology scrambled from her mouth. "Oh, my God, sir. I'm so sorry," she rushed out. Crystal shook her head, stepped back, and dropped her gaze until all she could see was the ridiculously sheer pink lingerie and heels she wore. Her uniform for working the private party rooms. "Please. I'm sorry."

"No harm done, darlin'." His voice was full of Southern charm, sweet and warm as fresh molasses. The smile in his tone drew her gaze up over the muscles his shirt did nothing to hide and, sure enough, he *was* smiling. And holy wow, this guy had a pretty-but-tough thing going on that was really freaking hot. His jaw and cheekbones were all hard angles, but his lips were full and playful, and his unusual gray eyes crinkled at the corners, like he might've been amused. "Say," he said. "We're company, and we got turned around when we went out to the bar. Any chance you know which way everyone went?"

Crystal forced her gaze away from his mouth and tilted her head back to meet those eyes. Maybe some of Big Al's visitors had come in through the front, too? But this guy just said they'd gone *out* to the bar, not come in through it . . . She looked over her pretty boy's shoulder into the eyes of two other men. An impatient intensity blazed out of both of their expressions, giving her the same authoritative vibe she'd gotten off of Al's guests a few minutes before. The guy in front of her arched a brow, more of that humor sliding into his eyes.

Her brain finally communicated with her mouth. "Uh." She glanced down the hall. "Well, some went to the private party room down that way, and some went downstairs with, um, the sick guy. I'm supposed to be getting him some food," she said, nearly breathless from the man's heat and his closeness and the niggling feeling in the back of her mind that something wasn't right about these men. But who was she to question?

Pretty Boy grinned. And, oh, boy, a playful sexiness just rolled off him until she was fighting the urge to squirm. Bruno would *kill* her—and probably this guy, too—if he saw how close they stood to one another. Her gaze flicked to the security camera above the curtained entrance, but it appeared they were just outside of its range. Thank God for small favors.

"That's where we're headed, too. Got a message to deliver." He winked and nodded his head to the side. "Just downstairs?"

Heart racing, Crystal swallowed and nodded. "On the left."

"You were very helpful . . ." His brows rose expectantly, and he gave her a crooked grin that tempted her to smile in return.

Bewildered, she stared at him, just soaked in all that easy charm and raw masculinity. And then she realized he was waiting for her to . . . *Oh!* "Crystal," she said. "You're welcome, sir."

Wearing a satisfied smile, he eased back a step. "Maybe I'll see you around."

Doubtful. "Okay." Seeing her chance to get away, Crystal took off again and didn't look back. Though the urge was definitely there.

Whatever. She had enough on her plate without fantasizing about a man she didn't want, couldn't have, and who probably wouldn't want her anyway.

Crystal made her way down the dim hallway to the far end, where offices sat behind a steel door. Unthinkingly, she entered the code onto the keypad, waited for the mechanical *click,* and stepped into the nerve center of Jimmy Church's gang operations. Or one of them, at least. Usually, the girls weren't allowed in here. But Bruno was one of the Apostles in Church's operation, just as her father had once been, and her association with those men earned her the privilege, such as it was.

She made her way through the empty outer office and to the second door down the hallway. With a knock on the frame, she leaned into the open door.

Bruno glanced away from the computer, and his expression slid into a scowl when he saw her. "Where have you been?" He rose and rounded the big mahogany desk that dominated the room and clashed with the wall of pin-ups: nude models, bad-ass motorcycles, and classic hot rods. Strip-club chic.

"Uh . . . I'm sorry. I've got two bachelor parties," she said, peering up at him and trying to gauge his mood.

With mountains of muscles built from steroids and hours spent lifting, Bruno Ashe was a wall of a man, his arrogance and ego filling the office and making him seem twice as big. Once, she'd thought his unruly brown hair softened the severity of his face, but now all she could see was the perpetual scowl he wore, made more pronounced by a scar from a knife fight on his cheek. God, how had she ever been attracted to him? How had she ever thought he was the answer to her problems? What she wouldn't give to go back four years and give her nineteen-year-old self a kick in the butt.

"Hmm," he said. "Next time you take care of me first."

Crystal found her fake smile and pasted it back on. "I'm sorry, baby." She rubbed her hand up his chest and died a little inside. "Can I take care of you now?" *Eight more months. Eight more months.*

Heat slid into his dark eyes, and he stepped closer until

he was looming over her. His arousal was obvious against her stomach. His brows rose in invitation . . .

And that one small gesture resurrected the memory of the man from the hallway. Just moments before, he'd had her pinned against the wall much as Bruno had her trapped against the door now. But Bruno possessed none of that man's charm and humor and breath-stealing good looks.

Crystal blinked the comparison away. What the hell was wrong with her? Bruno felt as entitled to her enthusiasm as he did her body. She forced the man out of her thoughts and wrapped her arms around Bruno's neck.

Bruno's cell phone vibrated, buzzing loudly against the top of his desk. Ignoring it, he kissed her, hard, demanding she open to him, give in to him. The ring cut off, then started right back again.

Groaning, Bruno pulled away with a look that commanded she stay right where she was, customers and everyone else who might need her be damned. He grabbed the cell like he wanted to strangle it. "What?" he answered. Lethal rage poured into his expression. "*What?*" Pause. "Who the fuck was it?" Pause. "How many? Did you get them?"

Crystal debated whether to stay or go. Whatever this news was, it was clearly going to occupy Bruno for a while. And given his black mood, she didn't really want to be around him.

As if her thoughts drew his attention, his gaze cut across the room to her. "You see anything unusual out there tonight?" he asked.

For a moment, she stared at him, not realizing he was asking her the question rather than the caller. "Oh. Me?" *Those men. Pretty Boy and his friends. Who went to the bar . . . but didn't have drinks.* Instinct placed the idea front and center into her head. "No. Nothing," she said. Because she didn't really know, and if she raised a concern and Bruno confronted those guys and they were legit? Uh, yeah. That would be all kinds of bad.

On the other hand, she'd just lied to Bruno.

Not that she didn't do it all the time. Crystal was well aware that much of her life was a lie, a charade, a play in a never-ending series of one acts wherein the climax determined whether she lived or died, remained free or got lost forever in the dark, seedy, underbelly of the world. Sad, sad fact that this place, this situation, this life wasn't even close to the worst there was.

And it was more than just herself she dutifully played her part for. Because when your father exacted a post-sentencing courtroom promise from you to do whatever it took to care for your younger, ill sister, you gave your word. And you upheld it like it was the oxygen you breathed. No price too great.

Not working at Confessions.

Not Bruno.

Not the scars on her back.

And the fact that her father had died in a prison-yard fight two weeks later had elevated the significance of her promise even more. Maybe that was why he'd demanded it of her in the first place. Maybe he knew something like that would happen, and it really would all fall on her.

Bruno turned away like she was of no further interest to him, and that was fine by her. "I want status updates every ten minutes. Find out if our other locations were hit, too. And find out who did this. I want their heads on a fucking platter, and I want them now." Given what it sounded like had happened, it was no surprise that Bruno was a volcano on the verge of erupting. As Church's director of security, this could fall on *his* head if he didn't get a quick handle on the situation. Bruno turned, and his eyes narrowed to slits. "Get out of here and close the fucking door."

Heart beating in her throat—from her lie, from the shock waves of Bruno's rage, from the news that someone had apparently attacked Jimmy Church's operations—Crystal closed the door, left the offices, and darted to the kitchen.

"Where have you been, Crystal?" Howie said, echoing Bruno but without any of the real annoyance of her boyfriend's tone. Confessions's longtime food-and-beverage manager had worked his way up from the bottom over a great many years, and as a result they'd known one another Crystal's whole life. He'd been friends with her father and fancied himself something of a father figure to her. She didn't mind.

"Sorry, Howie. Got held up."

She didn't need to explain. Not really. Knowing the way things worked around here, he nodded with a sigh. "Well, I had to put Macy on your parties. Both complained they'd been waiting—"

Her stomach dropped. "But I'm here now. You know I can—"

"It's done. With all that's going on around here tonight, you know they want everything running smooth as glass. So you're gonna have to split those tips. I'm sorry." His expression was full of genuine sympathy.

Damn. Church already withheld her hourly pay and half her tips to pay her father's debts, so having to split her tips further threatened to sink her stomach into her uncomfortable heels. Crystal refused to let it. If she allowed every little setback to knock her down, she'd be plastered to the floor by now. "Okay, I'm sorry, Howie. Listen, I need food for—"

The older man grasped a tray from the metal counter and handed it to her. "They called up looking for it," he said with an arched brow.

"Oh." She attempted a smile as she took the tray loaded

with a plate of chicken tenders, fries, and bottled water. Howie squeezed her shoulder, and she left.

Feeling like her head was on the chopping block, Crystal dashed down the private hall and rounded the corner that led to the basement steps. Damn, did she hate going anywhere near this part of the club. Horrendous memories and a desperate, miserable energy clung to the walls down here as if they were the varnish on the old, dark paneling. With a deep breath, she glanced around the tray and double-checked her footing on the first step down.

Commotion erupted from below, then a pounding sounded from in front of her. Two men barreled up the steps wearing masks. The first guy carried a gun aimed straight at her chest. And the guy in the rear held an unconscious man over his shoulder.

She rushed back, causing the bottle of water to fly off the tray, though her hands clutched onto the plastic as hard as her throat held on to the scream suddenly lodged there. Her brain attempted to process what was happening. Jimmy Church's operation had been infiltrated here, too? Jesus, who would risk pissing off the most notorious gang in Baltimore? And, *oh God,* no way this was a co-incidence after whatever Bruno'd learned on the phone. She'd win some big-time favor if she sounded the alert, if she could just get her voice to work.

All of a sudden, the men reached the top of the stairs, and, though they wore masks, Crystal recognized the steel gray eyes peering through the holes, the way that dark shirt hung over obviously defined muscles, the clean, masculine scent.

Pretty Boy.

Who the hell was this guy? And what kind of a death wish did he have?

Whoever these men were, they were busting Church's tortured prisoner out of here, and she couldn't help but think escaping this basement was an absolute good. No one deserved to be held against their will, tortured, abused, or—the thing that terrified her most—sold.

When she spoke, she wasn't sure what she would say until the words were coming out of her mouth. "There was a call. They'll be coming," she whispered, her chin dipped in case she was within the shot of the camera trained on the exterior door. "I have to scream now, and you have to hit me."

"*What?*" the first man rasped under his breath. Through the hole in the mask, his eyes were horrified by her demand.

"If you don't, they'll know I helped you. And I can't . . ." *What am I doing? Jesus, what am I doing?* "You have to. Please."

Hating her reality, she screamed so loud her throat hurt. She didn't have time for his morals, and neither did they. "*Please.*"

A storm rolled across those eyes. "Pretend to fall and cradle your stomach." The man swung a fist at her gut. She braced for an impact that never came. Relief and gratitude flooded through her as she played her part for the camera and threw herself backward, the tray of food flying to the ground with a thud. Her head and shoulder glanced off the wall, setting off immediate aches that had her moaning.

When she looked up, the space where the men had stood was empty.

But her scream had worked. Church's men came running. Crystal curled into a ball on the floor, attempting to make herself as small as possible to avoid getting trampled by the boots pounding down the hall toward the exterior door. The one through which two masked men had just stolen her corrupt and violent boss's prize prisoner.

With her help. Or, at least, without her hindrance.

Gunshots, shouts, and the squeal of tires against pavement erupted outside the heavy industrial door. More men ran past her. No one stopped or paid her any mind, like she was invisible. And in all the ways that mattered, she very nearly was.

Her head throbbed in time with the pulsing bass beat out in the main part of Confessions, the walls nearly alive with the sound. Fear and adrenaline barreled through Crystal's veins, making her shaky and unsteady as she pushed to her feet, trying not to step on the food scattered across the floor. Being upright exacerbated the ache in the back of her head. The one she'd caused herself. Because the man hadn't hit her like she'd demanded. He'd only pretended to.

Pretended.

Why had he only *pretended*? She'd *told* him to hit her. She'd had no choice. From the moment she'd seen him and his buddy hauling the unconscious prisoner up the basement steps, she'd known she would *have* to scream. On the injured guy's behalf, she was glad that he'd gotten free because she knew firsthand how many people got trapped in the clutches of Baltimore's Church Gang and never got out again, herself included. But no way could she be seen as helping them. Not if she wanted to live. And, more importantly, if she wanted Jenna to live.

Except, Pretty Boy had refused to hit her . . . A man who refused to hit a woman.

How freaking miserable was her life that a man such as that was so damn unique? Then again, maybe his seeming decency was just because she'd helped him.

"Crystal," came a voice full of menace.

Bruno. She adopted her meekest posture and cradled her stomach as if she'd really been struck, then turned toward her boyfriend and two of his lackeys, stalking down the hall toward her.

A wall of rage slammed into her a moment before his fingers dug into her upper arms. He nearly lifted her off the floor. "What the hell happened?"

Knowing how much he got off on his role as her protector, she let every bit of the fear she felt seep into her voice, swallowed hard, and shook her head. "I don't know. I was taking food downstairs, just like I'd been told. All of a sudden"—she gulped for air—"two armed men crashed into me, and one of them punched me and pushed me down." Crystal gingerly cupped the back of her head. "And then . . . I'm not sure. I . . ."

Bruno let out a sound that was almost a growl as he turned to the men behind him. "Check downstairs. Anyone else down there, shoot only to maim. We need answers first." The men hustled to obey, their feet heavy on the carpeted steps.

"What else did you see? Think." He shook her, the grip of his hands tightening, not an ounce of kindness visible in his gaze.

"Um, they were dressed in dark clothes. Had masks and guns. One seemed to be carrying something on his shoulder, but then the other guy hit me and I fell and they were out the door." No way she could admit to what else she knew. That she'd seen the faces under the mask when she'd given them directions, especially since she'd *known* something wasn't right. Such an admission would serve as a one-way ticket to hell of one variety or another—for her and maybe even her sister, too.

And she would do anything to make sure that never happened to either of them. Been there, done that, had the scars to prove it.

Bruno's callused hands eased on her skin. Suddenly, he yanked her into a fierce, breath-stealing embrace. "I will kill them for touching you," he said. The declaration was based more on outrage that his "property rights" had been violated when another man had dared touch her than actual concern. She knew that. But better his anger over her than suspicion of her.

Crystal burrowed into him, like she found solace in his arms. "I was so scared," she whispered, relishing the adrenaline shakes that gave credibility to her words. Sometimes she worried she was too damn good at acting, that maybe every time she put on one of these little shows, she lost a little more of whatever capability for honesty she'd once possessed.

As abruptly as he'd pulled her in, he pushed her away. She wobbled on her heels. "Wait in my office. I'll be back." Grasping her jaw almost painfully, Bruno kissed her hard. His lips and tongue demanded she respond, so she did. And then he was gone, out the same door through which the prisoner's saviors had gone.

Were they truly saviors? Were they even good guys? For the imprisoned man—whoever he was—she hoped so. Given Pretty Boy's revulsion at her words, her gut told her they were. And if there was one thing she'd gotten better and better at over the past four years of living this life, it was reading people, seeing them for who they really were. And her gut told her that the man with the gray eyes *was* a savior.

Just not hers.

No, when she found a way out of this mess—and she would, for both her and Jenna—it was going to be because *Crystal* got them out. No such thing as white knights or Prince Charmings or caped crusaders in her life, that was for damn sure. The one time she'd thought otherwise, she'd ended up with a man who had no qualms about hitting her.

Alone in the dim hallway, the events of the past few moments sank in. Trembling, thoughts scattered, body aching, Crystal made her way down the dim hallway to the office suite. As she had a little while before, she let herself in and moved through the inner sanctum to Bruno's office. Raised voices argued behind the door at the back of the suite. Crystal wanted no part of what might be going on in there. They'd wanted things *perfect* around here for Church's deal, and she suspected part of it might've been carried out the back door mere minutes before. If Church was in there, he was going to be hungry for blood.

And she was rather fond of hers.

She slipped into Bruno's office and held her breath as she closed the door so quietly, the latch didn't even make a noise. Her body molded to the black leather sofa that filled one wall, and cold suddenly painted over her skin as if someone had cranked up the air-conditioning. What she wouldn't have given for her comfy jeans and a sweatshirt instead of this ridiculous piece of lingerie.

Alone in the stillness of the room, the enormity of the risk she'd just taken for a complete stranger washed over her.

Tremors wracked her muscles, shaking her bones until the effort to hold it together hurt. So many times tonight she'd taken a chance. And for what? God, if she'd been seen talking to them, or hesitating before she screamed. Or if someone had noticed that the man hadn't actually punched her. Jesus, what if any of it had been captured by one of the security cameras?

She'd been conscious of them at the time, and her gut told her she was probably okay there. There were far more out front than in the rear of the building given that access was usually controlled so tightly. With two exceptions, the cameras all monitored the external doors. The only other cameras recorded who came through the curtain from the club floor and who went into the back offices. So, yeah. It was probably fine.

Please, God, let it be fine.

Hugging herself, she just barely managed to keep it together. Her gaze went blurry as she stared at a spot on the far wall and willed her emotions under control.

"Sara," she said, whispering her real name out loud. "Sara. Sara. Sara." Sometimes, saying the name out loud, the name no one but Jenna ever called her anymore, was the only thing that made her feel present in her body. Once, there'd been a girl named Sara, and her life had been good. One day, Sara would live again. "Sara. Sara. Sara."

Until then, she'd wait. And act. And survive.

Chapter 2

*S*till riding the buzz of last night's op, Shane McCallan ran down the empty street, dodging potholes, garbage, and the occasional discarded needle, and attempted to clear his head of the shitstorm that had parked itself in his cranium overnight.

The one that had featured his thirteen-year-old self, his eight-year-old sister, and the single biggest failure of his entire life.

Damnit all to hell and back, why had the nightmare returned?

Once a staple of his subconscious mind, he hadn't dreamed of Molly's disappearance for *years.* Not because the guilt didn't still eat at him—it did. And not because her loss didn't still weigh on his chest until it was hard to breathe, because that was true, too. Even all these years later.

But he'd perfected the art of driving himself into a state of exhaustion so acute his body shut down everything in favor of a few critical hours of REM sleep, his mind included. So he didn't dream anymore. *At all.* Not of Molly or anything else.

Until last night.

And good goddamnit if this wasn't just one more reason to hate Colonel Frank Merritt. If his former commander hadn't gotten greedier than a starving hog at feeding time, Shane would still have the job that wrung him out better than anything else he'd ever found, not to mention his friends, his professional reputation, and his honor. Instead, a year ago, Merritt had betrayed the Special Forces team he commanded to make a little coin on the side, resulting in the deaths of six good men on their team and the other-than-honorable discharge of the five survivors, himself included.

Turning a corner, Shane ran past a car up on blocks and stripped to its skeletal frame. He knew Baltimore had some rough neighborhoods, but this one was so run-down that both sides of the tracks were wrong. Why the hell had Nick and his brother opened a tattoo shop here, of all places? Abandoned buildings with boarded and broken windows and layers of graffiti covering the old brickwork were the norm. Close to the waterfront, the old, industrial area had probably once been hopping with port-related business. Now, it was just a sorry mess.

The blight and deterioration opened it up wide for criminal activity, which was why Shane had wanted to get out and eyeball the geography around Hard Ink for himself. Having taken a bullet during the getaway chase from Confessions last night, his shoulder wasn't in love with this idea. But it had only been a surface wound. No biggie. Still, it was goddamned ironic that the first time he'd ever been shot in his life happened *after* ten years of active duty service and innumerable deployments to all kinds of places nobody wanted to go. GSW or no, the former intelligence officer in him itched for a full rundown of their surroundings. Given the enemies they'd racked up in the past twenty-four hours, they needed all the intel they could gather. That the running might clear the cobwebs of the past from his mind was just a lucky twofer.

As his sneakers pounded out a rhythmic pace on the cracked blacktop, Shane pondered the return of the nightmare.

Maybe Nick Rixey was responsible for it. Wanting to help Becca Merritt, their former commander's daughter, find her missing brother, Shane's best friend—or former best friend, or whatever the fuck they were now—had called together what was left of their discredited and discharged Special Forces team for the brother's recon and rescue. And everyone from the team—himself, Edward "Easy" Cantrell, Beckett Murda, and Derek "Marz" DiMarzio—had dropped everything and come to Baltimore. Because that's what brothers did. Especially those forged by war and not blood.

So maybe the reunion, strained as it was by the fubar of a past they all shared and the danger of the present operation they didn't yet fully understand, was responsible for rattling things loose in his head that had long been secured in place.

Maybe.

Or maybe it was the operation itself. After all, it wasn't any great leap to think that finding and saving Becca's brother Charlie might've resurrected memories about Shane's own missing sister. The one no one had ever found and sure as shit hadn't saved.

Goddamnit all.

Where the street met the harbor, Shane rounded the next corner, mentally checking off another part of the map he'd studied before heading out. With the back of his hand, he wiped the sweat off his brow. Despite only being eleven in the morning, humidity choked the late-April air until it felt like he was running through molasses. Not that he really minded. Having grown up in southern Virginia, the heat was a welcome old friend. But the salt in his sweat stung the hell out of the injury on his shoulder.

Suck it up, McCallan.

Pushing himself harder, Shane picked up the pace, surveying the street as his thoughts continued to churn.

Or maybe someone else was responsible for shaking the subconscious skeleton from its closet. Maybe it was the woman he'd run into in the strip club where they'd found Charlie.

Crystal.

The first time he'd run into her—literally—she'd helped him unwittingly, thinking he belonged there. And, man, she'd been as beautiful as she was skittish. How a woman working in a strip club and wearing sheer lingerie managed to give off such a genuine, innocent vibe, he didn't know. But she had it—and then some. And the incongruity had been rolling around in his head ever since, like a pinball tripping sensors and ringing bells.

But the second time he'd run into her? When she hadn't prevented their getaway from the club? When it was clear he had no business there? Her terror had been apparent in the blaze of her green eyes and the tremble of her voice, but whatever mental calculus she'd run had come down in his favor. And she'd helped him—or at least hadn't hindered him—on purpose.

Yet, she so greatly feared someone there thinking she'd been complicit in his actions that she'd insisted he hit her.

The surreal nature of the request sent him reeling all over again. Shane couldn't remember the last time he'd been as gobsmacked.

Not even when Nick had called out of the blue after months of ignoring Shane's emails and phone calls and said he'd found a possible lead into the cover-up that'd gotten them booted from the Army.

The woman had freaking demanded he *hit* her.

Who *did* that?

And what kind of people did she know that made her expect he'd actually do it? It told him a lot about the green-eyed girl. That she was scared. And felt vulnerable. And thought punishment was a real threat.

That she was in trouble.

What the hell had happened to her after their cut and run? The possibilities were endless. And mostly piss poor.

And the wondering had nagged at him all night, right alongside his nightmares of Molly.

So, yeah, maybe concern for this woman, who was clearly caught up in a bad situation, had triggered all these old thoughts of his sister. Because Molly had never been found. He had no idea if she'd been killed right away. Or if she'd suffered a lifetime of imprisonment and abuse at the hands of some sicko. Or if she could be alive and in trouble, even now.

Like Crystal.

Another thirty minutes, and Shane had completed his circuit of the neighborhood around Hard Ink, his team's home base of sorts in their newest covert mission: to figure out how Charlie's abduction might be related to the cover-up of their commander's activities that got them a one-way ticket right out of the loving arms of Mother Army. Shane had been dubious as all hell that a connection actually existed, especially when he saw how into Becca Nick was. The man had clearly been thinking with his more southerly head. But the things Charlie told them after they'd rescued and patched him up last night made it clear that Nick was right.

Given the tension between himself and Nick, it rubbed Shane's ass a little raw to admit that, but there *was* a connection. And it gave Shane and the rest of his former teammates the first honest-to-God lead into the real reason behind their discharge. No way in hell he could walk away from that. None of them could.

Because they weren't just fighting for their own honor. They were also fighting for the honor of six good men who could no longer stand up for themselves. Doing right by those men wasn't a choice, it was a duty.

A half block out from Hard Ink, Shane slowed to a walk. The Rixeys owned the entire L-shaped building that sat at one corner. The place was a whole lotta nondescript red brick from its former days as a warehouse. Nick's younger brother Jeremy had rehabbed a fair chunk of the building, including the space for what was apparently a very successful tattoo business, at least according to Nick.

Shane had nothing against ink—in fact, he had quite a few pieces himself—but it still tripped him out to imagine that his hard-ass Special Forces teammate had the patience, precision, and artistic skill to put needle to skin himself. Man, they were a bunch of friggin' chameleons, weren't they? Changing and adapting as conditions dictated.

Just like they'd been trained to do.

And while Shane had landed on his feet with a decent job at a defense contractor, he almost thought Nick had the better approach in doing something entirely different from what they'd done in the Special Forces. Because being benched on the sidelines of a game you could only advise on but never again play sucked big, hairy donkey balls.

Like there were any other kind.

It was actually nice taking a little leave from the day job—he'd made the call to his superior right before setting out on the run. Question was just how much time this op was going to take. And was Shane going to have enough time or end up having to choose between a paycheck and justice. Because that was really no choice at all.

Rolling the aches out of his shoulder, Shane reached the driveway to their large gravel parking lot and caught movement from the corner of his eye. Jeremy Rixey was up on a ladder, while Nick and Marz stood on the ground calling directions up to him.

Every time Nick tried to talk, Jeremy started drilling into the brick. Trademark grin on his face, Marz adjusted the coiled black cable in his hands and shook his head as the brothers traded insults.

"Look, I'm just wondering if—"

Whirr, whirr, whirr.

"Dude, I know what I'm doing," Jeremy said when he paused the tool. "Either let me do this or get your moody ass up here instead."

Shane cut up the driveway toward them. "How many prior military does it take to drill in a screw?" he asked.

"None," Jeremy, the only civilian among them, called down with a smile and a wink. "Obviously." With their dark hair and pale green eyes, Jeremy and Nick looked a helluva lot alike though Jer's hair was longer and his skin bore far more ink. Nick didn't have any tats showing around the white T-shirt and jeans he wore—and neither did Shane, because tattoos were too readily identifiable in the field, but Jeremy had full sleeves, writing on his knuckles, and pieces on his neck, too.

"Becca saved you some pancakes," Nick said over the *whirr* of the drill. "But somebody probably snagged 'em by now. Where'd you go?"

Shane studied the man who'd been his team's second-in-command and his longtime best friend. After they'd been discharged and sent stateside last year, Nick had pulled a disappearing act and turned his back on Shane like they hadn't fought and bled at one another's sides for the past six years. And that bullshit had cut. Deep. "For a run and a little recon," he finally said. "What's up here?"

"Security cameras and motion-activated lights," Marz said.

Shane smiled at the guy. "Boys and their toys."

"Damn straight." Marz was their guru for all things computer and technology. The man had a scary kinda smarts where anything technical was concerned, which made him one of their key assets. Always had. In fact, it had been Marz who'd found a way to give them some eyes on the locations they'd raided to search for Charlie the previous night.

Fuckin' A, it was good to see the man healthy and standing on his own two feet again—even if one of them was prosthetic. Shane and Marz had talked from time to time, but before their reunion two days ago, the last time Shane had seen him was in the rehab unit of a hospital. Of all the survivors of the ambush that had revealed their commander's dirty little secret, Marz's injuries had been the most catastrophic. He'd lost part of a leg to a grenade, and Shane and Nick had worked together, despite Nick's own gunshot wounds to his back, to staunch the bleeding and keep him alive. Where the rest of them could be moody bastards, Marz was and always had been one happy, optimistic fucker. Drove them all batshit sometimes. But absolutely nothing got the guy down—at least not for long. The rest of them could learn a thing or two.

Shane scanned the brickwork closest to the street and found a new camera-and-light fixture already installed. "How many are you putting up?"

"All the way around the building," Nick said. "Street front's done. Just need to do two more points in the back."

"Okay, hand it up," Jeremy called. Nick grabbed the unit out of the box and climbed the ladder high enough to do the handoff. Marz put a steadying hand on the aluminum as he fed them the cable, then backed off as Nick neared the ground.

"We're also installing a fence around the parking lot," Nick said. "Jer's got a client with a fencing company, so he called in a favor, and the guy will be by to install it this afternoon. Easy and Beckett went with him to help haul the materials."

Shane nodded. "Shit, I wish I'd have known. They could've taken my truck."

Nick thumbed over his shoulder with a smirk. "Way ahead of you."

Frowning, Shane walked far enough to see that his big, black F150 was gone. He arched a brow at Nick.

"Don't give me that look. You would've offered. We just skipped a step." The guy's smile was tentative, like he was testing the waters and knew they might be infested with sharks.

"Sons o' bitches," Shane groused. But Nick was right. He wouldn't be here if he wasn't willing to do anything to help figure this situation out. And security had to be a part of that. "Fine. They scratch it all up, though, and I'm taking it out on your hide."

Nick's smile turned indulgent, and he nodded. "Well, you can try."

The drill let out an unhappy, high-pitched whine, and Jeremy cursed, drawing Shane's gaze. Shane let go of the retort sitting on the tip of his tongue as an idea parked itself in his frontal lobe. "You know, while we're at it, we should consider a few remote cameras on the approaches to this building. Give us a way to see what might be coming at us before it gets here. Saw a few places on my run that'd be perfect."

"I was thinking the same thing," Marz said. "Tell me where you want 'em, and I'll make it happen."

"I wish I could say this was all overkill," Shane said. But after last night, when they'd raided two locations of Baltimore's most notorious gang, stolen back Charlie, and engaged in gunfights with Jimmy Church's men, the shit was on, and it was deep. And it wasn't like they could go to the authorities, not after they'd found solid evidence that Church had the cops in his pocket. So, their enemies were highly sophisticated, apparently numerous, and not fully known—a trifecta of luck so bad that if it were raining pussy, they'd have gotten hit with a big dick. So, yeah, these precautions were right on the money.

Nick's gaze narrowed and went distant for a moment, then he nodded. "You and me both. But we've still got more questions than answers at this point, and too much at stake to take any chances."

It went without saying that Becca Merritt had to be on Nick's mind. Three days ago, her house had been ransacked and someone had tried to snatch her from her workplace at University Hospital, so she was living here while this situation got resolved. But something told Shane she'd be staying at Hard Ink even once everything was said and done. Any man with two eyes and half a brain could see that the search for Becca's brother had forged a tight bond between her and Nick. The kind that had a decent shot of lasting forever.

Shane totally got it. Because Becca had proven herself again and again in the short time he'd known her. By staying strong. By pitching in. By putting herself in harm's way to help their mission.

And by being the first person to ever apologize for the fubar that had stripped them of their careers, their uniforms, their honor.

Given all she'd done, Shane was as committed to her

safety as Nick. Especially because whoever had wanted their commander's children so badly wasn't going to give up. Someone believed Charlie and Becca had knowledge of their father's black ops in Afghanistan, and no doubt they'd keep coming until they got what they wanted. Or died trying.

"How's the shoulder?" Marz asked, as Jeremy made his way down the ladder.

"Eh. I'll live." Shane shrugged. "How's the leg?" He grinned. Marz had taken three gunshots in last night's firefight, all of them miraculously shooting through the bottom half of his right pant leg, the one that was mostly empty save for the metal rod of his prosthesis.

Marz barked out a laugh. "Good as new, baby."

Jeremy climbed down the ladder, shaking his head. "You guys are a little twisted."

"Says the guy wearing a T-shirt with a log-holding beaver asking, 'Are you looking at my wood?'" Shane said. Jeremy had a whole collection of dirty and irreverent shirts, apparently.

Everyone chuckled.

"Hey, I never said I had a problem with twisted." Jeremy hefted the ladder and moved it to the next position.

Everyone halted as a three-legged puppy came bounding down the driveway.

"Speaking of twisted," Shane said, earning a few more chuckles. Becca had rescued the German shepherd from scavenging the hospital trash cans a few days before, and now the cute mutt with a pair of inordinately huge ears had everyone wrapped around her oversized paws.

"Dude, no making fun of Eileen," Marz said, scooping her lanky black-and-tan body into his arms. Their shared missing-leg status had created a huge soft spot in the man's heart for the puppy.

"Who, me?" Shane reached over and gave her silky ears

a quick stroke. "Besides, how could I possibly make fun of a three-legged puppy with cartoonish ears named Eileen?"

"Last night you claimed credit for the name," Nick said. "Even though I was the one who sang Becca the song."

"Don't remind me. The memory of you down on your knees singing eighties anthems is burned into my brain forever. Besides, you're just mad that Becca liked my name best."

The smirk on Nick's face made it clear he was gearing up for a juicy retort, but just then, Becca rounded the corner from the back of the building. The woman was all-American-girl pretty, with blond hair, blue eyes, and a warm, bright smile. "You guys aren't making fun of Eileen, are you?" A chorus of negatives rang out, and Becca rolled her eyes. "You totally were. You're going to give her a complex." She nuzzled the puppy in Marz's arms. "It's okay, pretty girl. Don't listen to them."

"You *know* I wasn't doing anything but loving her. These guys, though . . ." Marz shrugged.

"Hey, don't throw me under the bus. I didn't say a word," Jeremy said, leaning the ladder back against the building. "It was these assholes." He pointed at Shane and Nick.

Shane had a defense on the tip of his tongue, but Becca turned her feigned outrage on Nick. "How could you?"

Nick nailed his brother with a glare as he stepped right into Becca's space. "I didn't say a damn thing, sunshine. Promise."

"Uh-huh," she said, trying to hold back a grin as Nick kissed her cheek.

Shane turned away and busied himself with filching a bottle of water from the box that held Marz's supplies. The H_2O was warm but did the job.

"Okay, you two. Get a room," Jeremy said.

"Aren't you the one who supposedly walks around naked?" Becca asked, crossing her arms.

Jer reached for the button on his jeans and tugged it apart. "No, but your wish is my command, sweetheart." He winked, stomping all over Nick's most exposed nerve. Shane rather respected the younger Rixey's ability to get under his brother's skin. Nick was usually buttoned up pretty damn tight.

Nick's glare slipped into an outright scowl as he pulled Becca in tight and buried her face in his chest. "Quick. Hide your eyes, or you'll be scarred for life."

Her laughter was free but muffled. "It's not my wish, Jeremy, it's not my wish," she said. She pulled back, face all squinched up, and asked, "Is it safe yet?"

"Yeah, yeah," Jeremy said. "Just know it's a standing invitation."

Nick darted around Becca and tackled Jer before he even knew what hit him. The tussle turned into a full-out wrestling match.

"They really *are* like twelve-year-olds when they're together, aren't they?" She shook her head, but the affection for both of the Rixeys was clear in her expression. "Whenever you guys are done, I was hoping someone would take me to the grocery store, so I can pick up everything I need for our special dinner."

Before they'd gone out on the mission to rescue Charlie, Becca had promised they'd celebrate his safe return with a big meal of everyone's favorites. It'd been a nice way of letting the team know she believed in them. Sitting down around a table and catching up with old friends, and some new ones, too, sounded like something they could all use.

"Gimme ten to shower, and I'll be happy to take you," Shane said.

Becca's eyes widened in surprise, making it clear Shane had some fence-mending to do there. He hadn't exactly given her the warmest reception when they'd first met because he'd let his feelings about her father color his reaction to her. Big mistake. She deserved better.

"Your truck's gone, remember? I'll take her," Nick said. Right.

"Why don't you both go?" Jeremy said. "Derek and I have this under control and, given everything, maybe you should both go with her."

Shane shrugged and, after a moment, Nick nodded. "Go take care of your swass and swalls, then, McCallan," Nick said.

Shane threw a punch as he passed the guy, but Nick dodged with a laugh.

"What the heck are swass and swalls?" Becca asked.

"Sweaty ass and sweaty balls," Shane, Nick, and Derek said in unison.

"Oh. Ew," Becca said amid the men's chuckles. "Yes, do take care of that, Shane."

He grinned over his shoulder and tossed off a salute. "Ma'am, yes, ma'am." Leaving the joking and laughter behind him, Shane hightailed it inside and took the industrial staircase two steps at a time. In the quiet of the stairwell, the questions that had plagued his run returned, but this time they came with something of an answer.

He couldn't do anything to save Molly. Sixteen years too late for that.

And he couldn't control his subconscious.

But he could find out what had happened to Crystal after they left. The question was just when to go, how to approach her, and how to keep from getting caught. Oh, and how to get the guys on board with the plan.

Easy as sin.

Right? Probably not. But Shane was like an old dog with a new bone when he wanted to be. And this was one of those times.

Chapter 3

$\mathcal{I}$'d like to propose a toast to Becca, for bringing us all together. And for this amazing meal," Shane McCallan said, raising his glass and hoping it would help make amends with her.

Becca smiled and ducked her chin as Nick pulled her in snug against his side. All around the makeshift plywood-and-sawhorse table, glasses went up along with appreciative comments about the incredible dinner Becca had spent the day preparing. A mountainous platter of fried chicken, huge crock of homemade meatballs, overflowing bowls of mashed potatoes and roasted vegetables, and a plate of fresh corn bread stacked a mile high filled the table, not to mention an apple pie *and* a chocolate cake. It was all the favorites everyone had asked for to celebrate Charlie's rescue.

And what they'd accomplished was worth a celebration because they'd been ass deep in alligators. Dumb luck had played far too great a role in everyone making it home safe and mostly sound. They only had a few scars to show for it, thanks to Becca's skilled nursing.

"You're more than welcome," Becca said, raising her own glass. "But I have to make a toast of my own. To each of you—" She swept her gaze around the table, from Nick beside her, to Shane at the end, to Jeremy and Easy across from her, and to Beckett and Marz on her other side. "This dinner does not begin to be enough to thank you for everything you've done for me and Charlie, nor are my words. But know I'll do everything I can to help you right the wrong that was done to you. And that you all have a place in my heart. So, to each of you."

The toasts were more subdued this time, but the expression on every man's face made clear the respect he felt for Becca.

"Now, let's eat!" she said with a big smile.

"I hope there's enough," Jeremy said, setting off a raucous round of laughter.

"You think he's kidding," Nick said. "Boy might be skinny, but he can pack away some chow."

As everyone filled their plates, Shane glanced around the table and took a long pull from his beer. The group of old friends—and a few new—ate and laughed and joked and shared stories. Hard to believe they'd only been reunited for a few days.

The food and the conversation were great, but the restless energy that had buzzed through Shane during his run, at the grocery store, and as they worked with Jer's friend to install the barbed-wire fencing still flowed through Shane's veins so fast and so thick he could barely sit still. Over this goat fuck of an operation. Over the cover-up that had changed everything for him. Over the woman he'd met last night and what might've happened to her after they bugged out of there.

Crystal.

"You okay, Shane?" Becca asked.

He smiled. "Happy as a pig in a poke. Food's delicious."

Becca laughed.

"Try to restrain your inner redneck, there, McCallan," Easy said with the hint of a grin. You might've thought a big black guy from inner-city Philly and a good old boy from the South wouldn't get along, but Shane and Easy had been fast friends from the beginning. In fact, Shane was responsible for crafting the guy's nickname out of the initials of his full name, Edward Cantrell. And Easy, well, Easy was responsible for almost single-handedly holding off the tangos who'd ambushed their convoy, giving Shane, trained as their team's backup medic, time to patch up the damage a grenade had inflicted on both Derek and Beckett.

Shane held out his hands. "Gotta be who I am."

Easy chuckled. "Well, be who you are without hogging the mashed potatoes. Pass 'em on down here."

Before long, everyone was clearing away their paper dinner plates in favor of clean plates for dessert. By the way they all attacked the cake, pie, and vanilla ice cream, you'd have never known they'd just demolished a veritable feast.

After inhaling his first piece of chocolate cake, Jeremy scooped another wedge onto his plate. "What?" he said as he dug in.

"Nothing." Becca smiled, affection for the younger Rixey plain on her face. "Eat up."

Nick stabbed his fork into Jeremy's cake and scooped a huge chunk for himself.

"Hey!" Jeremy yelled, scowling and tucking the plate against his chest and that ridiculously awesome beaver T-shirt.

Nick grinned and winked at Becca. Man, the guy had pulled a total one-eighty in the days since they'd been re-united. From sullen to almost playful. Well, as playful as war-hardened soldiers who had been cheated out of their careers by betrayal and corruption could be. Sonofabitch. But, one thing was for sure, Nick Rixey wore a new light-ness like a second skin.

No matter how tense things were between him and Nick, no matter how pissed he was at Nick's silent treat-ment for the past year, Shane couldn't begrudge the guy a slice of happiness. Not after everything they'd been through together.

Watching Nick and Becca smile and touch and just find solace in one another's presence set off an old ache in Shane's chest. Because he would never have that with someone.

God knew he didn't deserve it.

There were some things you could never atone for.

Molly's eight-year-old face came to mind. With her freckles, dimples, and pigtails, his sister had defined cute-ness. She'd looked up to him like the sun rose and set at his feet.

And he had failed her so spectacularly that the guilt and grief had been imprinted into his very DNA. *God,* in the list of moments he'd accumulate in his lifetime that he wished he could take back, telling her to go away and leave him alone would never, *ever* be surpassed. Because an hour later, she was gone. On his watch. Forever.

So solitude was his penance. Not that it was enough. Not that it would *ever* be enough.

Jesus H. Christ, this is supposed to be a celebration, McCallan.

A *click* sounded at the door to the warehouse-turned-gym, now their situation room in an operation they were still trying to make heads or ass out of. Nick's friend

Miguel Olivero entered. "Look who I found wandering the halls," he said in the jovial tone Shane already associated with the private investigator. Miguel ushered Charlie in through the doorway, Eileen hot on their heels.

Becca flew to her feet. "Charlie, what are you doing up?" She rounded the table and rushed to his side. The guy had been racked out in Nick's sister's room in the apartment across the hall since the early hours of the morning. Charlie looked about a thousand times better than when they'd grabbed him from the basement of Church's strip club, but it was still possible a hard wind could blow him over. Not surprising given he'd been dehydrated, tortured, and maimed at the hands of the Church gang less than twenty-four hours before. A ball of gauze surrounded his right hand, shielding the stumps of the two fingers he'd lost. Shane had to give him props, though, because the guy hadn't spilled a bean to the gang about the information his computer hacking had apparently revealed.

That someone or something named WCE had made a shitload of deposits totaling $12 million to a Singapore bank account in Frank Merritt's name.

"Eileen had to go out," he said, his voice like sandpaper. While Charlie's dark blond hair was just long enough to be pulled back in a knot at the nape of his neck, his blue eyes, height, and lankiness all resembled his old man.

After learning about the money, Charlie had suspected his father was on the take, so he'd dug into the old man's affairs, too, which led him to Nick. But his online "research" had apparently been noticed—by who they didn't yet know—because Charlie had been kidnapped by the Church organization and interrogated about a whole host of things, including how he knew about the account, whether he had the passcode for it, and what else he knew about his father's activities.

Becca and Miguel led Charlie to the folding chair next

to Jeremy, then Miguel took the last empty chair next to Nick. The eight of them made up the "team" responsible for saving Charlie's life. The newcomers dug into plates of food Becca had set aside for them.

As everyone cleared their plates, Nick excused himself, crossed the room to Marz's makeshift computer desks in the back corner, and returned with a legal pad. Sitting again, he said, "We need a game plan."

Murmurs of agreement echoed the sentiment.

"These were the questions we came up with last night. First, who or what is WCE? Second, how was Merritt connected to them and to Church?" He stabbed his pen against the paper as he articulated each of the questions. "What were they looking for when they ransacked Charlie's and Becca's houses. Who was Church's company at the club? And what do the codes we found in Becca's bracelet go to?" He scanned the group. "What am I forgetting?"

"We also need to find the pin to access the funds in Merritt's bank account," Marz said. Charlie nodded weakly as Nick made a notation on the pad.

Beckett sat forward, his shoulders like mountains and his expression like stone. He was one of the most reserved men Shane knew. Absolutely lethal in the field, he never met a piece of equipment he couldn't use, fix, or make work better. Second to Marz's prosthesis, Beckett bore the most visible scars from their ambush in the shrapnel marks around his right eye and the limp resulting from the complete reconstruction of his left leg. "It's a bigger question, but deserves a place on the list. Who made the cover-up in Afghanistan possible? Because that shit didn't happen on its own."

"That's the damn truth," Nick said as he added the question. "What else?"

Charlie cleared his scratchy throat. "Well, I thought of something else."

Conversation ground to an immediate halt, and all eyes swung to him. In a number of ways, he'd become the lynchpin to their investigation because he'd met their enemies, been on the inside, *and* his separate knowledge of Merritt's black ops got them around the nondisclosure agreement that they'd been forced to sign to avoid a one-way trip to Leavenworth. Anyone tried to accuse them of opening their traps about the truth, Charlie's own first-hand knowledge would offer a big old CYA.

"What is it?" Becca asked when the tension became a physical presence in the room.

The guy's gaze flickered around the table, nervousness rattling off him. "I just don't know if it's relevant."

"Everything's relevant at this point," Nick said.

Shane sat forward in his seat. "Damn straight." Everyone had acceded to Becca's wishes not to push Charlie, given his condition, but the former intel officer in him was chomping at the bit for a methodical debrief.

Looking at his plate, Charlie said, "I wasn't the only one they were holding." He let that information hang there for a moment, then continued. "In the first place they held me, there were three women. I didn't see them, but I could hear them crying, and other stuff." Pissed-off murmurs erupted around the room, and Shane tugged his hand roughly through his hair. "When they brought me to the club, there were another two in the room they put me in. Looked out of it, like maybe they were drugged. But then I passed out, and . . ." He shook his head.

Ice slid through Shane's blood. If there had been women in with Charlie, they were gone by the time they'd found him. Where had they been taken? "How old were they?" Shane asked.

"Didn't see the first women. Just heard them. The other ones were young, though. If they were twenty, I'd be surprised."

Shane's fists curled. Molly would've been twenty-four this year. It was close enough that the thought of those women—clearly held by Church against their will—conjured up all of the terrifying nightmares that had always plagued him about his sister's disappearance. He shuddered.

"Anything else?" Nick asked.

"I don't know why they were holding them, but I don't think it had anything to do with why they were holding me." Charlie pushed his plate away, most of the food untouched.

Easy scowled. "Lotsa reasons why an organization like Church's would be grabbing women. None of 'em good." Murmured agreements went around the table.

"Sounds like human trafficking," Shane bit out.

Nick raised a hand. "Why do you think there wasn't a connection, Charlie?"

"I heard them say that the girls in the room where you found me were for Azziz and to put them in storage for a delivery."

Put them in storage? What kind of sick fuck? "Which brings us back to my interpretation," Shane said with barely restrained rage. "Did you hear any more about this meeting or who Azziz is while you were with them?"

Charlie shook his head, but his gaze went distant. "Wait," he blurted out. "Right after they took my fingers—" His gaze cut to Becca's. "Sorry." Sadness filtered into her expression. "Um, after that, the one guy got a call. He confirmed a delivery on Wednesday night. I don't think he said a name, but I was kinda out of it. But he definitely called it a delivery, then, too." He shrugged.

Shane's brain turned this new information round and round and teased through the pieces, trying to figure out how they—

"That shit stinks. But as much as I hate to say it, I think you're right. Whatever's going on with those women, it doesn't sound like our battle," Nick said, heaving a troubled sigh.

Pulling himself from his thoughts, Shane's gaze whipped toward his former superior. "What?" Nick's expression was grim. Blood pounded behind Shane's ears in a thunderous rush, and he surveyed the group until he was sure his words would be calm, measured. "You think we should just leave them there?"

"I don't think we *should*. I think we have to, and I resent the hell out of that fact. But we are outmanned, outgunned, and operating around way the hell too many blank spots—"

"Jesus, Nick. *De oppresso liber,*" Shane spat the Special Forces motto like an accusation, unable to restrain his inner asshole where this topic was concerned. But they'd devoted their lives to freedom for the oppressed, and he had no intention of giving that up because his uniform had been stripped from him.

A storm rolled in behind Rixey's gaze. "Damnit, Shane. Don't think for a minute I don't burn to free anyone those scum might be holding. But there are only five of us. We don't have the men or resources to take on the world, no matter how righteous those battles might be."

Beckett sat forward. "Let's say it is human trafficking. Who are they trading the women to and for what? Plenty of trafficking in Afghanistan. Maybe they're using the girls to buy off the warlords or grease the wheels with Afghani customs officials. I don't know. But it might be worth learning more about whatever this delivery is on Wednesday night. How to get the women to safety, if there even are any, is a problem for another day."

Shane studied Nick's expression while Beckett laid out

his argument and saw the words hitting home. If Shane had come at Nick with logic instead of emotion, maybe the room wouldn't be so tense right now.

Nick nodded. "Fair point. We'll add the who, what, when, where, why of that delivery to the list."

His teammates all nodded, and damn if the regretful expressions they sent his way weren't a smack in the ass. The guys knew each other's weaknesses. They had to. So, they knew about Molly, knew Shane had a mile-wide need to save women in trouble, knew it was Shane's biggest exposed nerve. Which he'd just proven by attacking Nick when he hadn't deserved an ounce of the grief. Shit.

Shane gave a tight nod. "Then we have to get back inside Confessions. That waitress could be our key," he said, looking at Nick and thinking about Crystal. Would she know anything about those girls? Christ, was she a victim of trafficking herself? The thought nearly had the food he'd just eaten burning a hole in his gut. "She didn't give us away, so maybe she'd be willing to help us."

"You have to go back in?" Becca asked Nick, her fair skin paling to a shade just this side of death.

Nick opened his mouth to respond, but Shane beat him to the punch. "No, not Nick. Me."

"Shouldn't be either of you. Not Easy, either," Beckett said. "You've been in there. You could've been made. Me or Marz can go," he said.

Shane pushed up from the table. "No. You know damn well I know how to disguise myself. For whatever reason, she helped me. Twice. Might mean a whole lotta nothing. But she was skittish as hell. If for some reason she saw something in me she could trust, I need to be the one to talk to her again. ASAP." And not just because Shane was worried about the woman. But if she knew something about this delivery, and Beckett's argument was right, she could very well lead them to intel that would help them regain their good names and their stolen honor.

"Let him go," Marz said, shooting a look at Beckett. "He could be right. It's worth a try. I'll wire you up, and you can take in more hardware while you're at it. The devices we planted aren't doing shit for us. Maybe she could even plant some in the back?"

"I'll see what I can do." Shane slid the metal folding chair under the makeshift table, glad he'd found a mission-critical reason to check on the woman who had put her neck on the line for him last night. He didn't need his gut to tell him she was in trouble. She'd all but admitted it. Crystal's wide eyes, long red hair, and beautifully delicate features came to his mind's eye, and Shane couldn't get to her soon enough. "Thanks again for a great meal, Becca."

The weight of several gazes lit on his back as he crossed the gym to the door, but he paid the sensation no mind. He was doing what they needed done. So what if it also gave him a shot at learning what might be happening to the women who landed in that godforsaken basement?

He crossed the industrial hallway to a door on the other side of the landing, punched a key code into the box at the side, and entered the Rixeys' apartment. With its brick walls, high ceilings, and exposed ductwork, the space retained the old warehouse's character, but Jeremy had done a helluva job renovating to make it an inviting place to hang and shoot the shit. Too bad they weren't here for that.

At the very back of the large apartment, Shane found the no-frills guest room where he'd crashed the past few days. A row of duffels lined one wall, and he rifled through one until he found what he needed. In the hall bathroom, he spiked out his hair with the gel he only ever used for darkening his hair color and, with the right clothes, subtly altering his appearance. It was a testament to his belief in Nick that he'd brought all his guns, equipment, and supplies with him. But six years of living and fighting and bleeding with someone meant you trusted his gut when it sounded the alarm. Simple as.

A few minutes later, he was in black from head to toe. Boots. Jeans. Tee. Holster. Beat-up leather jacket. He slipped the butterfly necklace he always carried into his pocket, tucking it deep so it couldn't fall out. Back at the mirror, he threw on some shades to see the effect. Nothing like the clean-cut look he'd sported the previous night. He grabbed a fake ID, his Sig Sauer, an earpiece, and a blade, then made to fly.

Anticipation flashed through his veins. If the gang had roughed Crystal up after they rescued Charlie last night, that damage would rest on his shoulders. At least partly. At this point, he couldn't *not* go back and check on her. Just his sense of duty at work. What else would it be?

Nick was waiting for him in the living room, ass propped against the back of the couch and ankles and arms crossed. "I don't like your going in alone."

"Won't be alone. I've got the communication equipment from last night's op. And this is strictly fact-finding. No intent to engage."

Nick gave a tight nod. "Good. That's good." They clasped hands, a familiar understanding passing between them. Shane turned for the door. "And Shane?"

He paused. Too much to hope for a clean getaway.

"Eyes on the prize, brother. Are we clear?"

Shane hated that Nick thought he needed a reminder to keep focused on the mission, but after Shane's outburst, part of him wasn't surprised to receive it. He reached the door and tugged it open. "Crystal."

Shane bit out a curse under his breath. The pun wasn't lost on him as the door clanked shut.

Chapter 4

*O*n a short break, Crystal leaned into the dressing-room mirror and tilted her face into the light. The swelling had gone down, so between her makeup and the dim lights of the club, the customers didn't seem to be noticing that she'd been struck. Bruno was too damn strategic to use his fists on her face, but he had no qualms about using an open palm, nor about taking out his frustrations on the rest of her body.

And last night, having lost Church's prisoner *and* the guys who'd stolen him, he'd had frustration to spare.

Of course, he'd apologized, wrapped her in his coat, and escorted her home afterward. Normally, she drove herself crazy worrying about Jenna when she slept over at one of her college friend's apartments, but last night she'd been grateful into her very marrow that her sister hadn't been home to see what Bruno had done. Again.

When the abuse first started, Crystal had fallen for his apologies and made excuses for him. After all, he'd saved her from far worse. Now, she recognized the apologies as the reprieve they were, smiled and made nice, and bided her time.

Thanks to a merit scholarship that covered her tuition and a bunch of summer classes the past couple years, Jenna was on track to graduate from college in December. So they only had about eight months until Crystal could put her escape plan into action.

Where to escape to Crystal still hadn't decided, but the anonymity of New York City's teeming crowds looked really good. Maybe Crystal could find a job in the Garment District working for a big-name designer, and one day she'd have the resources and contacts to design her own collection . . .

"Hey, there," Brandy said, pulling Crystal from her fantasies and slipping into the space next to her. A cleavage-revealing white robe around her shoulders, the raven-haired woman had a beautiful, lithe body and a serious meth addiction, and had worked at Confessions longer than Crystal although as a dancer, not a waitress. "You doing okay?"

"Yeah, thanks," Crystal said, chancing a smile at her.

Brandy's gaze landed on her left cheekbone, and her expression faltered for just a moment. "Yeah? That's good," she said, her voice less successful at hiding what she'd seen.

"Is it that obvious?" Crystal grabbed her compact as she turned back to the mirror.

"No, not really. The fluorescent lights in here show every damn thing." Brandy fished through her cosmetics bag. "I know just what to do. Look here."

Embarrassment heating her cheeks, Crystal turned in her chair and faced the woman, who couldn't be more than a few years older than her. They were friendly but not exactly friends. To Crystal, friends were people you could trust implicitly. Around here, it just wasn't safe to give anyone that kind of power.

"Your skin is so pretty and so fair," she said, holding back the loose curls on the side of Crystal's face. "I always wanted red hair." She stroked a brush over Crystal's cheek.

"Why? Your hair is gorgeous and mysterious."

She shifted the brush to Crystal's other cheek. "And yours is rare and unique." Her hand sagged into her lap. "What happened?"

Crystal pursed her lips and shrugged. Brandy knew what'd happened. *Everyone* around here knew what had happened when she showed up with a mark on her skin. And they all looked the other way.

"You're too good for this place, Crystal. You know that, right?"

She gave a half laugh. "We're all too good for this place."

Brandy shook her head. "I'm being serious." When Crystal didn't say anything, the woman continued. "You're talented and smart. What were you studying to be in college?"

"How did you—"

"God, girl, your father was *so* proud of you, he wouldn't shut up about it. 'First in the family,' he'd say."

"Oh," Crystal said. Once, she would've glowed to hear such a thing about her father, but after she'd learned what he was into, it had gotten a lot harder to keep idolizing the man who had failed her and Jenna so spectacularly. It shouldn't surprise her that Brandy had known her father. Lots of people around here had. His position as one of the Apostles meant that he'd been well-known and well respected.

But then his imprisonment and death and the revelation about his indebtedness to Church put an end to college for her before the end of her sophomore year.

Now, school felt so long ago it was as if Brandy spoke of another person. What life would be like if getting along with her college roommate was her biggest problem. God, how naïve she'd been. About the world. About her father. About everything.

"I hadn't decided," she lied. But she just couldn't sully her dreams of becoming a clothing designer by giving voice to them in this place, especially given how she'd bastardized those dreams by occasionally making costumes for the dancers. Now it just sounded stupid. Childish. Impossible.

Brandy stroked more blush on Crystal's cheeks. "Well, I'm sure it was going to be something great." She grabbed a tube from her bag. "Let's do this, too," she said, rubbing some red lipstick on a sterile applicator.

Crystal turned back to the mirror and smoothed the bold color onto her lips.

"It's way more than you usually wear, but you can totally pull it off, and it hides the mark," Brandy said, echoing Crystal's own thoughts. The rouge and lip color made the rest of her skin paler by comparison, but Brandy was right. The color on her face now looked intentional, hiding the redness by highlighting it.

"That is better. Thanks," she said, glancing at her cell phone. Break time was over. "I guess I better get back out there before someone comes looking for me."

"Hang tough, hon," Brandy said, giving her hand a squeeze. "You have more of your father's strength in you than you know."

Crystal nodded and bolted for the door, suddenly feeling as if the walls were closing in on her. People around here didn't often talk about her father. His arrest, conviction, and death provided an unwelcome reminder of where this life could take them if they weren't careful. For her, his arrest and later death had been just the beginning of everything she'd lost, including her ability to trust. Because if you couldn't count on your own father to tell the truth and protect you, who could you count on? She'd had no idea what he'd been into until his arrest.

Back on the floor, Crystal switched off with Amber to cover the section in the back corner of the club. Monday nights were always on the quiet side, and for that she was grateful. She moved between the tables, taking orders, delivering drinks, and offering flirtatious conversation. Just another role to play. But as this one earned her money, she always gave it her all.

"Welcome to Confessions. What can I get for you this evening?" she said to the man sitting by himself in the next-to-last booth.

He lifted his gaze to her. And all the air sucked out of the room.

Steel gray eyes.

Pretty Boy.

She gasped and took an unthinking step backward. *Oh, God. What is he doing here?* Crystal forced herself to ease her posture. If she called any attention to herself right now, things could get bad. For both of them.

"I'll have a beer, please. Whatever's on tap. And Crystal?"

She almost asked how he knew her name, but then she remembered telling him when they'd spoken last night, when she thought she was helping someone who belonged here.

"Just breathe."

She turned away, her brain sorting through a variety of choices. Tell. Run. Avoid. All of which were fraught with potentially negative consequences for her. If she told them she recognized this man from last night, it would reveal that she hadn't told them everything she'd seen. Namely, the man's face.

The man's exquisitely handsome face. Chiseled jaw. Playful, full lips.

God, what was wrong with her? If he didn't get his sexy ass out of here, they were going to be in deep shit.

Walker filled her order, chitchatting with her the whole time. His chatter helped calm her nerves. *Just be cool. Nobody knows anything. Nobody sees anything. Just act natural.* As her panic receded, anger rushed in. She'd helped him. She'd risked herself. Enough was enough. He had no freaking right to put her in any more danger than she was already in. She scrawled a note on a napkin and returned to the man's booth with his beer.

"Here you go, sir." She placed the napkin down first, waited until she was sure he saw her message—*Leave now and don't come back,* then set the glass on top of it. "Will there be anything else?" She let every bit of the rage brewing inside her shine from her gaze.

It didn't seem to faze him. "I'd like to talk to you, darlin'."

She pasted a smile on her face and pretended the hint of Southern in his accent didn't make her go warm. "Well, I wouldn't like to talk to you." She turned on her heel—

And he caught her hand in his and reeled her in against his side.

Crystal gasped at the contact, and her chest went tight with a growing panic borne of an old, horrible experience. Then her brain registered that he wasn't hurting her, and he wasn't trying anything else, and she managed to beat back her anxiety enough to hold it together.

He was damn lucky she was a waitress and not a dancer, because the club had a hands-off policy toward the latter. At least out on the floor. But the waitresses, her included, tolerated a pat on the ass or a hand on her thigh because flirting brought bigger tips. Every time.

Pretty Boy's grasp probably looked playful from the

outside, so Crystal forced herself to throw her head back and laugh like she was enjoying the attention. And, truth be told, between the unusual gentleness of his grip and the hardness of his muscles where they were pressed together, a flash of heat shot through her. Ridiculous. Dangerous. "You have no idea who you're playing with," she whispered, anger at herself mixing with her ire toward him.

"I need your help. And I think I can help you in return."

She scoffed, leaned in closer, and prepared to let him know just what she thought about *that*—

"What happened to your cheek?" Anger slipped into his expression, sharpening the angles of his otherwise pretty face.

Well, shit. Not covered as well as she thought, then.

And why the heck would he care?

So, so gently, he stroked his knuckles over her cheekbone.

The tenderness of the gesture sent tingles through her belly. Bruno didn't always hurt her, but he was almost never gentle, either.

Softness and compassion weren't traits she was used to from a man. It was so foreign, she almost wasn't sure how to respond. For a moment, she pressed into the touch, but then her brain restarted, and she jerked away. She tapped her finger on the napkin. "I don't want to have to tell you again."

Without waiting for him to reply, she turned and moved to another table that blessedly needed her assistance. She had to keep busy, act normal, laugh, and make the men feel special—and, above all else, avoid the gray-eyed man until he finally got the message. Or her shift ended. Thankfully, she wasn't closing tonight and only had another hour to go. She could keep it together that long.

It was maybe the slowest hour of Crystal's life.

Everywhere she moved, she felt the man's gaze on her. The one time she gave in to the urge to look at him, he appeared absorbed in the dancers onstage, but somehow she knew it was an act.

Maybe it took an actor to know one?

The guy was watching her even when he didn't appear to be. She would've sworn it. Prickles ran over her scalp. Her awareness of him was so intense, it permeated the air all around her. This man was dangerous in all kinds of ways she didn't want to explore. Couldn't even if she wanted to. Which she didn't.

Then, ten minutes before the end of her shift, he threw a few bills on the table, shoved out of the booth, and strode across the club as if he weren't Jimmy Church's Number One Most Wanted.

And, God, if she'd thought his face handsome, the head-to-toe view was a total stunner. Tall, built, and all in black, the guy moved with a lethal grace that was quiet and powerful at the same time. She recognized the swagger a lot of the guys in the gang possessed, but his movements weren't full of the posturing she often witnessed in the men around here. Like he was *so* bad-ass he had no need to prove it.

Crystal forced her gaze away and breathed a sigh of relief.

Thank God he's gone.

She ignored the niggle of regret that settled into the pit of her stomach and made her way to clear his table and pocket his tip. At least for her troubles, Pretty Boy had left money—she could often keep a bigger portion of cash tips because the shift manager couldn't track them with specificity, as opposed to the credit-card tips he could account for to the last penny. She wasn't sure if the guy had been brave or stupid for returning after what he'd pulled the night before. All she knew was she hoped he didn't ever return.

Niggle.

She groaned as she returned to the dressing room and changed out of the skimpy halter shirt and tiny skirt that just covered her ruined back but left her cleavage, midriff, and legs bare. Stepping into her jeans and flip-flops was like seeing an old friend. When she got out of this job, she might never wear heels again.

Crystal reveled in whatever crisis had kept Bruno away from the club tonight as she made her way out the door, across the parking lot, and into the dull red pickup that had been her father's. Red, for the hair all three of the Dean women had had in common, not that she could remember much about her mom. She'd died in a car crash when Crystal had been so young her only real memory of the woman was her warm, happy smile. At least she'd managed to hang on to her mother's sewing machine. Knowing that her mom's hands had once worked at that needle made Crystal feel close to her every time she sat down to make her or Jenna a piece of clothing—one of Crystal's few interests that had survived from before.

The engine started on a loud rumble, and Crystal's hands gripped the wide steering wheel. The truck was so big it made her feel tiny, but a part of Crystal loved the fact that she owned a vehicle large enough to move all the important stuff she and Jenna owned. For when the time came to get away.

And it *was* coming. This year, she and Jenna were going to have the happiest Christmas ever. Because by then, they'd be somewhere new and far, far away.

In the grand scheme of things, eight months was nothing.

She just had to keep out of trouble in the meantime.

That meant no more taking chances. And definitely no helping strange, beautiful men. No matter what.

* * *

SHANE SIGHED AS he positioned his truck on the street so he wouldn't miss Crystal leave. The trip to the club hadn't been a complete waste.

Before he'd found Crystal, Shane had managed to place listening devices at the ordering station on the bar, near the bar's phone, and in both public restrooms. He'd also double-checked that the receiver-transmitter that Easy had wired into the exterior cable the night before was still intact. That piece was key, enabling Marz to do some sort of technical voodoo whereby he could remotely access the live feeds the mics picked up. Or something. Shane loved the man like a brother, but Marz's technospeak had the power to put him right into a coma. They still needed eyes and ears in the private spaces of Confessions, but it was a start.

Situated among a run-down strip of restaurants, dive bars, and stores gone out of business, the club's property dominated the whole side of the block, a hotbed of activity in the midst of the otherwise subdued street. It was one of those neighborhoods through which the cops never patrolled and taxis never drove without a call specifically bringing them there.

Shane studied the club's points of ingress and egress, assembling a mental catalog of the building in case he needed to return. But his thoughts keep coming back to Crystal.

She was more than a survivor—which the demand to hit her had already told him. She was also a fighter. Which was good. Whether she knew it or not, they were in this thing together, and she was going to need to be smart and she was going to have to be strong. That she'd come at him with all kinds of hellfire—all the while acting like he was just another customer—was reassuring. Not to mention damn hot.

Jesus, she was a slight little thing in his arms, tall and lean and warm. Beautiful curves and smooth skin. A man could lose himself in a body like hers.

And someone had taken a hand to her.

As he sat in the cab of his truck, a big bucket of rage parked itself in the center of his chest. When he'd seen the handprint under the extra layers of her makeup, it'd taken everything he had to not react in a way that would draw attention. He'd put her in harm's way enough. Clearly.

But one thing was for goddamn sure. Whoever's hand matched that print wouldn't need two gloves come winter.

Just like Shane had seen what she'd tried to hide, he'd learn who'd hurt her. In the Army, Shane had been known for seeing what others missed. Like the inked eagle sprawled across his back, he excelled at sighting his prey from far, far away and attacking with a speed and accuracy that never gave them a fighting chance.

The sonofabitch who hurt her would never know what hit him. On second thought, yeah, he would. Abusers were bullies. Cowards. And Shane wanted to see the fear in the man's eyes when he made him pay.

About twenty-five minutes later, movement caught his attention. A red truck made its way from the back of the lot to the gate at the street. With Crystal in the driver's seat. Bingo. She had to leave at some point, and it would be easier to talk to her away from all the eyes in the club.

Crystal turned onto the street and passed him. He let two other cars go by before pulling out behind her. Bright and big as the truck was, he didn't need to be aggressive with the tail. He could keep track of her just fine. And the fact that she was the Mother Teresa of drivers—obeying every traffic law to a tee—helped a lot, too. He found it oddly endearing since his foot was normally an anvil of pure lead when he got behind the wheel.

Speed was a fucking awesome distraction from the shit in his head.

Fifteen minutes later, she pulled into a garden-apartment complex just outside the city line. Shane kept going straight, ditched his F-150 about a half block down the street, then hightailed it on foot, keeping to the shadows, until he saw her truck.

Crystal sat behind the wheel. Still. Head back. From this distance, it almost looked like she was sleeping. He didn't want to scare her, but in case she lived with someone, maybe he should approach her while she was—

A strange moan caught his attention. His gaze whipped to the right, to the outdoor stairwell of the building he approached.

A girl sat on the next-to-the-bottom step. One moment, she had her arms around drawn-up knees. The next, she went rigid and started convulsing.

Shane was immediately in motion.

The seizure forced her muscles to contract, forming her into a ball that made her fall down the last two steps.

He went to his knees beside her, his medic training kicking in without a second thought. Gently, he rolled her to her side in case she vomited, then he whipped off his jacket and slid it under her head.

There was nothing else to be done until it was over. Damnit. The medical identification bracelet she wore announced her epileptic condition, so Shane held off on calling 911. If the seizure wasn't too severe, she might be lucid within another minute and could tell him how best to help.

Aw, damn. This girl has red hair like—

"Oh, my God, what are you doing?" came a voice from behind him.

Crystal.

This was *so* not how he'd wanted to reveal himself. "This woman is having a seizure."

She went to her knees beside him. "I'm here, Jenna. Hang on." Worry poured off her as the younger woman's muscles contracted, and her eyes rolled back. "She's my sister."

Yeah, he'd figured that much out. "She'll be okay," he said.

"I've been taking care of her for years. I don't need you to tell me she'll be okay," she said, her tone equal parts anger and fear, beautiful green eyes flashing. "What are you, anyway?" Her gaze dragged over the holstered gun under his arm.

"Former Army medic."

"I told you to leave me alone," Crystal bit out in a hushed voice.

"No. You told me to leave Confessions. Which I did."

"Yeah. And then you followed me home. Right?" She nailed him with a stare.

Shane's gut clenched. No defense there. Instinct told him the truth was the only chance he had to keep her from shutting him out for good. "Yes. I really need your help. I thought maybe it would be easier for you to talk away from the club."

Jenna's muscles went slack on a groan, recapturing their attention. Her eyelids lifted sluggishly, as if they were made of five-pound weights.

"Okay, sweetie, just hang in there. I'll get you inside," Crystal said, sliding her hands under the other woman's shoulders.

Shane gripped his thighs and forced himself still. "Let me help," he said, itching to just pick Jenna up since it was pretty damn clear Crystal wasn't going to be able to move her unconscious like this. But he sensed that doing it without her permission would bring down all sorts of shutters, and so far he wasn't making great headway in winning her over.

The debate played out across her expression, then her gaze dropped to Jenna's face. She stroked her sister's cheek and sighed. "Okay. But just because I know I can't get her up the steps like this. And she could be out of it for a good half hour."

Nodding, Shane scooped up his coat and the woman and rose to his feet. She couldn't weigh more than a buck twenty soaking wet. Jenna was totally out, exhaustion from a severe epileptic seizure often sent a person into a sleep state immediately afterward and left them drained for the next day or two. Crystal had a damn lot on her plate. Even more than he'd known.

For a moment, Crystal mother-henned over her sister in his arms, as if making sure he wasn't hurting her. With a resigned expression, she finally said, "This way."

As he followed Crystal up the set of concrete steps, he realized he'd learned something important about her tonight. She didn't like to receive help. And she didn't like to ask for it. But she would if her *sister* was the one who needed it.

Damn if he didn't respect that.

And, Jesus, if he'd thought Crystal sexy with too much skin showing, she was even sexier in the tee and faded jeans, her hair swept into a long ponytail. Damn, even the painted toes sticking out of her flip-flops intrigued him.

At the door, she stopped and looked around, like she was making sure no one noticed them, then she let him in.

The apartment was small and plain, but clean and organized. Crystal led him through the combination living-dining room decorated in shades of blue and past the galley-style kitchen to a narrow hallway at the back. Three doorways stood in the dimness of the space, a bathroom and presumably each of their bedrooms. They entered the one on the right, and Crystal clicked on the small lamp on the bedside table.

The orderliness of the rest of the apartment stopped at Jenna's bedroom door.

The room was like a bookstore with a double bed in one corner. One of those old, used bookstores where it was possible the removal of a single book from the shelf might bring the whole place collapsing in on itself. Towering stacks of books sat on every flat surface, including the carpeted floor, and one whole wall was lined with over-flowing shelves.

"So, she likes to read, then," he said as he gently laid Jenna onto the rumpled comforter. Colorful flowers and butterflies on a white background. A butterfly mobile hung from the ceiling in front of one window. Shane re-sisted the urge to check that Molly's necklace still lay safe in his pocket. And to think this girl's apparent fascination with his sister's favorite creature was some kind of a sign.

Crystal smirked and busied herself with the covers. "What gave it away?"

It wasn't the smile he'd been going for, but it was a start. He hoped.

Jenna's breathing was raspy—not unusual after a sei-zure, and Crystal sat on the edge of the bed and stroked her palm over the younger woman's forehead. "So, uh . . ." She frowned. "You were a doctor in the Army?"

Shane studied the reluctant expression she wore, the lines of worry settled into her forehead, the way the soft, red waves of her ponytail cascaded over her shoulder. "I cross-trained as a medic."

On a long sigh, Crystal shook her head and stood. "Well, thank you for helping her. I . . . I don't know how I would've gotten her inside . . ." Her gaze landed every-where but on his.

He frowned, sensing the good-bye from a mile out. "I'm glad I was here."

She hugged herself. "You should go."

And there it was. "Crystal—"

She gestured to be quiet and led him out of the room, gently pulling the door shut behind them. In the dimness of the hallway, she looked up at him, a war of emotions on her face. "You can't be here."

"Why not?" he said. Not only did he need her help, but the fact that she and her sister might need his had his feet rooted firmly in place. All of a sudden, his brain assembled the last few minutes into a puzzle picture he didn't like. "Wait. Is she not receiving treatment for the epilepsy?"

Crystal's eyebrows slashed downward, and outrage dropped her mouth into an oval. "Of course she's receiving treatment."

Shane held his hands up. "I'm sorry. I didn't mean to offend you. It just seemed like you might want my help. *For her,*" he added.

She didn't school her expression fast enough, and Shane saw the rightness of his analysis.

"Come on, Crystal. What's going on?"

She turned on her heel and walked the short distance to the living room. "You really need to go."

Shane sat down on the well-worn denim couch and crossed his boot over his knee.

She gawped. It was almost comical how expressive her face could be. When she let it.

"What's going on?" he repeated.

"I don't even know you."

"That's why I was hoping we could talk." His gaze scanned the room and landed on the large flat-screen mounted to the opposite wall. Beneath it sat a bookshelf with a variety of high-end equipment—DVD player, receiver, stereo, speakers. Sweet setup, but not a single piece of it matched the worn-out nature of the rest of the women's belongings. Odd, since Crystal didn't strike him as the type to splurge on luxuries, not when the woman's truck was likely so old it was flirting with a historic vehicle designation.

She arched an eyebrow. "You can't be here."

"You keep saying that."

"Because it's true. Jesus, if—"

Shane was off the couch and in front of her. "If what?" He tucked a few bronze wisps off her face and behind her ear, then let his fingers graze her cheekbone. The gentleness belied the storm whipping up inside him at the near reference to her tormenter.

She stepped back. "It doesn't matter."

Like hell it doesn't. Crossing his arms, Shane waited.

"God, I can't get rid of you." Exasperation had her throwing up her arms.

"I specialize in pain in the ass, darlin'." He smiled, forcing himself to gear down the intensity.

"Well, congratulations, because you clearly graduated with honors."

He grinned and watched as she twisted her lips to avoid doing the same. The problem was clearly that she didn't think she should talk, but his gut told him she wanted to. That she was dying to. "I just want to be your friend, Crystal."

All traces of humor disappeared from her face. "I don't have friends."

"You don't have them? Or you're not allowed to have them?" Shane worked hard to keep his voice neutral.

"The reason doesn't matter. And it's none of your business."

Goddamn. Had he ever worked this hard to get a woman to warm up to him? Far from making him back off, the strength of her defenses had him worrying about why she felt she needed them.

He closed the distance between them. "Okay, no friends, then. But I could still help you and Jenna."

She sighed and looked him in the eye. "We don't need your help."

Just then, a *thump* and a muffled cry sounded from the back of the apartment.

Chapter 5

Crystal was down the hall and through Jenna's bedroom door in an instant. After years of dealing with this, her body reacted instinctively anytime Jenna needed help. Sure enough, Jenna had fallen out of bed and now lay disoriented and struggling to untangle herself from her covers.

"Hold on, Jen, I'm here," she said, easing the blankets from her body. Jenna looked up at her with a confused stare that made Crystal's chest ache. The disorientation was normal after one of her seizures. Sometimes she even had memory lapses. She'd been having them more frequently the past few months, but it had been a long time since she'd had one this bad. What in the world had triggered it?

Crystal didn't know the answer, though she intended to question Jenna about her recent activities when she was well enough. Certain things could bring on an epileptic attack, and Jenna wasn't always as strict about avoiding those as she needed to be. All Crystal knew was she absolutely hated not being able to do more for her sister when the seizures hit.

"Can I help?" Pretty Boy asked from behind her.

Twin reactions coursed through Crystal. A knee-jerk desire to tell him she'd love his help because, *God*, it would be *so nice* to have someone to lean on now and then. And he was a freaking doctor, for God's sake. Or, medic. Whatever. Given Jenna's condition, his skills would've been at the top of a perfect-man wish list. If she'd ever made such a thing. Which she hadn't because dreams were for other people. She'd well learned *that* lesson.

But alongside that yearning for help came the soul-deep certainty that giving in to such a feeling was a one-way ticket to all kinds of trouble. Because this man and her boyfriend were obviously enemies, and Bruno wouldn't tolerate her being friends with—or, hell, even talking to—this guy even if they weren't.

Still, she did need to get Jenna in bed. And he *was* already here . . .

Clearing her throat, Crystal nodded without looking at him. "Would you help me get her back in bed, please?"

He was immediately beside her, heat and strength radiating off of him. "Of course."

Crystal chanced a glance at him and instantly regretted it. Because his expression was filled with pure earnest desire to help her. To help *them*. And, no, she hadn't forgotten that he was hoping for some sort of help from her, too. But he'd never once suggested any of this was a *quid pro quo*. She rose and gave him room to pick up Jenna.

He lifted her sister and, just like earlier, the gentleness and care with which he handled Jenna almost tempted Crystal to give in . . . to open up . . . One knee braced on the mattress, he leaned forward so he could place Jenna closer to the wall. So she wouldn't fall out of bed again, so she wouldn't hurt herself. Crystal didn't need him to explain why he'd done it because it was exactly what she would've done. And there was that temptation again. Causing her stomach to flutter and her heart to race.

Without asking, the man retrieved the blanket from the floor and laid it over Jenna like she was a baby he didn't want to wake. He was a big guy—tall, broad-shouldered, muscular—and the gun holstered under his arm said he was dangerous, too. But he was also the most gentle, kind man she'd ever met.

God, I need to get him out of here.

Holding a pile of books so it wouldn't topple, he eased the nightstand a few inches away from the side of Jenna's bed.

Crystal didn't know whether to scream or throw herself at him—an odd thought for someone who'd lived through what she had.

"Come on," she whispered. Not wanting to chance seeing him do one more thoughtful thing, she turned and marched to the door, then glared at him as he crossed the room.

The moment he registered her annoyance was clear because the concerned expression slid off his face in exchange for a confused one. "What?" he whispered, closing the door without making a sound.

And that was when she realized. She'd been on the verge of cursing him out and tossing his unfairly sexy butt out the front door. But she didn't know who it was she'd be cursing or tossing.

All this time he'd been in her house, and she'd never asked his name.

Smart, Crystal. Real smart.

And as much as she needed to stick with Plan A and make him *go,* that wasn't what came out of her mouth. "I don't even know your name," she bit out.

He smiled.

Oh, my God, did he smile.

It was a smile that made her think of lazy summer afternoons spent lying in the sun. Warm and sweet and reassuring.

"Well, pardon my manners, darlin'." He extended his big hand. She crossed her arms over her chest. "I'm Shane."

"Shane, huh?" she said, dropping her gaze to his hand as he lowered it to his side again. Because the combination of the Southern lilt to his voice with that smile and that face was too much to take in all at once. "*Just* Shane?" She peered up under her lashes.

For an instant, those gray eyes narrowed. Assessing. Weighing. No way he was going to tell her his real name. Not after—

"Shane McCallan." He said it in a low voice, almost a whisper, like he didn't want anyone but her to hear.

And Crystal nearly gasped. If he'd have hit her, she would've been less surprised. Because her gut said he was telling the truth. And, *God,* that meant he'd just given her all kinds of power. And the intense cast of his gaze told her he was well aware of that, too.

"Shane McCallan," she murmured, needing to try the name out on her tongue. Shaking away the sensation that the floor might be moving, she gestured him toward the living room.

"Wait," he said, a thumb pointing over his shoulder. "Mind if I use your bathroom?"

She couldn't stop the eye roll. Because, *suuure,* why the hell not? He might as well just kick his shoes off and stay for dinner at this point.

He winked and turned for the door.

"Light switch is on the left," she said.

He closed the door—quietly again—and Crystal stood

there for a moment. When she realized she was staring at
the door, like maybe she could will him out, she whirled
and made a straight shot for the living room. Where she
stood again, not knowing what to do with herself.

All at once, she became conscious of the apartment.
When her father went to prison, they'd lost the house she
and Jenna had lived in their whole lives to legal fees and
their father's debts to Church. And, with Bruno's help,
they'd landed at this inexpensive and not very nice apartment complex with a handful of their belongings they'd
managed to hang on to. She'd been damn proud of every
one of her garage-sale finds at the time, but now she
wondered what Shane saw when he looked around. And
would he wonder how a woman with a houseful of obvious hand-me-downs had afforded all the high-end media
equipment? The flat-screen TV, various components, and
stereo were all Bruno's doing. His patience with her no-
bells-and-whistles TV had lasted about five minutes.

Crystal fought the urge to plump the throw pillows, put
her running shoes away, and try to make the yellowed
blinds hang straight. She kept the place neat and homey
for her and Jenna, but Crystal never worried about what
others might think because she never had visitors. She
paced into the galley-style kitchen and had to resist washing the breakfast dishes.

Gah! Whatever!

The only person who ever saw the inside of the place
besides her and Jenna was Bruno. On a few rare instances,
one of his guys had stopped by to see him on business.
But Crystal could count the number of times that had happened on one hand.

Speaking of Bruno . . . Crystal tore her cell phone from
her pocket and woke up the LED screen. Her shoulders
sank in relief. She hadn't missed any calls or texts while
she'd been dealing with Jenna . . . and Shane. Bruno was

obsessive about her responding immediately when he contacted her. A missed message could have him showing up at her door.

And that would be really, really bad right now.

Good thing he'd made it clear he wouldn't be over tonight. And she felt confident in that. Because not only did he have a crisis to handle for Church, but he often stayed away for a day or two after he'd beat her. Like he didn't want to see the evidence of his handiwork on her skin.

Frowning, she slipped her phone back into her jeans and wondered what the hell was taking Pretty Boy so long. Even though she now knew his name, she suspected the nickname wouldn't disappear anytime soon from her thoughts.

Not that she'd be thinking about him or anything.

She rounded the doorway of the kitchen in time to see Shane turning out the bathroom light and striding up the short hallway toward her.

Guy had to be over six feet tall. And man, he moved in ways that made her *curious* about things she had no business being curious about. Like what someone so gentle and so kind and so mind-bogglingly sexy would be like in bed . . .

Heat immediately flooded her cheeks, the curse of her pale skin. At the same time, her stomach went on a roller-coaster ride. The thought of trying to be with someone else after what'd happened to her was like free-falling off the edge of a cliff—freeing and terrifying at the same time.

Shane lifted a single eyebrow, and it was like he *knew* she found him attractive. He was probably used to women throwing themselves at him, pretty as he was. His gaze trailed a quick but unmistakable path up and down her body, and she felt it like a physical caress. Her nipples pebbled under the thin cotton T-shirt, and arousal stirred through her blood in a way she hadn't felt in *years*. Maybe not ever.

And then he was right in front of her.

She wanted to retreat. She wanted to press herself against all that hard, male heat.

"So, what is it you want?" she asked instead, anxiety making the words come out more harshly than she'd intended.

Eyes like liquid silver, he stared at her so intently, she would've sworn he could see right into her soul. Then he shook his head, stepped to the bookshelf under the TV, and flicked a series of buttons on the stereo. Not so loud that it should disturb Jenna, a sexy, soulful song filled the air around them. "Do you like to dance, Crystal?" he asked in a low voice.

"Uh, what? Why?"

His smile was crooked, playful. " 'Cause dancing's something people do when they're getting to know each other."

"Really?" Maybe where he was from. Then again, she worked in a strip club. Dancing was something people did to make money. So, okay, maybe her view of dancing *was* a bit jaded.

"Absolutely. Ask anybody." The song faded away, followed by the announcement of a Southern rock station's call sign. A new song started, and Shane turned to her with a smile. "Dance with me."

Crystal peered up at him without the slightest idea how to respond. Because her body was saying *hell, yes!,* while her brain was screaming *bad idea, really, really bad idea.*

He stepped closer, arms raised, expression full of all kinds of invitation.

The next thing she knew, her right hand was in his and her left had slipped around his neck. *Ohmigod, ohmigod, ohmigod,* ran over and over in her mind. *What am I doing?*

But then he tucked her hand against his chest and tugged her against him with the hand that settled at her lower back. And the closeness stole her breath.

He moved them to the beat of the song, a slow, sexy, bluesy number she didn't know but would never forget. Some songs carried memories like the images were imprinted upon the very lyrics themselves, and she had no doubt this would be one of them.

All of a sudden, the air in the room felt ten degrees warmer. As they swayed to the beat, Shane's body pressed against hers from thighs to chest. With every step and move and turn, Crystal's breasts rubbed against the hard plane of his chest. Strong hands held and guided her body, making her want to feel them explore her everywhere. Arousal rose like a waking dragon inside her. Cautious. Curious. Dangerous.

This was wrong and stupid on so many levels. But, scary as it was, it *felt* so freaking good that she couldn't force herself to pull away.

One song. It's just a dance. Just a dance just a dance just a dance.

And, holy crap, she wasn't the only one aroused.

Against her belly, Shane hardened.

Crystal sucked in a breath, and he pressed his lips close to her ear. "We're just dancing here. That's all. I promise," he said.

But the adrenaline was already in her blood, setting her to a trembling she couldn't control. Part curious interest and part instinctive fear.

"Sshh," he almost cooed. "Just dancing."

The echo of her own thoughts from a moment before allowed her to draw a breath that almost calmed. They turned and swayed to the music, moving closer, pressing tighter, Shane's lips so close to her face that she could feel his breath shudder across her cheekbone.

He was a fire she had no business playing with. She knew that even as she leaned her face against his . . . and got exactly what she'd hoped for.

He kissed her.

Just a brush of his lips against her cheek, but a kiss all the same.

And as much as it made her head spin, it was the little catch of breath in the back of his throat that sent a jolt of electricity down her spine to settle low in her belly. Light as a feather, he caressed her cheek, her temple, her ear with his lips. With him, always such gentleness, so different from almost every other sexual experience she'd ever had. It made her feel safe to allow this to continue.

Between them, his erection was firm, long, totally unyielding. She shivered, caught between interest and fear, desire a river moving faster and faster inside her. The whole experience was a revelation—that her body had the capacity to respond this way, that a person existed who could pull these reactions from her.

For a moment, she gave herself over to the dizzying sensations. In her mind's eye, she saw them undressing, fumbling their way back the hall, falling naked and wanting on the bed. What would it be like, just once, to take something that she wanted without worrying about anyone else, without being afraid? Just one wild, secret night, all for her? What would *Shane* be like?

The way the room started spinning around her made it clear Crystal wasn't really up to finding that out. Not that it mattered. Because it would never happen anyway.

Crystal had been so deep into Shane, she didn't hear the song ending. The moment of silence before the next song began captured her awareness, made her realize what she'd been doing—what she'd been *wanting to do*—and she gasped and jerked her face away from Shane's worshipful lips.

"I know I can't stay," he said as if reading her mind. "Just give me one more song."

That was two songs more than she should've ever agreed to. She knew it. But that didn't stop her from nodding yes as the next song, a harder, faster, rock song with a driving beat, filled the room around them.

SHANE WAS WELL aware he was wandering off the reservation, but damnit all to hell and back, Crystal was pushing every one of his buttons. Her soft, warm body pressed against his. Her hands held him tight. Her gaze was an open book, begging him to stay, pleading with him to kiss her again, but also making it clear that those desires scared the hell out of her.

No part of his plan had been about seducing her. He didn't use sex to manipulate female informants. Ever. The music had been about blocking any listening devices that might've been planted in her apartment. And the dancing had been about getting them close enough to communicate despite the tunes.

It might've been an unnecessary precaution, but it didn't seem too great a stretch to think that whoever she was afraid of, whoever had hit her, whoever had given her reason to believe that Shane would be willing to do that, too, might be controlling enough to keep tabs on her. Even in her home.

And, given that his bathroom visit had been a cover for planting a few bugs of his own—one in the handset of her bedroom landline, one on the molding above the bathroom door, and one just now on the side of the stereo blocked by a collection of picture frames—he had surveillance on the brain.

Except her touch, her heat, her closeness has chased his rational mind into a corner until all he could do was *feel*.

As Crystal swayed with him to the music, her fingers softly, maybe even unconsciously, stroking the skin of his neck, he felt like a total prick for violating her space that way. And none of the good rationales made that feeling go away. Not that she was their best lead for learning what was going on inside Confessions. Not that his gut told him she wouldn't open up, at least not yet. Not that the devices might give him the ability to help Crystal and Jenna if some bad shit ever went down here.

In her beautiful, hesitant expression, he could see the war playing out inside her. To trust him or kick him to the curb. To push him away or pull him tighter. To accept his help or reinforce the fortress of walls she'd clearly built around her. And he knew those bugs were a risk.

In the final analysis, though, he'd done right by his team.

But that fact wasn't doing near enough to stuff a sock in the piehole of his guilty conscience.

Unthinkingly, Shane pressed his lips against the shell of her ear. His mouth went dry, and he had to restrain the urge to taste her there. To taste her everywhere. Goddamn. "What's your last name, Crystal?" he finally managed.

"What? Oh." Pause. "Roberts. Crystal Roberts."

Annnd there it was. The hesitation, the touch of perspiration on her hand, her pulse kicking up everywhere they touched. He didn't know who Roberts was, but it wasn't *her*. The lie didn't surprise him one bit, though. Just meant he'd read her right.

"Well, I really need your help, Crystal Roberts. Before I go, can I ask you a few things?"

The question shot tension through her body, but Shane kept them moving to the beat of the song. "I don't know."

"Fair enough. My asking doesn't mean you have to answer. Just remember that, okay?"

"Okay," she said, skepticism coloring her voice.

"Do you know why Church was holding my friend hostage?" he whispered against her ear.

"No."

Truth.

He nodded, his cheek brushing hers. "Do you know who Church was supposed to meet with last night at Confessions?"

She shook her head, inserting a tiny pause. "No."

Also truth. Though his gut told him she knew *something* even if it wasn't *who.*

"You're doing great. Just a few more. Were they holding anyone else with my friend?"

There went her pulse again. "Uh, no," she said, though there was an upward lilt on the end of that last word that gave it the hint of a question.

"Are you sure?"

"He was the only one I saw," she said, anger swirling into her tone.

Truth. And it was clear Crystal was practiced at answering questions in their most narrow constructs so that, in absolute terms, she could tell the truth.

Shane nodded. "Okay, okay. Just stick with me. Now, this next one's a doozy. There's no way to ask it without just asking it."

She released a shaky breath. "What?"

Their voices remained soft, hidden under the musical umbrella of the song. The conversation was holding Crystal on the very edge of her tolerance for risk. Shane could feel the truth of that in her touch, in her reactions, in her very physiology. But he had to ask. "Is Church involved in trafficking girls?"

Sure enough, the tension in her sweet body ratcheted up under his hands. "I'm just a waitress."

"I know," he said, keeping his voice soft, calm.

"Why do you care?" she asked, still dodging the question. And, in so doing, giving him the answer.

Sadness slinked through his gut at the realization that, in her world, caring was apparently so rare it was noteworthy, and maybe even suspect. He didn't need the firsthand experience of Molly's loss to be outraged that women were bought and sold like commodities on a shelf. He cared because he was a human being who couldn't stand injustice. And because he was a soldier who had the skills, training, and knowledge to do something about it. "'Cause maybe I could help."

She scoffed. "I can't decide if you're crazy or have a death wish."

He shrugged. "Both have been asserted by my very best friends, so you'd be in good company either way." Shane dipped his head until he could look Crystal in the eyes. Fear and panic danced in those green depths. "What does he do with the girls?"

She shook her head.

"You're just a waitress."

She nodded. The song—their dance—was seconds from ending.

"I know." He cupped her cheek in his hand, careful not to push against the bloom of red on the fine bone below her eye. "One more question then, because I'm almost out of time. Can you tell me about the delivery taking place Wednesday night?"

For less than an instant, her gaze widened. "No."

There was that precision again. He winked. "Let me rephrase. What do you know about the delivery taking place Wednesday night?"

"I . . . don't know."

"I might have gotten my friend back, but he's still in danger, Crystal. This meeting might be the key to something for him. For both of us." He let the question hang there, then . . . silence. Their song ended. For a moment, it seemed perhaps she hadn't noticed, because she kept moving. So he did, too. A commercial came on. An obnoxious car salesman shouted about sales and interest rates and zero down payments.

"Oh," she said, just noticing the change. Her arms withdrew from his body, and he missed her touch everywhere though she didn't actually step away.

"Well, our song's over." He reached for her hand but let her be the one to actually make contact. After a moment, she slipped her fingers into his palm. Shane lifted her hand to his mouth and let his lips linger against the smooth skin on the back of her hand. Without warning, he flipped her hand over and placed a small silver cell phone into her loose grip. "There's a single number programmed into it. It comes directly to me," Shane said quietly, patting the phone in his pocket. "It's a brand-new prepaid, so it's clean."

Her gaze lit on the rectangular device like it was a snake that might rear back and bite her.

Shane wrapped her fingers around it, relished the skin-on-skin contact for one last moment, then gently let her go. "Thank you for the dance. And the conversation. If you—or Jenna—need anything, use that." He nodded toward her hand.

Crystal gaped at him, only now her face was a lot less readable. But by *God,* she was a beautiful little thing. Hair like a low, warm fire on a cool winter's night. Skin like peaches and cream. Curves meant to be traced and gripped.

Stepping to her side, he brushed a kiss on her cheek. Without saying a word, he crossed the small room to the door. Man, he hoped he was playing this right. But he feared if he kept pushing, he'd send her fight-or-flight response into overdrive. And then those walls would go up high, hard, and fast in a way he might never be able to counteract. Backing off seemed the *only* way to go.

He gripped the doorknob.

"Hey . . ."

"Yeah?" he said, smiling over his shoulder.

Her mouth moved, but no sound came out. She cleared her throat, and the whisper that came out was nearly inaudible. "Thanks for helping me with Jenna."

He gave a single nod. And then he walked out the door.

Chapter 6

Shane planted himself in the shadows across the parking lot from Crystal's apartment. Would she leave? Would
someone arrive? He couldn't pull himself away for the
night without seeing if there would be any discernible re-
percussions of his visit.

A half hour passed, and everything remained quiet.
From the outside at least. Then, one by one, the lights
inside the apartment went out and the windows went
dark. It was after 1:30 a.m., after all. The lateness and the
darkness and the quiet were all perfect for the last thing
Shane needed to do before he left.

He crossed the lot and the scrubby grass in front of
Crystal's building, then circled the building to the rear.
Bingo. The electrical, phone, and cable wiring congre-
gated down the back of the brickwork at one corner.
Shane retrieved the receiver-transmitters and Swiss Army

knife tool set from the side pocket on his thigh and made quick work of wiring up the units so Marz could collect the feed from the devices he'd planted.

At the middle window above him, a dull glow just hinted at light behind the curtains, and Shane could almost picture the small lamp on Jenna's nightstand. Had Crystal gone back in to check on her? Or did Jenna need help again?

The latter question flooded a restlessness through him he really had no business feeling. Didn't mean he could make it go away, though.

Best solution was to bug out.

Shane ghosted through the night-darkened backyards to the side street on which he'd left his truck. For shits and giggles, he drove a circuit through the apartment complex and around the immediate neighborhood surrounding Crystal's place. Not that he ever expected to need the intel he gathered, but in his world there truly was no such thing as too much information.

He spent the ride home analyzing all his interactions with Crystal Roberts. The lie about the surname had him wondering about the first name, too. She did work in a strip club, after all. Didn't most of the dancers take stage names? Though she wasn't a dancer, at least not that he'd seen so far.

An image of Crystal onstage, dressed more scantily than ever before, crawled unbidden into Shane's brain. Moving that lithe body to the music. Gyrating around a pole. Removing clothing piece by tantalizing piece. While every man in the audience eye-fucked her—

"Sonofabitch," Shane bit out in the quiet of the cab. He shook his head and forced the image out. *Focus, McCallan.* He had no right to have an opinion about what she did or didn't do anyway. So what did it matter to him?

Buuullshit, a little voice said inside his head.

"Fantastic," he muttered. Because his subconscious was clearly aware of something he was working his ass off to ignore—that a nascent sense of investment, of responsibility was taking root where Crystal and her sister were concerned. Mission or no.

Twenty-five minutes later, Shane reached the driveway along the side of Hard Ink. Pressing the button on the black rectangular clicker he'd received just this afternoon caused the chain-link gate blocking the drive to swing inward, clearing his entrance to the parking lot beyond. His tires crunched over the gravel, and the truck's movement set off the new motion-sensor lights. Had they really just installed all of that this morning? Seemed like days ago. Or maybe that was just his exhaustion speaking.

Because Shane couldn't remember the last time he'd woken up in the morning feeling fully rested.

As he crossed the lot to the back door, he blew a kiss and flicked the bird to the closest security camera. He could imagine Marz's laughter—as well as the few choice words he was probably saying in reply.

Shane keyed himself in, passed the locked door to the long-closed tattoo shop, and jogged up the cement steps to the second-floor landing. He went straight to the gym, wondering who might be up that he could debrief at this hour.

Marz and Nick sat around Marz's desk in the far corner. Both men's gazes cut toward him as he stepped into the room.

"Hey," Shane said, crossing the wide space.

"Wassup, my brother? Besides your middle finger? Where's the love?" Marz said, reclining in his chair. He was the picture of ease, with his hands laced behind his head and his feet propped on the desk, the prosthesis his cargo shorts exposed crossed over his ankle.

"Blew ya a kiss, too," Shane said, grinning.

"You know I can't handle these mixed signals." Marz winked.

"How'd it go?" Nick said, rising from where he'd been propped against the desk's edge. "Make any headway with the waitress?"

She's not just a waitress. Shane forced himself to dial back the irritation Nick's label had unleashed. Crystal *was* a waitress. It was just that, in the few hours he'd spent with her, he'd also learned she was so much more. A survivor. A sister. A caregiver. A fighter. And Shane suspected he'd only scratched the surface.

But if he spilled any of this personal reaction toward her instead of speaking about her like the operational asset she was, Nick's radar would sound off all over the place. "A little. Not as much as I hoped, but I laid some good groundwork. And, I managed to get us some ears inside her place, too. Whatever good that may do."

Nick's gaze narrowed. "How'd you end up at her place?"

Shane recounted the entirety of his night, from bugging Confessions and his confrontation there with Crystal, to following her to her apartment, helping her sister, and finally questioning her after bugging her apartment. He conveniently left out the dance. And the feel of her body in his arms. And how hard she'd made him no matter how much he'd tried to rein himself in.

Marz immediately got to work on the computer, connecting to the transmitters and testing the feeds.

Shane held up a hand and started counting off on his fingers. "Here's what I nailed down for sure. Church is involved in human trafficking. Some part of it takes place in or via Confessions. And there *is* a delivery taking place Wednesday night. I think I need to sit on my hands for twelve to eighteen hours and see if Crystal reaches out. In the meantime, we get some ears on those transmissions and see if she has any conversations that might be useful. If not, I'll need to go back in and push a little harder."

Nick nodded. "Was she as skittish as at the club?"

"Every bit. Even in her apartment. She was pretty clearly afraid I'd be found there. No doubt by whatever scumbag took a hand to her and marked her face." Not wanting the others to see how much Crystal's abuse affected him, Shane scrubbed his hands over his face and tugged his fingers through his hair, still stiff with the gel.

Marz froze, his gaze cutting up to Shane, while Nick's expression slid into a scowl. "Shit. Someone beat her?" Nick asked.

Shane dropped his hands and felt a big bucket of pissed off park itself on his chest. "Yeah. Because of what we did."

"She said that?" Nick asked, his tone subdued, like he didn't want to rile Shane any more than he already was. Which meant Shane was doing a stellar job hiding how angry he was over this. Fantastic.

"She didn't have to," Shane said, needing to put an end to this topic. "Anyway, the degree of her fear and the fact that someone had no qualms marking her in a visible way both seem to point to some kind of association with a higher-up in the Church organization. And, if I'm right that this same someone outfitted her otherwise no-frills apartment with several thousand dollars in high-end media components, he's either a boyfriend or a sugar daddy or something. Least that's what my gut is telling me." Though, when they'd danced, Crystal sure hadn't responded to him like her heart had been claimed by another man. Because, *damn,* she'd been every bit as affected by their dance as he had. He'd put money on it.

"Sounds right," Nick said. "Seems like the sister could

be an in with Crystal, too. If the girl needs medical care she's not getting, you could no doubt white knight it and earn some favor."

Shane frowned. "If Jenna's not getting treatment or medicine, she's in some serious trouble. She had a full-blown grand mal seizure. Doubtful Crystal's pulling in health benefits as a waitress, so unless someone's picking up the tab, I have no idea how she'd cobble together money for the meds. They've gotta be damn expensive."

The clacking under Marz's fingers stopped. "Hold up a minute. If someone *is* covering the sister's doctors' bills and meds, that'd certainly give that person a strong hold on Crystal, and it would incentivize her loyalties toward them and away from us. If any of that's true, you sure we aren't barking up the wrong tree? 'Cause we don't have time to spare."

Marz had a point, so Shane bit back the knee-jerk irritation that threatened at the suggestion that Crystal wasn't reliable. Because his gut told him she was even if she needed a little time. Years of finding, managing, and working with informants gave him a sixth sense about these things that he'd learned to trust. "What you're saying all follows, except we don't know if any of it's true. Until we do, Crystal's our best option. And it's worth saying that she was more than a little interested in my medical training. Like maybe she saw an alternative in me. But I could only push so far without scaring her off. I'll figure out what's going on. Don't doubt it."

"I don't," Nick said. "But we can't put all our eggs in one basket. Tomorrow night, B-Team should visit Confessions and see what else they can learn and who else they might be able to tap for intel." B-Team was one of the three-man teams they'd created to run the operation that led to Charlie's rescue. They'd had two possible locations to investigate—Shane, Nick, and Easy on A-Team focused on Confessions, where Charlie had in fact been held, and B-Team's Beckett, Marz, and Miguel infiltrated one of Church's front businesses, a storage facility across town.

Out of nowhere, Charlie's recollections about his time in the storage facility slammed into Shane's brain. He braced his hands on the desk as the pieces turned in his brain . . . and finally clicked together. "Well, goddamn," Shane said.

"What?" Marz and Nick said at the same time.

"Church's storage facility. When we interrogated that thug on the boat the other day," Shane said, referring to the man whose attempts to kidnap Becca had landed him on the wrong end of Nick's favorite knife, "the guy said Charlie had been at the storage facility, and Charlie said he'd heard women locked up inside there with him. Jesus. Could a storage facility be any better of a place through which to traffic women? I bet there are box trucks in and out of there all the time, maybe even container storage. What if there are records at that facility that would give us more intel relevant to Wednesday's meeting? What the cargo is, who the cargo's intended for, maybe even where it's being delivered."

"Well done," Marz said, his fingers flying over the keyboard again. "Maybe I can get us into their server. If not, we'll need boots on the ground. Shane could be right, though. There's a reason they were so trigger-happy there." And Marz would know, seeing as how three of the Churchmen's bullets had turned the guy's pants into Swiss cheese.

"All right. This is good. We'll brief everyone in the morning and put together a plan. In the meantime, you two should get some shut-eye," Nick said. "We all look like the walking dead."

Marz chuffed out a weak laugh as he scrubbed his

hands over his face. "Roger that," he said, pushing out of his chair. "I'll start fresh on all this on the flip side."

"You guys make any progress here?" Shane asked. Marz's computer research was at the center of a number of mysteries they were trying to solve.

Marz blew out a long breath and tugged his longish hair behind his head. "I spent all night burying our IP address so deep you'd have to go to China to find it. Now I've got some spiders crawling the web for all possible meanings of 'WCE,'" he said, referring to the depositor's initials Charlie had found in his father's twelve-million-dollar bank account.

Shane pressed his lips into a tight line. Twelve million dollars. Apparently the going rate for selling out the men and the values you were supposed to defend. Fucking Merritt. Shane counted his failure to see his commander's true character as the second biggest mistake of his life.

After Molly.

Sighing, Marz continued. "Also been trying to unravel the mystery of Becca's bracelet without much luck yet." When they'd rescued Charlie the night before, the guy had only needed one good look at a bracelet their father had sent back from Afghanistan to see that the design actually embodied binary codes that translated to six-digit numbers. What those numbers meant, though, nobody knew. Marz pointed to a cardboard box sitting on the far end of his desk. "And I sorted through all the papers Becca had from her father, but nothing seemed to connect to the numbers." The frustration in Derek's voice was unusual, but understandable. They were looking for a needle in a Himalaya-sized haystack.

"You'll figure it out. Don't worry about it," Shane said. If anybody could, it was Derek DiMarzio.

"Appreciate the vote of confidence, but I feel like I'm spinning my wheels. Charlie might be able to help, though. After all, I'd missed the bracelet, and he'd only needed one look to realize its significance." Shane suspected Marz might be right since Charlie seemed to have been cut from the same scary-brilliant cloth. Marz shrugged. "Anyway, the transmitters are all up and running, so anyone wanting to listen in or review the recordings can."

"Thanks, man," Shane said, clasping hands and bumping shoulders with the guy.

"*No problemo.*" Marz repeated the action with Nick, then headed toward the door, his nearly even gait almost hiding the fact that, a year ago, Shane had held the man's femoral artery between his fingers when a grenade had blown off everything below his right knee.

When Shane looked at the guy, he saw many things—a survivor, a friend, a brilliant mind. But he also saw one of the few unequivocal things he'd done *right* in his life. It wouldn't make up for failing Molly or his team. *Nothing* could make up for that. But it sure explained why Shane always felt that just a little of the weight on his shoulders lifted when Marz was around.

Because it was surprising just how much a lifetime of guilt weighed when saddled around a man's shoulders.

What a fucking track record Shane had. No run-of-the-mill screwups for him. No. His mistakes were of the epically catastrophic kind. Every damn time.

Which was why, with every passing minute, Shane's instincts lit up all over the place when it came to Crystal. Saving her just might represent a chance to earn a little redemption. He felt the truth of that into his very marrow. Any other outcome was unthinkable. Intolerable. Liable to take him to his knees once and for all.

Shane forced himself from his thoughts and turned to Nick. "How come you're over here with us ugly mugs instead of holing up with a certain blond-haired cutie?"

A hint of humor flashed across Nick's face. "We were holed up until Charlie started feeling bad. He said he was okay, but Becca wanted to sit up with him for a while."

"Gotta respect that."

"Yeah. I can only imagine how I'd feel if it were Katherine lying in that room right now, having gone through what Charlie did."

Nick didn't mean anything by mentioning his younger sister. Shane knew he didn't. But it still totally sucker punched him. Because having failed to be there for Molly when it mattered most, he'd never get the chance again.

"Aw, goddamn, man, I didn't mean—"

"Ain't a thing," Shane said, shaking his head. "Just know if I can help with Charlie, you can count on me." Suddenly, Shane realized the gruffness in his words made them sound a bit like an accusation given their recent history.

Sure enough, Nick's expression told him he'd heard the same thing. Damn, would they never recover that old, comfortable easiness that once came so naturally? "Thanks. I hope you know the reverse is true, too. Always has been."

"I know you have my back." Which wasn't exactly the same thing as being able to count on someone, was it? When the shit was flying, sure. Shane had no doubt that Nick Rixey would have his six. But day to day, when the crisis was past, and it was just the regular slog of life, when they no longer had this catastrofuck of a situation to drown out the physical and mental pain this past year had inflicted? Yeah, he wasn't so sure about that.

Time would tell, he supposed.

A weighty pause filled the space between them. Nick crossed his arms and dropped his gaze to the floor. "But . . . ?"

Shane shook his head. "I don't need to say it, Nick. You know as well as I do what went down between us."

Rixey gave a tight nod. "I do. Question is, you gonna let me build a bridge or not?"

If only it were that simple. Shane didn't want to hold this grudge. Feeling hurt and betrayed took energy and headspace he didn't have to spare. But some emotions couldn't be willed away. No matter how hard you tried. He had a lifetime of experience to prove it.

"Come on," Nick said, walking away.

"What?"

"Just come on."

Sighing, Shane forced himself to move, no idea what Nick wanted and very little patience left to find out. Halfway across the room, he yawned so big his eyes watered, and his jaw cracked—

Something knocked him in the gut. "What the hell?" he said, his arms rising up to block the attack and finding . . . a pair of black boxing gloves resting in his grip. He glared at Nick. "Aw, hell no." He tossed them to the floor, his patience just about worn clean through.

"Pick them up," Nick said, tugging on a thick black glove.

"No." Shane stepped toward the door.

Nick moved in front of him, blocking his way. "Pick. Them. Up."

"I'm not fighting you." Shane nailed the slightly taller man with a glare. Throwing fists wasn't going to fix what was broken between them, and Shane wasn't a vindictive asshole. At least, not usually.

Jabbing both gloved hands against Shane's shoulders, Nick's light green eyes narrowed. "Put the goddamn gloves on, McCallan."

The shove made Shane's GSW sting like a mofo and tripped a wire in his brain, unleashing all kinds of things he'd been trying to hold tight. Anger. Regret. Hurt. Guilt. He shoved right back. "Screw you, Rix."

"That's the spirit. Now do as you're told and glove up." He knocked his gloves together and arched a brow.

Do as I'm told? "Fuck that noise. We aren't working for Uncle Sam. And you sure as hell aren't my superior anymore. What's your fucking problem, anyway?"

Pressing his lips together, Nick shook his head. "I'm not the one with the problem."

Shane scoffed. "Oh? Is that right? Then why'd you shut me the hell out the past year?"

"And *now* we're getting somewhere." Nick walked past him, and Shane flinched back, his adrenal gland doing its job and flooding plenty of fight instinct through his body. He was wound as tight as barbed wire. Nick scooped the gloves from the ground, turned, and chucked them at him again. Hard.

This time, Shane caught them before they made impact.

"Look, I know a firearm is your first weapon of choice. But as I don't need any more holes in my head, and I'd like to stay on this side of the great white beyond, you're going to have to make do with the gloves. You need this, Shane. *We* need this. So could you just put the fucking gloves on already and stop being a pain in the ass?"

"Right. *I'm* the pain in the ass," he muttered, his hands making quick work of lacing up without really telling them to do it. Nick was right, though. Shane did need this. For a whole lotta reasons. But the other man was a few rounds shy of a full clip if he thought throwing a coupla punches would clear the debris field between them.

The minute the second glove was secured, Nick was right in his face. "No holds barred." He slammed his gloves on top of Shane's, and Shane hammered right back.

And then it was on.

Shane threw the first punches, catching Nick in the jaw and the ribs, and blocked the uppercut aimed at his gut. Facing off again, Shane jabbed with his right, forcing Nick to cover himself in a way that exposed his left side—and the lingering injuries from his gunshot wounds that still gave him back problems. Shane jammed his knee into Nick's side. The deep groan that erupted from his opponent's throat tempted Shane's guilt, but then he wasn't the one who insisted on this, was he? And now that Nick had invited Shane's lizard brain out to play, it liked their little game here too much to back down.

Nick recovered quickly and came at him with a back kick that had broken ribs written all over it. Shane managed to rear back at the last possible second, but the action threw him off-balance, allowing Nick to take his feet out from under him. Shane slammed to the ground, his breath whooshing out and pain radiating up and down his spine. But even before gravity had all its fun, Shane was forcing his ass to move. He rolled and sprang to his feet, ignoring the dizziness that threatened.

And it was a good goddamned thing he'd found his feet again.

Because Nick was now full-on pissed off. He came at Shane like a freight train, swinging, kneeing, kicking. Nick's fury fueled his own, and Shane gave every bit as good as he got. Body impacts, grunts, and the scuffs of shoes on concrete echoed around the cavernous space. Man, but Shane was going to be feeling this little dance for days.

They circled, attacked, and retreated over and over, neither man holding the advantage for long. Nick clipped him in the mouth, and Shane felt the skin split and the metallic tang of blood on his tongue. So evenly matched, their fight turned into a war of attrition that threatened to go on and on. Exhaustion making his arms heavy and his responses slower, Shane used the memory of the train of unanswered calls and emails, each one leaving him feeling more alone and isolated, and found the will to keep going, keep fighting, keep exorcising the demons in his head that never let up for five fucking seconds.

It was just . . . all . . . too . . . goddamned . . . much. *Wham.* His fist connected with Nick's cheekbone like a sledgehammer. Nick's head whipped to the side, and his whole body spun as if in slow motion.

Nick caught himself just before he face-planted, though he stumbled until he crashed into the bench press.

For a long moment, Nick braced his gloves against the leather-covered bench and seemed to gather himself. He rose and faced Shane, and it was clear from the stiffness and slowness of his movement that he was hurting.

Shane didn't take a lick of pleasure from that fact.

Just the opposite.

The sight of his best friend bloodied and injured at his own hands drained the fight from him. Becca was going to have both their asses in a sling when she saw that the nearly healed cut on Nick's cheekbone was open again. The initial wound wasn't Shane's doing—that had been between Nick and Beckett.

"Goddamnit," Shane rasped, wiping the sweat off his brow with the back of his forearm. His mouth took over where his fists left off. "I needed you, Nick. I fucking needed you, and you weren't there."

Nick's head dropped heavily on his shoulders. For a long moment, labored breaths aside, he was still. Then his gaze cut up, and Nick nodded. "I know. I . . . know."

Shane waited, expecting more. Expecting . . . something. Anything. That Nick had needed him, too. That Nick was sorry. That he understood just how deep his silence had cut. "That's it? That's all you have to say?"

"What else is there to say?" Nick pulled off his gloves.

And there it was. Same story, different day. Guy still

didn't get it, did he? Shane tugged off his gloves, returned them to a shelf against the wall, and shook his head. "Not a damn thing, I guess."

Shane reached for the door handle.

"*Jesus.* What do you want me to say?" The agonized whisper had Shane turning back to his friend. "Do you want me to say I was so fucked in the head I became depressed? Do you want me to say I should've figured out what Merritt was doing? Because I know that shit is true. And that, since I didn't see the forest for the trees, I was so guilt-ridden I couldn't face you guys? That I thought you'd all blame me for ruining your lives and killing our friends?" Nick's eyes were bleak with anguish.

Shane's gut went tight as a hollowness settled into his chest. "Nick—"

"Or maybe you want me to say it was easier to ignore you than face the possibility that I'd lost you, too? Because you had to hate me as much as I hated myself, right? Or, how 'bout that the pain of the surgeries and the PT was so intense I got hooked on painkillers for about three months until Jeremy realized what'd happened, flushed them down the toilet, and called my doctor behind my back?" Nick scrubbed his hands over his face, smearing the blood on his cheek, and clawed his fingers through his dark, sweaty hair.

Christ. How the hell had the guy carried all this around for the past year without caving under the weight of it? Just went to show that you never really knew the size of the load another person carried. Except—Shane *should've* known. He was supposed to be Nick's best friend in the world. His brother.

Damnit. Shane should've forced the question.

As Nick stood there pouring his soul in a bloody mess onto the floor between them, it occurred to Shane for maybe the first time ever that he'd failed Nick as much as he'd always thought Nick failed him. If he'd only pushed through his own hurt and anger, maybe he would've realized that under normal circumstances, the Nick Rixey he knew would *never* shut him out. But things hadn't been normal, had they? Not by a long shot.

Sonofabitch.

Shane released a long breath, then crossed the space that separated them and lowered himself heavily onto the bench. "Sitcha ass down before you fall down."

Nick sat and dropped his gloves.

Bracing his elbows on his knees, Shane watched a bead of sweat drop to the concrete. "I wish I'd known." From his peripheral vision, he saw Nick nod.

"I know. I wish I'd been strong enough to tell you."

Shane's thoughts were in a whirl. Which made sense since the earth was shifting a bit underneath his feet, at least where his beliefs about Nick were concerned.

Knock, knock, sounded against the door that led to the hall. A moment later, it eased open, and Becca stuck her head through the breach. *Did she hear . . .*

Yup.

Her expression was a study in worry and concern. How much she'd overheard, he didn't know. But it was something, for sure.

"Um. Everything okay?" she asked, clearly knowing the answer to the question. She stepped the rest of the way in and let the door fall closed behind her.

Nick's glance slid from her to Shane. The man's eyes repeated the question. *Are we okay?*

Shane didn't want an audience to say the things he needed to say, and the words weren't there just yet anyway. So he said, simply, "Yeah, man. We are." It wasn't enough, but it was a start.

Nick rose. Shane wondered if Becca would catch that he'd braced himself on the weight bar to make it to his feet. Her expression darkened the closer Nick got. So, yeah, she'd noticed.

"Sorry, Becca," Shane said, rising to his feet. "Won't happen again."

Nick shook his head and caught her hands in his. "Be mad at me, not him. I started it. A guy thing."

She rolled her eyes but cupped his face in her hand as she looked him over. "Well, let's be done with the guy things, okay? We have enough enemies out there without fighting each other."

"Roger that," Shane said, regret making him weary.

"Okay, sunshine," Nick said, his voice sounding as exhausted as Shane felt. Nick followed her out the door but threw a look over his shoulder before he stepped into the hall. "You coming?"

"Uh." Shane tugged his fingers through his hair. "In a few. I think I'll just"—he shrugged—"listen in on the feeds from Crystal's and Confessions for a little while. Or something."

Nick gave a tight nod, and the door closed behind them, leaving Shane alone in the cavernous quiet of the unfinished warehouse. He licked at the crust of blood on his lip as aches screamed from every joint in his body.

But, god*damn,* the silence around him only amplified the roar in his head. Because the space between his ears was *loud* with the sound of all the words he couldn't take back, of all the things he should've said but hadn't, of all the things he wished he could say, but couldn't.

Like apologizing to Nick.

Like . . .

Like telling Molly, yes, she could play with him and his friends.

Like telling her he was sorry he'd sent her away.

Like having the chance to say good-bye.

Jamming his hands in his pockets, his fingers found

the chain of Molly's butterfly necklace. God, what he wouldn't give for five more minutes with his kid sister. Just five. Did she know how sorry he was? How much he loved her? That he'd devoted his life to making things right for others as a penance for getting so much wrong with her?

He stood there. Absolutely lost and completely alone. It was the stinging in his eyes that finally caught his attention, made him realize he'd been staring off into space. He wiped the burn away. Just a little sweat in his eyes. Damnit.

He hadn't kept Molly safe, but maybe he could do that for Crystal and Jenna. And maybe Crystal could lead him to information that would help him clear his name, his teammates' names, and the names of his six brothers who'd died. Because they were his family, too. That was a shit-ton of maybes, but Shane didn't have a choice. A lifetime of guilt and a soul-deep sense of duty meant, at the very least, he had to try.

Chapter 7

Crystal lurched into a sitting position, not sure what had woken her. From her makeshift bed on the floor of Jenna's bedroom, her gaze cut to her sister, all balled up against the far wall and sleeping soundly. Then what—

"Crystal! Open the damn door!" *Bang, bang.*

Bruno?

Adrenaline racing through her system from being startled awake, Crystal scrabbled off the floor and dashed through the apartment. What the hell was he doing here? And what time was it, anyway? Pitch black still cloaked the outside world, so it had to be the middle of the night.

A light that shouldn't have been there slanted in a narrow beam across the living-room carpet. Crystal flicked the switch to the front hallway's ceiling fixture and realized it had been the light from the landing streaming through the exterior door, already ajar about two inches. Only the security chain kept it from being opened all the way.

"Open it before I break it down," Bruno growled, peering through the gap.

"What's the matter?" she said, completely bewildered by his presence and his urgent anger. "Step back so I can undo the chain."

As soon as she did, he pushed his way in, shoved past her, and looked around, like he was searching for something.

Tucking her hair behind her ears, Crystal watched him for a long moment, not wanting to risk having him direct his ire at her. Though, given his foul mood, that was likely going to happen whether she did something to attract it or not. "Bruno, what's happened? What's the matter?" she finally asked.

He pivoted toward her. "Who's here?"

"What do you mean? Me and Jenna." But, true as it was, her stomach was already sinking. Given the night's earlier activities, his question couldn't be a coincidence.

His gaze narrowed, and his expression darkened. "We'll see about that, won't we?" Grasping her by the biceps, he yanked her down the dark hallway toward the bedrooms.

"Ow, you're hurting me," she said, as his fingers dug into her bare skin. "There's no one here. I don't know what you're talking about."

Dragging her to the threshold of her bedroom, he reached in and flicked on her overhead light. Her bed was still made, the lavender comforter all straight and flat, her pretty throw pillows in a neat row against the headboard. Her normal pillows were all on Jenna's floor . . .

Bruno stalked into the room and whipped open the closet so hard a big stack of fabric scraps from her sewing projects tumbled out. He braced like he thought someone might actually be hidden within.

What made him think someone was here? There had been

a few times over the years when she'd had a niggling thought that he seemed to know something he shouldn't, but never anything that so blatantly made her wonder if maybe some of his guys spied on her. God, she wouldn't put it past him. The thought brought a sting to the back of her eyes. Did she truly have nowhere she was safe, nowhere she could have a slice of privacy? Although no doubt Bruno would feel entitled to snoop as much as he liked since he'd taken over the rent when Crystal had once fallen so far behind they received an eviction notice. Even with Jenna contributing some of her work-study money, Church took so much of what Crystal made at Confessions that she often couldn't make ends meet without Bruno's "help." Which wasn't exactly free, was it?

Still, the thought of him *watching* or, worse, *listening* stirred up a storm cloud of anger and resentment in the space between her ears until she struggled to keep her expression and voice neutral.

"Where is he?" Bruno said, crouching to look beneath her bed, then storming into the bathroom and ripping the shower curtain back.

"Where is *who*? There's no one here. I was asleep."

"Oh, yeah?" Eyebrows arched, he pointed to her too-tidy bed, like he was so freaking clever.

She laid a gentle hand on his chest. "Just listen for one second. Please?" His expression was a volcano about to erupt. She rushed on. "Jenna had one of the worst seizures I've ever seen a few hours ago. I was sleeping on her floor in case she needed me." She eased her sister's bedroom door open and stepped back so he could look in. "See? I'm worried about her, Bruno. She was completely delirious afterward and still hasn't really woken up."

A frown carved deep into his face, he leaned into the room, his gaze going from Jenna's still form to the mess of blankets and pillows on the carpet . . . to the closed closet door. Holy crap, he still didn't believe her.

Before he charged into the room and scared Jenna awake, Crystal padded across the carpet, slowly twisted the handle, and opened the closet door to show him that the only things within belonged there. She kept her expression carefully blank, but her thoughts were filled with, *Asshole. Control freak. Jerk.*

But since he was the assholish, control-freak jerk who paid for their housing and Jenna's various medications and numerous checkups, she put up with him. At over five thousand dollars every three months, Jenna's treatments didn't give her much choice.

Not for much longer, though . . .

Because once Jenna graduated from college, she could get a job that would provide her health benefits and, for the first time in four years, Crystal wouldn't feel compelled to do something, be someone, or be *with* someone she didn't want to ensure her sister had the care she required.

She didn't resent Jenna. Not one bit. Everyone made sacrifices for the people they loved. Crystal wasn't special in that. It just worked out that between their father's imprisonment, the debts he'd owed Church that, after her dad died, Church decided *Crystal* should repay, and Jenna's epilepsy, Crystal's options were bad, bad, and bad.

The only silver lining in all of it was that their father had apparently extracted a promise from Bruno to take care of his girls while he was in prison, which Bruno had honored because her father had once saved his life. And that, combined with Jenna's ill health, had shielded her from sharing Crystal's fate. But Crystal lived in fear that Church could at any moment override Bruno and force Jenna to work, too. Or worse.

Now Crystal was in way too deep—in debt to Church, in debt to Bruno, and in possession of just enough knowledge of the Church gang's inner workings—to ever be able to walk away. Which was why she planned to run.

She closed the closet door and returned to Bruno's side.

With a jerk of his head, he urged her into the hallway. "She had the seizure in here?" he asked, his tone less aggressive.

"No, downstairs, at the bottom of the steps. Happened right when I got home from work." All at once, she realized she had to give him at least a little of what he'd been fishing for. It was a risk—because Bruno forbade any other men except his guys from coming inside the apartment—but he clearly knew something. In a flash of desperate brilliance, a cover story came to mind. "Wayne from downstairs came home during the middle of it and helped me get her inside. He stayed for a while to make sure we were okay, then he left." She let realization wash over her expression. "Is that . . . is that why you thought someone was here? But how . . ."

Bruno crossed his arms, rocked on his bootheels, and pressed his lips into a tight line. "No one's allowed here, Crystal."

Crystal could count the number of times Bruno had ever seemed uncomfortable on one hand, but now was one of those times. The fidgetiness was *so* not him. *Ha.* She'd turned the tables around a bit.

Not that she could enjoy the little victory for long. Last thing she wanted was for his discomfort to morph into a new reason to get angry. "I know. I'm sorry. And, anyway, I'm just glad you're here. I didn't think I'd get to see you tonight." She smiled and pretended doing so didn't kill a small part of her.

His shoulders untensed, just the littlest bit. "You know I had work to do."

"I know. Any progress?" she asked.

"We'll get the fuckers, don't worry." He heaved a breath and leaned heavily against the doorframe behind him.

The fuckers. As in Shane, who'd stood in nearly the same exact place maybe three hours ago. Crystal's stom-

ach flipped. "You seem tense. I know you've got a lot on
your shoulders."

"You relax me, baby. You always know just what to do."
He grasped her cheek in his hand and rubbed his thumb
over her lips. As his stare zeroed in on her mouth, Crystal
knew exactly what he wanted, and it made her stomach
roll. *Fuck my life,* she thought, just as a moan sounded
from behind Jenna's door.

Frowning, Crystal froze. There it was, again. "Hold that
thought," she whispered, then peeked inside the room.

Jenna crawled unsteadily toward the edge of the bed.
"Gon' be sick, gon' be sick," she whimpered.

Crystal darted inside and lifted the plastic bathroom
trash can she'd left on the floor by the bed. "Here you go,
sweetie." She managed to pull her sister's hair back from
her face just as Jenna vomited into the can.

When Jenna stopped heaving, she sat there, holding the
can in front of her. "Do you think you're going to get sick
again? Are you nauseous?" But Jenna just stared into the
bucket, still not coherent enough to respond to Crystal's
questions.

Before she threw up again, Crystal made a trip to the
bathroom for a wet washcloth and a towel. "Sorry," she
said to Bruno, now standing in Jenna's doorway. He shook
his head, obviously not pleased by this turn of events but
not angry, either. Crystal had to give him credit—he'd
always seemed to have a soft spot for Jenna, maybe because he had a younger sister of his own, and he'd seen
how the epilepsy ravaged Jenna with his own eyes. She
supposed it was one of the reasons she'd once felt so safe
with him.

Good thing Bruno didn't know what Jenna thought of
him now. And he could never know.

Kneeling on the floor by the bed, Crystal wiped Jenna's
brow with the cool cloth, smiling when the other woman

lifted her eyes and made contact. There was a flash of clarity in Jenna's blue-eyed gaze before it disappeared as another wave of nausea washed over her. She vomited into the bucket again.

"Little better now," Jenna mumbled, falling into a ball on her side.

Crystal carried the bucket to the bathroom and flushed its contents, then she washed it out in the bathtub.

She hated seeing her sister like this, hated not being able to do more to make her better, but a part of her wanted to throw her sister a party and bake her a cake. If Jenna hadn't gotten sick when she did, Crystal would probably be getting a rug imprint on her knees right now.

Not that she wanted Jenna to get sick, of course. But if it had to have happened, it couldn't have done so at a better time.

"I'm sorry," she said, hugging Bruno from behind.

"Don't be. I'll take a rain check. You gotta deal with this."

Thank God he'd been the one to say it. Now he couldn't come back at her later and try to say she hadn't wanted to be with him. She came around him and pushed up on her tiptoes to kiss his lips. "Thank you."

"Hmm," he said, clearly unhappy that neither his surprise raid nor his booty call had worked out the way he'd expected.

"Hey, I have an idea," Crystal said, smiling and hooking her arms around his neck. "I'm scheduled to work the late shift tomorrow night, but I have off on Wednesday. Let's go on a date. Whatever you want to do."

His expression softened. "Sounds nice, but I can't. Got a meeting Wednesday night."

The meeting. Shane.

She hadn't set out to ask about the meeting, but Bruno's mention of it immediately resurrected the sound of Shane's voice in her head. *I might've gotten my friend back, but he's still in danger, Crystal. This meeting might be the key to something for him.* "That's okay. We can go out after," she said, hoping her voice didn't sound any different because she could feel the quickened beat of her own pulse everywhere their bodies touched.

He shook his head. "Not sure how long it'll be."

"Well, where's the meeting? I could wait for you at a restaurant nearby. Even if you have to work, you gotta eat." What was she doing? She never pushed him like this. Why was she fishing for information? And what the hell did she think she was going to do with it if she learned something, anyway?

You know how to reach him . . . to reach Shane . . . The cell phone he'd given her sat hidden inside the air-conditioning vent behind her bedroom dresser. One of several stash spots she had around the apartment for things she wanted to keep secret from Bruno—the phone, a gun, money she'd been putting aside a little at a time for her and Jenna.

She wasn't flirting with Bruno for Shane, though, was she? She'd only proposed the date to mollify Bruno after the fiasco of tonight. Right? Right.

He wrapped his arms around her lower back and his hands landed on her butt. The little squeeze he gave proved her efforts were working. He was loosening up. "It's a good idea, but my meeting's not 'til nine, and there ain't nothing near the marine terminal, anyway. Besides, I'll have to handle some shit afterward."

Holy crap. She'd just learned the time and location of the meeting in one fell swoop. *Stop freaking out, Crystal. Nothing's going on here. You're just talking.* Right.

"Okay. Well, let me know if you want me to make you an early dinner here beforehand. Anything you want. If not, we'll just do this another time. I miss you," she said, forcing sincerity into her voice.

Jenna moaned in her sleep, drawing both of their attention.

"That might work. If I don't see you tomorrow at the club, I'll call you and let you know."

"Sure," she said, meeting his lips when he leaned down to kiss her.

"Well, given this"—he waved in the direction of Jenna's bed—"I won't stay here tonight. Let me know if she needs anything."

She smiled. "I will. Thank you." And in that moment, he reminded her of why she'd ever thought being with him was a good idea.

"But Crystal"—he grasped her jaw and tilted her face up to his—"if Wayne steps foot in this apartment one more time, he's going out in a box."

Annnd way to ruin it. "I understand," she said. "It was just an emergency. Won't happen again."

"Make sure of it."

With that, he dropped his hand, turned away, and left the apartment.

SHANE SAT AT Marz's desk, eyes trained on the computer, and listened to the conversation happening in Crystal's apartment.

And *holy shit,* Shane didn't know whether to drive over there, do a jig, or punch a wall. Because this conversation couldn't have been more revealing on so many levels.

Operationally, Crystal had managed to get the male to reveal the time and location of the Wednesday night meeting. That was huge. Question was, had she done it on purpose? And would she tell him what she'd learned? That would be the true test of whether he'd made any inroads with her trust.

But, personally, what he'd overheard confirmed a lot of his fears and suspicions about Crystal Roberts, or whatever her name really was. She had a boyfriend. A jealous one not above making threats, nor, likely, following through on them. Somehow said boyfriend had known about Shane's presence at the apartment, so clearly her place had been under surveillance before he'd planted his own bugs there earlier in the night.

Crystal's voice saying, "You're hurting me," still rang in his ears, sending ice down his spine and vengeful heat through his blood—not to mention giving him a lead as to who might've hit her.

But despite the stress and fear she must've felt, Crystal had handled the whole situation amazingly well. Every bit as good as if he'd been feeding her the words through an earpiece. From the lie about the neighbor with the similar-sounding name to her innocent-sounding questions to the way she'd mollified the guy. Shane was strangely . . . proud of her.

And worried for her.

And intrigued by her in a way he had no business feeling. Not with this shitstorm blowing all around them.

The sound of a slamming door came through the speakers.

"Asshole," Crystal said in a low voice.

Shane smiled. *That's my girl,* he thought. The smile dropped right back off his face. "Get your head out of your ass, McCallan. Not yours now. Not yours ever."

"Now what am I gonna do?" came through a few moments later, followed by a troubled sigh.

"Call me, Crystal. That's what you should do."

But only silence followed her question. His gaze trailed to the digital clock in the corner of the monitor—3:52 a.m. *Shit.*

If he didn't get some sleep, he was going to be wasted tomorrow. And since it seemed all the occupants of Crystal's apartment had settled in, there wasn't much benefit to sitting here any longer.

But first, he needed to write down this info so Marz would see it first thing because it hopefully freed them from having to infiltrate Church's storage facility again. He grabbed a legal pad and pen.

Delivery, 9 p.m. Wednesday, marine terminal

Job done, Shane ghosted through the Rixeys' apartment so as not to wake Beckett and Easy sleeping on the pullout couch and an air mattress in the living room, and made his way to the guest room he was currently calling home.

He needed a shower, but the bed had apparently developed magnetic powers because his ass was down for the count before he'd really decided to go horizontal.

THE NEXT THING Shane knew, morning had come, streaming soft golden light through the high warehouse window over the bed he could barely enjoy because of the ass-beating he'd taken the previous night. His face, ribs, and back throbbed in time with his pulse, making him suck in a harsh breath through his teeth when he forced himself into a sitting position. Damn, a year as a civilian, and he was getting soft.

Pushing into a standing position, his internal clock told him it was late. Sure enough, the LED on his cell phone showed nearly nine o'clock.

He fumbled through showering and dressing, letting himself linger a while under the stream of soothing hot water, grabbed a bagel off the kitchen counter, and beat feet toward the door to find the team.

"Hey, Shane? You got a minute?"

Becca.

He turned away from the door. "For you, always. What's up?"

"It's Charlie."

Shane could've guessed as much from the worry furrowing her brow and filling her blue eyes. "Nick mentioned he went downhill last night. How's he doing?"

"Well, that's what I'd like your opinion on. Do you mind?" she asked, her gaze lingering for a quick moment on the scab on his bottom lip. A souvenir from his rounds with Nick the night before.

He gestured for her to lead the way and followed her down the hall to the room where the Rixeys' sister apparently stayed when she came to visit. He couldn't imagine what a female version of Nick would be like. The thought almost made him smile.

Until he saw Charlie's face.

Fever red cheeks blazed over otherwise pale skin. His blond hair lay damp and darkened all along his hairline. Ten feet away and Shane could already tell the guy was in trouble.

"One oh two at last check," she said softly. "And rising despite another course of IV antibiotics overnight."

"How bad's the amputation site?"

"See for yourself," she said, carefully unwrapping the bandages.

Charlie's eyelids lifted once, twice, but he couldn't seem to keep them up no matter how many times he tried. He mumbled words too indistinct to be heard. The more Becca worked on the gauze, the more restless Charlie became.

Becca removed the last of the bandages and stepped aside.

Shane swallowed his *oh, shit* reaction, not wanting to escalate her already obvious concern. She knew enough to know what he was about to tell her. He leaned in to examine the wound. An angry, swollen redness that almost bordered on purple proclaimed Charlie's condition loud and clear. "Skin infection. Possible bone infection. Definite bone infection if the rest of this bone isn't amputated, here," he said, pointing. "And he needs some reconstructive surgery. A skin graft to close this up maybe. Probably why the infection is progressing despite the antibiotics."

She blew out a long breath and locked her hands on top of her head. Her position made him notice she was wearing a too-big man's T-shirt and rolled-up boxers that had to belong to Nick. An unexpected twinge of jealousy had him examining Charlie's wound again. He'd always loved the look and idea of a woman in his clothes, wearing his shirts to bed, the smell of his skin on hers, but he'd rarely had opportunities to make that little fantasy come true. And this situation wasn't making the immediate future look too good, either.

"Yeah," she finally said. A blanket lay balled up on a chair behind her, proof that she'd sat up some part of the night with Charlie.

Damn. Shane hated to have to say this . . . "He needs a hospital, Becca."

"I know."

He stared at her a long moment, just observing her mentally work through the problem. And he realized that more than just admiring the way Becca had handled herself these past days, he liked her. And he was glad she and Nick had found one another. "I'm sorry I was an ass toward you," he said.

She gave a small smile. "I know."

"What are you thinking?" he said in a low voice, not wanting to disturb Charlie. But now that they were done bothering at his hand, the guy was out cold.

"That he needs a hospital, but he can't go to one. Any admission automatically creates a paper and computer trail that Derek says is too risky. Not to mention that this injury is suspicious. They'd want to know how the amputation happened, and doctors and nurses are pretty good BS detectors. Plus, my attempted abduction last week means someone at UMC is on the take, and if that's true, it's probably not the only hospital in the city that's compromised."

"Our team's too small to transport him farther away," Shane said. "If some of us went with you to provide protection, it would short-staff the operation here. Especially with this delivery tomorrow night."

She sat heavily onto the chair next to Charlie. "Nick raised that concern, too. What a mess."

"Doesn't leave Charlie with many options, though." Sure as shit, Shane would've been going crazy if it was his brother in this situation. If this got much worse, they were going to have to chance a hospital, risks and operation be damned. Last thing they needed was another person dying on Frank Merritt's account.

It wasn't lost on him that for the second time in the past twenty-four hours, he found himself wondering how best to help someone else's sibling.

If the cosmos was trying to get his attention, it fucking had it already. For fuck's sake.

"Well, I have a Plan B, but it's still not a great option, and it requires bringing in someone outside our group. Nick's not going to love that idea," she said.

Neither did Shane. But he also knew that sometimes shit rained down so hard and so fast you couldn't shovel it all on your own. Nick would see that, too. "Who?"

"A longtime friend my gut tells me we can trust."

"It's at least worth having the conversation, first with Nick, then maybe with this friend. Any meet with the friend should happen somewhere off-site, though, and only if you take a protection detail." Because anyone associated with Becca's hospital was suspect until proven trustworthy as far as Shane was concerned.

Nick stepped through the door, his expression dark, intense, and flirting with pissed off. "A protection detail for what?"

Chapter 8

*C*rystal was showered, caffeinated, and thinking about what to make for lunch by the time Jenna emerged from her bedroom. Her sister shuffled down the hallway, still in her rumpled clothes from the previous night, and leaned into the kitchen. "Hey," she said, voice raspy and thin.

"Hey," Crystal said, pushing the fridge door shut. "How are you feeling?"

Jenna crossed her arms and hugged herself. "Tired. A little shaky. I'm okay, though." She attempted a smile, but the shades of gray in her normally blue eyes belied her attempt at optimism. "Thanks for being there for me last night."

"Of course. I'm always here for you. Why were you sitting outside anyway?" A hint of color pinked Jenna's cheeks, and Crystal chuckled. "You forgot your key again?"

"I left it at Rachel's. She's going to bring it to class this afternoon." Crystal just shook her head. "So, it was bad?"

Crystal frowned, not needing Jenna to explain what she meant. "One of the worst I can remember." She hesitated for a moment, but Crystal had to know. "Any idea what might've brought it on?"

Jenna tucked strands of sleep-tangled hair, a shade more fiery than Crystal's own, behind her ears. "Rachel and I stayed up late finishing our history presentation for today."

This was exactly why Crystal always worried when Jenna slept over at one of her friends' houses. But Jenna knew lack of sleep could trigger a seizure, and she'd be twenty in two weeks. Crystal couldn't mother her forever, no matter how much she wanted to sometimes. "So, you pulled an all-nighter," she said as gently as she could.

"Almost. I'm sorry."

Crystal nodded. "What can I get you to eat? Food might make you feel better." She turned back to the fridge. "I can make you some butter noodles if your stomach's still upset—"

"Wait. That's it? You're not going to yell at me?" Jenna reached around Crystal and grabbed a Sprite from the fridge, cracked it open, and took a small sip.

Jenna was the last person Crystal had left in this world. Arguing with her was nowhere near the top of her list of favorite things to do. Ever. "Nope. You know what you need to do and what you need to avoid. I'm not happy you stayed up when you know it's dangerous, but I also get why you did it. Wasn't like you were out clubbing or drinking. You know how important it is to take care of yourself without me saying it, and I'm guessing how bad you feel is punishment enough."

Jenna braced her elbows against the small stretch of

counter beside the fridge. "Yeah. Well, thanks. It's cool of you." She took another drink of soda.

Crystal smiled, feeling a weight lifted from her shoulders now that Jenna was doing a little better. "You're welcome. Now, butter noodles or something else?"

"Noodles, please. And thanks for always being so good to me. I know it must be a drag sometimes."

Settling the butter and parmesan cheese on the counter, Crystal turned back to her sister. "Don't say that. It's not. And, anyway, it's what family does. We stick together through everything."

Twenty minutes later, they were enjoying the comfort food at their tiny kitchen table. The carbs ensured that Crystal would have to add time to her workout. It was one thing to be required to wear revealing clothes. It was a whole other thing to feel like all her exposed parts jiggled as she moved. So she exercised pretty much every day whether she wanted to or not. It was also a great way to burn off the stress and frustration that came with living a life of lies.

Swallowing a bite of buttery, cheesy goodness, her gaze strayed to the living-room window. Nice as it was outside, maybe she'd go for a run instead of going to the gym—something else Bruno paid for.

A fork clanked heavily against a plate. "Sara!"

Jenna's voice made her jump. Instinctively, she looked around, as if making sure Bruno hadn't heard Jenna use the name. He was the one who'd insisted Crystal needed a new name—one with more sex appeal that would bring bigger tips. She'd gone along with it at work because she'd had to—Confessions was *his* domain. But she hadn't realized he'd intended to change her name entirely. It had only taken one instance of his reacting to her request to call her Sara outside of Confessions for her never to ask again. And for her to give in and *become* the name. Now, how messed up was it that she was so used to *Crystal* that, for a split second, Crystal didn't realize Jenna was talking to her? "What? What's the matter?" As she gawked, Jen's expression morphed from surprised to outraged to downright pissed off. "He hit you. Again."

Damn. The mark was so much lighter this morning, Crystal had hoped Jenna wouldn't notice. Once, Jenna had liked Bruno in a worshipful, big-brother way. When the violence started leaving visible marks, Crystal had been able to cover . . . right up until a set of finger-shaped bruises appeared on her arm. Since then, Jenna hadn't been able to stand being in the same room with Bruno. She always managed a decent cover story, but Crystal still worried every time that Jenna would lash out at Bruno, and he'd turn on her. If that happened . . . Crystal shuddered and inhaled to reply—

"Don't you dare try to deny it." Jenna crossed her arms over her chest as her eyes went glassy.

As much as Crystal hated Bruno's striking her, she hated Jenna's knowing about it more. And the likelihood that Jenna lost a little more respect for her every time it happened hurt so bad, she was sure her very soul must be bleeding. But it wasn't like Crystal could admit she only maintained the relationship to afford Jenna's epilepsy meds and to keep them safe from the Church organization. Because Jenna didn't know about the scars on Crystal's back. Nor how she'd gotten them. And she could never know. "I'm not."

Silence hung heavily between them.

"That's it? That's all you're going to say?"

Crystal settled her fork on the place mat, her appetite gone. "What would you like me to say?"

"What would I like—Are you kidding me? Uh, let's see . . . I would like you to say that you're going to call the police. I would love you to say you're getting a restrain-

ing order. I would freaking flip for you to promise you'll
never see him again."

She inhaled to take a breath, paused, then tried again.
"It's not that simple," Crystal managed.

Color flooded Jenna's cheeks. "Like hell! It's totally
that simple."

"Jen—"

"No." She shoved up from the table. "When is it going
to be enough, huh? When he puts you in the hospital?
When he kills you?"

In eight months. That's when it'll be enough. But Crystal
didn't say that, of course. She didn't want to do anything—
yet—to give away her plans, not even to Jenna. Because
waiting 'til winter wouldn't make sense to Jenna unless
she also understood the financial and safety considerations
Crystal juggled. And those were burdens Crystal didn't
want Jenna to have to bear.

Because Crystal was the big sister. She was the one
who'd promised their incarcerated father to do whatever
it took to take care of Jenna. Crystal might've been forced
to grow up fast and set aside her dreams at the age of
nineteen, but she refused to let that happen to Jenna, too.

But what can *I say? How can I make her understand?*
"Please sit down, sweetie. It's okay."

If possible, Jenna's expression became even more irate.
"It's not even a little okay, Sara." She shook her head,
spilling fat tears from the corners of both eyes. "You want
to know why my seizures are getting worse? Why I've
been getting behind on schoolwork and having to pull all-
nighters?" She plowed on before Crystal got the chance to
respond. "Because I am so worried about you, sometimes
I can barely think, barely sleep. Every time a new mark
shows up, I wonder if the next time, I'll lose you and end
up all alone."

Crystal rose, guilt and regret souring her stomach. She

knew that feeling. *God,* did she know that feeling. "Oh, Jenna. No. If you could just trust me—"

"Trust you? Not until you're willing to take care of yourself, too. Not until you're willing to stop being a *victim.*" She ran across the room and down the hall. Her door slammed, punctuating the word echoing in Crystal's ears.

Victim. Victim. Victim.

Crystal slumped into her chair as all the oxygen was sucked out of the room, and, for a minute, she couldn't seem to catch her breath. She didn't blame Jenna for being upset with her. If the tables were turned, Crystal would've been every bit as upset. Probably more. But that didn't change the fact that Jenna's words cut her deep because there was a small part of her that couldn't help but wonder if it had taken her this long to plan a way out because she was just . . . weak. A victim.

Maybe if she was stronger, she would've found a way out sooner. Maybe if she was smarter, she could've figured out a way to avoid becoming dependent on Bruno while getting Jenna the care she needed. Maybe if she was braver, she would've fought back instead of going along, biding her time until all her ducks were in a row.

She gasped, trying to swallow the sob that lodged in the back of her throat. Biting down on the inside of her cheek, she forced a few deep breaths until her brain reoriented its attention from the agony in the center of her chest to the slicing pain on the side of her mouth.

When she'd successfully fought back the urge to cry, to fall apart, to curl up in a ball and scream, she cleared the table. Put away the leftovers. Did the dishes. The mechanics of the movements calmed her, helped her set aside the hurt.

Someday, Jenna would understand. Maybe then, she'd be able to forgive Crystal all the things she'd done wrong

along the way. Until then, Crystal had to hold on tight
to the belief she was doing the right thing. It wasn't like
you could take a class on how to survive and escape your
relationship with an abusive boyfriend and a notorious
organized-crime ring while taking care of your chroni-
cally sick sister. Or else she would've been first in line for
that bad boy.

Doing the right thing.

Shane.

Why her brain brought him up at this moment, Crystal
didn't know.

Yeah, you do. Because helping him *was* the right thing.
It had been the night he'd rescued his friend from Confessions. And it was now.

Crystal wasn't a fool. She *played* ignorant really well,
but she'd picked up on a lot more than people gave her
credit for. Not just the never-to-be-seen-again women, but
the drugs and the guns and the rampant violence and in-
timidation. These were daily life for Bruno and the whole
Church gang.

Walking down the hall, she debated knocking on Jenna's door. But between her sister's anger and exhaustion,
Jenna wasn't gonna be in a talking mood for a while. And
if Jenna had any hopes of making her three o'clock history class, she needed to get some rest. So Crystal gave
her door a last look, then slipped into her own room,
closed the door, and turned the lock.

Looking around her room, Crystal's gaze went from the
lavender comforter she loved to her sewing machine on a
desk in the corner under the window, to the long dresser
covered in picture frames and trinket boxes. For a long
moment, she stared at the dresser like it might be filled
with snakes, then she dug deep for the resolve to do what
she needed to do. What she *should* do.

Getting a grip on the wooden molding of the old piece of furniture—along with her mom's sewing machine, another of the things she'd saved from their house—Crystal heaved with a grunt and pulled the end out from the wall about eight inches.

An air-conditioning vent sat low to the floor in the shadow of the dresser. Crystal knelt, undid the loose screws with her fingers, and tugged the metal cover free. Stretching, she reached her hand in until her fingers encountered one of her stashes—about three grand in cash she'd squirreled away bit by bit, a handgun she'd stolen from the club, and the cell phone that Shane had given her the night before.

She turned the square rectangle over and over in her hands, debating, summoning the courage. Because unlike the other times she'd helped Shane McCallan, this time it would be intentional, purposeful . . . planned.

Could she call him from inside the apartment? Maybe make it sound like she was calling someone else and hope Shane got it? She wished she knew exactly how Bruno had learned a man had been in the apartment, but she didn't. *Better not chance it.*

Retracing her way through the apartment, Crystal stepped out onto the cement landing the four units shared and eased the door closed behind her. The steps to the upper floor blocked her view of the street, which meant anyone watching from below shouldn't be able to see her either.

Taking a deep breath, she turned the phone on. One missed call. A few button presses revealed the call had come from the same number programmed into the phone. Shane.

He called me?
Why?

Curiosity mixed in with her determination. She pressed the call button and put the phone to her ear. Her gut told her she was safe standing there, but as the phone rang, her skin crawled as if a thousand eyes were watching. On the third ring, her stomach slowly descended. It figured that she'd worked up the nerve to do this and he wasn't going to—

"Hello?" Shane answered, his voice familiar, warm, and a little breathless, like maybe he'd run to pick up the call.

"Shane," she said quietly.

"Are you okay?"

Her heart squeezed at the fact that his first question was about her well-being, but then a car started up in the lot below and she nearly jumped out of her skin. *Be quick, be quick, be quick!* "Yeah. I, um, have information," she rushed out.

"Not over the phone," Shane said.

"What? Oh. Then how—"

"I'll come over."

And Crystal thought her heart had been racing a moment before. "You can't. Not to the apartment," she said. Not after last night.

"Okay. Where?" he asked.

Crystal's mind raced. "Out back of my apartment building. There's a trail that leads into the woods."

"That'll work. What time?"

"Um. Around two thirty?" That would ensure that Jenna had left for her three o'clock class at Loyola and that Crystal and Shane would have enough time to talk before she returned.

"I'll be there."

That's all she needed to hear. "Okay, then I should go."

"Yeah. And, Crystal? Thank you."

Heart in a full-out gallop, she hung up, nerves making her jittery.

Back in her bedroom, she turned off the phone, placed it deep inside the vent, and righted everything again, double-checking that the dresser settled precisely into the depressions in the old beige carpet. Using her fingers, she erased the marks in the rug's nap that revealed the dresser had ever sat away from the wall.

Her gaze cut to her alarm clock on the nightstand across the room. Two hours until he would be here.

A ripple of fear and anticipation shot through her stomach—along with an excitement she couldn't deny.

Chapter 9

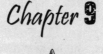

*S*tanding in the quiet of his bedroom, Shane stared at his phone, a sense of triumph heating his blood.

Crystal had called.

Just the thought that Crystal had apparently decided to help him flooded restless energy through his veins. Because it meant she was reliable. Even more importantly, it meant she was taking a chance on trusting him. Shane didn't know everything there was to know about this woman. Not by a long shot. But he was pretty damn sure she didn't trust easily.

Now he just needed to make certain he didn't do anything to damage that trust.

The listening devices in her apartment came to mind. The ones that had allowed him to overhear her conversation with Bruno and made it possible for the team to spend the morning researching the marine terminal and getting Marz's fingers to work looking for any other clues and connections that might help them.

No question the devices violated Crystal's privacy *and* her trust. And he felt twice as shitty about that given the trust she evidently planned to put in him. Already had, just by making the call.

But then his mind put those facts up against some others—namely, her scumbag's penchant for getting violent. And Shane's brain landed on the side of thinking the devices a necessary evil. Didn't mean they sat well in his stomach, though.

Deciding to allow himself five minutes to bask in the victory of Crystal's having called, Shane made his way out of his room and down the hall to the wide-open space of the Rixeys' combined kitchen and living room. Everyone had been hanging here after lunch when he'd slipped away to take the call, but they'd all made like ghosts and disappeared. He searched the gym and found more of the same.

He jogged down the cement-and-metal steps, his footsteps echoing in the industrial hallway, to the doorway of Hard Ink, the tattoo shop Jeremy and Nick co-owned. Whereas Nick only did some occasional work in the shop around his job as a process server—talk about your odd mash-ups—Jeremy was apparently well-known among tattoo enthusiasts, and the shop had an excellent reputation.

The back door to Hard Ink led into a large rectangular lounge with high windows and three brick walls. The longest wall held a kick-ass mural that read, "Bleed with me and you will forever be my brother." Shane's gaze traced over the red, black, and gray of the graffiti-like design and identified with the sentiment to his core. The team stood congregated around the center of the room, some standing, some half sitting on the round tables that filled the space.

"This is Nick, Derek, Beckett, and Easy," Jeremy said, pausing long enough between the introductions to allow each of them to shake hands with someone Shane couldn't see.

He joined the group and laid eyes on the man Jeremy was introducing.

"Oh, and this is Shane," Jeremy said. "Shane, Ike Young, the man with the magic hands."

With his shaved head, skull tats, full sleeves, and cutoff denim jacket, Jeremy's tattooist *looked* like he belonged in a tattoo shop. Shane and Ike shook. Guy seemed friendly enough.

"Pfft. He's not all that," Jessica Jakes said, walking in from the front reception area and elbowing Ike with a wicked smile.

"It's a good thing I like you, squirt," he said, putting his arm around Jess's neck and yanking her in tight. He absolutely dwarfed her in size—a combination of how petite she was and how huge Ike was.

"Of course you do. I'm totally adorable," she said, glaring at Jeremy as he rolled his eyes. What Jess lacked in height, she made up for in the size of her personality and the bite of her sarcastic tongue. Shane's gaze glanced over her, from the black braid that curved around the side of her neck and laid over her shoulder to the low vee of her tight, black shirt to the killer heeled boots she wore over a pair of curve-hugging jeans. When they'd met, Jess hadn't done a damn thing to hide her attraction to Shane, and he'd had half a mind to have a little fun with her when this mission was over.

Now . . . ?

Crystal.

His mind conjured up the softness of all that red hair, the heat of her curves in his hands, the press of her body against his.

Aw, hell.

Shane gave Jess another look and . . . nope. His interest wasn't there. Not anymore.

"And this is Becca," Jeremy said. She smiled as she shook Ike's hand, but worry and exhaustion shone in her eyes. This situation would've been a helluva lot of stress for anyone, but in the past few days, Becca had been injured, nearly abducted—twice, and now she was pulling all-nighters to stand watch over her brother. Thank God she'd managed to take a couple weeks' leave time from her nursing job. No way she could've juggled all that right now.

"So, Ike and Jess, just wanted you to meet the guys since they'll be coming and going from the building while they get their new security-consulting business up and running." The team had strategized this morning what to tell Jeremy's staff. They needed some plausible cover for why they were hanging around so much, and the consulting business well fit their military backgrounds and explained why they were buttoning up the security around here.

Jess pulled out of Ike's hold and crossed her arms. "Security consulting. What exactly does that mean?" she asked.

"Private investigation, computer and physical-security analysis and installation. That kind of thing," Nick said casually.

"Jess's dad was a cop," Jeremy said, neither his stance nor his voice as relaxed and convincing as Nick's.

She pressed her lips into a tight line and nodded. "Yeah," she said. "Well, good luck with it. I've got a client coming in ten, so I better get ready." She gave a small wave and left the group. It was maybe the most reserved Shane had ever seen her. The mention of her dad had almost seemed to take the wind from her sails. *Jess's dad was a cop.*

Why had Jeremy used the past tense? And, Christ, did they need to worry about Jess or her father being in any way connected to the police on Church's payroll?

As if hearing Shane's thoughts, Nick said in a low voice. "Her father died a number of years ago. She doesn't talk about him much." He turned to Jeremy. "We're heading out for a while. See ya later."

"Yeah, sure," Jeremy said.

Becca walked up to him. "Can I ask you a favor?"

Jeremy's smile was immediate and full of affection for Becca. "Name it."

"Can you keep an eye on Charlie for me? It's just that I don't know how long we'll be gone, and—"

"I'd be happy to. My next client isn't until four anyway. I can do the prep work I need upstairs."

"Thank you." She hugged him. "That makes me feel a lot better."

Nick gave Jeremy a nod that communicated his thanks, too.

"We better get going," Shane said. In addition to their humanitarian concerns about Charlie's condition, Marz was worried he wouldn't figure out the meaning of the binary codes without Charlie's help, so it hadn't taken anything for Becca to convince Nick and the team that Charlie needed treatment beyond what she and Shane could provide. Even leery as they were about bringing in an outsider. A veteran emergency medical technician nearly through with medical school, her friend seemed about as qualified as they could hope for. Better yet, he'd agreed to meet with Becca after lunch. But Shane didn't want to be late to Crystal's and risk her getting spooked.

The group of them made their way to the parking lot out back, and Shane updated the guys about his call. The whole team agreed Shane had to cultivate Crystal. Who knew what else she might share? Like a more specific location for Wednesday's meeting—Derek had explained just how ginormous the marine terminal actually was. Turned out what they knew of the meeting's location so far amounted to jack squat.

Despite their relative certainty that their presence at Hard Ink hadn't been compromised, Nick had asked all the guys to go to the meet to provide cover. Church had clearly infiltrated UMC, so Shane understood Nick's desire to err on the side of caution.

"Hey, whose bike?" Shane asked, nodding to the big black-and-steel beauty parked between his truck and Nick's black Challenger. Hadn't seen it back here before.

"Ike's," Nick said. "He belongs to a motorcycle club."

Beckett came to a halt as his gaze narrowed on the motorcycle. "An actual social club or an MC?" he said.

"What's the diff?" Marz asked.

"MCs often engage in organized crime to support their members. They're big businesses," Beckett said, his blue eyes going frosty. Shane turned a hard stare at Nick. Beckett owned a private security firm in D.C. and was never easily ruffled, so the big guy's concern was enough to fuel Shane's own.

"Oh goody. The Church gang on wheels," Marz said, echoing Shane's thoughts.

"Yeah," Nick said, nodding. "There are several here in the city. I encounter them every once in a while serving papers. Ike's group is an MC, but he keeps his club business separate from his work at Hard Ink."

Beckett braced his hands on his hips and glared at Nick. "And you didn't think to mention this? Is Ike something we need to worry about? Because we need problems from another direction like Noah needed more rain."

Nick shook his head, his expression and stance relaxed. "No. Ike's a good guy. Loyal to Jeremy. I've known him for a while, and I'm telling you it's not a problem—"

"All the same," Marz said. "I'd like to run some checks on Ike and this club when we get back." Beckett crossed his arms and nodded. Shane couldn't have agreed more.

"Fair enough," Nick said, opening the rear passenger door of Beckett's SUV for Becca. Then he, Marz, Beckett, and Easy piled into the big beast, too. Shane was riding solo so he could make Crystal's in time. As he backed out of his space, he gave the motorcycle a last look. Nick had better be right about Ike. Last thing they needed was a threat from within.

On the drive to the park, anticipation of seeing Crystal again had Shane's pulse beating a little faster, a little harder. He was walking on a knife's edge where she was concerned, between the team's need to use her for information and his own growing interest in her well-being.

As a rule, Shane didn't pursue women romantically just to get intel. A wink and a flirtatious smile. Sure. He excelled at that, and it was harmless. But even in the field, he'd refused to seriously lead a woman on as a means of gaining access to info. It crossed a line for him he couldn't stomach, maybe because of what'd happened to Molly. Who the hell knew. If that made him a less effective soldier, it also made him a better person. He believed that to his core.

Shane thought through everything that'd happened since he'd met Crystal at Confessions. He was attracted, no question. He was intrigued, without a doubt. So, he *was* interested. Whether he could act on that interest was one big question, and whether his interest in her conflicted with the team's agenda was another. And he didn't yet know the answer to either.

Within fifteen minutes, they'd made it to Patterson Park, a dozen-blocks-long square of green in the middle of the neighborhood east of downtown where Becca lived. Shane wasn't sure what she'd said to convince her friend to meet her here versus her house, or the hospital, or any of a dozen other places he suspected might've been less unusual, but since the guy had agreed, that was all that mattered.

Near the edge of the park closest to Becca's house, the team took up positions around the Pagoda, a hundred-year-old tower inspired by Asian architecture that stood at the edge of a wide field.

Easy, Marz, and Beckett took cover farther away, providing a perimeter, and the rest of them waited on the steps of the building. Despite the sunny spring afternoon, they were largely alone. In the distance, a group of sun-worshippers lay on blankets and on a far sidewalk, someone jogged with a baby stroller, but otherwise they had the privacy they'd wanted for this conversation.

About five minutes later, a man walked up the sidewalk that led from the street to the Pagoda. Everything about his body language and demeanor was open and straight-forward, and he smiled and waved as soon as he saw Becca.

She jogged down the steps, and Nick stuck to her like white on rice. "Hey, Murph," she called. "Thanks for coming."

"Becca. How you doing? How you feeling?" he said, coming up to her and giving her a hug.

"I'm okay," she said. "Let me introduce you to some friends and explain why I asked you to come," she said. "Murphy Jones, this is my boyfriend, Nick," she said. "Nick, Murphy."

Nick shook the guy's hand, a serious, appraising look on his face. "Nice to meet you. Thanks for coming."

Becca waved Shane closer. "And this is Shane, Nick's best friend and a former Army medic." As they exchanged greetings, Shane took stock of the man. Tall, thin, with short brown hair, probably late thirties. He made eye contact and was completely relaxed in his posture. Nothing about him seemed shifty or uncomfortable, leading Shane's gut to side with Becca's instincts that the man was probably trustworthy.

Remained to be seen how he would react to their requests, though. Because they were on the wrong side of crazy, especially if this guy happened to be a fan of strict adherence to rules.

Becca didn't hold anything back. "I'm in trouble, Murphy. And so is my brother."

The relaxed expression dropped from Murphy's face. "What kind of trouble? Wait. Is this related to what happened to you in the ER last week?"

She nodded. "Yeah. It's a very long and complicated story, but here's what I can tell you. My father was an officer in the Army and died in Afghanistan last year." *Along with a lot of other, better men,* Shane thought, anger stirring in his gut.

"I remember," he said, frowning.

"He was apparently into something he shouldn't have been, and, long story short, people are now after me and my brother Charlie because of it. Bad people."

Murphy's gaze bounced between the three of them, then returned to Becca. "Holy . . . shit. Why can't you go to the—"

"Police? Because we have evidence that some of the police are in on it. And apparently at least somebody at the hospital, because the guy that tried to grab me had access, an ID, and knew when I was working."

If the story she'd told so far didn't chase this guy off, Shane was going to be impressed. Even summarized, it sounded nuttier than a squirrel turd at a peanut festival.

For a long moment, Murphy pressed his fingers to his mouth. "Okay. Jesus. Why did you want to see me, then? How do I fit into all of this?"

"I need to ask you the biggest, craziest favor."

He blew out a breath like he was girding himself. "Okay, ask. We've known each other a long time now. If I can help, you know I will."

Shane's gaze made a three-sixty sweep around them. Everything was still quiet.

"I need you to examine my brother and help treat him." She and Shane ran down the list of his injuries with a bare-bones explanation of how they'd happened. Murphy asked some questions that they took turns answering.

"Long story short, he needs surgical intervention," Shane said, because the guy might as well know the whole of what they wanted from him. "We were hoping we could use your rig for what essentially amounts to field surgery." As he spoke, Murphy's face paled.

"Shit," he said, his gaze dropping to the sidewalk. When he lifted his head again, his eyes were full of questions. "Why can't you take him to another hospital?"

"Because his wounds are too suspicious," Becca said. "And this situation is so dire I don't honestly know who I can trust." And those were just some of the reasons.

"But you trust me?" Murphy asked.

Becca smiled. "I do. But I know I'm asking a lot . . . probably too much. I just don't know what else to do, and Charlie's running out of options." That was the damn truth. Worse, Charlie didn't have the time for them to stand around and dissect this from every angle.

The guy crossed his arms and stared off across the field.

Shane made eye contact with Nick and saw reflected back at him the same pessimism Shane felt. Sympathetic as he seemed, Murphy's questions and hesitation made his doubts clear. Not that Shane blamed him, but they didn't have the time to try to convince him, either.

After a minute, Murphy turned back to them. "You're asking me to provide care beyond my training in a setting not totally suited for that care and using hospital equipment without proper accounting or payment."

"In a nutshell," Nick said, as Shane nodded.

Becca sighed. "Pretty much. I wouldn't ask if my brother—"

"Shit." He shook his head. "I'll do it."

Shane did a double take. *Well, score one for the good guys.*

"—wasn't in such bad . . . What?" Becca asked, her eyes going wide. "You'll do it? Really?"

He gave an uncertain smile, like he'd just crested the hill of a roller coaster and hadn't expected the drop to be so great. "You're not trying to talk me out of it, are you?"

"No!" she said, throwing her arms around his neck. They all chuckled. "Thank you."

"Don't thank me yet, Becca. Agreeing to help and being able to do it are two different things," Murphy said. And as glad as Shane was that he'd agreed to help, he was also pleased to hear him keeping his promises modest. One thing you learned doing medical work of any kind was that there were absolutely no guarantees. Murphy seemed like a straight shooter, and Shane respected that.

"I know," she said.

Shane nailed the guy with a stare. "I'm not trying to talk you out of it, either. But I was sure you were going to decline. So, I gotta ask, what made you agree?"

Murphy didn't seem put off by the stare or the question. "I do what I do to help people who need it. If Charlie's in as much trouble as you say and can't otherwise get treatment, I feel duty-bound to see what I can do. Sometimes you gotta break some rules to do what's right." He shrugged and shifted feet, for the first time seeming a little uncomfortable, like they might disapprove of what he'd just said.

As if. They were living the sentiment themselves.

"That's what I'd hope you'd say," Shane said, shaking the guy's hand. Then he glanced at his watch. If he didn't go now, he'd be late. And he didn't want to chance Crystal's getting cold feet. "You two should take him to see Charlie. He won't know anything until he examines him for himself."

"Agreed," Murphy said, as Becca and Nick nodded. "I don't work until seven, so I've got time."

"All right. I've gotta take care of that other thing," Shane said. "I'll meet you all back at the place later."

After a quick round of good-byes, Shane headed across town toward Crystal's apartment, torn between anticipation of seeing her again and fear that she'd had second thoughts since she'd called.

This time, he parked in one of the visitors' spaces within the apartment complex, but one building down from Crystal's. A quick survey of the lot revealed everything was quiet. He crossed between the parked cars, jogged around the building, and trailed the edge of the woods until he found a path.

A quiet, *empty* path.

Did he have the wrong place? Maybe there was another trail.

He scouted farther along but didn't see any other place that seemed to fit Crystal's instructions.

He looked at his watch. He was three minutes late. And Crystal was nowhere to be seen.

Goddamnit. Had he missed his chance?

Chapter 10

$\mathcal{P}$eeking out her bedroom window, Crystal watched as Shane darted from a black truck toward the woods. The moment she laid eyes on him, her heart flew into her throat.

Because she was getting to see him again. And because she was helping him go up against Bruno and Church. Her stomach tossed.

I can't believe I'm doing this. She rested her forehead against the wall next to the window, the coolness of the plaster surface helping her focus. *Pull it together. This is the right thing.*

If she didn't get out there, he was going to think she'd stood him up. So, right. She should go. Now. Heaving a deep breath, she forced her feet to move. Out of her room, through the apartment, and down the rear stairs.

She expected to see him standing at the entrance to

the trail, but no one was there. Where had he gone? She hadn't imagined seeing him run back here, had she?

Turning, she surveyed the stretch of green that ran behind the buildings.

"Don't be frightened," a male voice said from behind her.

She whirled, pulse hammering behind her ears. "Shane," she gasped, her gaze raking over him. "I didn't hear you there." *God,* he was just as gorgeous in the light of day. Maybe more so.

His hair wasn't gelled as it had been the night before, so the blond in the long tips of it was more apparent. It was messy in a totally sexy way, like he'd been running his fingers through it. Her own fingers twitched because she would've loved to bury her hands in his hair and pull him in tight. Just once. To see what it would be like. To see how he'd react.

From his hair, her gaze dropped to his mouth. Namely to the dark red scab on the side of his bottom lip that hadn't been there before. And was she imagining it, or did he have a shadow of a bruise under his right eye? What the hell had happened to him in the fifteen hours since they'd last seen one another? Part of her was dying to ask, but one thing she'd learned early was to mind her own business.

The black jacket he had on was the same one from last night, which made her wonder if it once again shielded his gun holster. Her gaze dragged down. His blue jeans were the kind of old you just knew was worn soft, and damn did he look fine in them.

As she drank him in, he seemed to do the same in return. Like he was every bit as eager to lay eyes on her. His gaze was bright, intense, and tracked over her face and body like he wanted to soak in every detail.

For a long moment, she couldn't breathe, then he smiled. "Hi," he said in a low voice.

"Hi," she said as quietly, the breathlessness he elicited

from her making her feel a bit ridiculous. She was about to commit a major betrayal of her seriously dangerous boyfriend, not ask her high-school crush on a date, for God's sake. Suddenly, she needed a break from the intensity. Even without worrying about someone seeing them, Shane made her feel too exposed. "Come on," she said abruptly.

Stepping around Shane, Crystal started down a trail that cut through the woods. Some people ran through here to get to the running trails that surrounded the park on the far end, but Crystal never ran this path because something about the woods freaked her out. The isolation made her feel vulnerable in a way running on the street never did. But she figured because the trail wasn't part of her usual routine, it was safer. No one would expect her there, so no one should be watching.

At least, she hoped.

Looking over her shoulder, she found Shane right behind her. She took off at a jog, needing distance between them and the too many eyes of the apartment complex.

Shane's footsteps thumped behind her, and he easily kept pace. She hadn't given any thought to the fact that his jeans and boots weren't particularly suited to running, but he didn't complain.

Crystal guided them deeper into the woods until that sense of isolation she usually disliked engulfed them. Only, this time, it was exactly what she wanted.

About midway between her place and the park, they came upon a small clearing. Logs and cinder blocks circled a makeshift fire pit. A few empty beer cans sat off to one side. The rush of the warm breeze through the trees was the only noise around them.

Crystal slowed to a walk, braced her hands on her hips, and turned around. "We should be good here," she said.

Shane was right there. Fingers gently cupped her chin

and tilted it up. This close, the clean scent of soap and leather and man washed over her. "You okay?" he asked.

She nodded. Truth was, she wanted to be okay, but she was kinda jumping out of her skin. Because she was about to cross some lines from which there would be no return.

His gaze narrowed, and he leaned closer yet, his thumb stroking her cheek. "I don't like that you don't feel safe to meet in your own apartment," he said, gray eyes flashing.

Crystal shrugged. "Can't be helped. For now."

"You let me know how I can help with that. Just say the word. You hear?" No judgment. No unsolicited advice. Just a free and clear offer of assistance on her terms. His tone was a dark promise that curled around her and made her want to be closer, especially as his gaze warmed with unfettered interest that had her blood pumping harder. But that wasn't what they were here for. That wasn't what they were about at all.

But that didn't mean a part of her didn't want it. The foreign desire lanced panic through her blood and scattered her thoughts . . .

"How's Jenna?" he asked, dropping his hand, like he knew she'd gotten tripped up in his words and needed a reprieve.

"Wiped out, but up and about. She'd pulled an all-nighter . . ." Crystal let the words drift off, unsure why she'd told him the cause behind the seizure. Why would he care, anyway?

Shane frowned. "Well, at least you know the whys of it."

"Yeah," she said. "So . . ."

He stepped closer, close enough she had to tilt back her head to maintain eye contact. Normally, a man's invading her space triggered her fight-or-flight reflex. With Shane, the panicky fear whirled in the background of her mind, but there was an instinctive sense of safety, too. Probably ridiculous.

"Thank you for calling," he said.

"You don't know what I'm going to say yet."

For a moment, something seemed to flash through his eyes. But then it was gone, and she wasn't sure exactly what she'd seen. Probably nothing, as freaked out as she was. Besides, she didn't know him well enough to read his face, his eyes, his expression, the way she could Bruno.

"True, but no matter what, I know you're taking a risk. And I want you to know it's recognized and appreciated." The breeze blew a loose strand of her hair across her face, and Shane tucked it behind her ear.

Crystal's heart squeezed. In just a few words, he made her feel more valued than she'd felt in years. A wind gust kicked up around them, swirling more wisps of hair around her face pulled loose from her low ponytail. Why couldn't she have a life where she could be with a man like this? Maybe next year, once she'd started over. *Yeah, but then it won't be Shane . . .*

True.

And they'd be on the run, so it wasn't like she'd get to leave all the lies behind, was it? What kind of basis was that for a relationship?

Needing a break from the intensity of his gaze, Crystal glanced down at his chest. Under his black jacket, he wore a threadbare black T-shirt that looked as soft and comfortable as it did old. It was the kind of shirt that invited you to snuggle up against its wearer, or to steal and sleep in it. She almost smiled.

"When you let down your guard, you have the most expressive face," Shane said, caressing her cheek with his knuckles. The man seemed to revel in touching her in lots of different small ways. Rather than making her feel invaded, Shane's gentleness made her feel special in a way she wasn't sure she'd ever felt before.

All the same, Crystal schooled her expression, not

sure what she might've been giving away but knowing it couldn't have been anything good.

Shane laughed. "I guess if I want you to let down your guard, I shouldn't mention it, huh?"

She peered up at him. "Why would you want me to let down my guard?"

He studied her for a long moment. "For all kinds of reasons it might be counterproductive to voice, darlin'." His tone was part promise, part threat.

"Like what?" She braced her hands on her hips, but he just shook his head. "That's not fair. Tell me."

He closed the gap between them, the open edges of his jacket brushing against her light blue tank top. "Really want to know?"

No, you don't. You really don't, Crystal. Heart thundering against her breastbone, she nodded.

"Like you're beautiful. And I'm attracted to you. And I'm worried about you and your sister. For starters. How's that?"

For starters? Geez, what else could there be?

Her heart tripped into a sprint, and the heat rising to her skin had nothing to do with the warmth of the afternoon or the jog through the woods. She didn't know which affected her most, that he thought her beautiful, that he maybe wanted her as much as she wanted him, or that he actually cared about her and her sister. The combination was dizzying and terrifying and the kind of thing she might've dreamed up to hear from a man. But then she remembered the scars on her back and knew he wouldn't feel the same if he saw them. Or, worse, knew how she'd gotten them. She glanced away. "Oh."

Shane flashed that charming grin that had probably stolen a fair share of hearts in his lifetime. "Yeah. Oh."

As casually as she could, she retreated a step. The light of the afternoon dimmed, and overhead, the sky grew overcast. A spring storm was rolling in. Time to say what she needed to say so she could get home again. "So, uh, what I wanted to tell you was that I learned something last night," Crystal rushed out, needing to distract herself from Shane's honesty. And his interest. It hurt too much to flirt with something she could never have.

Hands landed on the bare skin of her biceps. "Crystal, breathe for me. Just relax." Shane gently squeezed—

Crystal sucked in a breath as the fingers on his left hand pressed into the very spot where Bruno had grabbed her the night before.

"What?" he said, yanking his touch away. Grasping her hands, he lifted and turned her arms, looking . . . She knew the minute he found the marks on the outside of her right arm. They weren't dark—not like the time Jenna had learned the kind of man Bruno really was—but the fury that rolled in across his expression told her he had a good idea what had caused them. "He hurt you again," he said, voice seething.

Shame made heat rise to her cheeks, and she knew they must be absolutely flaming from the feel of it. "Somehow he knew you were in the apartment last night. That's why I brought you out here."

"Who's *he*?" he growled, brows slashed downward. In the distance, thunder rumbled long and low, almost lazily.

Gently pulling her hands out of his, she hugged herself. "His name is Bruno."

He scoffed. "Figures. This can't go on, Crystal."

Jenna's words echoed in her ears, fueling her embarrassment and stirring up her anger, too. "I know," she snapped. "I'm working on it. And it's none of your business anyway." She pushed past him. This had been such a freaking mistake.

"Wait. Please don't go. I'm sorry," he called, his voice gentling.

The regret and earnestness in his voice froze her in place.

"I didn't mean to criticize you, Crystal. I just cannot abide violence against women. Period. Especially not someone I know." A long pause. "And definitely not someone I like." After everything that had happened to her, the words were a balm for her psyche.

Footsteps came up behind her, slowly, cautiously, like she was a wild animal who would bolt in an instant. And she supposed there was some truth to that analogy.

Torn between returning to the danger she knew or staying with the one she didn't, Crystal debated. Her heart told her Shane might well be the most dangerous man she'd ever met because he made her want, wish, maybe even dream. Not at all sure it was a good idea, Crystal slowly turned.

Shane was right in front of her. A rock in the middle of a raging sea, a refuge she might claim if she had the strength and the will and the nerve to fight for it. To believe she deserved it. She hugged herself.

"Hey," he said, cupping her face in his big hands. His fingers slid behind her neck and gently massaged.

She shook her head and glanced toward the treetops in an effort to pinch off the sting building behind her eyes. Why did she have to meet him now? She'd had a plan, and all she'd needed to do was follow it for a few more months. "You don't even know me."

"No. Not everything. But I know more than a little. And that much I like enough to want to know more." His fingers rubbed her neck, gently, soothingly.

And his words, well, his words were perfect. Maybe even too much so. *Too good to be true,* she thought. "I already told you I'd share what I'd learned. You don't have to play me."

His eyes narrowed, and he frowned. "You listen hard and you listen good, sweetness," he said, the words firm but the tone urgent, almost desperate, and laced with his southern accent. "I'm not perfect, and God knows I've made a lot of mistakes in my life. But I would never play with a woman's emotions to get information out of her. That kind of manipulation doesn't hold with me. Ever."

Sweetness. She'd heard everything he'd said. The passion with which he'd said it. The sincerity that burned from his gaze as the words had poured from his lips. But it was the term of endearment that reached into her chest and gripped her heart. For a long moment, they stood there, bodies touching, faces inches apart, his hands holding her in that firm-but-gentle way he had.

Thunder rumbled again, closer this time, and her heart was a drum beat double-timing inside her chest. If his hands didn't feel it racing, he'd have to hear it, because the sound was a loud *rush rush* in her ears. Beneath the sports bra and tank, her nipples went hard. If his gaze dropped, she knew he'd see, but she couldn't bring herself to feel self-conscious about it. Not when he was looking at her like he wanted to devour her.

His gaze dropped to her lips.

She shuddered, everything inside her but the smallest voice of reason crying out for him to do it. Just once.

"Tell me not to," he said, his voice a raw scrape.

"I CAN'T," SHE whispered in a shaky voice. "I don't want to."

Shane's body took over then, all urgent need and basic instinct. The rest of the world be damned. He pulled her in and kissed her, his lips devouring, his tongue exploring deep. Nothing held back. Nothing denied.

Not even as her lips reawakened the sting from the cut on his lip. Totally worth it.

Crystal's arms came up around him. She trembled against him, and Shane wasn't sure if it was caused by adrenaline or fear. Unable to tolerate the thought that she might feel forced, he eased off.

She moaned and held him tighter, like his retreat had made something snap within her. Their kisses deepened, and her body moved against his, sinuously, maddeningly, desperately.

They tasted one another again and again, giving in to the heat that had sparked between them from the moment Crystal had collided with him at Confessions. Little nips and bites of lips and teeth warred with long, sensual strokes of tongue that stole his breath and made him instantly hard. The sting in his lip, the throb of his GSW, the aches from Nick's asskicking, every bit of it faded away—no, her touch made it all *go* away.

The few times they'd spoken, Crystal had most often been guarded, tentative, fearful. Just as she'd been when he first kissed her. But, now, she was revealing a passionate woman who could be fearless, giving and receiving openly and without hesitation. Christ, the thought that this fierceness was the real Crystal slayed him because it meant she was burying and denying her true self, not because she wanted to, but because she had to.

No, because someone forced her to.

The thought reminded him of the bruises on her arm. Shane had known this woman for three days, and twice in that time she'd been hurt by another man. And both as a consequence for things Shane had done.

A crack of thunder echoed from the heavens, making Crystal jump and gasp into his mouth.

"I've got you," he rasped around a kiss.

Part of him wanted to say more, to tell her he had her and he'd keep her safe. But he couldn't make himself give up her heat, her sweetness, her obvious hunger—for him. So he made her a silent promise instead.

Never again, Crystal. He'll never hurt you again. Not on my watch.

Because Shane McCallan had made a mistake like

that once. And, as bad as Molly's disappearance had been, something's happening to Crystal would actually be worse because Shane knew it was coming. The one break he'd *ever* given himself over Molly was that he'd had no way to know she'd be abducted. Didn't excuse the role he played in allowing it to happen, but he couldn't have known. But with Crystal, while he might not know when or how this Bruno asshole would strike out to do the ultimate damage, it was all but a done deal at this point. Always was with guys like him. And Shane would go to the grave before he let it happen, before he failed another female for whom he cared.

Because he did care. Made no damn sense given how long he'd known her. And the timing was beyond piss-poor. But there it was all the same.

A red-hot need to protect Crystal, to defend her, to avenge her roared through his blood. It made him need to be closer, go deeper. One hand guiding her head, the silk of her bound hair sliding over his fingers, his other arm slid lower, wrapping around her back. He crushed her to him as their lips sucked and pulled over and over.

Crystal moaned, a needful, pleasured sound he wanted to hear again and again. She grasped at his shoulders, his neck, his hair, pulling and fisting it in a way that made him wild.

The breeze kicked up around them, and rain fell in gentle, random drops. Then a little harder, 'til the woods came alive with the sound of the falling water tapping on leaves and branches.

"It's raining," Shane forced himself to say. Not that he cared. He'd spent most of a decade living at the extremes. A little rain wouldn't faze him, particularly with a beautiful woman kissing him hot and stupid.

She smiled against his lips. "Is it?"

"God, Crystal," he groaned, kissing her jaw, her ear,

her neck. When she reclined her head, Shane yearned to comb his fingers through her long hair. Nuzzling her throat, he tugged the stretchy band free and reveled in the sprawl of those soft, red locks across his skin. He burrowed his hands in the thick curls as he brought his lips back to hers.

Thunder exploded overhead, and rain fell in a sudden, cool sheet.

Crystal gasped, her green eyes bright as she looked up at him, droplets hanging on her lashes and rolling down her beautiful face. Shane wanted to catch every one with his tongue.

As the rain soaked into their hair and clothes, Crystal appeared momentarily stunned and uncertain. And then a grin crept across her face until she could no longer hold back her full smile.

And it was like the sun emerging from behind the clouds, bright and warm and peaceful.

If he'd thought her beautiful before, smiling made her absolutely radiant.

Getting a grip on himself, Shane tugged off the jacket he'd worn earlier to conceal his weapon. "Here," he said.

"Keep it," Crystal said, smiling. "I don't mind." She tilted her face to the sky and closed her eyes.

Shane couldn't do anything but stare. Rain cascaded in a stream over her face and down her neck to her chest, revealing every feminine curve she had hidden behind the cotton and spandex she wore. He imagined seeing her like this, but in a shower, warm water sluicing down over perfect, naked skin.

Blood pounded into his erection until it was a delicious torture bordering on pain.

But so, so worth it.

The moment felt so special, so stolen, so secret . . . Damnit all to hell, Shane wanted to know her name. Her *real* name. But asking would probably send her scurrying for cover. *Not* worth it. No matter how badly he wanted to know it. How badly he wanted to know *her*.

For a long moment, Shane watched a trickle of rain run down her throat until he could think of nothing other than the taste of it from her skin. Sliding his hands over her ribs, his thumbs brushing the sides of her breasts, Shane licked and kissed and nibbled up the long column of her throat.

The moan she unleashed wrapped around his cock. As his lips crested her chin and captured her mouth again, his hands claimed the warm mounds of her breasts.

Crystal sucked in a breath, her green eyes flying wide. "We can't do this," she said, jerking back. Breathing hard, she looked over her shoulder, like maybe they could be seen through the quarter mile of forest. "I have to get back," she said.

Too fast, McCallan. Way to go. "I'm sorry—"

"Tomorrow night, nine p.m., at the marine terminal," she rushed out like he hadn't said anything. "That's what he said about the meeting. I think that's down in Dundalk on the water."

"Where at the terminal, Crystal? Do you know? It's a big place," he said, pretty sure he knew the answer already.

She shook her head, her movements almost frantic. "That's all I know. I hope it helps."

Damnit, he was losing her. "Crystal—"

She shrugged, eyes landing everywhere but on his. "So . . ." Her voice trailed off, and she turned away.

"Wait," Shane called. Her walk became hurried. "Crystal, wait."

She turned. "Give me a head start before you leave." Her face filled with a panicked pleading. "Please," she called over the falling rain. And then she took off.

"Fuck," Shane bit out, his gaze glued to her tight little body and dark red hair until the rain and the trees and the path finally obscured her once and for all. With a growl, he threw his jacket against a tree.

Which was, of course, totally fucking ineffectual as a way of resolving the giant pile of pissed off parked on his chest. At himself.

"Goddamnit," he grumbled as he hauled the coat off the ground.

Christ, McCallan, you could mess up a wet dream.

He stared up at the sky and let the rain beat on his face. Shane knew why he'd blown it so bad. He'd been thinking with the wrong damn head. And not a little with his heart, too. He damn well knew better.

Grousing and kicking at things, Shane humped his way up the rain-slicked trail. Within minutes, he'd returned to the opening to the back of the apartment complex. Crystal was nowhere to be seen, of course. Since he'd spooked her by coming on too strong.

What he really wanted to do was hike up those steps, knock on her door, and make her believe he had her best interests at heart. But his gut told him that'd be a big mistake. Huge. If he pushed right now, she might lock down for good.

Which meant he was going to have to sit on his hands and bide his time.

Retracing his steps to the next building over, Shane paused and surveyed the lot. Everything looked clear, but he still didn't know how this Bruno asshole had learned about his visit last night. If someone was watching Crystal's place, though, they weren't likely to be as interested in this building.

Why the hell did this woman have him wound so tight, anyway? At first, he'd been sure her vulnerability had been her appeal. She'd been a chance to add some tallies to his side of the great cosmic scorecard. And God knew he needed 'em. He'd been an asshole to ever reduce her to that, but it had been his own issues talking, not any true reflection of who Crystal was.

Now, it was more than that.

Maybe it was that she didn't just need help, but she gave it freely, too. To Jenna. To him.

And that she was strong. And brave. And smart. And . . . fuck's sake.

Finding the lot quiet save for the steady shower, Shane darted toward his truck. Inside, he grabbed a towel from behind the seat and scrubbed it over his hair and face.

He'd give her the night to cool off, then try to talk to her tomorrow. Apologize. He really hadn't meant to scare her off. Damnit.

Throwing the truck into gear, Shane left. A new thought crept into his head.

Maybe it was for the better that this had happened. Wanting to help Crystal was one thing, getting involved with her a whole other. And every time Shane let his emotions get involved, his brain turned to shit. Right now, that was something he couldn't afford. His team, his mission, and his honor demanded more. Demanded better.

And he was duty-bound to give them everything.

So, he'd help her if he could. But no more dancing, touching, or kissing, for God's sake. He had to go totally hands off.

Imagining not touching her again was like a kick to the gut, but no one ever said sacrifices were supposed to be easy.

So, fine. From now on, he'd keep his distance. With everything else going on, it shouldn't be that goddamned hard.

Chapter 11

You're back. Finally," Marz bellowed across the gym at Shane the minute he walked through the door. Hyped-up about something. Business as usual for the guy.

Shane joined Marz, Beckett, and Easy sitting on metal folding chairs around the computers in the back of the room.

"Go for a swim?" Beckett asked, smirking.

Shane glared. As if his wet jeans weren't chafing his hide enough, now Murda had to ride him. "Everybody's a fucking comedian," he grumbled, tugging his damp tee away from his skin.

"What crawled up your ass?" Amusement danced in Beckett's blue eyes.

Turning a chair around, Shane straddled it and sat. "My own damn stupidity."

"Things didn't go well with the woman?" Easy asked in

a flat voice. Sitting backward on the chair with his arms braced on the backrest, Easy's position mirrored his own.

Shane looked the guy over. Bloodshot eyes. Dark circles. All of them were run ragged, weren't they? The combination of the hell of the past year and the crisis of the past days. "Yes and no. Crystal volunteered the information I picked up on the bugs last night, so she confirmed her reliability."

Beckett arched a brow. "What's the no?"

Tugging his fingers through his damp hair, Shane heaved a breath. "She didn't have any further specifics on the marine terminal. And I pushed her too far." He waved a hand. No way he was sharing *how* he'd pushed her. He wasn't a glutton for punishment, after all. "It'll be all right. I'll fix it." Maybe. Blinking away that train of thought, Shane looked to Marz. "Why were you so happy to see me? You know, besides my general awesomeness."

Marz pushed out of his chair, big grin on his face, and held out his hands. "I'm getting married!"

Shane sighed. The expressions on the other two said they'd already been down this road. "All right. I'll bite."

"I think the appropriate sentiment is 'congratulations'," Marz said, crossing his arms and feigning insult.

"Just spill the brilliance of whatever this is about," Shane said.

"Only because you acknowledged its brilliance." Marz sat, excitement rolling off the guy. "I figured out how to solve the problem of getting us eyes and ears in the back of Confessions."

"By getting married?"

"By *pretending* to get married. And what does *every* pretend groom need?" Marz's grin was full of anticipation.

"A bride?" Shane said.

Marz rolled his eyes and waved his hands. "Okay, but what else?"

Shane looked between the three of them. And *then* the lightbulb went on. "A bachelor party," Shane said.

Marz clapped his hands. "Ding ding ding. Give the man a cigar."

Yup. The idea was, in fact, brilliant. Really brilliant. "I assume there are private rooms in the back for parties or something?"

"Precisely," Marz said, turning his monitor toward the other three men. The Confessions Web site promised discerning gentlemen a night they'd never forget with the sexiest, most exotic women in Baltimore.

Like, say, Crystal.

Shane swallowed the growl the stray thought beckoned. He read farther down the screen. "Says the rooms have to be reserved in advance."

Beckett looked up from his phone and gave a small smile, or what passed for a smile with the hard-ass. "He's way ahead of you, man."

"True dat," Marz said, reclining in his chair and lacing his hands behind his head. "While you were out chasing girls"—he waggled his eyebrows—"I got us a Plan B in the form of a bachelor party. We've got an appointment to see the private rooms tonight at eight." He tapped his hand against a small box. "And I put together a couple different types of devices depending on what kinds of access we manage to gain while we're in there."

"Nice. Did you actually schedule a date for a party?"

Marz laughed. "Told them I was doing the deed on Saturday to make the appointment time-sensitive. So the party is Friday night." He waved a hand. "We'll just cancel it."

"Who's going?" Shane asked.

"The four of us," Marz said. "Make it seem like a group

of friends just hanging out together." Beckett and Easy voiced their agreements. "I think Nick's gonna sit this one out. Charlie's going downhill, and Becca's worried. She's holding it together like a champ, but Nick's not going to want to leave them."

Damn. Shane had been so wrapped up in Crystal, he'd nearly forgotten about Charlie. And *there* was the problem in a fucking nutshell. "What did her friend say after he saw Charlie? Did you talk to him?"

"Murphy? I did," Easy said. "Seems like a stand-up guy. Recognized things were dire. Supposed to be back around eleven with his rig and everything y'all need."

Need. As in, for the surgery. Sonofabitch. What they were contemplating doing was a helluva lot more complicated than anything he'd ever handled before. What if it didn't work, and Charlie got worse? Even a blind hog had to find an acorn now and then. Wasn't it about their turn?

"We'll get you back in time to help with that," Marz said.

Which meant . . . *Aw, hell.* Would Crystal be there tonight? Shane scrubbed his hands over his face and tried to remember if she'd mentioned her work schedule.

"What?" Marz asked.

"Crystal. I should give her a heads-up. If I surprise her in there, and she gives away that she knows me, it could be bad for us and her." *Shit.* So much for giving her the night to calm down. But who could've predicted Marz would get fake-engaged in the three hours he'd been gone.

"Guess you better get to whatever fixing things you need to do, then," Beckett said, expression serious.

Shane struggled to yank his phone from his wet jeans pocket. He pressed a button and put the cell to his ear.

Straight to voice mail.

"Damnit," he said. He'd called her this morning to see

how Jenna was doing and gotten the same result. Though, if she was hiding the phone, maybe she'd turned it off, too. It was what he'd do in the same situation. "Marz, can you pull up some ears on her place." He glanced at his watch. After five.

A few keystrokes later, Marz nodded. For a long stretch of minutes, the apartment on the other end of the devices sounded quiet, only occasional, small shuffling noises to indicate someone might be there. All four of the guys stared at the speakers like there was something to watch, their seriousness reflecting their understanding of what could happen to an informant who was outed.

Knock, knock. "Jenna? Can I come in?" Crystal. Bingo. Silence stretched out before another round of knocking. "Jenna? Please?"

Shane frowned. Crystal sounded almost upset. He imagined the expression she'd worn right before she'd bolted from the woods, and his chest squeezed.

"Jen, this apartment is seven hundred square feet. You can't avoid me forever."

Marz arched a brow and held out his hands like he was asking what was going on. Shane shook his head.

Something rattled and squeaked. "Actually, I *could* avoid you if I wanted. So don't tempt me. What do you want?" Jenna, presumably.

"I just wanted to see how you were feeling," Crystal said, her tone conciliatory.

"I'm fine," Jenna said in that tone women used that meant they were the exact opposite of fine.

"Please don't be mad at me."

The regret in Crystal's voice reached right into Shane's chest and grabbed hold. He'd seen how much her sister meant to her. He could hear it in her voice, even as Jenna came at her with anger. There was a long pause, and Shane leaned closer.

"Is *he* going to be at your work tonight?" Jenna finally said.

"I don't know. Maybe."

"That's a yes. I have half a mind to march into Confessions tonight and tell him if he lays another hand on you, I'll call the police myself."

Oh, shit, Shane thought. What a fucking disaster that would be. "You will *not*," Crystal barked, apparently agreeing. "Do you hear me? You are *never* to step foot in there for any reason. You know how I feel about that. It's not safe."

"Oh, but it's safe for you?"

"God, Jenna. Grow up. I don't have a freaking choice." The words overflowed with a desperation that sucker punched Shane and made it hard to breathe. *She doesn't have a choice? What the hell does that mean?*

A gasp, then a sniffle.

"Aw, sweetie, come here. I'm sorry. I didn't mean to yell."

Someone was crying. "No. Gotta get used to taking care of myself sometime. Might as well be now," Jenna said in a strained voice.

"Jen—"

"I'm gonna lose you. Don't you understand?"

"No, you're not. I promise." Sharp knots formed in Shane's gut as the women fought. He identified wholeheartedly with Jenna's concerns, but he hated the guilt and pain he heard in Crystal's voice.

"You can't make that promise. Not with where you work and who you date. God, I hate Dad. I *hate* him. This is *his* fault." *Their father? What did he have to do with this?*

"Sshh, it's okay."

"No. None of this is okay. If he hadn't gotten himself killed, you wouldn't have gotten sucked into that world. But it's your fault, too. Because you *could* get out, but you don't. You just stay there and take it. You're just like him!" The longer Jenna spoke, the more heated her words became. She had some of the same fighter qualities as Crystal, it appeared, though Shane wasn't a fan of where that fight was being directed right now. Those words had heart-shredder written all over them.

Crystal's gasp told him he'd been right. Jenna's rant had hit its target.

A few long moments passed, with Crystal attempting unsuccessfully to talk Jenna down. And as much as Shane regretted the younger woman's behavior for Crystal's sake, her motivation came through loud and clear. Shane wasn't the only one who knew Crystal was in trouble. Nor was he the only one worrying. Jenna's fear was at least partially behind why she was lashing out. He would've put money on it.

A slammed door brought an abrupt end to the conversation.

"Shit," Crystal whispered. "That went great." The sarcasm did nothing to hide the sadness in her voice. "I'll be home after two, Jenna. Don't wait up. Please try to get some sleep tonight. Okay?"

Silence.

A series of muffled noises followed until another door closed. Crystal leaving, presumably.

Which meant they would run into one another at Confessions.

Fanfuckingtastic.

Feeling like the ground was moving beneath his feet, Shane nodded to Marz, who turned down the feed. How could Crystal be *forced* to work at Confessions? And by whom? By this Bruno asshole? By Church himself? Jesus. Shane thought he'd been worried about her before. With five little words, Crystal had just confirmed that her situation was even worse than Shane had feared.

"You thinking what I'm thinking?" Marz asked.

Still reeling, Shane met the man's concerned gaze. "Dude, I don't even know."

Marz pressed his lips into a tight line and shook his head. "Put the context of a strip club we know engages in human trafficking together with the comment Crystal just made, and it's pretty damn clear she's not fully free."

"Debt servitude, maybe?" Beckett said in a tone full of ice.

The more his friends speculated, the more he knew they were right. Sonofabitch. The realization of just how seriously in trouble Crystal was made him feel like he was breathing crushed glass. And *there* went the thought he could remain detached.

Forcing himself from the downward spiral of his thoughts, Shane focused on another part of what they'd learned—their father. "Marz, can you go through the phone records? See if you can find Crystal's real name. Then see if you can dig up who their father was and how he might be involved in all this?"

"Can do," Marz said.

"So, it sounds like Crystal's on her way to the club now," Beckett said, rubbing at his scarred temple.

"Yeah." Shane thought about how smoothly she'd handled his appearance in the club the night after they'd rescued Charlie. She could've freaked out or screamed or pointed or run away. A million things. But she'd masked her surprise, ordered him out without making a scene, and put on a good show to which no one gave a second thought. No reason to think she wouldn't handle herself the same way again.

Except, now, Shane knew her, cared about her. The worry he felt was probably more about him than her. And wasn't that a peachy revelation.

Easy cleared his throat and rubbed a hand over his bald

head. When he wanted it to happen, the guy had a knack for fading into the background of a conversation to the point you almost forgot he was there. Seemed like he'd been doing it a lot since they'd reunited. "This sister could become a problem for your waitress friend," he said. "She's got a bit of a temper on her. If Crystal's handsy boyfriend comes over, and Jenna loses it at the wrong time . . ." Easy let them finish the sentence for themselves. No matter how they filled in the blanks, though, the end results weren't good.

"Sounds like she was just blowing off steam," Shane said. "But point taken."

Nodding, Easy said, "I'm not saying we do anything, but it bears watching."

Murmurs of agreement sounded from all three of them, and Shane found himself glad to have their support where Crystal and her sister were concerned.

"All right. I need to shower and change if we're going back out. These jeans are starting to chafe," Shane said, to the guys' amusement. He was halfway to the door when something occurred to him, and Shane turned back. "Hey, Marz?"

"Yo."

"If you find out Crystal's name, don't tell me."

"Come again?" Marz said, as Easy's and Beckett's gazes swung toward Shane.

He made sure his tone was casual, unaffected. "I just want to hear it from her first."

Marz cocked his head and stared at him. Sure enough, a flash of recognition passed through the man's eyes. Shane's emotions had gotten involved, and now Marz knew it. "Whatever you say, hoss," he said. "I live to serve."

Shane nodded and beat feet for the door, silently thanking the man for holding back whatever commentary might've gone through his head a few seconds before. Last thing he wanted was for the team to worry he'd lost his objectivity because he'd gotten attached to the girl.

Even though, *damn,* he was kinda getting attached to the girl.

And wasn't that a red-handed smack in the ass.

CRYSTAL WASN'T SURE how the sensation of emptiness could be so painful. But her chest absolutely throbbed with it.

Had she ever seen Jenna so angry before?

No. Not even the day her sister had seen those first bruises on Crystal's arm though that day had been pretty bad, too. In her heart of hearts, Crystal knew Jenna was just worried. The girl had their father's temper but, unlike him, was usually quick to forgive. Not this time. God, Crystal wasn't sure how to make this right.

Not without dumping an anvil of worry and guilt on her sister's shoulders. And no way that kinda stress would be good for Jenna's epilepsy.

Because spilling to Jenna didn't just put her sister in the position of having to keep her mouth shut and play her part convincingly, it also meant revealing that Bruno paid for Jenna's medical expenses and explaining why their departure had to be secret. Which meant explaining how Crystal had been forced to work off their father's debts. And *that* meant revealing the scars on her back that Crystal had gone out of her way to hide the past four years.

For a moment, memories sucked Crystal back to the night it had all started. Some of Church's men had come to the house, nearly cleaned out from the previous day's auction of their home and its contents, to inform her that the sale hadn't raised enough to cancel out her dead father's debts. Apparently, they hadn't thought her cooperative or concerned enough—after all, the debts weren't *her* fault—so they'd grabbed her and forced her into their van. Next thing she knew, she was locked in one of the basement rooms of Confessions. Tools of various sorts hung on one of the pitch-black walls—some she could identify and some she couldn't.

And then the men had started coming.

The only saving grace in the whole thing was that Jenna had been away on the tenth grade's spring break field trip to Philadelphia. Over Jenna's protests, Crystal had insisted she go so she wouldn't have to witness all their belongings being sold off. And thank God she had. Because if Jenna had been home that night, there's every chance the Churchmen would've taken her, too. Somehow, Crystal didn't think that Jenna's being only fifteen and sickly would've stopped them.

Cold crept over Crystal's skin, and she shuddered. It had been Bruno who rescued her from the basement and kept Jenna from landing there herself. Thank God their father, before he went to prison, had called in a favor for having saved Bruno's life and gotten the man to promise to watch out for them. So Bruno had rescued Crystal and shielded Jenna to even the score and keep his word. But because he couldn't let them out of the debt repayment, he'd arranged for Crystal to get *other* work at Confessions. That was when she started waitressing. And, after a while, dating Bruno.

God, she could still remember her relief and gratitude toward Bruno. He hadn't just *seemed* like the answer to all her problems, he'd literally saved Crystal and protected Jenna from a situation that might've killed them or seen them sold off somewhere far, far away. Just like the other girls who'd disappeared into the club's bowels, never to be heard of again.

So, Crystal knew firsthand exactly what kind of danger lurked behind the scenes at Confessions. The threat of

that fate wasn't idle. Which was why she absolutely refused to tolerate even the thought of Jenna's stepping into
the club. God, when the girl had threatened to come to
Crystal's work *and* confront Bruno, Crystal had almost
tipped right over the edge into a full-blown panic attack.
Because back when Bruno first got violent with her, he
wasn't above reminding her how easily he could change
Jenna's fate. Just one call from Bruno, and Church would
have her hauled in.

And that's also why you helped Shane. Right. She just
hoped that didn't come back to haunt her.

Crystal couldn't imagine how she'd *ever* find the words
to tell her little sister *any* of that, though. Jenna would
never look at her the same way again.

No. It was far better for Jenna never to know exactly
what'd happened—what was *still* happening. For years,
Crystal had gone out of her way to hide her true reality.
She never changed in front of Jenna. Always locked the
bathroom door when she showered—a source of constant
complaint from Jenna given their one-bathroom setup.
And she'd gotten Bruno's permission to sew herself uniform tops similar to the standard Confessions uniforms
but that covered up her defects.

Since, you know, men were paying for the fantasy of
perfection at the club. And while the whip marks she
bore probably *were* a fantasy for some of the sickos that
sat around ogling the girls night after night, Confessions
didn't exactly advertise their support for that kinda thing
right out there in the open. No, those dark proclivities
could only be provided for in the shadows.

Say, in the club's basement . . .

Forcing her attention back to her reflection in the
dressing-room mirror, Crystal blew out a shaky breath.
Wallowing in those memories did absolutely no good.
Except maybe as a cautionary tale to help guide her

through her screwed-up life. As she stared at herself, Crystal had the fleeting thought that her life was a house of cards, one light blow away from falling to pieces and disintegrating to nothing.

"Enough," she whispered under her breath. If she didn't get her head together, she was going to mess something up and get herself in trouble around here tonight. But between the head-spinning deliciousness of kissing Shane and the fight with Jenna—not to mention being compared to their father . . . Crystal felt as fragile as cracked glass.

She gave herself one last look. Hair—curled and sprayed. Makeup—dramatic. Jewelry—costume crap she didn't care about losing. Uniform—skanky and scanty as always. Slipping her feet into the killer heels, she bent over and assembled the little silver buckles. Back in character for yet another shift.

The club had been open since noon, but it was still quiet when Crystal took the floor at seven. Which just figured. On nights when she might've considered giving all her tips to another waitress for ten minutes off her feet, business never let up. On nights when all Crystal wanted was to be so busy she wouldn't have five minutes to think, time crawled by.

Tonight, the last place she wanted to be was in her head with the memories of all the ways she'd screwed up.

Confessions's shift manager Darnell Parsons waved her over to the bar. "Prospective bachelor-party clients coming in to take a tour of the private rooms at eight for a party Friday night. You want to host them?" he asked, eyeballing her. With his warm brown skin and light eyes, the man was attractive enough, but he was possibly the most humorless, uptight man she'd ever known. "Well?" he asked, annoyance plain in his tone.

"Yes. I would. Thank you." The clients could request certain girls to work a party, so making a good impression during one of these visits could result in getting booked for parties where the tips ran way bigger than what you could earn on the main club floor.

Darnell nodded. "Go get the rooms up and running so everything's ready when they get here," he said.

"Yes, sir." Crystal darted toward the curtained doorway to the back hall. The minute she stepped through, she remembered how Shane had pressed her up against the wall right there, trapping her with his strength and his heat and his charm.

God, how could that have only happened a few days ago? If she thought on it, she could recall his scent and the way it had wrapped around her. Or, maybe, despite the long shower she'd taken after they'd gotten caught in the rain this afternoon, a part of him still lingered on her skin even now. Either way, one thing was clear. Shane had invaded her head and unsettled her body.

Crystal huffed an annoyed breath at herself and marched down the dim corridor. Feelings like that were exactly why Crystal needed to keep her distance from the man. He made her lose focus. He made her wish things could be different. And he made her want to throw caution to the wind and, for just once in her life, take what she wanted.

Openly. Wantonly. Unapologetically.

Which would be a freaking disaster. Or worse.

Past the door to the rear parking lot, a hall with black carpeting and red, padded walls stretched out like a long arm, the party rooms located along both sides.

Crystal entered the first room on her left and set about turning on the lights and the sound system. Despite variations in size and décor, the rooms were essentially the same. A small square stage sat in the center with a pole that extended to the ceiling surrounded by groupings of leather couches, chairs, and tables. Mirrors on the ceiling and along one wall. All the rooms had a private bathroom and wet bar in the rear of the space, though clients had to pay extra to have someone tend the party en suite.

She repeated the same setup in the other two rooms, knowing Darnell would want to take a chunk out of her hide if the client arrived before they were ready to begin the tour. Thankfully, Crystal was ready to play hostess with minutes to spare.

Soon after she'd taken up position by the bar, four men walked through the front door, two of whom she recognized. One of the men who'd been in the hallway with Shane the other night. And Shane, plucking a cowboy hat from his head.

He and his friends were approaching the bar not far from where she stood.

Oh, God. What the hell was he doing here?

Feigning nonchalance, she smiled at the men, forced her body to remain relaxed, and glanced away like two of the four of them weren't on the Church gang's most wanted list.

"Hey, buddy," one of them said to Walker, who'd been shooting the shit with a few regulars from his position behind the bar. Crystal peeked at the men from underneath her lashes. "We're here to see Darnell. Is he around?" The man who'd spoken was tall, bulky in the shoulders, with longish brown hair and an expression that hinted at a smile.

"I'll call him out here for you," Walker said. He gestured toward Crystal. "In the meantime, Crystal would be happy to show you to a table and take your drink orders."

She turned on her inner flirt, smiled, and batted her eyelashes. "Gentlemen, if you'll follow me, please."

Her heart pounding as loud as the bass of the music around them, Crystal guided them to a table near the curtained doorway. When it wasn't too loud or crowded,

Darnell preferred to introduce clients to the club out here so he could discuss the public amenities before showing clients what was available in the private spaces.

"What can I get for you boys?" she asked with a smile. And for the first time, she had a moment to soak them all in. And . . . what the hell were they wearing? Plaid shirts, big buckles, blue jeans, boots. The African-American man wore a beat-up John Deere baseball hat pulled low on his forehead. Shane balanced his cowboy hat on one thick thigh.

Looking at him, the men's appearances suddenly made sense. Disguises. Because Shane looked different yet again from the way he'd been every other time she'd seen him. That first night had been so hurried, but the next night when he'd shown up at the club, then at her apartment, he'd had a hard-edged, bad-ass vibe about him. Earlier today, his look had been more casual. Not average, exactly, because Shane could never be that. But now . . . well, let's just say he played country boy very convincingly, right down to the pronounced drawl with which he ordered his whiskey.

She couldn't meet Shane's gaze, though, because she really wasn't sure which of the competing emotions might bubble to the surface if she did. Hysteria. Anger. Maybe even humor at the getups.

By the time she'd returned from the bar with the men's drinks, Darnell was introducing himself and shaking each of the men's hands. As unobtrusively as possible, Crystal delivered the drinks.

"Now, who's the bachelor?" Darnell asked.

"That would be me," the friendly-faced man said, offering his hand. "Darren Morrison. Getting married on Saturday." They shook.

"Celebrating your last night of freedom?" Darnell said. Crystal had to resist rolling her eyes.

The man nodded. "You got it. When my boys suggested there was no better place to have a send-off than Confessions, I had to agree." The guys all smiled, including Shane. She had to admit, nothing about them flagged these men as being anything other than what they seemed. Good ol' boys out for a night of fun.

Crystal would just need to make sure her performance was as strong.

As Darnell dove into his spiel, Crystal stepped to the side of the group as far from Shane as possible. Soon, her manager was leading them into the back of the club, down the long hallway, and into the first of the party rooms. Inside, the men milled around, poked their heads into the bathroom, and tried out the couches while Darnell described how parties typically worked: one waitstaff, two dancers, special attention for the bachelor of various sorts, and the room itself for three hours.

Standing near the door, Crystal watched the men explore the room, totally convinced they were just a group of ordinary guys planning a party. They answered Darnell's questions about number of attendees, types of food and drink they wanted on hand, and the groom-to-be's preferences in girls like the subject matter totally engrossed them.

All of which led Crystal to wonder what they hell they were really doing here. Even if Mr. Groom was, in fact, having a bachelor party, it made absolutely no sense to do it here given that Shane and the other man had been involved in the rescuing of Church's hostage. No matter how she turned it around, she couldn't get their presence to make any sense.

"Mind if I use the john?" Mr. Groom asked Darnell with a smile.

"No problem," Darnell said.

As the man disappeared into the bathroom, her manager grabbed the remote and demonstrated the video system. A screen eased down along the one wall, and a menu of movie choices filled the screen. Sports, action/adventures, thrillers, war movies, and, of course, porn.

The guys laughed and joked around about the cheesy titles.

When the man rejoined the group from the bathroom, Darnell continued the tour into the next two rooms. Along the way, Crystal offered to refill drinks, answered the rare question directed toward her, and generally tried to fade into the background.

"Do you have a preference between the rooms, gentlemen?" Darnell asked as he finished showing the last room.

Shane led them in a conversation of the pros and cons of rooms until they agreed to reserve the first, biggest room. Crystal was almost bored as she followed the group of them up the private hallway toward the main part of the club.

The back door flew open and Bruno stepped inside. "Hey, baby," he said, grabbing her arm and pulling her into his body, so that she almost stumbled.

"Hey," she said, blinking away the sense of calm she'd managed to achieve. She had to go and tempt the fates with thinking the night was boring, hadn't she?

In that moment, Shane looked over his shoulder and caught what unfolded next. As he watched, Bruno pushed her against the wall. Grasped her jaw. And kissed her aggressively. Crystal felt like the kiss moved in slow motion.

Worse, she had to kiss him back. A biting sting sprang to the backs of her eyes as she sank into the kiss and threaded her arms around Bruno's neck.

Shane's stare was a physical caress against her skin. And his rage suffocated the very air she was trying to breathe around Bruno's invading tongue.

And, *oh God,* as if the man she wanted watching her kiss another man wasn't soul-killing enough, Bruno's hands started wandering. Down her sides. Pausing at her breasts. Cupping her ass.

She'd never felt cheaper in all her life.

Vomit made a slow crawl upward from her stomach.

From down the hall, the men's footsteps receded, then disappeared out into the main club altogether.

No doubt Bruno had just made her decision about whether to shut Shane out a hell of a lot easier. Because there was no way Shane would want her after seeing that. Not six hours ago, she'd stood in the woods in the rain and lost herself to Shane's touch, his scent, his kiss.

And now here she stood doing the same thing again with someone else. Or, at least, that had to be the way it looked to Shane.

Bruno patted her on the ass. "Gotta go, babe," he said, as if his actions hadn't just left her feeling gutted.

She forced a smile. "Okay. See ya." She watched him strut his way down to the offices and disappear inside.

Half-afraid she might really be sick, Crystal bolted. She pushed through the dressing-room door so hard it banged off the wall behind it. Across the room. Into the stall. Onto her knees.

As her stomach rolled, she stared at the placid water in the old, stained toilet. A cold sweat broke out across her brow and under her uniform, but the urge to hurl receded. Thank God.

She slumped on the floor next to the john, her back against the scratched and dented light blue wall of the stall. At least no one had been in here to witness that lovely scene.

Forcing herself onto her feet, Crystal breathed deeply a few times to make sure her tummy had really settled. Then she applied some new powder and blush to remove the sheen from her face. "Good as new," she said, hoping a little positive thinking would make her feel better. Not so much.

Damnit. She had to get her head on straight. *This* was *exactly* why her gut kept saying Shane McCallan was so dangerous. Frankly, there weren't many people whose opinions of her mattered. In fact, before Shane, she'd been able to count those who mattered on just one finger. Jenna.

She couldn't afford to let some man she barely knew scramble her wires like this. There was too much at stake.

With one last deep breath, Crystal pulled the dressing room door open. And walked right into a big, male body.

Crystal gasped. "You can't be back here!" She grabbed Shane's shirt with both hands and hauled him into the dressing room, then locked the door. "What the hell are you doing? You're going to get me killed." She'd meant the words figuratively, of course, but in point of fact, they possessed some literal truth.

His gaze was hard and lethal as steel. "I saw you run past the door."

"And?" she said, exasperation using up every bit of her patience.

"I was worried."

He was . . . worried? Even after he saw me . . . ? "Why?" she said.

He muttered under his breath, his fists clenching and unclenching. "I take it *that* was Bruno?"

Crystal's gaze dropped to the floor, the one she wished would open up and swallow her. She nodded.

"Well, I saw him grab you, Crystal. He might as well have mauled you—" Shane raked his fingers through his hair, messing up the neatly combed style that highlighted the blond.

Crystal grabbed his hands. "Don't do that. You're messing up your comb-over," she said. Using her own fingers, she straightened his hair, all the while the realization sank in that he wasn't mad because she'd kissed Bruno, he was mad because Bruno had kissed her.

Shane went still under her touch. Her face heated and, sure enough, his gaze blazed at her. She yanked her hands away. "You have to leave—"

"Not yet." A raw, aggressive masculinity poured off him, and Shane shook his head. "Not until you hear what I have to say." He stepped closer.

"But, Shane—"

"No. What he did out there, that wasn't okay with you. Jesus. I could see it in your eyes, your body, the way your fucking hands shook." He heaved a deep breath, like he was attempting to calm himself. "And if it wasn't okay with you, it's sure as hell not okay with me." Closer, yet. So close his chest brushed hers. "In point of fact, I have a major fucking problem with a male *forcing* a woman to do anything," he said, his eyes burning with molten silver. "But let me be clear, Crystal. Seeing him all over you like that would do bad things to me even if you wanted his attention. So my intentions here"—he pursed his lips and shook his head—"they're not all honorable. Because I want you. I want you so bad I can hardly breathe."

The room spun around Crystal, and butterflies looped within her belly. "Shane," she whispered, dumbstruck by his declaration. Nervous energy exploded within her until she thought she might burst into a thousand pieces. "Please. We can talk later," she rushed. "You have to go."

"You promise? Because I'm not done here. Not by a long shot."

The dark temptation of his words rushed heat through her blood, but the longer he remained, the more fear drowned out all her other reactions. "Yes, yes. Just go."

He nodded, anger receding from his expression, but something just as hot rolling in behind it. Desire.

Shane leaned down . . . and kissed her on the forehead.

And as much as she freaking *longed* for his kiss on her lips, what he'd done was even more perfect. The exact opposite of Bruno's aggression. He didn't just talk the talk, he walked the walk, too. And in her world, that meant everything. Words were cheap and easy.

Shane peeked out the door and took off.

Staring at the closed door in front of her, Crystal pressed her hands to her chest. Not wanting to lose the feeling suddenly expanding within. Because the constant sensation of emptiness that had left her cold for so many years was gone, replaced by something new. Foreign. Scary.

Something she should try to ignore.

Something she should push away.

Something that could hurt her in ways Bruno's hands and Church's possession never could.

Crystal—no, *Sara*—was very likely falling for Shane McCallan.

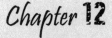

Chapter 12

Shane ducked through the curtain and held up his phone to the bouncer doing a fortunately piss-poor job of guarding the back of Confessions. "Found it," he said with a nod. The guy barely acknowledged him, but it was no skin off Shane's nose, because Crystal had promised she would talk to him.

And that promise had calmed some of the cyclone of rage that had whipped up inside him when he'd seen Crystal run past the curtain after Bruno had manhandled her. Goddamn but it had taken every ounce of discipline he'd *ever* had to restrain himself from marching back that hall and tearing the big goon off of her. Only the certainty that doing so would've been a disaster for their mission and for Crystal had held him in check. Still, the fact that Crystal had said she had no choice but to work here put her relationship with that asshole in a whole new light. And not a good one.

Shane threaded through the growing crowd in the bar, and their table came into view. Except . . . "Where's E?" he asked as he sat.

"Never a dull moment," Beckett said as he nodded toward the bar.

Following Beckett's gaze, Shane found Easy, obviously talking to someone at the bar, but the guy was so big Shane couldn't see around him. Not that Shane had a lot of room to talk after cutting out to check on Crystal, but they didn't really have time to chat up the clientele. And then Easy turned and guided someone through the crowd.

Not just anyone. Jenna.

"Oh, fuck a duck," Shane said under his breath, his scalp prickling. What the hell was she doing here when Crystal had told her explicitly to stay away? Had she actually come to confront Bruno? And, Jesus, the thought of her hanging out alone in a strip club known to traffic young, vulnerable women made Shane want to hurl.

"Charlie Mike," Marz said, the call sign telling them all to continue mission and basically stay chill. And roger that, because they had to get her ass out of here before she had a chance to confront Bruno or Crystal saw her and freaked out. Both had a higher-than-average likelihood of making tempers and other things go kaboom.

Arm around her shoulder, Easy gave a hopeful motherfucker looming behind Jenna a withering glare and guided her toward their table with all the ease in the world. She went along well enough, but questions and skepticism shone brightly in her blue eyes.

Shane got his first good look at Crystal's younger sister, at least his first look at her conscious. Wearing black jeans, black Chucks, and an old concert T-shirt gave her a college-grunge-meets-girl-next-door vibe that was drawing attention because it was clearly way the hell out of place for Confessions. And damn if she wasn't pretty close to a carbon copy of Crystal, except shorter, curvier, and with darker red hair.

"Who's your friend, E?" Shane said with a false enthusiasm in his voice as he rejoined the group.

"This is Jenna," Easy said as he offered her his seat. She slipped into it, her expression part curiosity and part recognition that she was maybe in over her head. "She's just waiting to see her sister, who works here." Gone was the subdued version of Edward Cantrell they'd seen the past few days. In his place was a totally engaged and deceptively calm man Shane knew was ready to pounce on the first thing that made a wrong step in his—or rather, *her*—direction.

And Shane approved. Because beyond the trafficking, they didn't know the whole universe of what Crystal thought made this place unsafe for Jenna. So high alert was the right way to play it.

"I see." Shane reached his hand across the table. "I'm Shane McCallan, darlin'. Nice to meet you." *Again.*

She returned the shake and gave him a weak smile. "Hi. I'm Jenna," she said, staring at Shane like she was trying to place him.

"Well, hell. While we're at it, I'm Marz," he said, extending his hand, too. "And this big ugly lug is Beckett."

"Ignore him," Beckett said with a small wave. "His jokes aren't as funny as his looks."

For a long moment Jenna traded looks with each of them. "Edward said you all were Crystal's friends?" she asked, her gaze returning to Shane. "But have we met before?"

"We've met," Shane said, as the girl frowned. And then he decided to just lay it out there, because all the ways her presence could make this situation go bad were eating at his insides. "But you were a little out of it." Gripping his cowboy hat, Shane continued. "I'm gonna cut right through the crap if that's okay with you, Jenna. Because I think you know where you're sitting right now isn't the safest place and that your sister would be less than happy to see you out here."

Jenna paled. "She told you about the fight?"

Perfect opening, Shane thought. "Uh, yeah. And we said we'd look out for you in case you really showed up."

Jenna frowned, and it was an expression filled with equal parts uncomfortable regret and restrained anger. "Well, I wasn't—" Sucking in a breath, Jenna blanched. The curtains flared, and Bruno surged through.

Shane tamped down his body's demands for vengeance when panic flashed across Jenna's face. So she *wasn't* here to confront him after all? Because she did not look like someone ready to pick a fight right now. Then what could be so important that she couldn't wait to talk to Crystal until she returned home?

"Put your hair up under this," Easy said, handing her his ball cap.

"No, E," Shane said, passing his cowboy hat across the table. "They'll make you."

Jenna whipped her hair into a ponytail and stuffed it under the hat. Easy tilted the brim lower over her face.

"Gentlemen, I'd say we are damn close to overstaying our welcome," Beckett said in a low voice Shane just made out over the music. Agreed murmurs went around the table.

They rose. And the manager guy appeared out of thin air. "Mr. Morrison?" he said, using the fake name Derek had provided on the credit card. "You're all set for Friday night. Please just call by five o'clock on Thursday with a head count."

"You got it." Marz shook the man's hand. "Thanks for showing us a good time tonight."

The man smiled, offered good-byes to the rest of the group, and disappeared as quickly as he'd come. Shane blew out a long breath. Thirty feet separated them from the front door. They started through the crowd in the bar area.

Making sure Marz was still behind him, Shane glanced over his shoulder just in time to see Crystal return to the club floor. From his position bringing up the rear, Marz noticed, too.

Crystal gaped as her eyes shifted from Shane to the woman walking in front of him. Maybe it was the clothes, or the purse, or a lifetime of living with and knowing someone, but Crystal clearly knew who was walking beneath Shane's hat.

Shane could almost feel Crystal's desperate urge to bolt across the room and pull her sister into her arms, and he realized that Crystal really had no way of knowing what was going on. Hell, from where she stood, it probably looked damn suspicious.

Just then, Marz put a finger to his lips and, when Crystal's gaze latched onto the movement, Marz put his thumb to his ear and his pinkie to his mouth, mimicking a phone.

Giving a single small nod, Crystal forced her expression into something a lot more casual. And it was a good thing she did. Because the next moment, Bruiser made a return trip from the bar and marched right up to her.

Every muscle in Shane's body tensed as Bruno's hands landed on her skin.

"It's cool, McCallan. Keep moving," Marz said with a hand on his back. And then they cleared the door and stepped into the cool of the nighttime air.

"Keep walking," Shane said from Jenna's left side,

echoing Marz's words to him. Easy flanked her on the right. What a fubar of a night. From being forced to sit on his hands and watch Crystal's distress when Bruno kissed her to the surprise of Jenna's appearance at the club, Shane was on his last nerve.

"But my car's over there," Jenna said, pointing down the street.

"What kind is it?" Shane asked, guiding her toward the sidewalk heading in the opposition direction.

"What?" Tucking a loose strand of hair back under the cowboy hat, Jenna frowned.

"What *kind*?"

Jenna slowed just as they passed a fence that blocked their view of the club. "Why—"

Shane stepped in front of the woman and tipped the cowboy hat back enough to make eye-to-eye. "Look, I'd rather not let you out of my sight until you're safe and sound at home. If there's one thing I know about your sister with complete and utter certainty, it's how much you mean to her. So I'd really rather that nothing happened to you on my watch, and that begins with getting you the hell away from here."

Crossing her arms, Jenna's glare softened but remained. "I don't know you. So I'm not going anywhere with you."

Scanning the street around their position, Shane crossed his arms, not willing to budge on his position. "Well, I know *you,* Jenna. I know you have epilepsy and your seizures are worsening. I know you had a grand mal seizure less than twenty-four hours ago and that you shouldn't be running around dangerous sections of town by yourself. I know you live in the East Side Apartments with your sister and that your parents are gone. And I know your sister's in trouble, and you're worried about her." As he spoke, Shane watched as Jenna's expressions morphed from rebellious to uncertain. "I'm worried about her, too.

And that puts us on the same side. So if you'll let me take you home so I can assure your sister you're safe again, I would very much appreciate it."

"Uh . . ." She glanced around the group, her gaze landing last on Easy beside her. He nodded.

"Now, please call your sister," Shane said, hoping Crystal had made her way to her cell. "She saw us leave, and Marz gestured to her that we'd call." Shane had really been hoping to spare Crystal the knowledge that Jenna had stepped foot in that hellhole, especially given the risks Crystal had taken earlier in the day to see him and pass on information about the meeting. She had enough on her plate.

"Oh, God, she saw me?" Jenna asked, her eyes going wide.

"She did, but she was cool," Shane said, finding yet another reason to admire Crystal. Tonight, she'd had no warning and no preparation that she'd see him on her workplace turf, where he knew his presence alarmed her given his role in Charlie's rescue. Crystal didn't know much about Shane, so she had no reason to believe him especially capable of flying under Church's radar. And yet, with all that, she'd been cool and sweet as lemonade on a hot, summer day.

Add all that to Shane's pushing her too far earlier, Bruno's aggressive kiss, and Shane's inviting himself into her dressing room, and she'd have been well within her rights to totally freak out by now. But she hadn't. Of course she hadn't. Because everything Shane knew about Crystal so far pointed to the fact that she was tough as fucking nails.

And as he stood there staring down her younger sister, it was plain to see that Jenna was cut from the same cloth.

"Jenna, call her," Shane said, gentling his tone. "I don't want her to worry because I don't think it's good for her to be at all off her game when she's in there. Do you?"

Recognition flashed through Jenna's blue gaze. She fished her cell from her small purse and pressed a series of buttons. After what seemed an inordinately long time, Jenna said, "Hey. It's me." Pause. Some of the tension drained from Shane's muscles, knowing hearing Jenna's voice would likely ease Crystal's concerns. A car went by on the street behind them and Shane did another one-eighty scan of their position. Beckett was doing the same thing. "I know, I know. I'm sorry," Jenna continued. Pause. "I just . . . I . . . I had to say I was sorry," she said, her voice suddenly tight and strained with sadness. She batted at an eye, and her gaze flickered up to Shane. "I didn't mean it," she almost whispered, and Shane was glad for the apology for Crystal's sake. He just wished Jenna had waited to deliver it in person—at home. Jenna's gaze whipped back to Shane. "I'm with them. They said they're your friends and want to take me home." With an arched brow, Jenna offered him her phone. "She wants to talk to you."

With a prayer that this jacked-up night didn't further damage Crystal's trust in him, Shane placed the cell to his ear. "Crystal."

"What the hell is going on?" she asked in a hushed voice.

"Long story, but if it's okay with you, rather than tell it right now I'd like to escort your sister back to your apartment."

"Yes, please. Oh, my God, thank you. She has to get out of here." A hint of panic was clear in Crystal's voice. "Will I see you . . . I mean, will you stay there with her?" she asked.

Shane glanced at his watch, and twin reactions coursed through him. A soul-deep satisfaction that she'd even asked—a hell of an improvement from where they'd stood this afternoon. And white-hot regret, because he had to return to Hard Ink in less than an hour for Charlie's surgery. "I can't. I have something I have to do in a little while. But why do you ask? Do you think she needs protecting?"

"No. I don't know. I'm just a little rattled."

Man, but the unusual fragility in her voice just slayed him. "Look, if it'll make you feel better, I can leave someone . . ." He surveyed the group.

"I'll stay," Easy said. "If that's okay with Jenna." She stared at the guy for a long moment, then gave a small shrug. "Don't worry, you won't even know I'm there."

Shane gave Easy a thumbs-up. "I'll leave a good friend named Edward. He'll keep an eye out 'til you get home."

"But that won't be until after two," she said.

Shane turned away and paced a few steps along the cracked sidewalk. "I told you I'd help you and Jenna. That offer didn't come with an expiration date or office hours. Understand?"

She blew out a long breath. "Thank you."

"You're welcome. Now get your head screwed back on straight and keep your wits about you. Everything's fine here, okay?"

"Okay. And Shane? I . . . uh . . . just, thank you." The connection went dead.

Handing the phone back to Jenna, Shane asked, "You with me?" Jenna nodded, more cooperative now. But Shane couldn't fault her for fighting back. Hell, he had half a mind to lecture her for walking out the door with a group of strangers in the first place. But that would be all kinds of unfair, wouldn't it? "Okay, then. Would you be comfortable riding with us, and Easy will follow in your car, or would you rather I ride with you to your place, and they'll follow?"

She glanced at the group of men surrounding her. "Uh, I guess—"

"We've got some activity out front of the club," Beckett said in a low voice.

"Pick, Jenna. Or I'll choose for you. Because either way, I'm not leaving your side until I know you're locked inside that apartment."

Jenna rolled her eyes. "I'll ride in your car, *I guess*," she said, then gave the make, model, and location of her vehicle. Fishing in her purse, she located her key ring and handed it off to Easy.

Shane nodded at Easy. "Remember that location is under some type of surveillance, E."

He nodded. "Roger that. I'll make like Casper."

Jenna watched Easy walk away and turned a glare on Shane. "You're kinda bossy. You know that?" she said.

Shane barked out a laugh as they set off for Beckett's SUV, parked just down the street. He threw Jenna a smile and winked. "I can totally live with that."

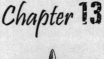

Chapter 13

*B*ack at Hard Ink, Shane hopped out of Beckett's SUV, with Charlie's surgery filling his mind. For the next few hours, nothing else mattered. Not Church or Merritt or the team or himself. Not even Crystal.

Because tonight was do-or-die.

Gravel crunching beneath his boots, Shane crossed the parking lot to the back door of Hard Ink, Beckett and Marz right behind him. Easy had stayed back to keep watch over the women's apartment until Crystal got home from work, giving Shane a little peace of mind that everything was squared away there. At least for now.

The three of them humped it up the steps, and Shane broke left for the Rixeys' apartment.

A hand landed on Shane's shoulder, and he paused at the door.

"You saved me. You can save him. Don't doubt it,"

Marz said, an uncharacteristic seriousness in his expression.

Eyes narrowed and brows slashed downward, Beckett's discomfort with any talk of Marz's injuries was clear. But that didn't keep him from offering his hand and saying, "Same goes for me. You got this."

Shane shook both men's hands and nodded. "No prize for second place this time," he said.

"You won't need it. Now go take a few minutes to clear your head before Murphy gets here," Marz said.

Before Murphy gets here . . . and shit gets real. "Roger that." Shane turned and pushed through the door. Difference between the medic work he'd done in the field and what they were doing tonight? He'd never had time to prepare for a crisis in the field. No such thing as time to psych yourself up—or psych yourself out. One minute it would be situation normal, the next everything would go to shit, and you dealt because there was no other choice. Men's lives were on the line, the bullets were flying, and the clock was ticking.

The living room and kitchen were quiet and dim, but light spilled out from Charlie's room down the hall. Tossing his hat on the couch, Shane headed straight there and found Becca, Nick, and Jeremy all standing vigil at Charlie's bedside. Not to mention Eileen, who'd made a black furball of herself at the foot of the mattress.

They exchanged hushed greetings as he entered. Shane crouched next to Becca, sitting by the bed. With his fever red cheeks and sweat-dampened hair, Charlie appeared much the same as before. "How's he doing?" he asked in a quiet voice.

"No change," she said, already wearing a set of scrubs and her game face. There wasn't going to be any room for *Becca the sister* during the procedure. But for *Becca the nurse*? Damn straight. They needed her there, and they needed her to be rock solid. From the look of resolve on her face and in her eyes, Shane needn't have worried.

"We're going to take care of him, you hear?" Shane refused to entertain any other outcome. Wasn't in his nature. Besides, you couldn't look at your own hands and believe them capable of salvation without a healthy dose of confidence, and not a little arrogance, too. He didn't look at it as playing God, but he didn't question for one minute that there was something divine, something miraculous in the ability to restart a beating heart, restore a man to consciousness, or bring someone back from the edge of eternity.

Becca nodded and gave a small smile. "Murphy should be here soon."

"Okay," Shane said, rising. Nick tilted his head toward the hall, and Shane followed him out.

"How'd it go?" Nick asked in a low voice.

"We've got eyes and ears on the inside now," Shane said. "Marz planted bugs in the ductwork which he thinks will pick up sound from at least several offices away and cracked the wireless frequency on some of the security cameras, too. He'll fill you in on all the details."

"Good. That's good." Nick tugged his hands through his hair. "Wish I could be in there with you and Becca. Hate sitting on the sidelines."

Shane would've felt the same way. "I get it, man. Best thing you can do is just chill out. Becca's gonna need you—bad—when we're done. No matter how this shakes out, the woman's staring down a major release of stress and emotion when it's over."

Not that Shane really had to explain this to Nick. They'd both been in enough snafus to be well acquainted with the adrenaline letdown that almost always followed. Experience it enough, you learned how to manage the flow. But hell if it didn't mow your ass down those first few times, no matter how much you thought you'd prepared for it.

"Yeah," Nick said.

Worried as the guy was—for Charlie, for Becca, for the whole team given their situation—Shane knew there was something he could do to take a little of the load off Nick's mind. The apology Shane hadn't quite been able to pull together the previous night. "Look, man, I wanted to—"

A rattle sounded at the front door, and Marz walked in with Murphy—and another man. Both in full EMT uniform. What the hell? Had Nick and Becca changed their mind about her friend's partner taking part in this?

"Goddamnit," Nick bit out, his scowl answering Shane's question. Nick leaned in Charlie's room. "Becca? Murphy's here. Brought company, too."

"Oh," she said, rising. She led them up the hallway, and Nick flipped on lights as they went.

Murphy raised his hands in a gesture of *mea culpa*. "I know what you said. But we're a package deal. No way to make this happen without Eric," he said.

Becca turned to Nick and laid a hand on his chest. "It's okay. I can vouch for him, for both of them. You know I wouldn't do anything to put Charlie at risk, or any of us."

Nick's intense gaze cut from Becca to Eric to Murphy.

Murphy shrugged. "Some lies I'm willing to tell, some I'm not."

Tense as Shane was over the unexpected newcomer, he totally got the sentiment. No doubt, falling off the grid midshift was going to require some creative storytelling on their part. But lies were the last thing you wanted standing between you and a partner you had to count on day in and day out. Which brought Shane back to the words he owed Nick Rixey. Soon.

For a long moment, Shane looked over the new player in

their little drama. Last name Rodriguez, according to the name tag on his shirt. Dark hair and eyes, stocky build, loose stance, made easy eye contact. Despite Murphy's immediate defensiveness, the guy appeared relatively re-laxed, like he had nothing to hide, and like he understood enough about the situation to accept the tension saturating the air around them. Shane's gut came down on the side of trustworthy.

"Fair enough," Nick finally said, apparently coming to the same conclusion. Besides, guy was here now. No choice other than to accept it and move forward.

"Jones filled me in," Eric said. "I have his back in this, and I'm happy to help." The guy looked from Nick to Becca. "I'm sorry to hear about your brother and what you're going through."

"Thank you, Eric. Thanks for being here. No doubt we'll need you," she said.

Nick squeezed Becca's shoulders, and she leaned back against him. "How do you want to start?" he asked.

For the next forty-five minutes, Murphy walked them through the procedure, using a PowerPoint presentation he'd prepared on his laptop, and the four with medical training talked through approaches and responsibilities. They weren't going to have a lot of time or a lot of space, so going in as prepared as possible was critical to the out-come they all wanted.

Charlie. Back among the living.

But even though their discussion left him feeling like they had a better than average chance of this working, talking could only take them so far.

After changing into scrubs, they loaded Charlie onto a stretcher. Guy was so out of it he didn't stir a bit as they transferred him, nor as they carried him through the apartment and down the steps to the ambulance parked just outside the back door of Hard Ink.

Together, they got Charlie hooked up to a variety of monitors inside the rig, started him on another course of IV antibiotics, and strapped him down at the chest and thighs to keep him from thrashing about should he unexpectedly wake up mid-procedure. At each step in the process, Shane kept an eye on Becca. But she had her head squarely in the game, and her determination served to reinforce his own.

They all gowned up, scrubbed in, and gloved up, then Murph administered a nerve block intended to preempt pain from the elbow down to the fingertips.

Shane nodded to Nick, standing outside the rig's back door. Behind him stood Jeremy, Marz, and Beckett, all of their expressions as grim and serious as Shane felt. "All right. Close us in and let's do this," Shane said.

The doors *clunked* shut, enclosing them in the makeshift OR with a patient whose life they'd just saved from the clutches of the Church Gang. No way they were losing Charlie now that they had him back.

It would kill Becca. And it would go a long way toward destroying the team, too. Because something special had happened these past few days. They were becoming a family born of choice rather than blood.

Murphy slid his mask over his mouth and nose. "Okay, lady and gents, we've got a guaranteed window of two hours where no one will miss us or the vehicle."

Shane met the guy's gaze and nodded. "Lead the way, Doc."

As Shane and Eric assisted and Becca monitored Charlie's vitals, Murphy made quick work of prepping the wound. Removing the exposed bone was a slow process accomplished in small millimeter chips using a pair of plierlike bone cutters. Then Shane and Murphy worked together on the delicate skin-grafting procedure. Since they had so little elbow room and wanted to keep the need for anesthetic localized, they'd transplanted the skin they needed for the flap from Charlie's forearm.

When the whole procedure was done, Shane stared at the repair with more than a little wonder. What they'd done had been clearly illegal, likely unethical, and absolutely necessary—and it had worked.

Now they just had to hope Charlie was strong enough to bounce back from the infection.

They opened up the back of the rig and shared the good news with Nick and Beckett, who didn't appear to have moved since they'd closed themselves in a good ninety minutes before.

Nick reached up and pulled Becca into his arms. "You did it," he said against her hair, and she clutched her arms around his neck.

"We all did," she rasped.

Shane patted her back and smiled, and she turned and hugged him next. "Thank you," she said.

The gratitude washing off her made Shane feel ten feet tall. "No thanks necessary, Becca."

While Nick, Beckett, and Becca carefully got Charlie to his room upstairs, Shane hung back and helped Murphy and Eric do a thorough cleanup job on the ambulance. Then they all headed up to the apartment to make sure Charlie was still okay.

As they shared a quiet round of congratulations— Becca's eyes never leaving her sleeping brother's face—a call came through on both of the EMTs' radios. "Perfect timing," Murphy said with a smile.

Stepping out of Charlie's room, Nick held out a hand. "We won't forget what you did for us. Thank you," he said, shaking both men's hands. Thanks and good-byes went around, then Murph and Eric left. Not only had the pair proven themselves good friends, but they could be damn important allies as this situation unfolded. And

with the authorities and the hospitals off the table, they
needed all the help they could get.

"Where are Marz and Jeremy?" Shane asked.

"Next door doing research," Nick said. "We should
share the news."

"You guys go, I'll stay with Charlie," Becca said.

Nick grasped her hand. "You should be at the celebration," he said. "We'll only stay a few minutes and come
right back."

She smiled and nodded. "Okay, just a few minutes."

As a group, they poured into the gym, and Shane for
one couldn't keep the grin off his face.

From his chair at the computer, Marz nearly jumped to
his feet. "It's over? How'd it go?"

"Went good," Shane said as he put an arm around Becca's shoulder and hugged her in against his side. "We did
good."

As they gathered around Marz's desk, she gave a fast
nod and batted at the corner of her eye. "Now we wait for
Charlie to wake up and beat this fever."

Jeremy set a box of files on the floor. "He'll do it, Becca.
Don't you worry."

Marz's smile was a mile wide. "That's right. Man, this
is damn good news."

Shane nodded. "Chalk one up to stupid luck."

Marz shook his head. "Wasn't luck out on the dirt road
that day, and wasn't luck tonight. You two are rock stars,
man. For real."

"Besides," Beckett said, stuffing his hands in the pockets of his jeans, "if it's stupid but it works, it isn't stupid."
They all chuckled.

"So," Shane said, eager to change the topic. "Any luck
here?"

Marz sat heavily. "Lots of things in the works. Surveillance camera feeds are all up from inside Confessions. I

managed to isolate the range of frequencies representing voices from the club's music and other background noise, so we've got audio, too. Sound quality isn't perfect, but it's better than nothing. And for shits and giggles, I set up a search query of all the companies doing business out of the marine terminal who have anything to do with Afghanistan, Singapore, or military hardware and materiel using the Port Authority registries."

"You've been busy," Beckett said.

Marz shrugged and rubbed his thigh. "Couldn't just sit around and wait, you know?"

A rustling sound caught Shane's attention, and he glanced around the desk to find Eileen wrestling a big stuffed bear out of a box. The puppy pulled it free but landed on her back, the bear on top. She growled and flipped out from under it. Shane laughed.

"Oh shit," Jeremy said, reaching for the bear. "No, no, Eileen."

The dog sank her teeth into the bear's neck and bolted.

Jeremy took off after her, darting between Beckett and Nick and around the gym equipment. Eileen growled and shook the bear as she dodged and weaved. Jeremy finally cornered her. "Gotcha, bad puppy. That's Becca's bear," he said, scooping the dog and bear up. "Let go, now," he said. Eileen licked his face as everyone chuckled. They all loved that mutt, but she seemed to have a special sweet spot for Jeremy and Charlie in particular.

"Don't worry about it, Jer," Becca said with a smile.

"All right, fess up," Nick said. "Were you and Marz playing dolls all this time?" Nick asked with a straight face.

"Ha, ha, asshole," Jeremy said as he flipped his brother off.

Shane snickered at the glower on Jeremy's face. "Is that an Army bear?" he asked.

"Yeah," Becca said. "My dad sent it to me from Afghanistan."

"Here," Jeremy said, drilling it at Shane like a football.

Shane caught it before it nailed him in the gut. "Fucker," he said, chuckling. Something metallic clanked to the floor.

"Oops," Jeremy said, putting Eileen down and retrieving a thin chain from the concrete. He held it up. Play ID tags. "Look what you went and did, Eileen. Bad girl. Bad, bad girl."

The puppy tilted her head and whined before sitting down on her haunches. Her tail wagged lazily. Dang if she wasn't the cutest three-legged German shepherd Shane had ever seen. Not that he thought he'd ever seen a three-legged German shepherd before. Or any three-legged dog. Still.

"Sorry, Becca. I'll get a replacement chain," Jer said.

"I might have one somewhere. I'll look," Marz said. "What's it say?"

Jeremy smiled. "Bear, Maxwell. His social security number. And 'B Positive.' "

Shane reached out his hand. "Hey, that's pretty accurate info. Lemme see. Maybe I can fix it." He dropped the bear to the desk as he examined the ball chain. "Oh. The connector's totally gone." He scanned the floor around their feet, but didn't see it. Flipping the ID tag around, Shane chuckled. "Maxwell Bear."

And then Shane froze.

The social security number was familiar . . .

"Holy shit," Shane said, doing a double take. "This isn't a SSN. Look how the digits are divided up." His brain racing, Shane held it out to Marz and everyone stepped closer.

Marz's eyes went wide. "Three groups of three instead of groups of three, two, four." He dug a sheet of paper from a stack on his desk and slammed it down with the tag so everyone could see.

Nick leaned in. "Holy. Shit."

"Oh, my God. That's . . . isn't that the number carved inside my mother's locket?" Becca asked.

Shane looked again, just to prove his brain hadn't played a trick on him. But, no. The ID tag still read 754–374–329 and matched one of the numbers they'd been investigating the past few days. The Singapore bank account number. The account holding $12 million in cash Merritt received running the black op that took their SF team down.

"It's the same," Becca whispered. "Why would it be on the bear's tag?"

Marz grabbed the bear from where Shane had placed it on the desk. The hat. The coat. The pants. The boots. Shane's heart pumped harder in his chest as Marz took off each article of clothing and inspected them carefully for writing or false panels. Nothing. When the bear was naked, Marz flipped it around and gave it a full physical. Still nothing.

Becca's eyes were wide as saucers. "What do you think it means?"

Marz shook his head as he stared at the bear.

Shane's thoughts flew around Becca's question. *No way this is a coincidence. What were you trying to tell Becca, Frank? And why did you feel you had to hide codes and account numbers and messages in so many secretive ways?* The bracelet. And now the bear.

"It means we have to start looking at things a whole lot different." Marz squeezed the toy from ears to paws. "And it means your bear has to die, Becca," he said as he looked up at her.

She gaped and stared at the bear for a long moment. Finally, she said, "You think something's in it?"

Shane's scalp prickled as the rightness of her words ran through him.

Marz smiled. "I think something's in it."

Becca nodded. "Well, all right. But if it has to die, can we do the killing over in the apartment so I can keep an ear out for Charlie?"

TEN MINUTES LATER, they'd checked on a still-sleeping Charlie and congregated around the island in the kitchen. The beer and whiskey flowed.

Shane was still riding so high from the success of Charlie's surgery that he didn't think sleep was anywhere in his immediate future, despite its being well after one o'clock in the morning. And now the adrenaline rush of their discovery with the bear.

"To Becca and Shane," Nick said, raising his glass. Everyone followed suit.

"To Charlie," Shane said, diverting the attention from himself with another round of clinking glasses. After all, he'd just been doing his job. Shane tossed back a swallow of whiskey and enjoyed the warm bite of it hitting his tongue.

"If I drink any more of this, it'll knock me out until Sunday," Becca said, pushing her bottle of beer away. "And I should keep an eye on Charlie through the night."

"You don't have to do it alone," Beckett said in a quiet voice, those ice blue eyes trained on Becca. "I'll help." Shane had a pretty strong suspicion that, like himself, the big guy was also trying to make some amends where Becca was concerned. He'd been almost as standoffish when they'd met, and soon thereafter he'd gotten in a fistfight with Nick that she hadn't appreciated one bit. And she'd let them all know it, too.

The memory of Becca's fierce defense of Nick almost made Shane smile. Not many people took on Beckett Murda and lived to tell the tale. But she had.

"Me too," Nick said. "We're in this together."

She smiled and tucked in against Nick's body. "Thanks, guys."

Nick wrapped his arm around her and kissed her hair. "Now, back to the bearicide," he said, pointing at the toy in front of Marz.

"This is some serious cloak-and-dagger," Shane said, studying the tag again.

"Merritt always was a brilliant tactician and strategist. That's clearly at play here. Question is, why?" Beckett said as he crossed his big arms. And he was right. Merritt had been a soldier who understood war, who knew how to use his assets and mitigate his weaknesses. Shane had always admired that about him. Part of the reason it stung so bad that the man had betrayed him. All of them.

Marz nodded. "Right. Which is why it has to be significant that he had a special ID tag made with the bank account number in place of the SSN. Then sent it to Becca."

"I can't believe it," Becca said, rubbing her thumb over the stamped numbers. "First the bracelet and now this."

"I know." Marz met each of their gazes. "That's why I think there's something in the bear."

A rush of anticipation shot through Shane, and he braced his hands on the counter. "Well, what are you waiting for? Open this bad boy up."

Stepping back, Nick retrieved a pair of kitchen shears from a drawer. "You sure it's okay with you?" he asked Becca.

"Heck, yeah," she said, as Marz accepted the scissors into his grip. "My father wouldn't have done this without a reason."

"Agreed," Marz said. "Here goes nothing." He burrowed the sharp point of the scissor blade into the seam that ran up the stuffed animal's back, then slowly opened the body, the legs, the head.

Shane peered over his shoulder, trying like hell to avoid blocking Marz's light but dying to know what they were going to find. What it was going to be, Shane wasn't quite sure. But it had to be something good, something *important*. Because there was no other reason for Merritt to go to all this trouble except as a signal to pay attention and dig deeper. At least, that's what Shane's gut told him. "Who thought we'd be doing another surgery tonight?" he asked.

"God help the patient with Marz as the doctor," Beckett said. And it was really damn good to see a bit of normalcy returning between the pair. Beck hadn't handled Marz's amputation well and had turned into even more of a clam than usual after the ambush.

Low, tense chuckles went around the room.

"Here goes nothing," Marz said as he began massaging his fingers through every bit of white stuffing. As Marz searched, Shane's heart kicked up inside his chest. "Double-check me," he said to Shane, pushing a mound of fluff in front of him.

Shane was only too happy to help. His fingers literally itched to encounter whatever it was that'd been hidden. The stuffing was silky soft and thick, forcing Shane to pull it apart to make sure he hadn't missing something.

Nothing in the body. Nothing in the legs. Nothing in the arms.

Marz started on the head. "Come to Papa," he said, anticipation and excitement clear in his voice. Except . . . He finished pulling through the last of the stuffing. Nothing. Shane came to the same conclusion as he double-checked him.

The bear was empty.

"You gotta be fucking kidding me," Marz said. Disappointment deflated the air around them.

"Check the body," Shane said, refusing to believe this

was a false lead. What would be the fucking point? They each took a section of the bear's unstuffed body and turned the pieces inside out. Still nothing. "Well, goddamn."

"It doesn't make any sense," Becca said, her voice suddenly strained. And it nearly broke Shane's heart to see her struggling to hold back tears. One broke free, and she batted it away, then Nick turned her in his arms and pulled her against his chest. "I'm just tired," she said in a raspy whisper.

Nick nodded, his troubled expression mirroring Shane's own feelings. "I know. Tomorrow's another day. Thanks for everything all of you did today," he said, meeting each of their gazes. "Come on, sunshine," he whispered against her hair.

She nodded and offered the rest of them a watery smile. "Thanks, guys," she said, as they left the kitchen and headed back down the hall toward Nick's room.

"I guess I'll call it a night, too," Jeremy said. "And Marz? I've got clients until about noon tomorrow, but I'm free in the afternoon if you need more help."

Marz dragged his gaze away from the ruins of the bear, his expression as close to pissed off as you ever saw it. "Absofuckinglutely. Consider yourself spoken for." Jer gave a nod and said his good-nights as Marz scooped the pile of fluff into his arms. "Well, I'm too annoyed to sleep. Think I'll go scan more of the surveillance feeds. Those fuckers have to say something about tomorrow's delivery sometime."

"One would think," Shane said, feeling like they'd missed something but unable to make his brain focus through the fog of exhaustion.

"Why don't you just throw that away?" Beckett asked, frowning at the stuffing overflowing Marz's hands.

He shook his head. "It's Becca's. I'll leave it to her to decide what to do with it."

Beckett followed Marz to the apartment door, but looked back over his shoulder. "You wanna hang?" Beck asked.

Shane scrubbed his hands over his face. What he should do was go the hell to sleep. But despite the aches and fatigue of his muscles, the dull throb of his gunshot wound, and his fuzzyheadedness, sleep was the last thing on his mind.

Crystal.

She'd be getting off work soon . . .

And she'd promised to talk to him. *Really* talk to him, this time.

With Charlie's surgery behind him, his thoughts were free to roam again, and they went back to the image of that Bruno asshole running his dirty paws all over her.

The whirlwind in his brain wasn't going away until he saw her again, that much was clear.

"Nah," Shane said. "I'm going to go check in with Easy. Make sure everything's cool there."

"Okay. Well, don't forget to wear a raincoat," Beckett said, totally deadpan.

Marz's expression froze for a second before cracking into a wide smile and uproarious laughter.

"Fuck off." Shane realized even as he said it that his annoyance probably confirmed Beckett's suspicion. First Marz, now Beckett. This cat wasn't going to stay in the bag much longer, was it? So be it.

Beckett gave a slow grin.

Shane rolled his eyes and beat feet for his room. He'd check in on Charlie, then he needed a quick shower and a change of clothes before he headed out, before he saw Crystal again.

Chapter 14

Crystal was so strung out with worry over Jenna that she hadn't even bothered to change out of her skanky uniform. Instead, she'd traded her heels for flip-flops and thrown on an old hoodie she'd left in her locker. It was after two in the morning, after all, so it wasn't like she was trying to win any fashion awards.

Nervous energy had her tapping her fingers against the steering wheel as she turned into her neighborhood. There'd been almost no traffic, and she'd lucked out on a whole string of green lights, but it still seemed like the longest. Trip. Home. Ever.

Why the *hell* had Jenna come to Confessions?

How many times had Crystal told her to *never* go there, whether Crystal was working or not? Bruno had protected Jenna from getting sucked into Confessions, and the best way to ensure Jenna stayed out, stayed safe, and stayed off the gang's radar was for her to stay away from the club. No exceptions.

God forbid anyone in the organization developed an interest of any sort in Jenna. The very thought sent a cold chill right through Crystal's bones.

And who was this Edward guy Shane had left with Jenna? A small part of Crystal was waiting for the other shoe to drop, but most of her said they could trust Shane—a kinda amazing conclusion given how suspicious she tended to be of pretty much everyone and everything. And since Shane had vouched for the man, it was probably fine.

If only her racing heart and flip-flopping belly would believe that.

The entrance to her apartment complex came into view, and Crystal released a deep breath. She was going to feel ridiculous when she got home, saw everything was just as it should be, and found Jenna long asleep.

A light flashed. Once. Twice. Three times.

Crystal squinted through the glare of the passing streetlamps.

And there, on the corner just past the apartment complex's driveway, stood Shane McCallan. He lowered his cell phone, the light swinging away, and waved.

Twin reactions coursed through Crystal. Excitement at seeing him again, at the fact that he'd apparently been waiting here for her. And a little suspicion, too, because *why was he waiting here for her*?

Oh, God, had something happened?

Both reactions sent Crystal's heart racing. She pulled up alongside him and rolled down the window. "What's wrong?"

Wearing a heather gray shirt stretched taut across his chest and shoulders, Shane gave her that sexy, charming smile. "Nothing, darlin'. Everything's fine. I checked in with Easy, I mean, Edward, about fifteen minutes ago, and he reported everything's quiet at your place."

"Oh." The truck's engine idled loudly. "Well, then, what are you doing here?"

He tilted his head and nailed her with a hot, intense stare. "You said we could talk."

Her stomach flipped. What did he want to talk about? His words from the dressing room came to mind. *I want you so bad I can hardly breathe.* Her heart beat a little harder still. "But, Jenna—"

"Is fine." He arched a brow. "You're not going back on your promise, are you?"

She shook her head. "No. But, um, where . . ."

"Why don't you park over there," he said, pointing at an open street space in front of a string of row houses. "We can just talk in your truck, if that's okay."

"Uh." Crystal looked at the door to the glove box, hanging open because it wouldn't stay closed anymore, and at the cracks in the vinyl bench seat beside her. Like her apartment, she'd never really given much thought to the truck's appearance until now . . .

"Or we can sit in mine," Shane said. "It's just down the way."

Crystal nodded. "Yeah. Um, let's do that." As she pulled into the spot, she shivered, excitement rushing through her at the chance to be with him again. This time, somewhere quiet, private, alone. Well, sorta, anyway. She turned the engine off and removed the key, and in the quiet of the cab, she forced herself to take a deep breath. *It's just a talk, for God's sake.* Then why did it feel more significant?

She cracked open the door . . . and remembered what she was wearing. The *one night* she didn't change into normal person clothes, she got the opportunity to hang out with a nice guy. A *hot* guy. And here she was dressed like a freaking tramp.

Knock, knock.

Crystal's gaze flew to the window beside her, and Shane was there, smiling at her with a questioning gaze. Well, wasn't like he hadn't seen her in this before.

She nodded, and he opened the door the rest of the way. Swallowing her embarrassment, she swung her almost entirely bare legs out and hopped down. "I, uh, didn't take the time to change," she said.

He took her hand. "I don't care about that, sweetness. Come on."

There was that nickname again. And the acceptance, too. And, oh, man, his hand was big and warm and reassuring around hers, his thumb rubbing over her knuckle again and again. She never wanted him to let her go.

Don't get attached. You know there's no way this works out.

Maybe. Probably. But that didn't mean she couldn't enjoy him while he was here, did it? She shivered despite the fact that she was playing with fire.

"Are you cold?" Shane asked, pulling her body closer to his as they walked down the quiet street, lined on one side by mostly dark row houses, and on the other by the fence and hedges that separated her apartment complex from the road.

"No, I'm okay," she said, giving him a small smile. He was always so tuned in to her. Just like he'd noticed how much she hadn't wanted Bruno's kiss. Hell, Bruno was kissing her and hadn't noticed her hesitation. Or hadn't cared.

"I'm right here," he said, pointing a key fob at a big black truck. The lights flashed twice in response. "M'lady," he said, opening the door for the second row of seats with a playful smile. "There's a blanket on the floor there."

She climbed in, his hand warm on her lower back, the leather soft against the backs of her thighs. He closed the door and came around to the other side, then joined her at the opposite end of the big bench seat. And just then she figured out why he'd had them sit in the back instead of the front—because a console separated the two halves of the front seat. Which meant he didn't want anything separating them . . .

She shivered again, nerves and excitement making it hard to sit still.

"Here," he said, shaking the soft fleece blanket out and draping it across her lap.

"You're so . . . different," she said, not really intending to voice the thought. She peered at him sideways while she fiddled with the blanket.

Shane smiled. "Different good, I hope."

Heat flooded into her cheeks, so she turned her gaze out the window. A streetlamp stood two cars lengths ahead of them, but Shane's truck sat shrouded mostly in darkness along a row of hedges. It was so . . . peaceful sitting here with him, even as her nerves jangled and her heart raced.

"How was your night?" Shane said, pulling her gaze back to him.

She shrugged with one shoulder. Hours and hours of serving men food and drinks while she pretended not to notice the hard-ons tenting their pants or feel their fingers stealing touches of her skin. "Same old, same old. Yours? Everything go okay with that thing you had to do?"

He gave a nod, a small, tired smile on his face. "Yeah. Thankfully, it did."

Part of her wanted to ask what it was he'd had to do, but it wasn't any of her business. "Good," she said. A long moment of silence passed with Shane's gaze roaming over her. It took everything Crystal had not to fidget. "So, um, what did you want to talk about?"

Despite his almost relaxed posture, Shane didn't hesitate, and he didn't pull any punches. "Why do you tolerate Bruno?"

Damn if *tolerate* wasn't the exact right word choice. If the question hadn't been so fraught with land mines, Crystal almost might've smiled. "You're just going for it, huh?"

He nodded and arched a brow. "Damn straight. You said we could talk, so I'm talking. Now it's your turn."

For a long moment, Crystal debated whether to answer. Why bother? Part of her knew it was an exercise in futility because it wouldn't change a damn thing. But another part of her, the part that really hadn't had *anyone* to share this incredible load with, just . . . wanted . . . one person to hear her. One person to empathize with her. One person to actually know her. She cleared her throat. "He helped me when it counted," she said, hoping she could leave it at that.

Shane frowned, and his gaze cut from her cheek to her arm, or, rather, to the spot where the bruises were covered by the sleeve of the hoodie. He chuffed out half a laugh. "I spent a lot of years in the Army doing intelligence work. You're as skilled at answering questions as any of the operatives I ever worked with."

That's because it's a survival skill. One perfected after years of tiptoeing around Confessions, the Church Gang, and Bruno. "I can't tell if that's a compliment or not," she said. "And I thought you were a medic."

"I trained in both." He shifted his back against the door to face her and tilted his head. "Why do you work at Confessions? And give me something more than 'it pays the bills,' please."

It pays the bills, all right. The ones racked up by her father. Which didn't leave much left over for her own. "Nope. Can't do it. Because that *is* the reason." When he pursed his lips, she lifted her hands as if in surrender. "Honest."

He heaved a long breath and nailed her with a thoughtful stare. "How old are you?"

The unexpected question pulled a bit of a smile out of her. Crystal shook her head. "A hundred and four." Shane's brow arched over an amused expression, and she shrugged. "That's how it feels sometimes. I'm twenty-three."

His eyes went wide. Apparently, she'd surprised him in return. "You seem older than that."

A niggle of discomfort slinked into her belly. "Disappointed?"

"You could never disappoint me, Crystal. Let's get that straight right now. You just have a seriousness about you that reads older. I like it. A lot." He nailed her with a gaze full of heat and promise.

Crystal hugged herself. "Like I said, a hundred and four. Why? How old are you?" Late twenties she'd guessed when she'd thought about it at all. Bruno was in his thirties, so she was used to hanging around older men.

He smiled. "I'll be shaking hands with the big three-oh in a few months."

"Wow. You're *old*," she said.

Shane threw his head back and laughed. "Touché, darlin'. Touché." His playful, appreciative smile tempted hers. She never teased Bruno because he took almost any attempt at humor as a personal slight. She'd learned that lesson long ago.

After a few moments, Shane's smile faded away. "Why did it worry you so much that Jenna came to Confessions?"

The age question had been such a softball, she'd nearly forgotten how good he was at asking ones that left her feeling cornered. "Wait. I want to ask another question," she rushed out, twisting the edge of the blanket in a knot between her fingers.

Shane lifted his hands from his lap, indicating he was open to it. "Ask away."

Looking him over, she debated for a moment. God, he was really freaking gorgeous sitting there in the near dark. With those big, broad shoulders, the contours of his biceps visible beneath the sleeves of his shirt, and the strong thighs filling out his jeans. "Okay. Here's what I want to know. Why do you care about any of this? You don't even know me and Jenna."

Shane shook his head, and the smug smile he wore was as sexy as it was irksome. "You wasted that one, because I already told you. I care because I like you. And I'm getting to know you better and better."

The words lifted her up and crashed her back down again. Because she adored his interest in her, but it could never come to anything. And, anyway, he didn't know everything there was to know about her. If he did, all that growing care of his might disappear. "Okay, then why were you planning a bachelor party at my club?"

He laced his fingers across his flat belly, still the picture of ease. Really sexy, really attractive ease. The kind that made a woman want to see if she could rile a man up. One way or another.

Her gaze raked over him, from powerful thighs to flat, hard torso, to broad shoulders. When she got to his face, she found an amused smile and an arched brow. *Busted.*

"Truth," she said in warning because he'd caught her ogling. No way was she letting him think he could distract her so easily. Even though, Shane *was* six-plus-feet of crazy sexy distraction.

"Okay. We were there because we needed more information about tomorrow night's delivery," he said, meeting her gaze. "And we took some steps to try to get it."

Her mouth dropped open, and she closed it just as quick. Crystal couldn't believe he'd been so forthright.

"Oh." But what the heck might those steps have been? She hadn't seen them do anything unusual or suspicious.

"My turn again?"

She tucked her hair behind her ears. "Uh, sure."

"Why were you so worried about Jenna's coming to Confessions? Truth."

She guessed she couldn't dish out that demand if she wasn't willing to pony up in return. "Because it's not safe for her. I don't want her getting tied up with the people there at all."

"It's not safe for her, but it's safe for you?" he asked in a steady voice, but the bulge of his crossed arms belied the tension the topic wrought in him.

A sense of déjà vu washed over Crystal. Jenna had asked her something very similar earlier in the day. Or yesterday, at this point. "The truth is, no, it's not particularly safe for me, either." Shane's brow raised, like maybe she'd surprised him with her candor, too. "But I'm already caught up in it, and Jenna's not. She's going to graduate from college, pursue a career, and have a life free of strippers and . . ." All the bad things from which Crystal wanted to protect Jenna jumbled together in her mind and stole her voice. It was just . . . so much.

Shane sat forward, his expression intense, his eyes hot, liquid silver in the light of the streetlamp. "And what? Come on, Crystal. Talk to me." His hand landed on her knee, warm and heavy and grounding. And for just a moment, she had the strongest urge to ask him to call her by her real name. *Sara, call me Sara.* Just once, she'd love to hear it from his mouth.

God, not even my name is mine to do with what I please. Because she couldn't let herself be that person while she lived this life.

It was a choice, a struggle, a reality Crystal never wanted Jenna to face. Frustration and desire and fear and anger built up in her chest and squeezed her throat. "Damnit," she finally bit out, dropping her gaze into her lap. "I—I—" In that moment, she realized there was literally no one else in the world to whom she could voice her fears and dreams. She swallowed hard and blurted it out. "I want her to have a life free of strippers and drug dealers and gangbangers and killers and hit men and . . . and . . . girls getting *taken* and *used* and *sold*." The words spilled out faster and faster as she spoke, like the unusual expression of honesty knew it had to hurry before Crystal shut it down again. She shuddered, her scalp prickling with a nascent panic she'd induced all on her own.

"Crystal—"

She gave a fast shake of her head. "No more," she said in a strained voice.

Sighing, Shane scrubbed his hands over his face.

Forcing herself to take a deep, calming breath, Crystal eyed Shane for a long moment. "What?" she finally asked in a voice just greater than a whisper.

He dropped his hands into his lap. "Would it freak you out if I told you I really wanted to hold you right now? I know you're in trouble, Crystal. I don't know how to help, and it's killing me—"

"Okay," she said, because she *yearned* to feel his arms around her again. And because she knew she couldn't handle any more conversation. Unlike the typical twenty-three-year-old, Crystal couldn't talk about movies or TV shows or what she'd done with her friends last weekend. She *never* went to the movies, rarely watched TV, and had no friends. Her conversational reach extended to superficialities on the one hand or life-and-death topics on the other.

"Okay?" His expression looked so happy, like she'd done something special for him when it was clearly the other way around.

Crystal nodded, but then wasn't sure exactly what to do. No man had ever cuddled her before. Not ever.

Shane reached for her. "Come here, darlin'," he said, nearly hauling her across the seat until her back came up against his front, her body situated between his legs, her legs drawn up in front of her. And, good God, he was hard and warm everywhere she was soft and cold. Crystal couldn't help but burrow against him.

He released a satisfied sigh as his arms wrapped around her stomach. After a minute, she let herself relax and rested her head against his shoulder, one of her arms lying atop one of his. And then he laced their fingers together.

A sting rose against the backs of Crystal's eyes. For some reason, what they were doing hadn't felt so intimate until he'd done that. Stupid, really, but feeling connected to someone else wasn't something she was used to.

With his other hand, Shane played with her hair, stroking it back off her face, tucking it behind her ear, wrapping a long length of it around a finger, then releasing. From there, his hand trailed over her arm, just a comforting rub, like he was trying to warm her.

So this is what affection feels like. Yep. But don't get used to it. Easier said than done. Because Shane's touch was like water to someone who'd been stranded in the desert. Crystal wasn't sure how she'd be able to stop with just one sip.

"What just happened?" Shane asked in a low voice against her ear.

"What do you mean?" she asked.

"You just tensed up, sweetness. Am I making you uncomfortable?" He lifted his arms away.

Instantly missing him, Crystal grabbed his hand and brought it back against her stomach. "No. Not at all. It's . . . nice."

"Then what?"

She shook her head. "It's nothing. Stupid."

"Turn around here a little bit, Crystal. Please?" Nerves made her stomach flutter, but she turned on her hip so that her left shoulder was tucked into the crook under his right arm, her thigh propped up a little on his. He nudged her chin upward until she met his gaze. "Nothing you could think or say to me would be stupid. Ever. Please don't devalue yourself that way because I never would."

Crystal's throat went tight. Because Shane—in all his goodness, in all his decency—was the real deal. And it was both amazing and tragic that she'd ever met him. "I don't know what to say," she rasped.

His hand slid up, warm and strong against her cheek. "Just say okay."

"Okay," she whispered, because in that moment, she was totally powerless against Shane McCallan. He could ask anything, do anything, and she'd be right there with him. Her eyes dropped to his lips and her memory resurrected the feel of them against her own, the delicious minty taste of his tongue in her mouth, the incredibly arousing sounds he made in the back of his throat as he devoured her.

Against her hip, Shane's erection grew, and a wave of desire rushed through Crystal's body.

"Don't look at me like that, Crystal," he said, his voice a raw scrape. It wasn't a demand or a threat. It was a plea. And the thought that this big, strong, powerful man was begging her for anything was thrilling.

"Like what?" she asked, dragging her gaze up to his. In the diffuse light of the streetlamp, she could tell his eyes were absolutely blazing, and it only fueled the arousal rising up inside her.

"Like maybe you want me the way I want you." Tilting his head, he nuzzled his face against hers, the tip of his nose trailing over her cheek, his breath ghosting over her lips. "Like maybe you'd let me kiss you and touch you." A quick brush of his lips against her temple and ear. "Like maybe you'd let me *in*."

Crystal could barely breathe for the way her heart was pounding and her pulse was racing. She slid a hand up his chest to his neck, wanting, needing, just absolutely yearning to have this. Just this once.

Leaning into him, Crystal held his gaze and adored the way his expression filled with such expectant satisfaction, like she'd surprised him. Pleased him.

She pressed her lips to his.

The groan he unleashed was needful, almost triumphant. His arms came around her gently and pulled her in. And it wasn't enough. She needed to be closer. Deeper. She needed more of Shane McCallan.

She might never get another chance.

A flicker of unbidden panic whipped through her body. Bruno had been her only lover for the past four years, and she'd only been able to take him inside her after months' buildup of trust and familiarity of touch. That was back before he'd shown his true colors. Or before she'd shed her naïveté. Maybe they were the same thing. Who knew?

Stop thinking about Bruno and get out of your head. Just feel. You deserve this. You need *this. Besides, cart before horse, much?*

Shane pulled away and rested his forehead against hers. "I didn't come here expecting this. Hoped, maybe." He smiled. "But I really just needed to see you."

"I'm glad you came," she said, combing her fingers through the sides of his hair, then holding his face in her hands.

"What do you want, sweetness? I'd give you anything." Over her hoodie, his hands rubbed up and down her back, hip to shoulder, hip to shoulder.

Crystal couldn't find the words, so she tilted her face and claimed his lips, and this time the kiss unleashed a fire that seemed to flash through both of them. She shifted into a kneeling position between his thighs, and he hauled her into his lap so that she straddled him. The position brought the hard length of his cock between her legs and she gasped and moaned at the feel of him so close to where she was wet and wanting.

They pressed closer, held tighter, kissed more deeply until all Crystal knew, all that existed in the world, was this moment, this place, this man.

Shane's hands moved over her body. Fisting in the long lengths of her hair. Gently cupping and massaging her breasts. Stroking her bare thighs. Crystal adored the way he seemed to *need* to touch her. How powerful and necessary human touch was. How life-giving and affirming. And how simply mind-blowing was it to discover that touch could be a giving thing, not just about taking, that touch could be healing, and not just about hurting, that touch could comfort, and not just exert control. Even when things had been better with Bruno, they'd never been like this.

And to think she'd found someone who could teach her something so fundamental that she'd never known before. Or, maybe, she'd known but hadn't believed.

Now she did. Because of Shane. No matter how little time she got to have him in her life, she would always be grateful that he'd shown her what it *could* be like. With the *right* person.

Gripping her hair in his fist, Shane reclined her head, opening the line of her throat to his worshipful lips and tongue. He trailed a path of liquid fire over her flesh that left her dizzy, totally awash in sensation. He tugged her hips in tighter, and Crystal moaned at the friction the movement created. He was deliciously hard and thick between her legs. Unable to resist, she rocked herself against him as he laid her back farther so he could kiss the small part of her chest the V-neck of the hoodie revealed. Slowly, he drew down the zipper, trailing kisses lower and lower until the heat of his breath fanned over her nipple through the thin fabric of her uniform.

Just as slow, Shane raised her back up, bringing their bodies together again. Crystal ran her hands over his chest and stomach, but what she most needed was to feel him, skin on skin. Pulling back from their kiss, she tugged at the hem of his shirt, silently asking for permission.

"Anything you want," he whispered, taking her belly and her heart on a loop-the-loop.

Lifting his shirt just a little, she threaded her hands underneath, reveling in the feel of smooth, masculine skin over well-defined muscle. She traced her fingers over the ridges and through the soft trail of hair that disappeared beneath the waistband of his jeans and led up to a light covering across his chest. Her arms further lifted his shirt until Shane finally reached over his head in that one-handed way men had and tugged the fabric free and clear. He dropped it to the floor of the truck beside them.

Shane sat back against the corner where the door met the seat and watched her look at him. Because she couldn't *not* look. As cut as he appeared with the shirt on, it was nothing compared to his bare flesh. The man had a leanness to his definition Crystal found so damn sexy. His body possessed none of the fake, overblown musculature of Bruno's steroid-built body but had every bit of the strength.

Her gaze and her fingers fell to a tattoo over his heart. She couldn't quite make out the details in the dimness, but it appeared to be a dagger. "What's this?" she asked, wishing she could see it better.

Shane grabbed her hand and pressed a lingering kiss to her open palm. "An old, sad memory."

The sadness was apparent in his voice, too. It made Crystal want to hold him and protect him in return. "I'm sorry," she said, wanting to know more, but not wanting to be asked anything else in return. So she figured it wasn't fair to push him.

"Don't be." He tugged her in for another kiss, and now everywhere her hands landed, they encountered warm, hard flesh. She wanted to feel him against her breasts and her stomach, but she would never be able to bring herself to take off her tops. When Bruno took her from behind, even *he* had her keep on the shirt she wore. No, she could be satisfied with what she had, because getting to experience this stolen moment was absolutely intoxicating, particularly as Shane devoured her in another molten-hot, breath-stealing kiss. "You're so damn beautiful, Crystal," he murmured.

You wouldn't think so if you saw my back, said a little voice.

His hands landed on her hips and rocked her once, twice, three times against his cock, chasing away the destructive thoughts and replacing them with pure erotic sensation. Somehow, his touch and his kiss and the way he moved against her managed to be both urgent and gentle. She loved the combination because it gave her the reassurance of his desire and the security that she was safe.

It was perfect for her. *He* was perfect for her.

Except he wasn't.

Burying her face in his neck, Crystal concentrated on the heat and pressure building between her legs. It had been so long since she'd last orgasmed that she wasn't sure she could, but damn did it feel absolutely amazing to try. She gasped and moaned as he rocked her harder, faster.

"I want you to come," he whispered against her ear. "I want to hold you in my arms and feel you fall apart. Because of me."

"Shane," she rasped, as her fingers clenched the muscles of his shoulders.

"That's it, sweetness, hold on to me." He kissed her neck and gripped her hips harder and met her rocks with thrusts of his own.

"Oh, my God," she said. Sensation swirled through her belly and congregated more and more in her clit until she knew, she absolutely knew, that Shane was going to make her come.

The orgasm was like a bomb detonating underneath her, exploding her into a million pieces and throwing her to the stars. Crystal moaned and held her breath as wave after wave of bliss washed through. Shane claimed her mouth in a fiery kiss that stole what little breath she still had. When the intensity receded, she found herself wrapped so tightly around Shane's body, she wasn't sure they would ever again come apart.

And she was totally okay with that.

Because earlier in the night, she'd worried she was falling for Shane. And now she knew she'd been wrong. Not falling. *Fallen*.

Crystal collapsed against Shane, and his arms held her there like he didn't want her to move any more than she did.

This warm, soaring pressure in her chest had to be love. Not that she had a lot of experience with the emotion. Not romantic love, anyway. But she couldn't think of anything else that would leave her feeling so invincible and so vulnerable at the same time.

And it wasn't just because of the orgasm, miraculous as that had been. It was Shane's goodness and protectiveness and attentiveness. It was his sensitivity and decency.

It was his gentle, comforting, arousing touch. The way he called her sweetness. That charming smile.

The fact that he was six-plus feet of gorgeous man was just the cherry on top.

She'd been so comfortable, so blissed out, that Crystal hadn't become conscious of the wandering of his hands until after they'd slipped under her hoodie and the tank to her uniform and stroked upward, just lazy, massaging drags of his fingers against her bare skin.

Oh, no! She jerked back out of his arms so hard she had to brace on her hands to avoid falling flat on her back across the seat.

But Shane's darkening expression told her she hadn't moved fast enough. He'd felt the scars.

Crystal's throat went tight as tears of humiliation and disappointment threatened. Of course this moment of happiness couldn't last. Not for her. She swung her legs off him, slid across the seat, and went for the door.

"Crystal, wait," Shane said, grasping her by the elbow.

"Let me go," she said. Last thing she wanted to do was cry in front of him, but the emotional roller coaster of this day had left her fragile and shaky. She had to get away.

"What the hell was that?" he asked in a disgusted tone. God, she didn't want to see the expression that went with the voice.

The leather of the seat creaked like he was sliding closer.

It's midnight, Cinderella. Your coach just turned into a pumpkin.

Shane's hand landed gently on her back.

Without another thought, she yanked her elbow free, pushed open the door, and jumped out of the truck so fast she pitched forward and had to catch herself on her hands. Gravel and macadam bit into her palms, leaving them raw and burning.

"Crystal!"

She took off at a dead run. Up the sidewalk and across the street. And, as little rocks and other debris flayed the soles of her feet, she realized she'd left her flip-flops in Shane's truck.

Lost her shoes. Just like Cinderella.

Except her life was no fairy tale. Not by a long shot.

"Crystal!" Shane's voice—desperate, closer.

She wrenched open her truck door, scrabbled in, and shut and locked the door. Her hands were shaking so bad that it took three tries to get the key from her pocket and into the ignition. By then Shane was at her door and knocking on the window.

"Please don't go," he said, voice muffled by the glass and the pounding beat of her pulse in her ears. "Crystal, please." He smacked the flat of his hand against the glass. "Please talk to me."

The truck started on a roar. She hit the gas, and the truck lurched forward, forcing Shane to jump back.

For a good thirty seconds, Shane ran after the truck. And it was staring at him in the rearview mirror that made her realize she was crying, sloppy streams of tears that streaked mascara under her eyes.

When she looked in the mirror again, he'd stopped. Hands on his hips, head hanging low, he just stood there. And then he turned in a slow circle, like he was lost. A huge tattoo she couldn't quite make out covered his back. Crystal hated how defeated he looked, hated that she'd been the one to do that to him.

After everything he'd done for her.

Chapter 15

$\mathcal{W}$anna talk about it?" Easy asked from the passenger seat.

"No," Shane said, entirely aware his tone gave a lot away but too fucking tired and pissed to care. Not pissed at Crystal. Pissed *for* her.

Goddamnit, he could barely breathe for the Humvee of rage parked on his chest.

Shane's fingers might've only been on her back for a few seconds, but he'd felt enough to have a damn good idea what was going on underneath her clothes.

Lines of scars.

Some shallow, some knotted and deep.

Lots of things might've made them.

Problem was, he'd seen the backs of men who'd been struck by a whip while serving various places overseas. And whips left a distinctive pattern of diagonally placed straight lines. And that was too damn similar to what his fingers had traced on Crystal's bare skin.

As if Shane hadn't been horrified enough by her swollen cheek and bruised arm.

With every fiber of his being, Shane hoped he was wrong about what he'd felt. He might never feel a greater happiness than to know his imagination had run away with him, and he had it all wrong. But instinct and intuition had his stomach rolling and the whiskey he'd drank earlier burning a hole in his gut. Add that to Crystal's reaction to his discovery, and Shane knew he wasn't wrong.

And that was another thing his brain couldn't stop chewing on. Why had she panicked so badly? Why had she run away? She'd nearly thrown herself from his truck, and no way her near fall and barefoot flight hadn't chewed up the skin on her hands and feet. When he'd finally caught up to her at her truck, she'd been crying so hard he'd worried she wouldn't be able to see to drive. Jesus, after the privilege of sharing a moment of passion with her, the evidence of her pain had just about broken his heart.

He peered down at the pair of white flip-flops resting on the seat beside him. They had a small fabric flower on the strap over the toes. He remembered them from the night he'd carried Jenna up the steps. As he drove through the quiet, mid-night streets of Baltimore, Shane debated the best form of death for the asshole who'd done this to her. Bruno.

Shooting? Too fast and impersonal. Poison? The scumbag might not be conscious of the fact he was dying. Drowning? Not painful enough. Cutting off his hands and dick? Messy but poetic.

"You like her," Easy said, his voice pulling Shane from his murder fantasies.

Well, hell. And then there were three teammates who

suspected the truth. No sense in doing a duck and cover now. He glanced toward his friend. "Yeah."

Easy nodded and ran a hand over the side of his head. "Then you gotta get her out of there."

Gripping the wheel harder, Shane heaved a deep breath and strove for a bit of levelheadedness amid the rage whipping up inside his chest. Everyone knowing he'd crossed an emotional line was one thing. But responding emotionally was another. "I know, but it's complicated. And we've got just about enough of that on our plate these days."

"I won't disagree with you there. But most of the time, there's a difference between what's right and what's easy. Maybe you should think about bringing her to Hard Ink."

Shane cut his gaze across the cab to find Easy staring at him, a tired, almost weary, expression on his face. "I don't know that I could convince Crystal of that. Or Nick."

Crossing his arms, Easy shook his head. "I don't know, man. But how many more people gotta die?"

That was for damn sure. Zane, Harlow, Axton, Kemmerer, Escobal, Rimes. His six teammates who'd died in the ambush on that dirt road that day. Merritt, though he'd brought that shit on himself. If the surgery hadn't worked out, Charlie might've been on that list, too. Might still, depending on how well he responded to the meds.

Molly.

Not that she'd died as a part of this fubar, but she was one more reason Shane refused to allow Crystal to be next. Or Jenna, because he knew enough to know that loss would devastate Crystal to her very core. But it wasn't like he could drag them to Hard Ink against their will.

Given what he suspected about Crystal's situation at Confessions and with Bruno, the idea of doing *anything* against Crystal's will sat like a jagged rock in Shane's gut.

"You talk to Jenna at all?" Shane asked as his thoughts churned.

"A little. This whole thing being the clusterfuck that it is, I checked the apartment when we got back. She gave me a little shit for that. And then she gave me a little more for planning to watch over the place until Crystal got home. And then a while later she came outside looking for me and gave me shit because she couldn't find me right away."

Shane arched a brow and slowed for a red light at an otherwise empty intersection. "What did she want?"

Easy cracked a slow grin. "To see what I was doing. I asked what part of covert she didn't understand, and she turned around and stomped away, right before she looked back to ask if I needed to use the bathroom or anything."

"What did you say?" Shane said, chuckling. Shane hadn't gotten to spend much time with Jenna yet, but she seemed to have a feisty streak, part impetuousness, part fighter.

"I just stared at her until she rolled her eyes and went back in." Easy rubbed his fingers over the hint of his smile on his lips.

Turning onto Hard Ink's street, Shane imagined the look Easy had probably given her. The one so intense it made you want to apologize even though you hadn't done anything. The one that had made the newbies in camp stammer and back away. And here it had just made Jenna annoyed.

Easy chuckled under his breath. "She was fine, though."

Shane grinned, only too happy to turn the tables. "Interesting choice of words."

"What?" Easy asked. "Aw, come on, man. You're cracked out of your head. I didn't mean it that way."

Waiting for the fence to open and allow access into the Hard Ink lot, Shane nodded. "Sure, sure. Of course not." But *something* had to explain the fact that Easy had said more on the subject of Jenna than on anything else since they'd reunited.

A fist lit into Shane's biceps, and he couldn't help but

laugh through the ache. "Ouch, motherfucker. Don't kill the goddamned messenger, now." He pulled into a spot and killed the engine.

A satisfied smile on his face, Easy reached for the door.

"Hey, E?"

"Yeah?" he said, his smile fading.

Shane girded himself to give voice to what he'd learned—or what he was pretty sure he'd learned, anyway. He wanted the guys on his side if Crystal's situation escalated because no way was he leaving her to fend for herself. If she'd have him, if she'd let him in, he'd want her by his side. And, for now, that meant at Hard Ink.

"What is it, Shane?" Easy said, all the humor gone from his voice.

"She's got"—he swallowed, hard, just from the memory of her ruined flesh under his fingers—"she's got scars all over her back."

Easy went still. "What *kind* of scars?"

"I didn't see them, but I felt them." He finally looked at Easy, whose gaze narrowed and brow slashed down. "So I can't be sure."

"But?"

I'm pretty damn sure. "I think she's been whipped."

Easy's expression was dark, lethal, rankly pissed off. "Then you need to do something about it. I'll back you up, a hundred percent. However I can help, you just say the word."

Shane gave a tight nod. He needed to keep himself buttoned up on this and not fly off the handle. He didn't want to scare Crystal. He didn't want to make the team doubt his objectivity. And he certainly didn't want to do anything that might further jeopardize Crystal's or Jenna's safety.

"You need to come clean with the team on all this," Easy said. "That's the only way forward."

"Yeah," Shane said, feeling the lateness of the hour in every bone in his body. "Roger that." Laying all this out there and trusting his teammates with it was the right way to go. They'd have his back. They always had. "I will. First thing in the morning."

Easy nodded, and they both shoved out of the truck. The decision invited a sort of peace into Shane's psyche, calming at least a little the whirlwind of rage he'd felt since he'd discovered Crystal's scars.

Inside Hard Ink, they made their way up the stairs, surprised to hear low voices coming from the gym.

Shane keyed in the code and followed Easy inside.

"Look, they threw a party and didn't invite us," Easy said, crossing the room.

What the hell was everyone doing up? Nick, Becca, Jeremy, and Beckett all sat around Marz, the only one in his street clothes from earlier in the night and still at work on the computer. Becca in pajamas, she and Nick were stretched out on a blue gym mat on the floor, Jeremy sat on a chair close to Marz, and Beckett reclined in one chair while he propped his feet up on another. Even Eileen was here, currently doing an impression of a fur ball curled up on the blanket covering Becca's legs.

"No rest for the wicked," Marz said, pulling an earbud from one of his ears. He glanced up from his monitors, a tired smile on his face.

"Everything okay with Charlie?" Shane asked.

Becca nodded from where she sat on the floor between Nick's legs. "Yeah, thanks. I just couldn't sleep for worrying about him."

"That pretty much went for all of us," Nick said. "Eventually, we all congregated over here rather than risk disrupting his sleep over at the apartment."

Shane nodded. "Has he woken up yet?"

Becca smiled, and it was so good to see happiness

brightening her face again. "Yeah. And his fever's down, too."

Beckett nodded. "We'd been overdue for some good news."

Damn straight. Shane thumbed over his shoulder. "Is he due for a check? I could go look in on him."

"No," Marz said. "I set him up with a walkie-talkie. He's lucid enough to give a shout if he needs something."

"Besides, don't you have some business here?" Easy asked, nodding at the group, a pointed expression on his face.

Right. No sense waiting for the morning with everyone up and at 'em now. Shane pulled a folding chair closer, sat, and rested his elbows on his knees. His head hung on his shoulders, and it felt like it weighed a hundred pounds. The combination of exhaustion and worry and anger.

"What's up, man?" Nick asked, concern clear in his tone.

Shane lifted his gaze and met Nick's. No sense beating around the bush, not when most of the team already knew. "I'm falling for Crystal." Despite the fact that he felt every pair of the eyes land on him at the same time, Shane resisted the urge to squirm or look away. He wasn't used to hanging his laundry out for everyone to see—*hell,* he wasn't used to having laundry of this kind at all, but he wasn't ashamed of what he had to say, either.

Nick's entire initial reaction involved a single lifted eyebrow, but Becca's smile was big and immediate. She glanced around the room at the others, and Shane's gaze followed. Marz wore a small smile and nodded like he approved of Shane's admission. Jeremy frowned, like he wasn't sure why Shane had made this a topic of general conversation. And Beckett's expression remained a careful, serious blank. Easy stood at Shane's side, a physical manifestation of the promise he'd made a few moments before in the truck.

"And?" Nick asked. Shane wasn't surprised the man suspected there was more. Nick Rixey's instincts were almost always spot-on, and Shane knew that was why the guy had been so hard on himself about Merritt's deceit. But then, they'd *all* missed that, hadn't they?

"And . . . things are complicated." Shane tugged his hands through his hair and remembered the amazing sensation of Crystal's hands stroking and pulling. "Here's what I know: Someone is abusing her—probably this guy Bruno—"

"Oh right," Marz said, retrieving a printout from a stack by his keyboard. "I looked into him while you were gone. Bruno Ashe. Age thirty-four. Known member of the Church Gang. Criminal record. Probable Apostle-level position according to the gang report Becca's friend lent us last week."

Shit. Why didn't that surprise him? Shane nodded and counted off on his fingers. "Okay, so then, a senior Churchman is abusing and controlling her. She's afraid to meet or talk in her own apartment. Today we overheard her tell her sister she had no choice but to work at Confessions, which is sounding more and more like she's somehow being forced given Bruno's position." Shane shook his head. "And then tonight, I got her to open up a little. She admitted she knows Confessions is filled with gangbangers and drug dealers and killers. And she confirmed—again—that girls are falling down a black hole at Confessions and never being heard from again."

"Oh, my God. That's terrible," Becca said. "This is the waitress who helped you all the other night?"

"Yeah," Nick said, hugging Becca in against his stomach. He met Shane's gaze, and Nick's eyes were equal parts calculating and sympathetic. "I'm gonna say something, Shane, because it needs to be said. I'm not trying to be an asshole or to downplay what is clearly a horrendous situation that Crystal's caught up in."

Knowing what was likely coming, Shane gave a tight nod. Tension seemed to thicken the air around them, because they *all* knew where Nick was about to go—at least the team did.

"Molly," Shane said, saving Nick the trouble.

"Molly," Nick said with a nod.

Jeremy frowned and looked around. "Who's Molly?"

"My kid sister," Shane said, eyes back on Nick. "I'm not gonna lie. She's never far from my mind, and this whole thing might've started out as a chance to make something right that I'd once gotten wrong, but that's not what's at play now." Shane looked each of his teammates in the eye, wanting them to see his sincerity. "Nick." Shane's throat went tight, and he had to clear it. Twice. "I *like* Crystal. And, at some point—I don't know when, she's been whipped."

Becca's gasp joined the men's low curses.

"Before this thing escalates, and she gets caught in the cross fire, I want to bring her here. If she'll come." Lacing his hands together, he waited for the blowback.

Nick inhaled to speak, but Jeremy beat him to it. "This is my house, Shane. I don't know everything that's going on, but I'm telling you right now that your friend is welcome, and if you need another pair of hands to pack up her stuff and move it over here, just name the time and place. Because what you just described is some major bullshit. And no one deserves to live like that." Green eyes blazing, Jeremy crossed his arms and nailed Nick with a stare, silently daring him to challenge.

And just then, Jeremy Rixey became Shane's brother in every way that mattered.

Nick nodded, anger making sharp angles of his face. "I couldn't agree more," he said in a tight voice.

The tension deflated from the room faster than a popped balloon. Relief flooded through Shane's system. Part of him had been braced for a fight. The more people who stayed here, the more resources they required and the higher the vulnerabilities they possessed. He would've understood if the whole lot of them had come at him with a list of totally reasonable reservations.

But they'd been there for him. And Crystal.

"You realize she's a package deal," Easy said in a low voice from beside him. "Jenna?"

"Yeah," Shane said. He suspected Jenna was going to be the sticking point for Crystal. But first things first. Get both of them to safety. And then figure out how to pick up the pieces. That is, if Crystal and Jenna agreed. And he feared it was a big *if*.

"Well, so were me and Charlie, but you all took us in," Becca said. "I don't see why that would make a difference. There's plenty of room in this building, isn't there?"

Jeremy nodded. "The apartment above ours has electricity and water. Bathroom's in, and the drywall's mostly up. Floors are all cement, but . . ." He shrugged. "It ain't pretty, but we could certainly buy a couple of beds for up there and let people spread out a little. It's not like we're using the space for anything else—"

"Hold up," Marz said, gesturing for them to quiet down. He scooped the second earbud back to his ear, pressed his fingers against the little black bud, and leaned toward the monitor he'd been eyeing from time to time. "Say it louder, asshole," he whispered to himself as he punched a sequence of keys. He closed his eyes and pressed his hands to his ears again. "Pier thirteen," he said almost to himself, and then his gaze whipped up, wide and excited. "I got a voice saying 'we're on for Pier thirteen tonight.'"

Holy shit. Was Marz saying what Shane thought he was saying? "You got the location for the delivery?" Shane

asked, moving around behind Marz's chair. Easy and
Beckett joined them, then Nick and Becca, until they
were all crowded in together.

Marz's hands flew over the keyboard of a laptop sitting off to the side, the only machine not engaged in the
audio and video surveillance of Confessions. He typed in
"Pier 13 Baltimore." A listing of search results appeared
on the monitor. Every one related to the same address on
Newgate Avenue, at the northwestern end of the marine
terminal.

Running one last search, Marz sat back, and the whole
group of them watched as a satellite image of Pier 13 took
shape on the screen.

"Right there's where we're headed, boys." Marz pointed
at the monitor, his tone victorious. "Right there is where
we start to get some answers."

"WHY, WHY, WHY?" Crystal murmured to herself as she
peeked in on the bubbling pan of lasagna. Five more minutes, and it would be done. Which meant that she had no
more than fifteen minutes before Bruno would be here
for dinner. The one she'd invited him to the other night
when she'd been trying to gather information about the
big meeting at the marine terminal he had in a few hours.

Because she hadn't wanted him to get suspicious of her
questions. And she'd needed him to believe she wanted to
spend time with him. *And* because she'd been trying to
appease his anger about a man having been in the apartment.

So when Bruno had called after lunchtime and said he'd
like to come over after all, there wasn't really anything
she could do but agree.

How was it possible that conversation had only been a
few days before? It seemed like a lifetime ago.

Twisting the hot pads in her hands, Crystal thought

back over the week. On the outside, she appeared just the same. Same woman. Same job. Same sorta boyfriend. Same miserable reality. But on the inside, it was like there'd been a flood, and when the waters receded, everything had been reshaped and relocated into a totally different landscape.

The buzzer on the oven screeched. Crystal flinched from her thoughts and shut it off, then she very carefully removed the glass dish from the wire rack and set it on the stovetop to cool.

Lasagna was Bruno's favorite. It was a shame, really, because as much as she liked it, if she ever got away from him, she might never eat it again.

As the scent of warm cheese, spicy sauce, and garlic bread filled the air of the small apartment, Crystal could reduce every bit of the raging storm that was her life right now to two words: Shane McCallan.

The man for whom she'd asked the questions.

The man she'd gone and fallen for. Like an idiot.

The man she could never, ever have.

Not that he'd want her after he'd felt the ruined mess that was her back. If he hadn't thought her a spineless loser before, he surely would now.

The backs of her eyes stung with regrets and grief, and Crystal let herself wallow in those feelings for exactly one more minute. When the LED on the stove clock flickered from 4:58 to 4:59, she forced herself to box that crap up tight and put it away. For good.

She needed to be a convincingly adoring girlfriend tonight, in every way Bruno expected. In *any* way Bruno expected. Which was why she'd worn her skinny jeans and the black shirt she'd made with the deep vee in the front that he liked so much. Tonight was all about pleasing Bruno. Grabbing a Sprite from the fridge, she gulped down a large swallow, washing away the sour bile that crept up the back of her throat when she thought of what that likely meant.

You can do it, Crystal. You've survived worse.

True. But using that as a benchmark was a helluva way to have to live your life.

Eight months. The hustle and bustle of New York's Seventh Avenue popped into her mind's eye. She'd been there once for a long weekend her freshman year of college, and the dynamism of the city had imprinted itself on her forever. Surely, she and Jenna would be safe in a place so large, so busy, so crowded with people.

A key sounded against the door handle, then the door opened.

She pushed the musings away. Showtime.

Crystal swept out of the kitchen with a big smile on her face. "Hey. You're here."

Bruno smiled and grasped her face in his hands. "Yes, I am, baby. And something smells good," he said, kissing her roughly and walking her backward into the kitchen.

Too wet, too much tongue, too much alcohol on his breath, she thought, completely aware she was using a very particular point of comparison in the form of a sexy former soldier with the most charming smile she'd ever seen. But none of that mattered right now, so she threw herself into it and laughed as he backed her into the counter. "Me?" she said, laughing.

Bruno pulled a piece of cheese from the corner of the dish and popped it into his mouth. "Well, you're okay, too."

She smiled because since he thought that was funny, she had to react like it was. "You hungry now? Because everything's ready. I can dish it up right away."

He stepped back and whipped off his leather jacket, revealing the double holster hidden underneath. "Yeah. Starving," he said, leaving the kitchen. His coat and guns fell on the couch with a heavy thump. He sat at the small dining table and tapped out a message on his cell phone. Waiting to be served.

Despite the fact that Crystal's stomach was seriously flirting with a full-scale rebellion, she plated two servings of lasagna and bread and carried them to the already-set table. "What would you like to drink?" she asked, realizing as she said it she'd slipped into her waitress voice. Which when you thought about it made a lot of sense. She lived to serve.

Thumbs still moving over his phone, Bruno shrugged. "You know what I like," he said without looking up.

She returned to the kitchen and grabbed a can of Natty Boh from the fridge for Bruno and her Sprite. Back at the table, she set the drinks down with a smile and joined Bruno at the only other chair.

Bruno dove right in, taking big forkfuls despite the fact that the sauce was too hot, causing him to suck in mouthfuls of air and gulp down swallows of beer.

"Is it good, baby?" Crystal asked, not yet having touched her own.

He grunted affirmatively and forked in another mound of noodles and sauce. God, he even *ate* aggressively. How had she never before noticed? With the sounds of Bruno's eager eating filling the room, Crystal sliced the edge of her fork into the corner of her portion of lasagna and scooped a small bite into her mouth.

It must've been good, because Bruno was absolutely hoovering it down, but it tasted like cardboard in her own mouth.

"How was your day?" she asked.

"Um," he said around a swallow. "Okay. Busy getting ready for tonight. You know how it is."

"Yeah. You always have so much on your plate."

He sucked a bit of sauce off his thumb. "That's why I have you. To relax me. Help me blow off steam."

Yes, that's what Crystal was good for. At least as far as Bruno was concerned. She smiled and tucked into another bite, but all she could think about was Shane's wanting to talk to her, wanting to get to know her. For an instant, she wondered what it would be like to cook dinner for Shane, to have him over to her apartment, to go out on a date with him. Would he hold her hand again? Would he want to hold *her* again? Would they talk all night or just sit in the quiet peacefulness of one another's arms?

"Crystal? *Crystal?*" Fingers snapped in front of her face. "Where the hell'd you go?"

"Oh, sorry," she said as warmth crept into her cheeks.

"More," he said, pushing his plate toward her.

She scurried out of her seat and grabbed the plate. "Of course. Coming right up." She nearly collapsed against the counter. *Get your head in the game, Crystal.* With a deep breath, she got Bruno's seconds and ran them out to him. "Here you go. I'm so glad you like it."

He grunted around a bite. God, was he always this much of a cretin?

Probably. Definitely. Now it was so prominent because she had something—someone—to compare him against.

Pushing away the thought, Crystal forced herself to eat more than half of her portion of lasagna while he responded to another series of text messages. She didn't want to do anything to draw Bruno's attention and make him wonder any more about her behavior.

"Jenna around tonight?" he asked, wiping his mouth on the paper napkin and throwing it onto his empty plate.

"Not 'til later," she said, knowing where this conversation was going. "She's staying on campus to do some research at the library." And thank God for that. Because after the way they'd been fighting the past few days, the last thing Crystal wanted was for Jenna to witness her little performance here tonight.

"Hmm." Bruno tipped his beer against his lips and took a long pull from the can, eyeing Crystal the whole time.

"Dessert?" Crystal asked, acting like she didn't know where his thoughts were going. She rose and reached for their dirty dishes, but Bruno grabbed her wrist and hauled her around the table and in between his spread knees.

He grabbed her breasts and kneaded. "Definitely dessert."

Too rough. Too scary. Too much about him—always. The gentleness and affection of Shane's touch was maybe her favorite thing about him, which was why Bruno's groping now felt so hard to bear. "Well," she said, clearing her throat and trying to hide a wince from a particularly hard squeeze. "The nice thing is that you can have your cake and eat it, too."

Bruno stopped and his gaze dragged up to her face. "You made cake?"

Sucker. She smiled. "Yup."

"What kind?"

"Red velvet with cream cheese icing." Bruno's eyebrows flew up. The first time she'd ever made him red velvet had been his birthday four years ago, which had only been about two months after he'd pulled her out of that hole in the basement of Confessions. It was the first night she'd let him between her legs, although she'd quickly freaked out when he'd tried to position his weight there. It had taken another month before she could manage sex with him. She cried for an hour afterward. He'd only stuck around for the first ten minutes of it.

So many things she loved had been ruined by their association with Bruno Ashe.

But not Jenna. Never Jenna.

"Yeah, cake," Bruno said. "Thanks, baby." He patted her ass and let her go.

Releasing a breath she hadn't realized she'd been holding, she cleared the table and took the dirties to the sink. She removed the cover from the cake plate and stared at the creamy swirls of white frosting—then she cut him almost a quarter of the cake.

She carried the hunk of sugar out to him with a fresh can of beer and sat opposite as he devoured it.

Why aren't you having any?" he asked around a too-big bite.

"I made it for you. Besides, I have to watch my figure, you know?"

"Yeah, I guess you do." His gaze dragged over Crystal's breasts, and it made her want to shrink into herself.

As his slice of cake got smaller and smaller, her heart raced and her stomach knotted. It was like facing a trip to the gallows. She knew what was about to happen was inevitable, but that didn't keep her soul from howling in protest.

And then his forked clanked against the empty plate.

"More?" she asked brightly.

He licked his lips and shook his head. "No. I had enough cake. Now I want dessert." Bruno lifted his hands, urging her to come to him.

For a moment, her muscles refused to respond. But then her survival instinct kicked in, and she got her butt out of the chair and rounded the table to stand at Bruno's knees. He helped her straddle his lap and pulled her down as far as her snug jeans and his thick thighs allowed. He fisted his hands in her hair and slowly pulled her mouth to his.

And then his lips smothered hers, and his tongue penetrated her mouth. Crystal was drowning in the sweetness on his breath until she felt like she was suffocating. Bruno grew hard between her legs and slid down in the chair to force them more tightly together. He gripped her hips, hard, and ground her down against the ridge of his erection, unleashing a grunt into their kiss.

Crystal's throat went tight and her eyes stung, but she responded the way she always did, the way he expected. She kissed back. She moaned. She writhed. But everything within her revolted against his touch and his taste and his scent. Her skin crawled, her mouth soured, her nose recoiled. No matter how hard she tried, she couldn't get out of her own head. Usually, she could tolerate, she could compartmentalize, she could rationalize. *It won't last long. It's not that big of a deal. You've done it before. Once, you wanted him.*

Now, none of those worked. None of those appeased. None of those made her feel any less like she was back in that basement room of Confessions, watching a total stranger undo his belt and leer at her like she was his for the taking whether she wanted him or not. She had been then. She was now.

"Get up, baby. I don't have a lot of time," Bruno said, pushing her off his lap. "And I gotta get inside you. It's been too long."

Crystal found her feet, though her knees felt soft, like they couldn't possibly hold her weight. The walls seemed to spin around her.

Bruno grabbed her, kissed her, pulled at her clothing. Her shirt went up, her bra got tugged down. His hands were everywhere, big and hot and harsh. He opened the button on her jeans. Then the zipper. He shoved the denim down over her hips. It chafed at her skin.

"Turn around and brace yourself," Bruno said in a ragged voice.

And that was when Crystal got out of her head. Out of her body, actually. She had the weirdest sensation of floating, and then somehow she was on the other side of the room. Or, at least, it seemed that way, because instead of seeing the dull white of the plaster wall in front of her face, she saw a couple about to have sex up against a wall, as if she'd become a casual observer not involved in what was going on. The woman's bottom and thighs were bared, as well as her lower back, showing just the tail ends of her scars.

The man shoved down his own jeans, baring the heavy, corded muscles of his glutes and thighs. He reached a hand in between them and grunted in frustration. She was too tense, too closed. He yanked her hips farther away from the wall. Another moment of attempted consummation. More frustration. Because her body wasn't responding. *Refused* to respond. He smacked her ass hard enough to leave a red handprint against the fair skin.

"Damnit, what the hell's wrong?" Spitting into his hand, he reached between them again.

Keys rattled at the door.

Crystal-the-observer slowly turned her gaze away from the couple, who hadn't yet heard the sound, and watched the door ease open.

Bruno gasped. "What the fuck?" He jerked his pants back around his waist. "Jesus, Jenna, what are you doing here?"

Crystal boomeranged back into her body. *Oh, God, oh, God, oh, God.* It was damn close to every nightmare she'd ever had converging into a real moment in time.

Jenna's expression was total abject horror—brow furrowed, mouth agape, cheeks flushing with anger. "I *live* here. What are *you* doing here?" Her eyes were like blue fire as they whipped between his open fly and Crystal's disheveled clothing.

Oh, God, Jenna, stop. Crystal pulled her jeans up but couldn't get her fingers to master rebuttoning them. "Sorry, Jen. We just got carried away, didn't we, Bruno?"

She smiled up at him, trying to distract him from what Jenna had just said, and the tone with which she'd said it. "Can I get a rain check?" she asked, wrapping her arms around his neck.

His eyes unnarrowed, just the littlest bit. "Yeah, yeah, tomorrow. Or maybe Friday. I gotta see," he said, his voice just a few degrees above frigid. "Wrap that food up for me."

"Uh, yes, sure. Of course."

Jenna glared at Crystal as she crossed the room, and Crystal threw her a look pleading for her to rein in her anger for just a few minutes. Once Bruno left, Jenna could dump as much of it on her as she wanted.

Crystal's hands were a jittery mess as she grabbed plastic bowls and matching lids from a cupboard and hefted big slabs of lasagna into one container and thick wedges of cake into another. She pulled a handled brown bag from under the sink and packaged everything up for Bruno.

"What's your problem?" came Bruno's voice from the living room.

Crystal's stomach plummeted to the ground. For a long moment, there was silence. Crystal returned to the living room, still death-gripping her hope that things wouldn't get worse. "Here you go," she said, as he finished donning his jacket.

"You wanna know what my problem is?" Jenna asked.

All the blood rushed from Crystal's face. She felt it, because the room started spinning again, and she perceived sound like it had traveled through a long tunnel. "That's enough, Jenna," she said as harshly as she could.

Bruno wrenched the bag from Crystal's hands and stalked toward her sister. He grabbed her jaw. "Yeah, I'd say that's more than edamnnough, Jenna. Learn not to bite the hand that feeds you," he said, shoving her away.

She stumbled back a step, and he pushed by her, yanked open the door, and slammed it shut behind himself.

Pale and shaking, Jenna gaped at Crystal for a long minute, then she slipped the security chain across the door. "You want to explain what that was all about, Sara? Why I just got accosted in my own home?"

Crystal grappled to respond, but whatever force had been holding her upright for the past fifteen minutes stopped working at that very instant.

The room went wavy, her skin grew clammy, and her knees buckled. Crystal's body went into a free fall.

The tenor of Jenna's words changed. From anger to panic. "Sara!" Jenna rushed to Crystal's side, to where she'd fallen in a heap in front of the couch.

Crystal curled into a ball and hugged herself as hard as she could.

"Sara? Sara, please," Jenna said, stroking her hair and her face and her arm. "Tell me what to do." More stroking, and Crystal became conscious that Jenna's fingers were wet from where they'd wiped at her cheeks. Someone was making the most mournful sounds, long, low wails of grief and loss. "Sara? Did he . . . did he rape you?"

No, he didn't rape me, she thought, shaking her head against Jenna's thigh. The one bright spot in this whole mess. Her body had locked up so completely that he hadn't been able to penetrate her. Though, had Jenna not come home when she did, Crystal knew Bruno wouldn't have been deterred much longer. It hadn't always stopped him in the past.

"I'm gonna call nine-one-one, sweetie. I'll be right back," Jenna said, stroking her hair again.

"No!" Crystal said, twisting to grip Jenna's wrist before she rose. "No, don't. I'm okay." Her voice sounded warped, strained.

"You're not okay," Jenna said, a deep frown on her face. Though it was one of fear and concern, not anger.

Crystal shook her head. "He didn't rape me. He didn't hurt me. I promise," she rasped.

Jenna eased back to the floor. "You didn't look okay. When I came in . . . *God*. Sara, you looked like you were three seconds from a panic attack."

"I know," Crystal said, hiccuping. "I know." She pushed onto her hands, but the sudden movement left her dizzy.

"Don't rush," Jenna said. "Just lie here with me for a little bit." When Crystal laid her head in Jenna's lap again, Jenna rubbed her back. "You're the one usually taking care of me," she said.

"Yeah," Crystal said. "I never mind." Her breathing shuddered, and the crying left her wrung out and headachy. She had to pull herself together.

"Well, I don't mind either. I just really hate seeing you this way. Nobody should get to do this to you," she said, keeping her voice as calm as she could as she rubbed wide circles over Crystal's back. Jenna's hand slowed. Stilled. "Sara?" she asked in a high-pitched voice.

Crystal closed her eyes. She'd been so wrapped up in herself, she'd forgotten. For a moment, she'd just let herself be comforted. And now Jenna knew. Now, Jenna had seen.

Slowly, the cotton of Crystal's shirt slid farther up her back, just a few inches, as Jenna leaned around her.

Jenna gasped. "Oh, Sara. Oh, my God. What is this? Oh, my God."

Crystal's tears started again, and she burrowed into Jenna's lap and wrapped her arms awkwardly around her waist. Jenna leaned down and returned the embrace as best as she could. They cried together for a long time.

When Crystal's body simply had no more tears left to

give, she slowly rolled onto her back, her head on Jenna's legs. "I didn't want you to know," she said, her voice a raw scrape. "I didn't want you to . . . think . . . less of me."

"Less of you? How could I?" Jenna asked, shaking her head. "My God, I would never have thought this was your fault. Because it's not. How could it be?"

"I know," Crystal said, her throat tight again. "I was just so ashamed." She covered her mouth with her hand, and Jenna stroked her palm over Crystal's sweaty forehead.

"Will you tell me now?"

The thing she'd never wanted to do. Crystal was supposed to have shielded Jenna from all this. Let her live her life free from the knowledge of this reality. It was part of what she'd promised their father, at least that's what she'd always told herself. Too late now. The failure sat like a ten-pound weight on her heart. Crystal's head moved down in a nod without her telling it to, but it was the right thing to do. "I'll tell you," she whispered. "I'll hate it, but I'll tell you anything you want to know."

Chapter 16

*T*he sun had set, and the team had been in position for almost two hours when the first vehicles pulled into Pier 13, a long stretch of concrete slab that ran from the road along a mammoth and abandoned industrial granary to the pier that stretched into the dark waters of Baltimore Harbor beyond. A gray van, two black Suburbans with tinted windows, and a box truck circled into the lot behind the granary.

"Hold your position everyone. Engage only if hostiles engage first. We are fact-finding only," came Nick's voice through Shane's earpiece. From his sniper roost on an old barge moored to one side of the pier, Shane watched as men climbed out of the trucks and fanned out in a defensive circle. Ten in all. Heavily armed.

Against their six.

Near the middle of the group loomed the man Shane

had seen kissing Crystal at Confessions. Bruno Ashe. He stood at the right hand of a tall, thin black man in a sharp-looking suit. Shane's gut said that had to be Jimmy Church. Who else but a self-appointed Messiah, the name he called himself inside his organization, would radiate that kind of self-assurance or warrant the kind of deference the rest of the men paid to him?

Eyeballing the white box truck, Shane wondered if Church was giving or receiving tonight. Maybe both. And, really, it didn't matter. Shane just hoped the nature of the delivery and those with whom Church was making the trade would help them figure out what the hell Merritt had been up to and how they could use that intel to regain their good names, their reputations, and their honor.

Shane scanned a one-eighty circuit from left to right. Though he couldn't see any of the team, he knew Nick and Marz provided the team's eyes from the sky from their positions inside broken windows on opposite ends of the granary's second floor. Beckett hid at ground level behind a trailer that might once have served as some sort of office. Easy crouched in a nook where a lower concrete gangway ran along the far side of the pier, shielded by the shadows of the NS *Savannah,* the first nuclear-powered passenger ship, apparently, that had long been docked there. And Nick's PI friend, Miguel, had the water approach covered from his position out in the harbor on his fishing boat. Jeremy had Beckett's SUV hidden about a quarter mile away, giving them access to both a water and a land evacuation of the site in case they needed the options.

Nick had been reluctant as hell to bring Jeremy out in the field, and of all people, Shane totally got his wanting to keep his brother safe. But the reality was they were seriously understaffed for the mission they'd created for themselves. And to his credit, Jer was only too happy to help however he could.

"Note that all eyes are on the water," Marz said. "Keep alert for a marine landing."

"Roger that," Miguel said.

Given that the *Savannah* took up most of the far side of the pier, that probably meant their unknown hostiles would dock on the same side as Shane's barge, making his position the closest to deal with them should the need arise.

Damn good thing they'd had the day to prepare for this operation.

After Marz had nailed down the meeting's location via the audio surveillance of Confessions, the whole group had gotten a few hours shut-eye, then spent the day learning everything they could about the pier. Miguel, Nick, and Easy had taken the older man's boat out along the whole stretch of waterfront comprised of several piers. Once they'd seen that the dock appeared no longer in use, they'd dropped Easy off to wire up a few booby traps in case things went south and they required a little explosive assistance to cover their asses.

Meanwhile, Beckett and Shane had familiarized themselves with the land approach, learning there was only one road in and out of that part of the terminal. Both groups had loaded up on photographs of the geography, allowing Marz to merge those with the aerial images he'd pulled off the Web to compile a whiteboard-sized graphic from which they could strategize and prepare for every possible contingency.

All of that meant Shane hadn't had five minutes to try to see Crystal, and the radio silence was eating at his innards. Last thing he wanted was for her to think those scars had chased him off when his reaction was exactly the opposite—he wanted her by his side where he could protect her from ever being hurt again.

"Look lively, gentlemen," came Miguel's voice over the

coms. "Two powerboats coming in from the southeast and heading your direction." Shane looked to his right out over the expanse of the barge to the black waters beyond. He scanned the horizon and finally found the green, red, and white navigation lights demarcating the vessels in question.

"Are you close enough for a head count?" Nick asked.

"Negative," Miguel said.

Soon, the hum of the boats' motors traveled across the water, the sound getting louder by degrees as they neared. Shane's muscles tensed in readiness, and every one of his senses sharpened with awareness, the reactions instinctive after years of being in similar situations out in the field. Breathing and heart rate steady, he tamped down the excitement that threatened to bubble up at the anticipation of getting some answers. Everything needed to be by the book to ensure that the team's presence remained covert, they got the photographic information Marz needed to research identities, and everyone got home safe.

Two motorboats entered the golden light cast by the lamp at the end of the pier. Cabin cruisers, the kind with galleys and sleeping berths belowdecks, easily thirty-six or forty feet long. Shane took a quick inventory of both boats. "At least three hostiles on each vessel," he said in a low voice. "Lots of firepower."

"Copy," Nick replied.

That made it sixteen against six. The nearly three-to-one ratio was way the hell less than ideal, but hopefully everything would go as planned, and it would never come into play.

The boats passed alongside Shane's position, and some of Church's men moved toward the waterside as the new arrivals docked and disembarked in an orderly, methodical fashion that said they'd done this before.

"Make that four per boat," Shane said as a single man

emerged from down below on both boats and held a sentry position on deck. Two other men stayed near the boats, while the rest moved closer to Church.

The round of greetings between Church and his men and the newcomers, generally friendly in nature, revealed a fair degree of trust. Question was, who the hell were these guys? Was one of these the man named Azziz that Charlie had heard about while kidnapped? And did they have anything to do with Merritt?

"You getting this, Marz?" Shane asked.

"Affirmative," came his voice, tight with concentration.

For a few minutes, the two obvious leaders—Church and whoever the number one was from the boat—exchanged social small talk about one another's family and business. From his position on the barge, Shane could hear much of what they were saying. Finally, the newcomer's leader said, "Have you got what I need?" American English, no accent.

Church gave a curt nod. "Of course. I can assume the same from you?"

"As always," the man said. Tall, Caucasian, dark hair, nothing about him seemed familiar or noteworthy. But the best operatives often perfected coming across as unmemorable.

Church signaled with his hand, and the box truck's engine started. The vehicle backed toward the dock's edge nearest the boats, stopping less than ten feet away. Church's men congregated on either side as some of the newcomers returned to the decks of the boats.

"Who's got a good visual on the back of that truck?" Marz asked. "I'm dark, now."

"I have a partial," Beckett said from his ground-level location behind the trailer.

"I got it," Shane said. "I'll get some pics." As the only other team member holding an elevated position, Shane had come prepared with a high-powered digital point-

and-shoot, just in case. He fished it out of his pocket and eyed the scene through the viewfinder.

Luggage appeared from the hull of one of the boats—two wheeled suitcases. As he shot a stream of stills, Shane burned for them to open the cases and see if the contents could provide more information.

Bingo.

The men laid the cases on the ground and unzipped them. Church crouched down and retrieved one of what appeared to be maybe two dozen plastic-wrapped kilo bricks of product. He slit one open with a knife and tested it. Nodded. The underlings closed the cases again. Shane couldn't be sure what was in those bricks—meth, cocaine, heroin, all of them could be transported that way. But given that Afghanistan accounted for at least 90 percent of the world's heroin, a potential connection to their fubar of a situation remained.

Church rose and stepped to the side, then Bruno knocked twice on the back of the truck and lifted the door. It rolled up with a clatter. Bruno removed four black suitcases from the truck's bed and set them in front of the boatmen's subordinates. Shane captured the whole exchange with the camera.

"Nice," Nondescript Man said with a smile. "It was a good shipment, then."

"Very," Church said. "You keep delivering such pure product, and I can get top dollar."

So then Church's cases likely held cash. Basic drug deal. Shane focused on close-ups of a few more faces, then lowered the camera.

"Okay, hand 'em down," Bruno called, standing at the back of the truck. Six of Church's men lined up, guns facing outward, and formed a human gauntlet from the end of the vehicle to the edge of the pier.

What the fuck is this? Shane thought, shooting the scene again.

Prickles rose on Shane's scalp, then he went ice-cold to the core. Two men who had apparently been inside the truck's cargo area took turns passing the bodies of unconscious women into the arms of the remaining Churchmen, who passed them off to the boatmen.

"Aw, Jesus Christ," Shane whispered, not fully realizing he'd said it out loud until Nick asked what was going on. *Oh, no. Oh, no.*

"They're pulling bodies out of the back of that truck," Beckett explained. "Women." Shane was glad for the explanatory assistance, because if he opened his mouth right now, he was likely to vent the inferno of rage erupting inside him.

"We gotta do something," Shane finally managed, as the third woman—a blond—was passed down the line. Shane's throat went tight. Is this what had happened to Molly? Had this been her fate?

"Stand down, Shane," Nick said. "That is an order."

A fourth. Short, dark hair. "We can't just let them . . ."

"Shane, listen to me," Nick came again. "We don't have the manpower. We don't have the guns. We're not in the right position to intervene."

Shane's chest squeezed. "Nick—"

"No. We'll get them *and* us killed," Nick said, the calm gone from his voice. Shane heard the anger and the reason and the fear—and he knew the latter was all about whether Shane would lose his shit and go rogue.

One by one, the boatmen carried the women belowdecks. Hands shaking, heart jackrabbiting inside his chest, Shane shot every one with the camera. But he felt raw and ragged, like he'd been torn in two, because part of him was dying inside for the inability to stop what he was silently witnessing—an assembly line of human trafficking that deposited nine women total into the bowels of the boats.

None with red hair. And goddamnit all to hell and back,

he *loathed* himself for caring about that, because Crystal's safety in this instance held his heart intact but didn't at all negate the loss that nine fucking families were in the midst of feeling right this very second.

And Shane was intimately familiar with that feeling. He'd carried it with him for sixteen long years.

The two men who'd apparently guarded the truck's human cargo jumped out and secured the door, and one turned toward Shane's position and stepped into the light.

Shane did a double take, totally gobsmacked to see a familiar face among the Churchmen. He shot a series of images. "You won't believe this shit, but I'm looking at Manny Garza right now," Shane said, forcing normalcy into his voice. Garza had been Army Special Forces, too, and Shane, Nick, and Beckett had crossed paths with him on a couple of ops in Afghanistan at least three years before the ambush. Last Shane had heard, Garza had washed out.

So what the hell was he doing *here*?

"Sonofafuck," Nick bit out. "Are you sure?"

Shane watched the guy move. His wavy hair was longer, but his light brown skin color, facial expressions, and body movements were completely recognizable as the soldier he'd known. "Affirmative."

And now Shane's rage brewed for another reason. Afuckingnother of their own was on the dirty side of this situation. First Merritt, now Garza. How far into their own ranks did this shit extend?

Shane didn't think he was imagining the tension radiating from the rest of his team. They might've been hidden from his sight, but he was well enough in tune with all of them to know he wouldn't be alone in his reactions to the night's turn of events.

"You got a source for your other needs?" Nondescript Man asked. "Because I've got a recommendation if you want it."

Church shook his head. "Appreciate the offer, but I prefer to keep this business separate from that business. You understand." *This* business was clearly the drugs and the women, but what the hell did Church mean by *that* business? Guns, maybe? That was the remaining cornerstone of the criminal business trifecta.

"Entirely. Well—" The boatmen's leader extended his hand, and Church returned the shake. "A pleasure, as always." The man's underlings retreated to the boats.

"Indeed," Church said with a nod. "Go with God." The Messiah turned and beat feet for one of the Suburbans, Bruno and another linebacker type flanking him on either side.

"You staying, G?" Nondescript Man asked.

Garza hung back from the rest of the Churchmen. "Yeah." He clasped hands with the man, and the familiarity between them was clear and deep. "We got another delivery Friday night. You know he wants me to keep an eye on everything over here. Prefer to be with you guys, though."

He? He who? Church? This Azziz person? Someone else entirely? Was Garza with Church or the boatmen? Or was he an emissary from one to the other? Shane's brain rattled off a stream of unanswerable questions. And hadn't this whole thing been that way—every time they managed to cut the head off one mystery, three others sprouted.

"Roger that," Nondescript Man said. "Watch your back."

"Always," Garza said, nodding. Then he hurried to the passenger door of the box truck and hopped inside.

The last of the boatmen went aboard. They reeled in the lines, then the boats were turning around, preparing to head out into the dark cover of open water.

On land, the engines in the four vehicles revved. Once the boats cleared the end of the pier, the vehicles pulled out one by one, lining up into a convoy.

Staying low, gun drawn, Shane scrabbled across the

barge following the direction of the boats. "I might be able to take out their motors," he said.

"Negative. Negative. Stand down," came Nick's voice. "Church's men are still in range. We cannot engage."

Peering over his shoulder, Shane saw the row of taillights just coming along the side of the granary, barely out of the lot.

For one last moment, Shane held on to the hope that he could save those women's lives. Letting go of that hope was like driving a dagger into his heart. It left him grasping his chest and gulping down air. Loosening the grip on his gun, Shane went down on his knees, his head hanging on his shoulders. Long minutes passed, during which he forced himself to stay in that place, to *feel* what it felt like.

To feel what *failure* felt like. Again.

Then, looking to the sky, Shane made a vow. If he couldn't save the victims, he would find a way to avenge them. One way or another, Church was going down. And somehow, some way, Shane would be the one to make it happen.

CRYSTAL WOKE FIRST. Gently rolling on her back, she stared up at the early-morning light making patterns on the ceiling. The butterfly mobile turned slowly, bringing the yellow one closer, then the orange.

Turning her head, she found Jenna still asleep beside her. They'd talked and cried into the middle of the night, until Crystal's throat was raw, and they were both damn near dehydrated from the outpouring of their grief.

Crystal told Jenna everything. She hadn't held anything back. What would be the point? Jenna had seen the scars. She'd seen the evidence of Bruno's abuse. And now she knew the reasons Crystal had put up with it.

At some point, they'd fallen asleep. Neither of them wanting to be apart from the other.

And though Crystal's heart was warmed by the end of

the loneliness that sharing had brought about, another part of her hated that it had come at the cost of Jenna's innocence, at the weight of her having to shoulder some of this burden.

Jenna's bright blue eyes blinked open. "Hey," she said, her voice scratchy.

"Hey," Crystal said. "You sound like I feel."

With a hoarse chuckle, Jenna nodded, then her expression turned serious. "How are you?"

"Okay. You remember what I said, right?" Crystal asked, needing to hear Jenna say it again.

"Yeah." Her eyes went glassy.

Crystal turned on her side, bringing them closer. "None of this was your fault, either. You are *never, ever* to blame yourself for any of this, do you understand?"

Her lips trembling, Jenna nodded. "I know. But I still feel bad. If it wasn't for me—"

"No," Crystal said, her belly twisting into knots. As much as she'd always worried that Jenna might think less of her if she knew all the things Crystal had done, *this* was the thing she'd most feared—Jenna's feeling somehow responsible because of her illness and the cost of her treatment. "Dad's debts trapped us here. Not your epilepsy. Please, please believe me."

"Okay," she said, pushing herself into a sitting position. "Okay." She tucked long strands of red hair behind her ears and met Crystal's gaze. "So what's our plan?"

Crystal forced herself into an upright position, too. "What do you mean?"

"I mean, what's our plan? We have to get the hell out of here." Jenna turned toward her and sat cross-legged amid the messy covers.

"Sshh," Crystal whispered, then reached over to the iPod dock and queued up some music to cover their conversation. Just in case. "Keep your voice down."

Jenna acquiesced just as she had the night before when Crystal had insisted they take a similar precaution. It was more likely that Bruno had known about Shane because he'd had a guy watching her apartment. He'd done stuff like that before. But at this point, Crystal came down on the side of full-blown paranoia and decided she couldn't be too careful.

Crystal grasped Jenna's hand. "We can't leave yet. I told you, we wait until you graduate and I have more money saved up, then we go."

"That's crazy, Sara," Jenna whispered. "Bruno's too unstable. It's not safe for you."

"You have a full scholarship at a great school. If we go now, you won't graduate. And to get a job with benefits, with good health insurance, you need a degree. We can wait."

Jenna shook her head. "I can finish anywhere, anytime. It's only the rest of this semester, the summer, and next semester."

"Exactly. Which is why we should stay. You're getting a free education. We won't have that anywhere else. Besides, if we go now, you'd lose all the time you put in this semester." Crystal believed to the depths of her soul that their getaway plan needed to be methodically and carefully planned. She was the one who really knew Bruno, Church, and the danger they faced if they misstepped along the way. But convincing Jenna that Crystal was right was like getting a teenager to believe their parents had any wisdom.

God, she really was like a 104-year-old, wasn't she?

Jenna blew out a long breath. "Okay, I have a compromise solution."

Crystal looked at her, willing to hear it but doubting she'd be convinced. She waved a hand, indicating Jenna should share.

"I've got two more weeks of classes left, then finals.

We go right after that. Then it's just the summer classes I planned to take and one last full semester, and it's mostly electives at that. I could do those anywhere."

That was four weeks. "I don't know if I can get us ready that fast," Crystal said, considering Jenna's proposal more seriously than she thought she ever would. Though she'd always imagined them running to New York City, she didn't have a job or an apartment lined up for when they got there, and she'd hoped to have more money saved. Most importantly, she hadn't found a way to get them fake IDs and new paperwork. Everyone she thought might be capable of such a thing was too damn loyal to the Church gang to risk asking. But damn, four weeks sounded like heaven.

But it also means you'll be leaving Shane that much sooner.

True. And that hurt. Bad. But no matter what, she wouldn't get to have him for long. And Jenna's safety was worth the sacrifice. Besides, if by some miracle Shane wasn't disgusted by her back, and Crystal did get to spend more time with him, she'd just fall harder for the sexy ex-soldier. And then losing him would hurt that much worse.

"You're considering it," Jenna said with a smile in her voice.

Crystal rolled her eyes. "Maybe."

"Hey, I know. Why don't you ask Edward and his bossy friend for help," she said. "They helped us before."

For a moment, Crystal heard Shane's voice coming through her cell phone that night. "*I told you I'd help you and Jenna. That offer didn't come with an expiration date or office hours.*" And she recalled the sadness and frustration in his voice when he'd said he didn't know *how* to help her. So maybe Jenna was right.

"They did. That's true."

"I really think they were good guys, Sar. Don't you?

And they definitely seemed like they could kick some ass." Jenna's blue eyes were almost pleading.

Yeah. She thought so, too. Crystal nodded, her stomach flip-flopping at the idea of seeing Shane again. Especially after the way she'd run away from him the other night. "Okay, I'll talk to Shane and see what he thinks."

Jenna grinned. "Shane, huh?" Somehow, those two little words managed to draw heat to Crystal's cheeks. Her sister's eyes flew wide. "Oh, my God!"

"Sshh," Crystal said again.

Laughing, Jenna leaned closer. "You like him?"

Her sister's perceptiveness threw Crystal off-balance. "I . . . I . . ."

"You *do*!"

Crystal grabbed Jenna's hands. "Okay, okay. Whatever," she said, playing it off. No point encouraging girl talk about a guy Crystal could never have. "The most important thing in all of this is acting like nothing's changed, Jenna. You have to promise me. Go to your classes. Hang out with your friends. Go shopping. And whatever you do, make nice with Bruno if you see him again."

Jenna sat back and nodded. "Okay, I will."

"Promise me?"

"I promise," Jenna said. "As long as you promise we're not waiting eight months."

Crystal blew out a long breath and met her sister's determined gaze. She wasn't a little kid anymore, was she? In just a few weeks, she wouldn't even be a teenager anymore. She was a brave, smart, strong woman, and Crystal admired her. And in this moment, Jenna was right. "I promise. You got a deal."

"We're gonna be all right, Sis. Don't worry." Jenna smiled.

"Yeah, we are," Crystal said. And for the first time in a long time, she came pretty close to believing it.

Chapter 17

*W*hen the knock finally sounded against Shane's bedroom door, he'd expected it. After they'd returned to Hard Ink the previous night, the only talking Shane had been up to was to share what Garza had said about another delivery happening Friday night. Then Shane had handed off his camera and called it quits on the day. The other guys had stayed up to debrief the op, but Shane's mood had been for shit, his emotions were too volatile, and his brain was so scrambled, he wouldn't have been of any analytical use to anyone anyway.

Late, late in the night, he'd finally managed to calm the storm raging in his head long enough to fall asleep for a few hours, but his dreams had been a relentless, horrifying, and heartbreaking search for Molly that always had him showing up moments too late or running into a dead end.

He woke up more tired and strung out than when he'd gone to bed, so he'd lain in the early-morning gloom spilling in from the high window and tried to get his head screwed on straight.

No luck yet.

The knock came again.

Shane sighed and sat up against the headboard. It was then that he realized Molly's butterfly necklace was still wrapped around his fingers from the night before. He'd been turning the chain round and round, looking for a little peace or wisdom or insight. He was still looking. "Come in," he called.

The door eased open, revealing Nick, so recently out of the shower his hair was still wet, and damp spots showed through his black T-shirt where he hadn't bothered to dry off. "What's up?" he asked.

Shane just shook his head. "Need me for something?"

"No, man." He came all the way in and closed the door behind him, then he leaned against it and crossed his arms. "That scene last night—"

"Don't," Shane bit out, more harshly than he'd intended, but he really couldn't help himself. The memory of the women's bodies being delivered into those boats made him feel a whole lot like a giant exposed nerve. And everything—his clothes, the covers, even the very air—rubbed it raw and made it hurt.

Nick pushed off the wall, crossed the room, and sat heavily on the edge of the bed. "I'm going there, Shane. And you need me to."

Shane drew up his sweats-covered knees and rested his arms on them, the necklace dangling from the fingers of his right hand. "Damnit, Rix. I said, don't—"

"There was nothing we could do. There was nothing *you* could do," Nick said, turning toward him.

"I know," Shane said. And he did. His rational self

knew Nick was right. But that didn't keep his heart from splintering inside his chest.

"Shane?"

He dragged his gaze up from the little silver chain and met Nick's intense stare. "Yeah?"

For possessing such an unusually pale color, Nick's eyes could be warm with sympathy when he wanted them to be. And now was one of those times. Shane should've realized what was coming. "Would you finally tell me what happened the day Molly disappeared?" Nick asked.

The question sucker punched him hard in the gut, stealing his breath and beckoning a rolling wave of nausea. The team knew Shane's little sister had disappeared when Shane was a teenager and that he felt responsible, but not the details. In fact, the last person he'd told the details to had been an Army shrink during his SF in-processing.

"Why?" Shane whispered. All he could manage.

Nick raked his hand through his damp hair, once, twice. "Because what happened to her is eating you up like a cancer, and the harder you try to beat it back, the more aggressive it becomes. This situation is strumming that string so hard, I can't help but think it's gotta snap." He shook his head. "I missed the thing with Merritt because I didn't trust my gut. And right now, my gut's saying you're in trouble. I thought so before last night, but now, just looking at you, I know it's true."

Thoughts whirling, heart beating almost painfully in his chest, Shane braced his elbows on his knees and held up the necklace. Shane couldn't remember when Molly had gotten it, but she'd loved it because it wasn't a little girl's piece of jewelry. It was a grown-up necklace, which meant the pendant had hung low on her chest. But she hadn't minded. In fact, she'd thought she looked *fancy*. Her word.

Taking the butterfly into his fingers, he smoothed his

thumb over the heart-shaped wings made of purple and white rhinestones.

"I found this—" Shane began, his voice catching. "I found it down the street from my house, lying on the curb." He turned the butterfly over and over in his fingers. "She would never . . . never have dropped it on purpose."

Wondering *how* it had come off? That was the stuff of which nightmares were made.

For a moment, Shane got sucked back into time, to that hot summer day. Late July. Him and Henry Waller and Kevin Ryan, his two best friends from his baseball team, were up in his room playing video games. His father had a round of golf that morning, and his mother was down the street at a bridal shower. Just for a few hours. And, besides, at thirteen, they occasionally left him to babysit Molly.

The first time Molly had knocked on his door, she'd wanted permission to get a snack. So Shane had okayed the Goldfish and juice box and sent her on her way.

The second time she'd knocked, she'd asked if she could play with them. Or, if not play, watch. But what teenage guy wanted his eight-year-old sister hanging out in his room with his friends? So he'd told her no and sent her on her way.

The third time she'd knocked, he'd been so annoyed at the constant interruptions that he'd wrenched open the door and told her to leave them alone. And, then, to drive home the point, he'd told her to *go away*.

The better part of an hour later, another knock sounded at his door. It was his mother, home from the shower and looking for Molly. As he'd searched and searched, he'd been so sure she was hiding to get him in trouble as payback for not letting her play that he'd been mad. But as the hours passed, the search widened, and his parents' eyes filled with fear and panic, and he'd realized that Molly wasn't playing a game.

Shane had found the necklace late that afternoon, and he'd had to turn it over to the police to test for fingerprints it didn't have. They'd returned it to the family a few weeks later, and Shane had kept it on him ever since.

"Jesus," Nick said.

Only then did Shane realize he'd recounted the story out loud. And that something wet had rolled down his cheeks. He scrubbed the errant moisture away and pinched his fingers against his eyelids, catching a bit more wetness against his fingertips. The last time he'd shed tears over Molly had been the night of what would've been her thirteenth birthday. Because it was the age he'd been when he'd lost her, when he'd sent her away, and she'd gone. Never to be heard from again.

"You were a kid, Shane. You didn't want anything bad to happen to her. You didn't cause it. You couldn't have predicted it. *It wasn't your fault.*"

Words he'd heard from a shrink. From his parents. They'd just never sank in. "But I—"

"No. The *only* one to blame was the sociopath who took her." Nick scooted closer. "Look at me, man. If you had a son, and the same thing happened to him. What would you tell him?" Shane shook his head, and Nick pressed. "What would you tell him? Would you look that little boy in the eyes and blame him?"

"It's different," he said, voice strained, mind reeling.

"How?" Nick said.

"It just is."

"Look that little boy in the eyes, Shane, and tell him who's responsible." With both hands on the sides of Shane's face, Nick forced their gazes to meet. "Tell him," he said, voice gentler.

"I don't know," Shane said, his breath coming in a shudder. "Not . . . him. Not him. *Not him.*"

"Not him," Nick said, dropping his hands. "Not *you*." He lowered his gaze to the floor, as if he knew Shane felt too exposed, too vulnerable, too embarrassed at the emotional display, at the weakness of his tears.

Shane gulped in a breath and turned his face toward the wall, where he made quick work of removing all traces of the wetness that had somehow appeared there again.

"And you weren't responsible for the loss of those women last night, either. None of us was. But you know who was?" Nick gave him a sideways glance.

That one was a no-brainer. Shane nailed him with a cold, hard stare. "Church."

Nick nodded. "Church." He didn't need to say anything more. Because Shane knew. If they were going to hurt Church and right the wrongs done against them and their dead teammates, he had to get off his ass and get out of his head. "Marz wants to confab as soon as we're all up and moving," Nick said, pushing off the bed.

Shane forced himself up, too. "Wait. I owe you some words," he said, rubbing a hand over the winged-heart tattoo he'd gotten in Molly's memory. *This* Shane could make right here and now, and he wasn't waiting another second to get his best friend back once and for all.

Frowning, Nick shook his head. "I don't—"

"The whole last year, I blamed you for falling off the radar. I blamed you for dropping out of my life when we got back in country. I saw your silence as just one more betrayal—"

"I know, and I'm so—"

"No. I was wrong, Nick. Because I was the one who failed you. I should've known the Nick Rixey I'd known all these years wouldn't fall off the grid without a damn good reason. And instead of going the extra mile and finding out what was really going on, I made assumptions that weren't true. You deserved better than that. You deserved me being a better friend to you than that."

Nick rubbed the back of his neck and nodded. "Okay." His gaze cut to Shane's. "Thanks."

"We're okay?" Shane asked, extending a hand.

"Yeah. More than." He returned the shake, pressed his lips into a tight line, and narrowed his gaze. "We're also kinda fucked up."

Shane barked out a laugh and scrubbed his hands over his face. "We are *all kinds* of fucked up, bro."

Nick moved toward the door and checked his watch. "Getcha ass moving. We have work to do." He let himself out of the room without looking back.

Closing his eyes and taking a deep breath, Shane let his head hang forward. He felt drained, exhausted, and a little hollow. But his head was quiet, and his heart a little lighter.

Shit on a fucking brick, he hadn't realized the weight of what he'd been carrying until he passed some of it to another to share. And not only that, but resolving this thing with Nick once and for all eased a whole other part of his soul.

And he knew something else that would help, too. Seeing Crystal. Telling her what he wanted. And making it clear it was *her.*

FRESH OUT OF the shower, Shane was lured to the kitchen by the warm, buttery scent of pancakes. Nick, Beckett, and Easy sat along the breakfast bar, talking over coffee as Becca plated up the hotcakes.

"Morning," he said from the edge of the room.

"Hey, Shane," Becca said, smiling. "Hungry?"

"Thanks," he said. "But I think I'll just start with some coffee." He fixed himself a cup and stood at the side of the bar.

"How are you?" Beckett said in a low voice.

Shane's gut tensed, but no sense avoiding the obvious, that being the fact he'd come close to going off the rez last night. "My head's on straight again," he said. "I'm sorry about last night."

Beckett shook his head and stared into his black coffee. "I appreciate the apology, Shane, but don't think for a minute it's necessary. That scene last night was brutal for me to watch, too. And, straight up, I don't have a missing sister or a girlfriend stuck working for a known trafficker. If I did, I don't think I'd have held it together as well as you."

Shane swallowed the lump in his throat and nodded. "Thanks," he managed.

Beckett's cell rang, breaking up the seriousness of the moment. Thankfully.

"Fucking Marz," Beckett said with amusement in his voice. He put the phone on speaker and answered. "Are you seriously calling me from across the hall?"

"I seriously am, motherfucker. What the hell are you people doing?"

"Becca made pancakes," he said, offering a rare grin to the group.

"Becca . . . *what*?" Marz hung up.

"Five-dollar bets on how fast he'll get over here," Beckett said, setting the stop watch on his phone. "I say twenty-five seconds."

"Forty seconds," Shane said.

"Thirty," said Easy.

Nick chuckled. "A minute."

When the door opened, the whole lot of them erupted in laughter before Marz stepped all the way through.

Beckett held up his iPhone. "Thirty-eight seconds," he said, grinning. "Damn."

"Aw, I'm closest. Pony up, suckers," Shane said, collecting a stack of fives from all the men.

"You sonofabitches bet on me?" Shaking his head, Marz made for the only open chair at the breakfast bar.

Beckett nodded. "On how long it would take you to haul ass over here at the mention of food."

As Marz hefted himself up onto the tall stool, Becca settled a plate of hot, steaming pancakes in front of him. "Thank you, Becca. You're a sweetheart." He winked.

"You're welcome. We were going to come get you," she said, smiling.

"Yeah, we definitely were," Nick said, elbowing him. He scooped a big bite into his mouth.

"Uh-huh. Right after you finished eating them all," Marz said, pouring a healthy serving of syrup atop his stack. "I know how you assholes are." He sliced his fork into the soft cakes and took a big bite. "Oh, these are good, Becca. Thank you."

"No problem. You guys ate on the go all day yesterday, so I figured you could use something hot to start off today."

Marz nodded around another sweet bite. "Oh," he said as he swallowed. "Mattress delivery is here. Jeremy went to meet 'em."

"I'll go see if he needs help," Shane said from where he leaned against the bar.

"Just chill out, McCallan," Marz said, eyeballing Shane like maybe he was worried about him. "Ike's helping him. And the deliverymen."

Shane nodded. Might as well get another cup of coffee, then.

"Make any progress on the facial-recognition work?" Nick asked Marz. They'd taken hundreds of photographs last night so Marz could run a comparison of the images against online arrest-record databases. Fortunately, all that information, including the booking photographs, was public record.

"Jeremy entered the pictures of the fifteen unknown men from last night's op into the facial-recognition search I set up. It'll take a while to start seeing results."

"Find anything on Garza?" Shane asked. He still couldn't get over the guy's appearance. Finding prior SF mixed up in all of this just ate at his gut. Where was the honor? Where was the integrity? To think his brothers had been killed by some of their own. Shane shook his head.

Marz swallowed a bite. "Short answer is no. Long answer is that Garza's a freaking ghost. No phone numbers, no Web presence, no social-media accounts, no memberships in any of the various SF forums or alumni groups. That only leaves a hack into Army and Veterans Affairs personnel records, which is some serious shit."

"Didn't Charlie say he'd done that?" Nick asked, pushing his plate away.

"Yeah. Just didn't want to bug him until he was on the mend," Marz said. "But I want to pick his brain about how he did it without bringing a detachment of MPs down on his head." Marz sipped his coffee and shook his head. "I also had to restart the Port Authority registries search. Keeps crashing."

"It lives," croaked a voice from the side of the room. Charlie. In a pair of scrub bottoms and a white T-shirt, and holding his bandaged hand and forearm against his stomach. A round of cheerful greetings sounded out from everyone.

Shane gave him a once-over—a little pale and a lot drawn, but conscious with none of the feverish symptoms of just thirty-six hours ago. He counted that a major victory.

"Sit here," Beckett said, emptying his seat and pushing his plate to the side.

"Thanks," Charlie said, sliding onto the end seat.

Becca came around to his side and put her hand against his forehead. "How are you?"

"I feel like somebody cut off my fingers," he said, a tired but amused expression on his pale face.

The men all gave a low chuckle. Gallows humor was common among people who had to deal with life and death on a daily basis, so Shane respected Charlie's ability to address his new reality head-on. They all did.

Becca ruffled his hair and rolled her eyes. "I'm serious."

"Me too," he said, bumping his shoulder into her. "Got any left?"

Her expression brightened. "Yes, definitely." She plated him two big, golden pancakes and Marz slid him the bottle of syrup.

"Good to see you up and around, man," Marz said, leaning forward so he could see Charlie.

Charlie nodded. "I'm going a little batshit lying in there."

"Well, when you're ready, I'd love to pick your brain about some things."

"Shower first," he said with a small smile. "If I'm still standing afterward . . ."

Finishing his pancakes, Marz nodded. "Fair enough." He pushed off the stool and deposited his plate in the sink. "Thank you, ma'am," he said, squeezing Becca in against his side. "You're too good to us."

She shook her head. "I'm with Charlie. I can't just sit around and do nothing. Feeding you guys isn't much, but at least it keeps me busy."

Nick rose off his stool, came around the island, and settled his plate in the sink, too. "An army can't march on an empty stomach, sunshine. We appreciate it. And don't forget you've been funding this whole operation. So none of this would be possible without your support all the way around," he said, pulling Becca into his arms. From the very beginning, Becca had offered up her father's life-insurance monies without reservation. After all, bullets and computers and pancakes didn't grow on trees. "And this won't last forever."

"No," Easy said. "But it's not clear how long it *will* last. How's everyone situated if this drags out?"

"I've already told the firms that hire me for process serving that I'm going to be unavailable for a few weeks," Nick said.

"I put in for two weeks' leave," Shane said. "And I'll ask for more if we need it."

Beckett braced his hands against the counter near Charlie. "I farmed out what I could, pushed back what I couldn't hand off to someone else, and have put out the word I'm not taking on any new clients right now," Beckett said, referring to his private security firm in D.C.

Like Beck, Marz was self-employed, too, doing computer-security consulting. "Same thing," Marz said. "I finished the two most time-sensitive projects I had on my plate the other night, and let everyone else know I'm off the grid for a while."

Charlie rubbed his good hand over his messy blond hair. "Shit. I've got some people probably wondering where I am," he said. "I need to send some emails today. Oh." He looked around the group. "I need to get my laptops from Becca's basement."

Nick frowned. "Tell me where they are, and I'll run over and get them later. But as far as the world is concerned, you're a missing person. Until we figure more of this out, maybe it's better to leave it that way."

"Oh?" Charlie rubbed his palm over his forehead. "If you say so, I will."

"Is it safe to go to my place?" Becca said, looking up at Nick.

"To stay? Probably not." Not after the place had been

tossed twice in the past week. "But a quick in and out should be fine. I'll be careful," he said, kissing Becca's hair.

"How 'bout you, E?" Marz said.

Shane studied the guy. From one burdened man to another, he didn't think he was imagining that Easy looked like the weight of the world sat on his shoulders.

"Oh, uh. I've been working for my father, so it's cool." He twisted his paper napkin in his hands.

"Yeah? A family business?" Beckett said. "What is it?"

"Philly's largest auto parts dealer," he said in a flat voice.

Auto parts? Not exactly where Shane would've expected their weapons and explosives specialist to end up, but who was he to judge?

"Well, sounds like we're squared away for at least a little while," Marz said. "I'm getting back to it. When you people are done lollygagging, come over and let's make a plan."

"Lollygagging?" Beckett said, smirking. "Has anyone used that word since 1952?"

"I'm bringing it back, baby," Marz said, flicking Beckett the middle finger over his shoulder.

Jeremy entered just as Marz reached the door. "All set," Jer said, as he and Marz joined the group at the island. "We've got three brand-new beds ready to use upstairs." Jeremy headed to the kitchen and poured a cup of coffee.

"Thanks," Nick said. "Marz said Ike helped you."

"Yeah," Jeremy said, nodding. "Wanted to know if I was starting a harem. I just told him I wanted to rent the apartment furnished when it was done. He was cool."

"Okay," Becca said, tugging at the hem of Jer's shirt. "What's this one say?" *I put the long in schlong.* "Omigod, Jeremy." Everyone chuckled as Becca's face pinked.

Nick put his arm around her. "It's not his fault. My parents dropped him on his head when he was a baby."

Jeremy took a long pull from his mug. "Becca, you know you're way too sweet to be with my asshole brother, right?"

She shook her head. "Don't put me in the middle, you two." She grinned at Jer. "I have enough batter for a few more pancakes if you want some."

"Nah, I ate cereal earlier. Gotta watch my girlish figure."

Marz braced his hands on the counter. "Hey, Jer, I've been meaning to ask. What can you tell me about Ike and his motorcycle club?" Shane had been wondering this since that first day he'd admired Ike's bike.

"Why?" Jeremy asked.

"Can I be straight with you?" Marz asked.

"Of course," Jeremy said, frowning. "What's up?"

"There are social clubs and outlaw clubs, right?" Marz said. "Most of the OMCs started in the sixties, real anti-establishment types. Most of them provide their members a livelihood via some criminal activity—drugs, guns, prostitution, gambling, you name it." Shane's gut sank at the description. Man, the last thing they needed was a fight on another front.

Jeremy nodded, his expression darkening, like he knew where Marz was going with this.

"The Raven Riders are in the Maryland gang report Becca's friend gave us last week, Jer. They're outlaws. So I need to know if he represents a liability or a threat in our own house, so to speak. Hell, for all we know, the Riders could be in bed with Church." Marz looked from Jeremy to Nick and back again.

Damn, wouldn't that be a gagglefuck?

Jeremy crossed his arms. "Ike's as good as they come. I've known him for seven years. Never brings any trouble to Hard Ink. And I've met some of his friends from the club, too. Seem like good guys."

Nick nodded. "I agree."

Marz shifted feet, like maybe his leg was bothering him. The guy was so competent on his prosthesis that you could almost forget he wore it. As Marz grimaced and shifted again, it occurred to Shane that maybe all wasn't as copasetic in Marz's world as it seemed. The thought sank through his gut. "They may be, Jer. I'm not questioning that. Just saying we have to be hyperaware of who knows about us."

"Okay," Jeremy said. "That's fair."

"In fact, let's take a look-see right now," Marz said, pulling his iPhone from his pocket. After a minute, he said, "Looks like the Raven Riders are associated with the Green Valley Speedway west of the city?"

Jeremy peered down at the screen. "Yeah. The main club's out there. I've been to a few stock car races. They also have drag racing and motocross."

"The Raven Riders own a speedway?" Shane asked. That was big business. Question was, what were the activities that had landed them in that gang report?

"It's cool," Jeremy said, nodding.

"So, if the club's twenty miles from here, what does Ike do in the city?" Marz asked, still scrolling through the page on his phone.

Jeremy shrugged. "I don't know, man. He works for me. Told you, his club business doesn't interfere here. But, I get it, look into them more if you like, just keep it discreet for Ike's sake."

"Can do," Marz said, nodding. Shane was glad Jeremy and Nick had no reservations about the guy, but he couldn't help agreeing with Marz that, right now, they couldn't be cautious enough.

For the next thirty minutes, they hashed out what they

did and didn't know. And damn if that list wasn't lopsided as hell—and not in their favor. One thing they did know was that there was going to be another delivery tomorrow night. So once again they were in need of the when and where, which put Marz back on surveillance duty for the next twelve to twenty-four.

"Maybe Crystal could be useful with the details again?" Marz suggested, looking at Shane.

Aw, hell. How was he going to learn what she might know when the last time he saw her, she'd run away from him? But he owed his teammates—the ones standing around him and the ones cold in the ground—his best effort. "I'd be willing to ask what she's heard."

"Good. Because shy of that—"

The muffled ring of a cell phone sounded out.

"That's me," Shane said, fishing the cell from his pocket. Relief and excitement shot through him, at once easing the tension in his shoulders and spiking his heart rate. "Speaking of . . . it's Crystal." Three minutes and a short, awkward conversation later, Shane had the answer to his question. "I'm meeting her in thirty," he said.

Shane couldn't help but pin a lot of hope on this meeting. Hope that he could ensure her safety by convincing her to stay with him at Hard Ink. Hope that he could assist their mission by learning about the second delivery. Hope that that delivery would provide more answers to help them right the wrongs they'd all suffered.

And, goddamnit all, they were overdue for a little sunshine and good luck.

Chapter 18

*C*rystal stood outside the coffee shop tucked into the corner of the strip mall and hugged herself. Despite never coming all the way down to the blue-collar burbs of Brooklyn Park and standing halfway behind a cement column supporting the overhanging awning, she felt exposed and vulnerable. But that was probably just because she was taking charge of her life—for once—and doing something way outside her comfort zone.

Asking for help. From Shane McCallan.

Looking up at the cloudy morning sky, Crystal forced herself to take a deep breath and calm down.

She was okay. Jenna was okay. Everything was okay.

Crystal pulled the phone Shane gave her from her purse to check the time. She'd never carried it on her before, but since they were meeting, she wanted him to be able to reach her if something came up or he was running late, which he wasn't. Yet. She sighed and dropped it back into her bag for the third time in as many minutes.

A big black pickup pulled into the parking lot and made its way to the back corner. Shane. Relief and excitement flooded through Crystal as she stepped out of the shadows and watched the truck park in the second row. Through the windshield, she saw Shane smile and wave.

She couldn't help but return the gestures. Smoothing her hands over the floral top she'd worn, another of her own creations, she felt feminine and even a little pretty. It had taken her four changes to figure out what to wear to see him. Stupid that she'd put so much thought into it. It wasn't like this was a date or anything.

As Shane threaded between the cars and crossed the lot, all Crystal could do was stare. At the determination in his sexy, powerful stride. At the way those jeans hung on his lean hips and came down around a pair of loosely tied brown boots. At the way the breadth of his shoulders pulled the slate blue button-down tight across his chest. Hands in his pockets, he gave her a crooked smile that made her belly flutter and her cheeks heat.

"Hey, darlin'," he said as he stepped up onto the sidewalk.

"Hi," she said.

The word was barely out of her mouth when Shane's arms came around her back and he pulled her in tight. Without thinking about it, her arms went around him, too. He felt warm and strong and reassuring.

"I missed you," he said.

She couldn't remember anyone other than Jenna ever telling her that before. A sense of fullness expanded inside her chest. "You did?" she asked, breathing in the masculine spice of his skin.

Shane pulled back enough to make eye contact. "Yeah. I did." Cupping her cheek in his big hand, he leaned down slowly, bright gray eyes looking into hers, and kissed her once, twice, three times. Small, warm presses of his lips to hers that left her breathless and yearning for more. Would he kiss her like this if he'd been disgusted by her back? He stepped away, pulling her from the thought, and took her hand in his. "You have time for a cup of coffee?"

She smiled, absolutely adoring how sweet and considerate he was. *That's not why you're here, Crystal. For the tenth time, this* isn't *a date.* Right. "Yeah. Just enough," she said.

"Come on, then." Holding her hand, he guided her to the door, which he held open for her. Then, with his hand on the small of her back, they stepped toward the counter and got in line behind a man ordering a tray of drinks to go.

"What would you like?" Shane asked.

"Coffee's fine," she said, then she caught him ogling the case of pastries and laughed. "I think the question is what would *you* like?"

His gaze swung from the treats to her face, and his eyes flashed hot. "I'm looking at her." Crystal's heart stopped, then took off at a sprint. *He . . . would like . . . me?* Shane winked and said, "But for right this moment, I might settle for that big peach muffin." He rubbed his stomach. "I skipped breakfast and could eat a horse."

"Better get two, then," she said.

"Aw, you're gonna go and spoil me talking like that." Smiling, he put his arm around her shoulders and squeezed her against his side.

"Can I help you?" the pretty brunette behind the counter asked. The woman smiled at them both and was plenty polite to Crystal as she placed her order, but the clerk was so openly smitten with Shane it was almost funny. He joked with Crystal, tried to talk her into a pastry, insisted on paying the bill, and rubbed her shoulder while they waited, never seeming to notice the young woman's obvious admiration. He probably didn't even realize he'd done something special in that moment, but his actions made Crystal feel respected in a way she never felt when she was around Bruno. Hell, Bruno had no qualms at all about blatantly checking out other women when they went out together. Which wasn't often.

Enough about Bruno. Enjoy the moment. There won't be many more of them.

They retrieved their drinks and Shane's softball-sized muffin and went to the little bar at the side to fix their coffee. Two creams and two sugars for her, three sugars for him. She smiled when she realized he was paying attention to how she took it.

She could get used to a man who treated her this way. *Just don't get used to* this *man.*

Shane led them toward the back of the small shop and paused beside the last table. "This okay?"

"Yeah," she said, slipping into the booth. He slid in opposite her, his long legs spilling into her side under the table. Crystal sipped her coffee and peeked at him above her cup.

God, he was so freaking gorgeous. Nice. Gentle. Playful. The list of things she liked about him went on and on. It made her chest fill with a pressure it surely couldn't hold.

"You look pretty in that shirt," he said. His kind words and friendly gaze made her squirm.

"Oh, uh, thanks," she said, not offering up that she'd made it. Sewing was one of the few pre-Bruno parts of herself she still possessed, and she felt protective of it, probably overly so. Grappling for a different topic of conversation, she blurted, "How did last night go?" Immediately, she worried she'd made a mistake when something dark and pained flashed through his expression.

"Some good, some not so good," he said, shaking his head and looking down at his muffin. "Turns out Church's people have another meeting sometime Friday. Maybe things will go better then."

"Oh." She *had* made a mistake. *Way to go, Crystal.* Not that he seemed angry that she'd asked, but he definitely seemed upset. Had she heard anything about Friday night? She didn't think so. "Maybe I can help again," she said, wanting to bring back his happiness.

He looked up at her, and the angle made her realize how long his eyelashes were. *Her Pretty Boy.* And he really was. "If you hear something, that's great. But don't do anything to put yourself at risk. We'll figure it out."

She nodded, but her mind spun on what she might be able to do. After all, it was only fair since she planned to ask him for help. "Here," she said as she pulled a chunk of the muffin top free. "Open up."

His face brightened, and he smiled. "Yes, ma'am." He licked his lips and opened his mouth.

And the swipe of his tongue scrambled Crystal's brain. She chuffed out a nervous laugh and went with it even though her heart raced and her hand shook. Leaning across the table, she placed the muffin on Shane's tongue. And she didn't think she was imagining the heat in his gaze as he chewed slowly, like he was savoring it, and made these little appreciative noises in the back of his throat.

"More," he said.

Rolling her eyes but secretly pleased with this game, Crystal broke off another piece and brought it to his lips. When he opened, she popped it in, but he leaned forward and caught the tips of her fingers with his lips when he closed again. She laughed.

She recalled the dinner with Bruno the night before and . . . *God* . . . there was no freaking comparison. Not once in four years had she ever felt comfortable or free enough to be herself at his side. And the more she thought about it, the more she realized she might not know exactly who the real Crys—the real *Sara*—was anymore.

All she knew was that she greatly preferred the version of herself who came out around Shane, the one who laughed and joked and occasionally even got up the courage to do what she wanted, take what she wanted.

"You taste good," he said, the smile clear on his face even as he took a long drink of coffee.

"You're a terrible flirt, aren't you?" It wasn't a complaint. Crystal found it sexy and fun and flattering.

He winked. "You bring out the best in me, sweetness."

She ducked her chin, hoping to hide the heat she suspected was pinking her cheeks again. Sighing, she pressed the button on her phone to check the time. Just as she thought.

"You said you had *just enough* time for coffee," he said. "You have to be somewhere?"

Crystal nodded and brushed her hands against her jeans. "Unfortunately. I got called in to work a luncheon. I should leave in twenty minutes."

Shane twisted his lips, like maybe he was disappointed. "Okay. What did you want to talk about?" he asked, taking another bite of muffin.

"Right," she said, tucking her loose hair behind her ears. She grappled for the right words, but finally decided to go with the simplest and most direct. "I need your help."

He reached across the table and covered one of her hands with his. "Name it."

It was that easy? Sure, he'd offered—several times. But she was so unused to people being there for her that she realized she hadn't fully believed him until this moment. "Um, okay. Something happened last night and—"

"What? Are you okay? Jenna?" A storm rolled in across Shane's expression, and his gaze roamed over her face, her bare arms below the sleeves of her top.

She laid her free hand atop his. "We're both okay, but I realize that we need to start planning a way out." Instinctively, she lowered her voice and looked over her shoulder. "Now. I thought we could wait, but . . ." Crystal shook her head.

An intensity she didn't understand poured into Shane's gaze. "I think that's smart."

She might be stupid for asking him this, but she figured anyone skilled and savvy enough to take on the Church gang might know what she needed to do. "I know this is a lot to ask, and I know you might not know anything about this."

"What? Just ask. If I know, I'll help. If I don't, I'll figure it out with you."

With? Not *for,* but with. Like they'd do it together. Like maybe they were partners. She pushed the wishful thoughts away. "Do you know how I can get fake IDs for me and Jenna? And maybe some other paperwork, too?"

An emotion she couldn't read passed over his expression. "Documentation for a new identity?"

"Yeah," she said. "Exactly. Whatever that entails."

Shane frowned. "I think it's great you're looking for a way out, Crystal. Truly. But . . ." Shane seemed to struggle for words. "I was hoping . . ." He closed his eyes, gave a rueful laugh, and tugged his hand through his hair, making the lighter blond ends all messy. Totally sexy. "You'd think I was a tongue-tied teenager asking his girl to the prom."

Crystal smiled, but she was totally bewildered by what he was trying to say. "I don't understand."

He leaned forward and grasped both her hands in both of his. "Come stay with me. I have plenty of room for both of you. The guys you met at Confessions that night are what's left of my Special Forces team. We're sharing a building right now. We could keep you safe. Both of you. You wouldn't have to run."

For a long moment, Crystal's brain couldn't process what he'd said. Stay with him? And his—*wait*—his Special Forces team? Because it would be safer. Right. She shook her head. "I couldn't impose you on and a bunch of others like that. I know you have a lot going on. And I want to get Jenna settled somewhere for real."

Shane squeezed her hands. "It wouldn't be an imposition at all. You and Jenna wouldn't be the only women there, if that's what you're worried about. My best friend's girlfriend lives there, and Becca's great. She'd love you." His gaze grew more intense. "This is . . . I need you to know . . . I don't have any expectations here. I'm offering you two a safe harbor, no strings attached."

Torn, Crystal shook her head again. The offer was too much, too tempting, too . . . she didn't even know. But it made it hard to sit still in the booth. It seemed like the kind of thing she'd let herself believe in, then, *poof!*, it would just disappear, and she'd feel abandoned and disappointed. And stupid for having believed in the first place.

It wasn't that she didn't trust Shane, exactly, because she did. She wouldn't be here if she didn't. But when you learned you couldn't even trust your own father, it was near impossible to believe a man she'd known less than a week—no matter how good-hearted he seemed—would do something that big and amazing for her.

Bruno seemed safe once, too . . .

And even though her rational mind knew she was comparing apples to machine guns, the thought wound its way around her brain until it rooted deep.

All of a sudden, panic bubbled up in her belly, and she regretted opening her mouth. "I'm sorry. I shouldn't have

bothered you," she said, grabbing her purse, scooting to
the edge of the bench seat, and rising. She'd figure out
another way to get what they needed.

Shane flew out of his seat and blocked her exit with
his big body. "Don't run away again. Please." Slowly, he
reached for her hand, like he knew she was on the verge
of losing it and didn't want to do something to push her
over the edge. "I didn't mean to pressure you. I'll help
you. However you need. Just know staying with me is a
standing offer. Okay?"

Crystal looked into Shane's steel gray eyes—really
looked—and saw nothing but sincerity. She blew out a
shaky breath. "Okay."

"Will you stay and talk? For just a few more minutes?"
he asked.

Her muscles relaxed as she shifted her knees back
under the table, and Shane returned to his side.

"Got a pen?" he asked, grabbing a small stack of
brown napkins from the dispenser against the wall.
He accepted the ballpoint from her hand. In rapid-fire
fashion, he asked her a series of questions about her and
Jenna: fake name—Jessica for Jenna and Amanda for
Crystal, because another fake name was just what she
wanted, birth date, hair color, eye color, city of birth,
blood type, social security numbers, and more. When he
was done, he folded the napkins and slipped them into
the pocket of his jeans. "If I forgot anything, I'll let you
know. But that ought to allow me to get started."

"Okay. Thank you," she said. "How long do you think
it'll take?"

"Not sure. Probably not long. Let me confirm when I
find some sources and know more."

"Of course," she said. And though he was saying all the
right things and helping her, she couldn't shake the feeling that she'd made him unhappy. Or maybe sad. And it

put a rock in her stomach that the coffee wasn't helping. "I'm sorry I don't have more time today."

"Maybe later?" Shane said, hope in his voice.

"After this lunch, I have to go back five 'til eleven," she said.

A weighted pause sat between them. Crystal longed for the playfulness of before.

Shane nodded. "I'll walk you out." Outside, he took her hand again and led her to her old red truck. The car beside hers had parked crooked, forcing her and Shane close beside her driver's door. Then Shane stepped closer still, until he had her pressed up against the steel made warm by the late-April air. "My offer of help is unconditional. Remember that." She nodded, her heart beating fast against her breastbone. He kissed her. The softness only lasted for a moment, then it was like something snapped inside him—snapped inside *both* of them.

Caressing her cheek, Shane's tongue swept into her mouth, exploring, tasting, twining with her own. His other hand stroked her long hair, while her hands found his waist and burrowed under the untucked shirt to find the bare, hard muscle of his stomach. He groaned into their kiss as he pursued her again and again, kissing, nipping, sucking on her lips. Intense but gentle, like he was a man with an unending appetite and the patience to match. Against her stomach, the long length of his erection hardened, sending Crystal's heart into a fast sprint.

It was just a kiss. But it was the kind of kiss that made a woman feel claimed, desired, powerful. And even as he thrilled her, he was the kind of man who made her feel safe—no part of her doubted that if she said *stop,* he'd be off her in an instant. His clean scent, lean muscles, and gentle touch combined to make it impossible to forget it was *Shane* who held her in his arms. And it all allowed Crystal to do something she'd never done before—enjoy, want, and wish for more. Her nipples tightened, and her core clenched, and Crystal would've given anything to have had the afternoon free, then to have had the courage to spend it with him continuing what they'd started in the middle of this cloud-covered parking lot.

Shane pulled away, his forehead against hers, his harsh breaths caressing her wet lips. "You better go," he said, looking at her like going was the last thing he wanted her to do. He retreated a step and gestured for her to move to his other side, then he opened the door for her.

Hating the distance between them, Crystal climbed into her truck and reached for the door, but Shane leaned into the breach.

"I think about you and I worry about you all the time, Crystal. And it's not just because I want to help you. And it's not just because I want to protect you. I care about you. A lot. No matter what, don't forget that."

I feel the same way, she thought. *And probably even more.* But she couldn't give voice to those thoughts. That would make them all too real. And after years of ignoring and boxing up her emotions, she was bad at feeling them, scared of admitting them, and worse at expressing them.

"'Bye," she whispered, instead. As she started the truck and watched Shane walk away in her side-view mirror, she had the biggest sense of having just lost a once-in-a-lifetime opportunity. Silly, really. They'd be seeing each other again. And he'd agreed to help, so she should be happy.

Right? Right. So, then, why wasn't she?

THE BUSINESS LUNCH was just that—a liquor-laden schmoozefest of three-piece suits trying to impress some mucketymuck by slumming it at a strip club. Harmless and good-tipping. The perfect combination.

They'd finished eating a half hour ago, and Crystal was

keeping them well lubricated with top-dollar, top-shelf labels as the girls danced.

Despite the fact that the nine of them were relatively easy to handle and that her tip escalated with every new drink order, Crystal was itching for the men to leave. Because something had taken Bruno and the rest of the Apostles off-site until later this afternoon. This was her chance to try to help Shane the way he was helping her. She spent time alone in Bruno's office all the time. Nobody thought anything of it.

So she had a very rare, very important window of time.

But she couldn't do anything until these guys decided to return to their upper-middle-class lives on the other side of town.

Twenty minutes later, the older man at the head of the table finally pulled out his platinum credit card and handed it to her to settle the bill. *Thank God.*

At the register near the bar, Walker gave her a smile. "They treat you okay?" he asked.

"Tame as kittens," she said with a grin. And then she thought, *I'm going to miss you, Walker.* There weren't many people she would miss from this life, but Walker might be one. He'd always been nice to her, looked out for her—looked out for all the girls, really. As ordinary as that seemed, though, it had been the exception rather than the rule in her life.

Until Shane.

Crystal waited for the credit-card slip to print and wondered who else she'd miss. Howie, the food-and-beverages manager, was another guy around here who'd looked out for her when he could, or offered her cautious words of advice when he couldn't. But really . . . that was about it. Her feelings for the rest of the people she knew here were either neutral or negative. It was a sad testament to how much she'd been floating through her life the last few years.

But that was about to change.

The printer chugged out the receipt. Crystal placed it inside a leather folder with the man's card and returned to the table. "Thank you very much, gentlemen. Come again," she said with a smile and a wink that earned her a few appreciative chuckles.

When they were gone, she set about clearing the table as she would any other day. No faster. No slower. Back at the register, she opened the billfold and nearly shrieked with happiness—the men had not only left her a huge tip but they'd left it in cash. A little of her regret at not being able to spend the afternoon with Shane melted away. At least the time spent had been worthwhile. Quickly, she folded and slipped one of the three fifty-dollar bills into her skirt, securing it with the band of her panties on her hip, then she handed the billfold to Walker. The normal process for accounting for her cash tips so Church could take his cut. Walker accepted it with a quiet nod and Crystal swallowed her usual resentment toward losing income she'd earned for a debt she hadn't created.

"See you in a few hours, Walker," she called, forcing normalcy into her voice. With lunch out of the way, she could put her plan to help Shane into action. Which explained why her heart had lurched into high gear. "I'm on at five."

He pushed his dark hair back off his face. "Right on. See ya."

Taking a deep breath, she made for the dressing room and quickly changed into her street clothes. She hadn't had time to pick up Jenna's prescription from the pharmacy this morning, so she had to get it and drop it at the apartment before her evening shift began. And that wasn't an errand she could do in her uniform.

Making sure she had everything, she left the dressing room. But instead of turning right to head down the hall to the back door, she turned left, came to the secured door to the senior office suite, and punched in the key code.

The metallic *click* caused another spike in her heart rate. Blood rushed loud behind her ears. Head down, pace normal, she made her way to Bruno's office like she had so many times before. She often waited in his office for him to take her home after a shift, so no one would think twice about her being there. Nothing unusual here. Nothing going on. At least, that's what she wanted any security cameras that might be tracking her movements in here to see.

Just docile, submissive, trustworthy Crystal hanging out in her longtime boyfriend's office.

Once she closed herself inside Bruno's workspace, she relaxed. She knew for a fact that none of the Apostles' offices were monitored by camera. That way they could keep their drugs and their women and any other unusual proclivities private. They'd earned that right through many years of working in the Church gang. It was a sign of trust and respect.

She wanted to be long gone before two o'clock, just in case Bruno got back earlier than expected. That didn't give her long. Five minutes. Ten, tops. Problem was, she had no idea what she might be looking for.

Coming around Bruno's side of the desk, she carefully sorted through the papers on top, first observing how they'd been situated before she touched them. Schedules, spreadsheets, inventory lists. Nothing that looked interesting. Then again, Bruno wouldn't leave sensitive documents sitting out on top his desk, would he?

Crystal sat in his desk chair and pulled out the drawers one by one. On the right side, office supplies filled the top two drawers and dozens of keys on rings suspended from little bars filled the third. Shifting to the left side, Crystal found the big drawer on the bottom largely empty, the middle one filled with various kinds of medicine, and the top one filled with more paperwork. She shuffled through it, and the label on a folder caught her attention.

Charles and Becca Merritt

Becca. Hadn't Shane said his friend's girlfriend was named Becca? It could totally be a coincidence. The name wasn't *that* unusual. Still, Crystal turned the papers on top the folder sideways to mark its spot in the pile and slid it out.

Maybe a dozen pages of information sat within. Home and work addresses, surveillance pictures . . . She paused on a close-up of a blond-haired man looking over his shoulder. Crystal had seen this man. Bruised, bloodied, and bandaged, yes. But she had no question that this was the guy Shane had rescued from Confessions last weekend.

That was all she needed to see. Rather than take the time to read everything, Crystal fished her iPhone from her purse so roughly the bag fell to the floor, but she couldn't worry about that right now. She opened the camera app and took shots of every page. She repeated that process with another folder labeled *Merritt* and a third labeled *Nunya,* whatever that meant, because it had been sandwiched between the other two. With each shot, her adrenaline surged until she was shaking so bad she found herself having to take multiple pictures because the images blurred. Then she returned everything to where she'd found it.

Time's up.

Crystal wasn't the least bit sure she'd found anything useful, and nothing about Friday night, but she'd tried. Damnit. She could only hope there was something here that would help Shane the way he was helping her. Rushing around to the far side of the desk, Crystal cursed when she saw the contents of her purse spilled across the floor.

She dropped to her knees, grabbed her things, and stuffed them messily back in the bag. With one last look to make sure nothing appeared out of place, Crystal forced a deep, calming breath and opened the door. The outer office was quiet, still. They hadn't returned yet.

Walking casually was absolute torture since her muscles nearly screamed with the desire to bolt out of there and never look back. But that would raise immediate suspicion. With four weeks left before they could go anywhere, she had to keep playing her part.

The outside air tasted like freedom. The farther she got from Bruno's office, the more assured she was that she hadn't been detected, and the easier it was to *be* normal, not just *act* it.

Which was a good thing since she had a list of normal things to do in the next three hours before she returned. Pharmacy, a quick trip to the grocery store, then home to drop it all off. And at some point, she needed a good ten or fifteen minutes to text Shane all the photographs she'd taken so she could delete them from her phone. No way she could go back to Confessions with those images on there. She'd be a nervous wreck all night. Bruno had been known to thumb through her text messages (entirely from him and Jenna) and emails (almost all advertisements, Nigerian bank-type scams, and penis-enhancement treatments) from time to time.

So she better get to it.

SHANE'S GUT WAS tied up in knots because he'd botched the ask to get Crystal to safety at Hard Ink.

Sitting at Marz's desk for the past ninety minutes, he'd run his choice of words through his mind again and again and he'd come to one dumbfounding conclusion—he'd never made it clear that he *wanted* her here with him. Not because she was in trouble, not because he could protect her, but because he was a man wanting a woman and a chance.

Fucking idjit.

Since Marz had pulled a string of nearly all-nighters, they'd convinced him to go get some sleep. But first, he'd shown Shane how to run the Port Authority registries queries he'd been working on to try to identify any relevant businesses of interest at the marine terminal. Shane was more than willing to help, even if his brain was slowly oozing out his ears in boredom.

Next to him, Jeremy sketched on a big sheet of paper while he waited for the mug-shot research he was doing to produce results. Shane leaned closer. The guy was talented, that was for damn sure. The design was of a big tree full of leaves, but at the top, the leaves turned into blackbirds taking flight and baring the uppermost branches. The birds were dynamic, and the whole image was powerful and melancholy.

"For a client?" Shane asked.

"Yeah," he said, not looking up from the drawing.

"Maybe I'll get you to do me sometime." Shane hadn't gotten a new piece in a while, but he'd always liked the feeling of the needles crawling across his skin.

Jeremy's face slid into a slow grin, and his tongue flicked at the piercing on the side of his lip. "*Do* you?"

"You know what I mean, asshole," Shane said, chuckling. His cell rang, and he grasped it off the desk. Crystal. Maybe she'd changed her mind about staying with him. "Hey. Everything okay?"

Silence.

"Crystal?"

The line went dead.

Shane redialed, but the call went straight to voice mail. Probably just a spot of bad reception. No doubt she'd call back in a few.

"Everything okay?" Jeremy asked.

"Yeah. She just dropped me."

Five minutes passed. Ten. Tension settled into Shane's shoulders, making his muscles tight and his joints stiff. He rolled the shoulder with the healing gunshot wound, but it didn't help.

He dialed again. Straight to voice mail.

As he stared at his phone's screen, Shane's intuition shot up a red flag.

Glad Marz had shown him how to turn on the audio feeds from Confessions and Crystal's apartment, Shane minimized the screen with the registries query—now at 42 percent. Almost three o'clock, so Crystal was probably done with the luncheon but not yet scheduled to be back for her evening shift. Where would she go?

"Mind if I play this on the speakers, or would you prefer I get some headphones?"

"I don't mind," Jeremy said, frowning up at Shane's computer. "What is that?"

"Crystal's apartment." Music played in the background, like maybe a door separated it from the listening device picking it up. No voices. No sounds of movement.

Another ten minutes passed, and Shane dialed one more time. Same result. And now his gut was calling an outright foul.

Something's not right. Why the hell hadn't he asked for the number to her iPhone? The thought had passed through his mind whenever she'd checked the cell for the time. But Crystal was skittish, and her nerves had been out in force during some of their conversation. He hadn't wanted to add to her stress by asking for it.

Shane glanced at the speakers and crossed his arms tight over his chest. This was going to make him crazy. He shoved out of the chair. "I'm going to go find her."

Jeremy's pen fell still, and his expression was all concern. "You really think something's wrong? I could come with."

"Appreciate that, man. But stay here and keep at this—we need the data you're producing. I'll grab one of the guys."

Jeremy nodded, disappointment flashing across his face. "Good luck. I hope everything's okay."

Shane cut across the gym, planning out a strategy. Should he go to Confessions and look for her truck first? Hell, why hadn't he put a GPS tracker on the vehicle? Rookie oversight. The thought had him doing a one-eighty and marching back to Marz's desk. Beckett had brought tracking devices with him, so Shane knew they had them. It was the work of a few minutes to find the box in which they were stored, then he took off again.

"Shane?" Jeremy called across the gym. "Wait. Come here," he said.

The growing alarm in the man's voice hauled Shane back to the computer, back to the feed pouring through the speakers.

"I want this place searched top to bottom," came a bitter male voice. One Shane recognized. Bruno, with that same suspicious, paranoid tone he'd had the night Shane had been there.

Shane's gut twisted.

Something crashed. A scream.

"What the hell are you doing—" Another scream. "Get the fuck off me—" The sickening sound of a slap or a hit. The voice was so warped by fear and anger, Shane couldn't tell if it belonged to Crystal or Jenna, but it didn't matter.

"Jesus Christ," Jeremy said. "What the hell are we listening to?"

Shane didn't stick around to answer. Because he knew. That call he'd gotten hadn't been from Crystal. Somehow, Bruno Ashe had gotten ahold of the burn phone he'd given her. And Shane's calls had given the scumbag all the ammunition he'd needed to suspect Crystal of—what? Disloyalty? Cheating? Lying? Any of the above. *All* of the above.

He tore across the gym and into the Rixeys' apartment. Much as impatience and urgency ripped through his gut, Shane needed backup, because Bruno hadn't been alone. Shane's entrance was so abrupt that everyone froze and looked at him.

"Shit's going down at Crystal's right now. I need you," he said to the lot of them.

The room exploded into activity. Within three minutes, the whole team was armed and loaded into Beckett's SUV. Within four, they were on the road to Crystal's.

"Call Jer and see what he's hearing," Shane said over his shoulder to Nick.

Rixey dialed immediately. "Jer? Put your phone up to the computer speaker," he said in tight voice. A moment of silence passed, and then sounds poured out of Nick's phone. Shouts. Crashes. Screams. Crying.

Nausea rolled through Shane's gut. He couldn't lose Crystal. He couldn't go through that again.

Beckett drove like his house was on fire. The others checked and double-checked their weapons.

It was a fifteen-minute trip under the best of circumstances. Except, it was after three o'clock, and Crystal lived on the eastern side of the city. There was every likelihood they were going to run into some early-rush-hour interference. Sonofafuckingbitch.

Why the hell hadn't he laid it all out there when he'd

been with Crystal this morning? If he'd handled that conversation right, she and her sister would be with him right now. They'd be safe.

And Crystal would know that Shane loved her. That he was *in love* with her. The fact that she might never hear that from his lips—no. He couldn't even entertain that possibility.

A yelp and a groan. A low, sadistic laugh.

Instead, one of them was being terrorized by a man Shane absolutely burned to kill with his bare hands. When he and Bruno finally met face-to-face, Shane was going to bathe in the bastard's blood and dance on the dust of his bones.

Suddenly, the noise died down from Nick's speaker. Shane turned in his seat. "Did you drop it?"

Pressing a button, Nick examined the screen and shook his head. "No, just got quiet there."

And that's when Shane heard words that turned his blood to ice. "Bring her. We're gonna have a little fun."

Chapter 19

$\mathcal{D}$riving into her apartment complex, Crystal pressed the button on her phone to check the time. The clock on her truck's dashboard had stopped long ago. Quarter 'til four. She should have just enough time to drop off Jenna's prescription and the three bags of groceries, and to text Shane the pictures so she could delete them from her phone.

As she parked, scattered raindrops fell on her windshield. She peered up at the gray skies and hoped the rain held out long enough for her to get inside. Looping the bags over one wrist, Crystal grabbed the meds and her purse with the other and heaved out of the truck.

Times like this, she really wished they lived on the ground floor. She hefted her load up the steps and juggled everything as she worked to thread her key into the lock and push the door open with her foot.

"Hey, Jen, I'm home," Crystal called. "I brought your medicine." And just in time, too, since she only had one pill left.

Crystal rounded the door from the entranceway—and froze.

The apartment was a wreck.

"Jenna!" she screamed, dropping everything and sprinting through the debris covering the floor. Books. Broken glass. Soft pillows ripped open. "Jenna!" Something caught Crystal's foot and she tripped into the doorway of her sister's room.

Wreckage covered the floor there, too. A bookshelf had toppled over.

Oh, God, no. Oh, God. Oh, God, no.

Dizziness and nausea threatened, but Jenna wasn't there. Crystal whirled into her own room. The damage was worse. Bedclothes scattered. Mattress tossed and torn. Every drawer overturned—though the dresser remained in place, her brain noted. Her closet almost emptied.

Still no Jenna.

Bruno. Bruno did this. She couldn't possibly know that, but she did.

"Oh, God. What do I do? What do I do? Think," she said to herself in a fast stream.

Shane. She needed Shane.

Blood rushed through her ears as she retraced her steps into the living room. Her purse lay amid the discarded bags of groceries. With shaking hands she opened it— wallet, iPhone, makeup, lip balm. Where was Shane's phone? She sorted through the debris on the floor, but nothing.

Had she left it in the truck?

All at once, the image of the spilled contents of her purse on the floor of Bruno's office flashed into her mind's eye.

She gasped a hard breath, and goose bumps ripped across her skin. "Oh, no. No, no, no." Crystal couldn't be that unlucky, could she? She couldn't have done something that led to *this*. But the more she thought about it, the more she worried she had—the more she *knew* she had. A sob tore up her throat, and Crystal smothered it with her hand, feeling streams of wetness on her face.

Footsteps.

Crystal's gaze flew to the apartment door, still open a few inches from when she'd come in, her hands too full to close it.

Whispered voices. More footsteps. Multiple people. Coming closer.

Had Bruno been watching for her truck? Waiting for her to come home? Had he returned to finish what he'd started?

Crystal lunged toward the door just as movement passed behind it. With all her might, she slammed it closed, but something kept it from latching—a body pressing from the other side.

She cried out and dug her feet into the floor, pushing harder. The minute she let up, her opponent would come flying in. He'd be right on top of her.

"Crystal. Crystal? It's Shane."

The words drilled through the loud buzz in her ears. "Shane? *Shane?*" Heart thundering, she let go of the door and stepped back.

He was right there. With four other men, all of them armed, weapons drawn, expressions wary, braced for battle. His arms around her were too strong, too tight, absolutely perfect. "Jesus," he said, pulling her to the side so the rest of the men could enter.

A sob ripped out of her, smothered against his chest. Movement and voices came from behind her, but Crystal couldn't think about any of that. Shane's heat, his scent, the cotton of his button-down against her face—that was the universe of information she could handle in that moment.

Jenna.

Crystal wrenched back. "Jenna's gone," she said, her voice warped by tears and fear and grief. "I think Bruno has her."

Something terrifying appeared in Shane's steel gray eyes. Sympathy. Regret. Confirmation. "He does," Shane said in a low, cautious voice.

Confusion scattered her thoughts. "Wait," she said. "How—"

"Clear," came a male voice from the back of the apartment.

"Clear," another man said.

"Clear," came a third. "Apartment's empty."

"Wait!" she yelled as the men spoke.

Five pairs of male eyes swung to her, and the room went silent.

Shaking her head, Crystal met Shane's gaze. "How do you know? How do you *know* he has her?" Shane heaved a breath and his shoulders fell. "*How do you know?*"

"I bugged your apartment. That first night I was here."

The words came to her as if through a tunnel, distant and tinny. "What?" He'd been spying on her? She retreated a step, pulling herself away from his touch. Shane spied on her . . . just like Bruno. "You . . ." She shook her head again, her mind so badly wanting to reject what he'd said.

"This damage wasn't quiet. A neighbor has got to have called the police," the huge man said, looking from Shane to a dark-haired man she hadn't met. Crystal couldn't remember the big guy's name, though they'd met at Confessions. "We should relocate this conversation."

She pushed on like the man hadn't spoken. "Why would

you do that? I helped you. I risked myself for you. I risked Jenna." Static roared inside her head and white-hot rage filled her chest. Lunging, she swung her fists at Shane. "It's your fault this happened!"

"Crystal. Stop. I'm sorry," he said, taking her blows. "I know. Just stop, you're gonna hurt yourself." His voice was tight, sad, desperate as he caught her wrists in his hands.

"I thought I could trust you," she said, not meaning to voice the thought but not regretting it one bit when Shane flinched.

"You can. I promise."

"Oh, you *promise*? Well, then." She threw up her arms, her heart breaking twice over. First, for the loss of Jenna, and second for the loss of the *idea* she'd had of Shane. How stupid she'd been. How reckless. And now the only person in the world she loved—and who loved her—had been kidnapped . . . and who knew what else. Tears squeezed her throat until it was hard to breathe. "I did everything you asked of me. You didn't have to make me . . ." *Fall in love with you.*

"I will explain. Later." Shane grasped her by the arms and looked her dead in the eyes. "I know I fucked up, but those bugs were here in part so I could help if something like this happened. We heard Bruno bust his way in here. That's how we knew. We tried to get here in time to save Jenna." He swallowed hard, like failing to do so cut him. Deep. "We tried. But right now, we have to get you out of here."

"I'm not—"

"Crystal, you don't have a choice. Bruno will come back. But where we live is safe. And we can figure out how to get Jenna back."

Get Jenna . . . back? They could do that?

For the first time in long minutes, the chaos in her mind

subsided. The rage dulled. The hurt faded away. A new image flashed into Crystal's mind—Shane and the dark-haired man hauling the injured blond guy up the steps and out of Confessions. "How?"

His thumbs rubbed gently over her arms where he held her. "I don't know yet. That's what we need to figure out. And we shouldn't waste any time."

Saving Jenna was all that mattered. Crystal nodded and followed Shane to the door, only darting back to retrieve her purse and her sister's prescription. *Oh, God. She doesn't have any medicine with her.* But Crystal couldn't think on that long, because the five men circled tight around her and guided her out the door, down the steps, and a short distance across the lot to a big SUV.

Crystal ended up in the backseat between Shane and a big, athletic-looking man with dark brown skin and an absolutely lethal expression on his face. Edward. The one who had guarded Jenna the night she'd come to the club.

When he caught her looking, he met her gaze, and his brown eyes were fierce. "We will do *everything* we can to get Jenna," he said, as the truck tore across the lot, the sound of the engine like a freight train.

The vow kept the worst of the panic at bay, but not all of it. Because she'd been held against her will by the Church gang. She knew what most of the worst-case scenarios looked like. Saw the reminder of it every day in the mirror. And her soul bled at the idea that she and Jenna would have any of that in common.

All her work. All her precautions. All the sacrifices Crystal had made to keep this very thing from happening. None of it had mattered. In the end, she hadn't kept Jenna safe. She hadn't kept her promise to their father.

The rough ride jostled her in the seat. No matter how hard she tried, she couldn't hold it together. A whimper caught in her throat, and hot lines of tears spilled from her eyes.

"Come here," Shane said in a low voice, lifting his arm around her shoulders and tilting her chin toward him with his other hand. "It's not okay right now. I know it's not. But it will be."

"We have to get her, Shane. We *have* to." She heard the pleading in her words and felt it pouring out of her eyes, and she wasn't ashamed to beg. Not for Jenna's life. "Please. I wouldn't be able to live if anything happened to her."

Shane nodded, and his expression was equal parts enraged and heartbroken, just like she felt. "I know," he said.

As the world raced by outside the windows of the SUV, his words rekindled her anger. "No, you don't. You *don't* know. You *can't* know what it's like to have your sister ripped away from you, and to have that be your fault!"

Shane grimaced like she'd punched him. An odd tension Crystal didn't understand filled the truck's cabin.

"Yeah, I do. I know exactly what that feels like." His soft declaration ratcheted the tension further. Crystal looked around at the other men, trying to figure it out, but they'd all turned away.

With deft flicks of his fingers, Shane unbuttoned the top of his shirt and tugged the left half to the side. His actions revealed the tattoo she'd asked about that night in his truck, the one she hadn't been able to make out and he'd said represented a sad memory. Crystal's stomach rolled as her gaze traced over the image of a winged broken heart stabbed through by a dagger.

Grief rolled into Shane's gaze. "When I was thirteen, my eight-year-old sister Molly disappeared from our house while I was babysitting her. I'd told her to leave me alone. The police searched actively for about three weeks, but the false leads that broke and rebroke my mother's heart went on for years. We never saw Molly again." Grasping Crystal's hand, he brought it against the warm, hard skin of his chest over his broken heart. "I understand," he said in a strangled voice, his eyes glassy.

"Oh," she said, his pain washing over her until it was hard to breathe—and harder to restrain herself from comforting him. "I'm sorry." Crystal threw her arms around Shane's neck and scrabbled into his lap. "I'm so, so sorry."

"So am I," he said against her hair. "But you have to know. I would lay down my life to make sure we get Jenna back."

Face-to-face, they held each other, whispering words of comfort and apology. Crystal had been so right and so wrong. Even if he'd done something he shouldn't have in bugging her apartment—and that still stung, Shane *was* a good man. She hadn't read him wrong. But Bruno Ashe? He was an evil piece of shit. "I didn't mean what I said," she rasped, needing him to know, to believe. "It's not your fault . . ."

Shane shook his head. "You were right that I invaded your privacy. And I'm sorry," he said, stroking her hair and wiping a tear with his thumb. "But I was so afraid for you that I justified what I did as being for your own good. I understand if you can't forgive me or trust me, but you have to at least know that I never meant any harm."

"I know," she said. "I believe you." Crystal buried her face in his neck and breathed him in. His scent, his heat, his strength grounded her, gave her what hope there was in this hopeless situation.

No, she had to believe there *was* hope. She simply refused to accept any other outcome.

Jenna had wanted to pack up and leave this morning. Crystal had been the one to urge caution. Thinking back to that conversation nearly broke her heart. They could've been gone by now, and Jenna would've been safe. So if she lost Jenna—when it was her carelessness in Bruno's office that had set off this whole chain of events, she knew one thing for sure.

Crystal would never, ever forgive herself.

SOUL-DEEP RELIEF FLOWED through Shane's blood as he held Crystal in his arms. She was a slight little thing, and soft. And her presence went a long way toward quieting the ancient grief and guilt always stalking around at the back of his mind.

Less than an hour before, terror that he'd never feel this with her again had gripped him all the way into his DNA.

The drive to her place had been sheer torture. His sprint across the parking lot and into her building had felt like wading through wet concrete. But the minute he'd seen her dart behind the door, knowing it was her because she'd worn the same shirt as earlier, Shane had been able to breathe again.

It was an incomplete relief. A hollow victory. Because they hadn't reached Jenna in time.

And now she was gone.

But Shane meant what he'd said to Crystal. If giving his life would restore Jenna's, he would make that sacrifice. He refused to let Crystal suffer what he had all these years.

Hopefully, it wouldn't come to that.

A bone-jarring rattle as they crossed railroad tracks at a fast clip. "I haven't seen a tail, have you?" Nick asked.

Beckett shook his head. "We're clean as a whistle."

Peering out the window of the SUV, Shane recognized the run-down landmarks of Hard Ink's neighborhood. They were almost home. Which was good, because the team needed to make plans, and he and Crystal needed some alone time to finish their conversation.

He hadn't thought twice about discussing his tragedy

in front of the guys. She'd needed to believe in his ability to understand what she was going through, and he'd been willing to do what it took to earn that belief. Simple as.

But Shane had more to say—a lot more. He hadn't said he'd understood just because he'd once been through the same thing. He'd said it because Crystal's pain was his pain, too.

Apparently, that was what happened when you fell in love.

Beckett guided the truck through the fence and into Hard Ink's lot. "We're here," Shane said.

"Okay," Crystal said, her voice weary and weak. Shane kissed her hair, willing to do anything to make this better for her.

"We've got company," Marz said from the front seat. Shane braced, peering over his friends' shoulders through the windshield. The biker dude who worked at Hard Ink had just stepped out the back door, helmet in hand.

"It's only Ike," Nick said.

"I know," Marz said, as Beckett pulled into a spot not far from Ike's Harley. "Just wish we knew more about what his club was into. I know you and Jeremy think he's fine, and he probably is. But I'd feel better confirming that he and his brothers aren't in bed with Church." Made sense to Shane. Everything they'd learned so far made it clear how far Church's reach extended around this city. It'd be close to a miracle if they weren't connected somehow. And they'd been damn short on miracles so far. The last hour proved that.

Nick looked from Marz over his shoulder to Easy and Shane. "Known the man for a while. Maybe I should just talk to him. See what I can find out." Given how tight they were on time, that was probably the path of least resistance. Besides, Nick's gut was usually spot on.

"Agreed," Shane said.

Marz shrugged. "Your call, hoss."

They spilled out of Beckett's truck and congregated at the rear just as Ike neared. The man's smile and greeting died on the vine as his gaze landed on the holstered piece on Beckett's side he hadn't tried to hide. Then Ike's brown eyes went stone cold.

"Sorry," Nick said. "It's cool, Ike."

Ike's gaze scanned the group and landed on Crystal, tucked under Shane's arm. "Everything okay here?" he asked. And that measured response to Beckett's aggression and the hard-edged tension rolling off of all of them earned Ike a measure of respect in Shane's book. The guy was tight and levelheaded. He hadn't flown off the handle where a lot of tough guys might've.

"We had a bit of a situation," Nick said.

Ike tilted his head and nailed Nick with a stare. "What's going on?" He gestured at the group with the hand holding the helmet. "I'm not getting much of an old-friends-setting-up-a-new-business vibe here," he said, referring to the cover story they'd told earlier in the week.

"Yeah." Nick raked a hand through his hair. "About that."

"You have something you need to say, Nick? Because I'm sensing some shit is going down for you. And that makes me concerned about blowback for Jeremy. Does he even know?" Ike shifted feet, growing agitation clear in his posture and the tone of his voice.

"He knows," Nick said. "Turns out I brought some ghosts home with me from Afghanistan. Ghosts by the names of WEC and Jimmy Church. Mean anything to you?"

Ike braced his hands on his hips. "You gotta be shitting me. You're on the wrong side of Church? That crazy motherfucker thinks he's some kind of second coming of Christ."

"So you know him?" Shane asked, his instinct sitting up and taking notice of Ike's hostility. Maybe there was an opportunity here. An enemy-of-my-enemy-is-my-friend kinda thing.

"Yeah, I know him." Scrubbing a hand over his bald head, Ike turned and paced, shaking his head and cussing a blue streak under his breath.

"He's a Raven," Crystal said, lifting her head off Shane's chest and staring at the back of Ike's cutoff denim jacket. A big black, white, and red patch of a raven perched on a skull with a knife through the eye socket covered his back. In black letters above and below, the patch read,

RAVEN RIDERS
MARYLAND

Smaller lettering above the state name read, "Death on Wheels."

Ike pivoted, and his gaze cut straight to her. "Yeah. What of it?"

Shane tugged Crystal tighter against him, not appreciating the ice in Ike's tone being directed as her.

She held out a hand meant to appease. "Churchmen hate Ravens," she said. "Right?"

"Feeling's mutual," he bit out. "Has been for years."

"So you don't have to worry," she said, looking up at Shane. "Ravens don't get in bed with Churchmen. Ever." This woman was smart, savvy, strong. So much to respect about her, and Shane knew he'd only scratched the surface. Her being able to confirm Ike's independence from Church was a huge load off the team's shoulders. Tension deflated from the air.

Ike chuffed out a laugh. "Lady knows what she's talking about."

A cell phone rang. Crystal gasped. "Oh, my God," she cried. "What if that's Jenna?" Shaking, she tore open her purse and removed the iPhone. The name on the caller ID read *Bruno Ashe*. "What do I do?" she asked, wide eyes flashing to Shane.

"It's Bruno," he said loud enough that the team knew what was going down. As everyone gathered closer round, including Ike, Shane cupped Crystal's cheek. "Answer it on speaker so we can hear. You'll do fine."

"Hold up." Marz held out his phone with the camera set to video recording. Smart thinking. Now they'd have the audio to play back just in case.

"Go ahead," Shane said, nodding.

Crystal answered the call. "Bruno," she said, her voice audibly shaken.

"Missing anything, baby?" he said, so smug and almost gleeful that Shane wanted to dive through the phone and tears his balls off by reaching down the asshole's throat.

"What did you do with Jenna?" she asked. "She doesn't have her meds, Bruno."

"Oh, you mean the ones I've been paying for the past four years. And how did you repay me for that generosity?"

"I didn't do anything wrong," she said, hugging herself tight. The fear and pleading in her voice made Shane bleed for her. His chest felt on fire inside.

"Who's the guy?" he nearly growled.

Her eyes flashed to Shane's. He nodded and mouthed, "Doing good."

"What guy?" she said.

Bruno made a sound like a growl. "Don't play me, Crystal. The guy with the fucking prepaid. The one I found under my desk. Interesting place in its own right, don't you think?"

How in the world had Crystal lost the burn phone in Bruno's office? Unease crawled down Shane's spine.

"A friend. Just a friend," she said, pressing her hand to her face. Shane surveyed the group and found rage and disgust on every face. He was glad they had his back in this fubar. And hers.

"Did you fuck him?"

"What? No. You know I haven't," she said. What a fucking piece of trash this guy was. How the *hell* had Crystal ever gotten tied up with him? But Crystal was a class act and didn't take his bait. "Bruno, where's Jenna? The stress of this could cause a seizure. Why would you do this to her?"

"Eh, it already has." Shane felt Crystal's distressed gasp in his gut. "She's out of it. Oh, and I put her up in your *favorite room.*"

What the hell did that mean?

The blood rushed out of Crystal's face, and she swayed. Shane caught her against his side as she moaned. "What? Bruno, no. Please."

"*I* didn't do this to her, bitch. You did. Don't forget that for a second."

Tears flooded Crystal's green eyes. "Bruno, please."

"Here's the deal, Crystal. You have a day to turn yourself in to me, for you to take her place. If you're not here by tomorrow night, I'll sell her, and you'll never see her again. And I'll still come after your scrawny ass."

"*No!*" she cried, sagging against Shane's body. The line went dead, and Crystal's knees buckled altogether. Shane swept her into his arms and cradled her against his chest as she wept. The sound of her pain slayed him. And it made him all the more determined to make the man responsible for it pay. With his life. "We have to go to Confessions," she sobbed. "Take me to Confessions."

Not a chance. "We can't trust a man like him to negotiate in good faith, Crystal. But we'll figure this out. I promise," he said, as she cried. No way Shane would ever entertain the idea of turning Crystal over anyway. Looking to his team, he said, "I want to get her inside. We can hash this out there."

Expressions ranging from enraged to outright homicidal, everyone agreed.

"Can I come?" Ike asked, his expression matching the rest. "I'm not making any promises, but maybe we can help." *We,* not *I.*

Shane didn't know a lot about motorcycle gangs, but what he did know was that they tended to be heavily armed, unafraid to fight, and mobile. "It's fine by me," Shane said. "We could use the friends."

Nick nodded. "I agree." Easy eyeballed the guy and nodded, too. Beckett and Marz were the last to come around, but Shane saw in their eyes that they'd run the calculus of what an alliance with Ike and the Ravens could mean and come to the same positive conclusion. "Come on up, man," Nick finally said. "And thanks."

Inside, Nick led them to the gym, and all the men followed him in, leaving Shane and Crystal alone on the landing.

"Put me down," Crystal said. "I'm okay."

Shane gently placed her on her feet but kept his hands on her waist just in case. "My room's over there," he said, pointing in the direction of the Rixeys' apartment. "Why don't I show you around, and you can rest a while."

She shook her head. "I want to know what's going on. What the plan is." Crystal hugged herself tight. "He means what he says, Shane. If I don't go, he *will* sell her."

"I know what he's capable of, sweetness. I've seen some of it for myself. We'll find another way. Trust me."

"I do. But I still want to stay with you. Hear the plan. Otherwise, I'll go crazy."

"Then that's what we'll do. Whatever makes this easier on you, okay?" He brushed her cheek with his knuckles, and she nodded. "Come on." He punched the code into the gym door and grasped her little hand in his.

Nick, Marz, Beckett, Easy, Jeremy, and Ike stood and sat around Marz's desk at the back. Nick's voice carried across the gym as he finished giving Jeremy the basics of the situation, including the fact that Ike knew a little of what was going on.

Shane noticed Ike soaking up the location information posted on a whiteboard behind Marz and the mug-shot identifications duct-taped to the brick wall. And let him look. Might as well know exactly what he'd be getting himself and his club involved in.

Shane made a round of introductions for the sake of both Crystal and Ike.

"I have something for you," Crystal said, handing Shane her cell phone. "I snuck into Bruno's office after lunch and found some papers that seemed relevant to your friends. If you hadn't mentioned Becca's name over coffee this morning, I might've missed it. I took pictures." She shrugged. "I hope there's something useful."

"Crystal, that's . . . amazing," Shane said, threading his hand into her hair and pulling her closer so he could kiss her forehead. That explained the lost phone. Guilt and regret slithered through Shane's gut. Had he done something to make her feel she needed to take such a chance? And, God, what bravery to have done it. Because what she'd done was something none of them could've done easily, and maybe not at all. "Thank you."

"I'll take that," Marz said. "Return it after I download all the pics?"

Crystal nodded, and Shane loved the way she felt in his arms and against his skin. He pulled two chairs together so he didn't have to stop touching her. She seemed to crave it as much as he did, always leaning into his caresses or closing her eyes as if savoring them. He put his arm around her shoulders and encouraged her to lean into the crook of his body. The sigh she released sounded like comfort and satisfaction. With everything that was going on, Shane felt ten feet tall that he might be able to give that to her.

Then they brought Ike up to speed and brainstormed the situation. Bruno's timeline freed them from having to rush out tonight with an ill-planned and undermanned rescue mission. And they always had the audio and video surveillance from inside Confessions to keep him honest. Just as valuable, the asshole's gloating about Jenna's location gave them confirmed intel for the escape and evac that lay before them.

"What did he mean by your *favorite room*, Crystal?" Marz said, his voice gentle, almost apologetic.

Shane's gut clenched. He'd known they were going to have to broach that topic at some point, but he'd also seen how those words had almost physically impacted her. A cold foreboding clawed up his spine.

Her gaze flickered uncomfortably to Shane before she responded to Marz. "Four years ago, I was, um, imprisoned in a room in the basement of Confessions for almost a week. It's the room at the far end of the hall from where your friend was held," she said, meeting Nick's gaze. But not Shane's, and he hated every one of the reasons he could imagine for her sudden skittishness around him. Wanting to ease her any way he could, he grasped her hand in her lap and stroked his thumb over her knuckles again and again. And tried to keep his mind from imagining what had happened inside that room.

Please, God, don't let that room have anything to do with the scars on her back. But even as he sent up the prayer, Shane's instincts prickled. Jesus Christ.

"Well, we have the perfect in to get there," Marz said. "My bachelor party."

Elation flooded through Shane's system. He'd nearly forgotten. "Fuck, Marz. That's genius. They won't suspect us. We'll have the perfect cover. *And* it'll get us in the back part of Confessions with access to the downstairs stairwell."

Animation filtered into Crystal's expression. "That's good," she said. "Getting into the back undetected is half the battle." She turned to Shane. "The party's perfect."

Shane fucking loved seeing Crystal engaged, willing to fight. It meant she could weather the stress of the situation. And it was damn sexy, too.

"Wait. In the middle of all this, you're throwing a party?" Ike asked, disbelief darkening his expression.

Marz chuffed out a laugh. "No. It's a ruse. We pretended to be planning a party as a way to plant surveillance inside. Now we can use the scheduled party itself to get Jenna." He flew forward in his seat. "Aw, hell, I didn't call with the head-count information. Let me do that right now." The call didn't take long. Marz confirmed the party, made the reservation randomly for twelve people, and was off the phone again in under five minutes. "All set," he said with a smile.

"Good. Now, what do we do about the second delivery?" Beckett asked, resting his elbows on his knees. "That's supposed to be tomorrow night, too." And probably at about the same time, if the previous night's meeting was any guide.

Shane nodded. "Yes, that's what Garza said."

"Question is," Marz said, "what's our goal? More fact-finding, which is valuable since we're still identifying the players at this point. Or are we hoping to intervene this time?" Shane's gut clenched. If there were more women involved, he didn't think he could stand by and watch them get stolen away.

Nick turned to Ike. "Well, I think the answer to that question depends on whether we have any assistance."

"I'm lost again," Ike said. Nick caught him up on what had happened Wednesday night and what little they knew about Friday. Ike blew out a long breath. "You guys are fighting a war with a goddamned stick," he said, shaking his head.

"Doing the best we can with what we have," Easy said, tension sliding into his voice.

"I believe it," Ike said, looking each man in the eye. "But it wouldn't be smart to run the rescue with just the group of you. It'd be suicidal to try to handle both tasks on your own. Impossible, probably."

Nick folded his arms and nailed Ike with a stare. "Agreed. Not sure what kinds of options we have, though."

The question hung in the air for a long moment.

Ike sighed and rubbed the back of his neck. "I have some resources at my disposal. But they're not cheap. And they don't ride without putting it to a vote. That'll take a little time."

The mention of money made Crystal's expression drop. Shane squeezed her leg, trying to let her know it would be okay.

"You know exactly how much time we have," Nick said. He glanced around the room. "What kind of resources are we talking? And what kind of cost?"

"Something like this? Safest to involve the whole club. That's twenty-eight men with weapons, ammo, and the know-how to use them. Cost is probably mid-to-high five figures. Or, if whatever this delivery is goes our way, a cut of the assets." Ike shrugged. "That's just how it works."

On the one hand, Shane resented the price tag attached to the offer of help. On the other, Ike and the Ravens, if they came through, might represent the boots and guns they needed to be competitive against Church, whoever those boatmen were, and whoever WEC was, once the team discovered their identity.

Shane saw the subtle nods go around as Nick silently surveyed the men. It was unanimous. Nick turned to Ike. "We're interested, and we've got the resources you're describing." Thanks to Becca's willingness to use her father's life insurance for this mission. And, once they found the password to Merritt's Singapore account, they'd have even more. "Now we just need to know how soon the Ravens might be able to make a decision."

Chapter 20

It was only seven thirty at night, but Crystal felt like she'd been awake for days. Maybe longer. Despite the way her brain raced with worry over Jenna and with anticipation over the plan Shane's friends had put in place to rescue her, Crystal's limbs felt heavy and sluggish, her eyes stung, and her body just . . . hurt.

Yet none of that compared to what Jenna had to be going through. God, she'd had a seizure from the stress of the attack. She must've been so scared. And now she was alone in that pit of a room, the walls, floor, and ceiling all painted a deadening, solid black, along with the bed and the bedding. At least, that's the way it had been four years ago. A sensory-deprivation chamber meant to disorient, break down, and heighten a person's reactions to what took place within.

God, please let her be alone. Crystal shuddered and

prayed that, just this once, Jenna's epilepsy might prove
an advantage. If her seizure had been bad, she could be
semiconscious at best all night and into tomorrow. Maybe
the postseizure symptoms she often had, the raspy breathing, vomiting, moaning, and tremors, would dissuade
anyone from bothering her. It wasn't much of a hope to
hang on to, but it was something.

As soon as the discussion and brainstorming came to
an end, Ike rose, shook everyone's hands, and promised
to be in touch. The man might've been in a rival gang,
and his size and hard edges—with the bald head and
large expanses of ink—might've been a little intimidat-
ing, but he'd also been gruffly kind and openly sympathetic to what'd happened to Jenna. Not everyone was
like Bruno and the other Apostles. It was a good lesson
to remember.

"All right," Nick said, rising. "We're going to need to be
sharp tomorrow. So everyone sleep tonight." He seemed
especially to direct that comment at Derek, sitting at one
of the computers.

"Trust me. I will. But I'm gonna keep an eye on the
feeds from Confessions while I finish up the last of
these searches and download Crystal's pictures," Derek
said. Crystal had liked him since the night at the club.
He was friendly and funny and easygoing. All of these
guys were so different from the ones she'd been forced
to hang around the past few years. Her gaze slid to big,
quiet, serious-looking Beckett, working on his cell phone.
Except for maybe that guy. He was a little scary.

"Good. I'm going to go check on Becca and Charlie.
Feel free to grab me if you need me," Nick said, then he
turned to her. "It's nice to meet you, Crystal. I'm sorry it
wasn't under better circumstances. But we'll try to make
that right tomorrow."

She shouldn't have been stunned by his kindness, but

she kinda was. "Thank you," she managed. "Thanks to all of you."

Murmured expressions of welcome went around, and Nick headed out.

"Would you come with me?" Shane asked, something warm and intense in his gaze.

"Yeah." Part of her feared being alone with him—for the first time with no danger of being caught, but part of her craved it.

Crystal gave the other guys a small wave, then she and Shane cut across the big warehouse room. It was an odd space. Only partially finished. Mostly a gym, Marz's obviously thrown-together computer station filled one corner and an equally thrown-together table that appeared able to seat ten or twelve dominated another. "Where exactly are we?" she asked. She'd been in little position to pay much attention on the ride over here, but it felt strange not knowing where she was.

Shane opened the door for Crystal. "Off Eastern Avenue not far from the harbor. Above a tattoo shop called Hard Ink that belongs to Nick and Jeremy."

"And you all know each other from the Army?"

He entered the code at a door across a wide industrial hallway. "Not Jeremy or Ike, but the rest of us."

As in the five men from a twelve-man team who had survived what sounded like a horrific attack.

When Nick had recounted to Ike the events that led to the group of them being in this situation, Crystal had listened with interest and sadness for Shane. As if the loss of his little sister wasn't enough, Shane had also gone through that ambush, lost a bunch of his friends, then had been forced out of the Army. That was a lot for anyone to bear.

Yet it hadn't made Shane angry or bitter or prone to lash out. It made him want to help others from going through the same. And it made Crystal want to hold Shane, comfort him, and protect him the way he was protecting her.

"This way," Shane said, leading her through the living room. The apartment was really cool. Masculine and modern. Tons bigger than the shoebox she and Jenna shared. Or, had shared. After they got Jenna back, could they even risk returning there for their things? Her stomach plummeted thinking they might have to give up their most cherished belongings, her mother's sewing machine, the clothes she'd made, Jenna's huge collection of books, their family pictures. All the money she'd saved. But she couldn't worry about that right now. One thing at a time.

And the first thing—by far the most important thing—was getting Jenna back. Crystal's insides nearly vibrated from the frustration and anxiety of having to wait. But it wasn't like she had much of a choice because she didn't believe Bruno would really let Jenna go if Crystal breezed in the front door. And having heard Shane's friends talk through the options, she'd been convinced that going in under the cover of the bachelor party gave them all kinds of advantages.

But in the meantime, it was a little hard to exist in her skin. And it felt wrong to eat a meal or go to sleep or enjoy Shane's company while Jenna was in such grave danger. *If you don't take care of yourself, you won't be able to help Jenna when she returns.* There was truth in that. With two such serious seizures so close together, Jenna's health was likely to be rocky in the coming days.

To actually manage food in her belly or falling asleep, she was going to have to lock away her worry for Jenna. Temporarily. Easier said than done, though.

Maybe Shane could help. Maybe allowing herself the distraction of his company and his touch and his kind words was *exactly* what she needed.

Maybe wanting him—even now in the middle of this life-and-death situation—wasn't the betrayal to Jenna that her conscience held it up to be.

Light spilled from under a doorway just ahead, and two people walked into the hallway as she and Shane neared.

"Oh, good. I was hoping I'd get to introduce you two tonight," Shane said to a pretty blond-haired woman standing with Nick.

Shane's introduction was hardly out of his mouth when Becca threw her arms around Crystal's neck and hugged her. "Thank you so much for helping the guys get my brother out of there. I'm so sorry to hear about your sister. Nick just told me," she said with such sincerity and concern.

Crystal was so unused to friendly, affectionate touch that at first she flinched in response to Becca's expression of gratitude. But the other woman didn't seem to notice. "You're welcome," Crystal said, her throat tight with sadness again. "I guess you know what this is like."

Becca grasped Crystal's hand. "I do. And if they could get Charlie out, they can get Jenna, too. Don't lose hope."

"I'll try." The conviction in Becca's voice almost made Crystal believe it.

"We were gonna grab a bite to eat," Nick said. "You guys want anything?"

"Crystal?" Shane asked, his big, warm hand on the small of her back.

Something about his touch there made her feel special, claimed. "Um, I wouldn't mind a drink, but my stomach's too jittery for food right now."

Shane guided her to the kitchen, showed her the mountain of drink choices in the fridge, and grabbed her a Sprite and a glass of ice.

Nick pulled a half gallon of chocolate chocolate chip ice cream from the freezer. "You change your mind later,

Crystal, just help yourself to anything. Make yourself at home. Okay?"

"Thanks," she said, feeling a little shy in the midst of all the kindness but also incredibly welcomed, too.

"Thought you were getting food," Shane said.

Nick pointed at the container of dark chocolate chip ice cream with the scoop. "What are you talking about? This *is* food."

Becca laughed, and it made Crystal chuckle, too. Crystal was glad there was another woman here to talk to and that Becca knew exactly what she was going through right now.

Shane grabbed a bottle of water and nodded Crystal toward the hall. "Come on," he said. "I actually live near D.C., but Nick invited us all to crash here when this situation started last week." He pushed open the door and crossed to the nightstand to turn on a lamp. Low, warm, golden light cast over the room, which just had a queen-size bed with a dark comforter and a dresser within. Unlike the well-lived-in living room and kitchen areas, nothing hung on the walls. But it was clean and safe, and Shane was here. That was all Crystal needed.

Except, as much as she wanted to be alone with Shane, now that she was, she didn't quite know what to do with herself. Would they sleep here together tonight? Nerves and desire fluttered through her belly, especially when she remembered she only had the clothes on her back.

"I don't have any clothes," she said.

Shane waved a hand at the series of duffels lining the one wall. "You're, uh, welcome to borrow any of my stuff to sleep in or wear. I know it'll be big, but we'll figure out something more workable."

Sleeping in Shane's clothes? Heat skittered down her spine and made her shiver.

Sitting on the edge of the bed, Shane patted the mattress. "Sit down, Crystal. I won't bite," he said, that smile she loved curving his lips upward.

"Well, that's a shame." Shane's eyes flashed with masculine interest, and Crystal pressed her fingers to her lips. "I, uh . . ." She shook her head. What had possessed her to say that? She might as well have just thrown out a challenge. Or an invitation. And as intrigued as she was—as she'd been the whole time she'd known him—about what it would be like being intimate with him, she couldn't help but worry she was setting herself up for a big fall.

What if she froze up or freaked out? What if, once he actually *saw* the scars, he lost interest?

"Crystal?" he said, patting the bed again.

"Right," she said. "Sorry."

Once she sat, Shane shifted toward her, bringing his leg up between them and grasping one of her hands. "I have some things I'd like to say if you think you might like to hear them. But if you're just feeling too overwhelmed with everything, too worried about Jenna, and you'd rather I didn't add to it, we can talk another time."

Anticipation kicked her heart into a staccato beat. "No, I'm okay to talk."

Shane rewarded her with a smile she felt all the way down to her toes. "Good. I'm glad." He looked down to where his fingers stroked her hand. "The first thing I want to say is that until you no longer want it, this room is yours. There are some empty beds upstairs, but here you can lock the door and—"

Crystal dropped her gaze to her lap. He didn't want to stay with her?

"What just happened there?" he asked, concern slipping into his gaze. "I said something wrong."

"No," she said, forcing a smile. "It's okay. It's great."

Shane blew out a breath and shook his head, his frustration clear. And though Crystal regretted upsetting him and felt that old panic slinking around the back of her mind, she believed in her heart of hearts he wouldn't lash out at her.

Next thing she knew, Shane had pushed her backward on the bed and leaned over her without resting any of his weight against her. "I want to make sure I have your attention."

Her heart broke into a sprint from their position, from her desire to feel him atop her, and Crystal arched a brow. "I'd say you do."

"Good. I've seen you with Bruno, and I've seen you while you're working. And I know you put on an act that's exactly what people want to see. Doing that made sense in those situations. But, Crystal, you never ever have to pretend with me. Disagree with me. Challenge me. Get mad at me. Tell me you need space. I'll be okay with all of it. I want the real you, not an illusion or a performance. Does that make sense?"

The backs of her eyes stung at the insight of his words. "Perfect sense," she said. "I'm just so used to doing it."

He nodded, an intense expression on his handsome face. "I get that. It was a survival skill. But nothing will threaten you here. You can be yourself."

Emotion caught in her throat, along with an anguished whimper. "I'm not sure who that is anymore," she said in a tight voice.

Compassion filled his eyes. "Maybe I can help you figure it out. If you think I can, I'd like that."

She gave a quick nod and batted away the tears that leaked from the corner of one eye. There was one thing she could do to be more herself, but would he be mad that she hadn't told him sooner? God, she'd told him so many lies and half-truths, not because she'd intended to deceive, necessarily, but because she'd lived a life where secrets ensured survival.

"Now, why did what I said about the room bother you?"

Her gaze dragged down his chest, needing a break from the intensity of his eyes. Crystal wasn't sure she'd ever known anyone as observant as Shane. "I liked that you said it could be my space, but I guess . . . I was hoping . . . that we could share it. But I totally understand if you'd rather—"

His hand against the top of her hair, Shane settled his body against the side of hers and kissed her on a groan. His lips were commanding but not rough. His tongue, caressing but not aggressive. She threaded her arms around his neck, wanting to make sure he didn't go anywhere. God, it had only been a matter of hours, but she'd missed this closeness with him.

When he pulled away, he traced his nose along the contours of her face. "I would love to share this room—*this bed*—with you, but I don't want to make you feel pressured. I want you, Crystal. I've told you that before. But I don't have a right to you. No man does. It's your choice. And even if you say yes now, to anything, you can always change your mind, okay?"

She hadn't yet told him much about what the last four years had entailed, but it was clear that Shane had deduced a decent number of things for himself. More important, though, was the fact that he seemed to know exactly what she needed to hear. And that made her feel safe to consider sharing herself with Shane in a whole variety of ways.

"Okay," she said, nodding. "Well, I like this a lot," she said, pressing her lips to his. "And I like when you touch me. And I'd like to sleep with you in this bed." She shivered, the unusual expression of her most honest feelings spiking adrenaline through her system. As she talked, he stroked her hair and face, and it made her feel adored. "I . . . I want you, too. But I, um . . ." Crystal shook her head.

"I'm not sure that I'm ready for more tonight." Nearly holding her breath, she forced herself to meet Shane's gaze, and his eyes absolutely radiated desire and respect and understanding.

Shane brought her hand to his mouth and kissed her knuckles, once, twice. "I understand. Thank you for telling me where you are." He winked and waggled his eyebrows. "For the record, I like the kissing and the touching, too."

Crystal laughed and felt her cheeks warm. "Good to know," she said, dropping her hands on either side of her head. Out of nowhere, a yawn tackled her. Crystal turned her head so she didn't yawn in Shane's face. "I'm sorry."

"Don't be. We could get changed, get ready for bed. That way if you start drifting off, it doesn't matter?"

"Yeah, sounds good," she said.

With a final kiss, Shane lifted off of her. And though she missed him immediately, her stomach did a loop-the-loop for the idea that in a few minutes, they were going to be lying in that bed for real, under the covers, together. He extended a hand and pulled her to her feet.

Crouching at one of his big green duffels, Shane yanked open the zipper. "What would you be most comfortable sleeping in?" he asked. "I've got plenty of T-shirts and sweats." He rifled through a stack of folded clothing and pulled a few things out.

But Crystal's gaze landed on the blue button-down on his back. Maybe it was ridiculous, but the idea of sleeping in something that he'd been wearing, that still held the heat of his body and the scent of his skin, sounded so thrilling that her brain refused to shake the idea. And he *did* say that he wanted the real her.

Crystal stepped forward and gently grasped the edge of his collar, and then she tugged.

"What?" he asked, looking up.

"I want to sleep in this," she whispered. "I mean, if you don't—"

Shane rose to his feet abruptly, and they stood so close that he towered over her. Roughly, he unbuttoned the shirt, starting at the top and working his way down. "Don't you dare say anything in the neighborhood of an apology for telling me what you want. Because I think this is a damn good idea." His gaze nearly scorched her as he spoke, spiking her pulse and heating her blood.

He whipped the cotton from his body revealing beautiful, masculine perfection. His chest and abdomen were made of sculpted muscles, graceful and powerful at the same time. The hard, curving lines beckoned her hands, which lifted without her telling them to. Her fingers landed on his belly, and he sucked in a breath that drew her gaze to his eyes.

Desire roared off him in the heat of his gaze, the opening of his mouth, the flicking of his tongue against his lip, his more rapid breathing.

In a slow revelry of movement, Crystal smoothed her hands and fingers over his skin, exploring the cut of muscle above his hips, the ridges covering his stomach, and the hard pads of his pecs. The feel of him made her mouth water and the nerves between her legs tingle.

She pressed a kiss to the winged-heart tattoo, so grateful he'd shared the image and the story behind it when she'd needed it most. Shane shuddered out a harsh breath.

It was clear from the bulge filling the front of his jeans that she was tormenting him—not that he complained. But that didn't stop her from wanting to explore more of him.

Shifting to his side, she rubbed her hands up his arm where she found another tattoo on the outside of his right biceps, two crossed arrows beneath an upward-pointing dagger. Something military, maybe? Something hot, definitely.

As she stepped all the way around him, the large tattoo she'd only seen at a distance came into view. Crystal gasped. "This is magnificent," she said, tracing her fingers over the wings of the aggressive bald eagle that covered his skin from his neck most of the way down his back. Its sharp beak was open as if in a screech, and its talons seemed poised to grasp its prey. "Why?" she asked.

"Eagles are the kings of the birds of prey," came his deep voice. "They're known for seeing what other creatures cannot and closing in on their prey before it even knows it's being hunted."

"And you admire these things?" she said, stroking her fingers down his spine and watching his muscles twitch.

Shane looked over his shoulder at her. "They were qualities that made me a damn good soldier. And the best feeling when you're out in the field isn't knowing your teammates have your back. It's knowing that you have the ability to have theirs."

Honor and conviction filled his words and gave her more evidence of the pure quality of this man's character, heart, and soul. "They're also majestic and beautiful and noble," she said, coming around his other side. Just like him. She frowned at a healing wound across the top of his other shoulder. "What happened?"

"Gunshot, the night we rescued Charlie. Just a scratch," he said.

Nodding, she slipped the shirt from his fingers and smiled.

"My turn?" he asked.

The smile dropped from her face. What he would find under her shirt was not beautiful.

He leaned down and cupped her face in his hand. "Every one of the men on my team has scars. And you know what those scars are?"

Heaving a shaky breath, she shook her head.

"They're proof of survival. They're badges of honor. They're marks of strength." Shane swallowed hard. "You don't have to show me, Crystal. But you do need to know there's nothing on your body I won't love and respect. Because it's you."

The words reached into her chest and soothed her heart.

Was she going to live her life in fear forever? Hide forever? Or maybe, just maybe, could she trust someone to know the real her? To *love* the real her. Jenna had accepted her; maybe Shane would, too?

Crystal tilted her head to the side. "It's not pretty."

"You're the most beautiful woman I've ever seen, Crystal. You're brave and you're strong and you're sweet despite having been through hell and back. Nothing could change my opinion of that." He stepped away. "There's a bathroom right down the hall."

She didn't have to ask what he meant. He was giving her an out. Question was, did she want to take it?

That she was even considering revealing herself made her heart gallop and her stomach squeeze like she'd crested the highest hill on a roller coaster. With the exception of finding Jenna missing, it was possible she'd never been more terrified than she was at that moment.

"Shane," she said, like his name was a life raft. And then she tugged the floral shirt over her head and dropped it to the floor along with his button-down. Her hair tumbled down her back and over her shoulders, soft and ticklish against her skin. White spots prickled at the corners of her vision, and Crystal forced herself to slow her breathing. Which got easier the moment she realized that Shane had not moved his gaze from her face.

"You don't have to do this, Crystal. You don't have to prove anything to me."

"I'm tired of being afraid," she said, her breath hitching.

Shane shook his head. "The definition of courage is action in the face of fear. By that definition, sweetness, you're the bravest person I know."

A fat tear streaked down her face. How had she ever found someone with such innate goodness? Even if she only got to have him for a short while, she would remember him for the rest of her life as the man who had held her hand and helped her step onto the path to finding herself again. Reaching up behind her, she released the clasps on the white satin bra she wore and let the straps tumble down her arms, and then to the floor.

Shane's Adam's apple bobbed in a tortured, audible swallow, like he was as nervous as she was. The thought made her smile. "Touch me, Shane. Please?"

SHANE WAS NOT sure how he'd earned the honor of witnessing this woman's strength and courage, nor the privilege of seeing her body and making her believe every part was beautiful. But he was determined to be worthy of both.

As much as he wanted to finally lay eyes and hands on her back, instinct told him to ease her into the exploration.

So he cupped her face in both hands and brought their lips together, which closed all the distance between their torsos, too. And, God, she was soft and warm against him, arousing and comforting at the same time. Kissing her softly, he let his hands drag down her throat and trace the fine line of her collarbones. From there, his fingers traveled over the curves of her shoulders and down her arms in a slow, teasing drag that made the fine hairs on her skin stand up.

Crystal trembled under his hands, but she stood firm, bright green eyes trained on his.

From her arms, Shane's hands found the feminine curves of her waist. He smoothed his hands up and down from ribs to hips and back again, the heels of his palms caressing the sides of her breasts on each pass. Dragging his hands inward, he ran his knuckles over her smooth, flat belly, once again struck by how slight she was. It lured his protectiveness to the fore, reaffirming his commitment to do for her what it seemed no one had ever done before—take care of her, protect her, build her up.

On each upward stroke, Shane allowed his hands to brush the bottoms of her small breasts. Perfectly suited to her frame, he yearned to feel their warmth and their weight in his palms, to taste the pebbled flesh of her nipples in his mouth. But every instinct warned him to go slow and give her the chance to become accustomed to his intimate touch.

Shane had never wanted a woman so much, and they'd barely touched one another. With her gorgeous red hair and her flashing green eyes and her tight little body, Crystal was a total knockout. But it was the survivor in her that really spoke to his soul, that brought him peace and gave him purpose.

"You honor me with this trust, Crystal. I would never hurt you," he said. This time, when his knuckles caressed her breasts, he turned his wrists and cupped the soft mounds in his hands.

Crystal jerked like he'd hurt her. "Wait. Stop."

Shane tore his hands away and retreated a full step. "I'm sorry." Damnit. He'd pushed too hard and fast again.

Breathing hard, she shook her head. "No. This isn't right," she said, her arm muscles tense, her hands fisted by her hips.

"I didn't mean to make you uncomfortable." He bent and retrieved his shirt from the floor and handed it to her.

"No, it's not that," she said, stepping closer and rubbing her palm over her forehead. "I don't know how to . . ." She dropped her face in her hands.

Shane was at a loss. If she hadn't felt pressured, what accounted for the agitation rolling off her? "Talk to me, Crystal."

"No. No, Shane. That's just it." Covering her breasts, she hugged herself, and the look of fear and despair on her face nearly broke his heart. What could— "I lied to you. My name isn't Crystal."

"Your name's not Crystal?" he said, triumph surging through Shane's blood so hard and so fast he could've roared it to the rooftops. He knew it. *He knew it.* Since that first night in her apartment, he'd known she'd lied about her surname, and he suspected "Crystal" had been part of her Confessions persona.

"Are you mad?"

Shane couldn't hold back a smile. "Aw, darlin', it's okay. I suspected that from the beginning. I was just waiting for the day you felt comfortable enough to tell me. Come here," he said, aching to comfort her. A hand in her hair, he pulled her into his embrace.

"You knew?" Her arms clutched at his back.

"I was pretty sure," he said against her temple. Shane pulled away just enough to look her in the eyes. "I'm really happy you decided to tell me." He smiled, a jolt of anticipation lancing through him, and realized she needed him to throw her a rope. He held out his hand and turned on his Southern charm. "Hi, I'm Shane McCallan. I'm so pleased to meet you."

Her cheeks flamed but her smile was grateful. She took his hand. "Hi, Shane, I'm Sara Dean."

Sara. Yeah. The name was real and sweet and feminine. "Sara Dean. A perfect name for such a beautiful girl." Damn, but he was just about flying. This moment was why he'd told Marz not to reveal her name.

"I'm sorry," she said.

"What for, Sara? Protecting yourself?" Shane shook

his head, his chest full with emotion. "Never be sorry for that. If you hadn't done such a good job all this time, we might never have had the chance to meet."

She threw her arms around his neck and pulled him down for a molten-hot kiss that set his body on fire. The aggressiveness of her lips, the tightness of her grip, the yearning, needful moans spilling into his mouth reflected a woman taking a chance, taking charge, taking control. This woman, his Sara, was like a phoenix rising from the flames, and somehow this magical creature had pulled him inside the ring of fire and allowed him to stand witness to the miracle of her rebirth.

When she pulled away, they were both panting hard and smiling. It was a moment of such lightness and ease that Shane could've lived in it forever.

Sara—amazing how easily his brain accommodated to knowing the truth of the woman who held such sway over his heart—slipped her hand in his and squeezed. "There's one more thing I need to share." As Shane watched, she stepped around him, crossed the room, climbed on the bed, and stretched out on her stomach hugging a pillow beneath her head.

Showing Shane her scars. Letting him look his fill.

He knew battle-hardened warriors without that much courage and spirit.

But, aw, Christ. The injuries were worse than Shane had been able to feel by a factor of five. He hadn't been wrong about the cause, though. Sara had been severely beaten. Multiple times with at least two instruments, he guessed.

A boulder parked itself on his chest, but he forced himself to move across the room and crawl up on the bed beside her.

"You okay?" he asked, brushing her hair over her right shoulder so that he could see the whole canvas of her back.

She turned her face toward him, but made no effort to make eye contact. "Yeah. Now, I am."

"Will it bother you if I touch you there?"

"No. I can't even feel some of it anymore." And looking at where the deepest cuts had been and the most knotted scar tissue remained, Shane could guess where. "Do you really want to?" she asked, her voice a little grossed out.

Shane didn't answer with words. And he didn't explore with his hands.

Leaning over her, he pressed a firm kiss against the most gnarled scar just below her left shoulder blade. She gasped. "My beautiful Sara," he said. Middle of her back, just left of her spine. Kiss. "Beautiful, beautiful Sara." The tail end of the lowest scar. Kiss. "So very pretty." As she trembled beneath him, he repeated the ritual for each distinct mark he could make out. Twenty-two in all. Seven darker, redder, deeper lines had been carved into her skin by one tool, and at least fifteen paler, flatter, stripes had been permanently etched into her skin by another.

Only when he'd kissed every one did he touch her with his hands, light strokes of his fingers and palms to learn the landscape of her. "Do you have lasting pain?" Shane asked, barely recognizing the almost hoarse voice that came out of him.

"My upper back gets fatigued easily if I try to carry too much," she said in a low voice. "And my left shoulder always feels tight. Sometimes, there's a lot of twingy achiness that comes out of nowhere."

Lying on his side, Shane stretched out beside Sara, his face aligned with hers, his hand lightly stroking her back.

"Do you want to know?" she whispered.

"Yes," Shane said, even though a part of him was already dying inside. Before the first words left her mouth, he reined himself in, slipping on his medic hat and borrowing a bit of the professional distance you were trained to develop when working life-or-death situations.

He didn't want to scare her with his rage.

Slowly, almost mechanically, Sara recounted the downward spiral of events that spun out of her father's arrest and the revelation of his massive indebtedness to the Church gang after his death in prison. The loss of her house, her belongings, her freedom. When she got to the moment when the first of the men had entered the basement room of Confessions, Shane turned onto his back and urged her to lay her head on his shoulder so he could hold her close. Over the course of four or five days, seven men came to Sara's room. Often individually, once a group. She was raped, caned, and whipped before Bruno finally pulled her out, took her under his wing, and found her another way she could pay her father's debts.

Shane's chest burned with rage and regret. It was every worst-case scenario he'd imagined come to life. Prostitution, sexual slavery, forced labor. What *hadn't* she gone through in the past four years? Sara's voice drew him out of his thoughts.

Being forced to work at Confessions was when Sara slowly faded away. After Bruno's rescue, she formally dropped out of college, cared for her teenage sister, and, at Bruno's insistence, took on a new name. "By the time I realized what had happened to my life, it was too late to get it back again."

"I'm so sorry, Sara," Shane managed, hugging her in tight and kissing her forehead. "If I could take it away and bear it for you, I would."

She tilted her face toward his and met his eyes. "You just did," she said. After a moment, she burrowed into his body, and her muscles relaxed against him.

Shane reveled in the fact she'd felt safe enough to bare her body and her soul to him this way. He swallowed hard as a revelation overwhelmed him. "I've never felt closer to another person than I do to you."

When she didn't respond, Shane lifted his head to find her eyes closed and her face slack. After the day she'd had and the memories she'd shared, he didn't blame her one bit, and he didn't mind, either. They'd have plenty more time to talk and to love.

Sara had fallen asleep without a shirt, so Shane tugged the edge of the covers up over her bare skin. They never had managed to get changed. No matter. Whatever she needed, he was willing to do. For Sara.

Sara. Sara. Sara. The name suited her beauty and her quiet strength so well.

Emotion lodged in Shane's throat.

He didn't just want to be there for her tonight or tomorrow or during this mission, however long it lasted. Miraculously, Shane was flirting with thoughts of forever. When this was all over, she could come back to Northern Virginia with him. Or if she wished to live somewhere else, he'd consider that, too. Wasn't like he loved the job he had. But he definitely loved Sara. Now he just had to find a way to convince her that she didn't have to go on the run. That he could provide her *and* Jenna—when they got her back, because they would—a safe future.

Because he couldn't live with any other result.

Chapter 21

$\mathcal{Y}$ ou're wearing my shirt," came Shane's gravelly voice from behind her.

Only the palest of sunlight filtered in through the window. It was still early. Sara lay with her back against his front and smiled. "I woke up in the middle of the night and changed."

He hummed approvingly and snuggled his face into her neck. Little kisses rained down against her skin there. Shane stretched behind her, and he thrust his hips into her bottom.

Hello, Mr. McCallan. He was hard and thick and ready.

Arousal shot through her body, peaking her nipples and setting her blood on fire—and waking her all the way up.

Jenna. Fear slammed into her anew. Her thoughts raced with worry over what had happened to her sister overnight. The possibilities were endless, and too many of them were unthinkably horrifying. God, Sara wished there was something she could do.

Shane's hand rubbed across her stomach, small circles that had Sara wishing he'd wander up or down.

They *would* do something. Tonight. The plan was mostly set. So couldn't she let herself be in this moment with Shane?

As if he'd read her wants, Shane's hand slid up to caress the valley between her breasts, ratcheting her desire for his touch everywhere. Testing the waters—of her own reaction, not his—Sara ground herself against him.

His groan spilled into her ear and spiked her desire. No panic. No flashbacks.

Nothing but Shane's incredible body and kind heart making her feel safe enough to consider taking a chance. The other night, he'd given her one of the most incredible orgasms of her life, and they'd been mostly dressed. Now she wanted more.

She rocked backward again, and a thrill shot through her belly when he met her thrust with one of his own. What would it like to be with him for real, nothing standing between them? "Oh, Sara," he said gruffly.

That's right. *Not* Crystal. Not anymore. And God did it feel good to reclaim herself after such a long time of locking herself away.

It was Shane who'd helped her find the courage to come back to herself—or at least start to. She wasn't naïve. She knew it might be a rocky road. But she couldn't get to the destination if she never took the first step.

Part of the journey had been embracing Sara in place of Crystal, part of it had been coming out of hiding about what had happened to her, and part of it involved reestablishing control over her body.

And that had her thinking about the incredibly sexy and very definitely aroused man holding her tight against him.

After everything he'd done for her, Sara was ready for more of him. For *all* of him. And given how full her heart was with love for him—because that's definitely what it was—Shane was the only man she wanted.

Shifting onto her back, she peered up into Shane's heavy-lidded gaze. "I want you," she said, the foreign admission of desire sending a zing of energy through her.

In the dim morning light, Shane rolled over, bringing his chest atop hers. The initial press of his weight created a phantom wave of panic that receded almost as quickly as it'd come. The minute her brain registered his scent and the increasing familiarity of his touch, she'd calmed again.

"God, I want you, too," he said, claiming her mouth with a hungry kiss that soon grew urgent. Shane kissed, nipped, licked, and stroked until Sara was breathless and wet. He worshipped her neck, her collarbones, and, undoing the top few buttons, her chest.

With no secrets between them, Sara was able to relax as Shane kissed the soft mounds of her breasts, flicked at her nipples with his tongue, and sucked the rosy buds in deep. Her heart kicked into a staccato rhythm fueled entirely by desire, something she hadn't felt in so, so long.

Sara stroked Shane's hair and explored his shoulders and back. She loved the feel of him, and loved even more that she felt free to participate in this act in a way that was never true with Bruno. "Come here," she said, pulling him back to her mouth.

He didn't hesitate one second. Sara lifted her head to kiss *him,* taking his face in her hands, pushing her tongue into his mouth, swallowing the delicious groan her actions unleashed. When he finally pulled back, more light had filtered into the room, allowing Sara to see that his scorching gray gaze mirrored her own desire back at her. That someone so handsome and so good could know all the things about her she'd thought so ugly and undesirable and still want her was a miracle for which she'd always be grateful.

Shane's fingers massaged her temples and stroked the sides of her hair. "I need you to tell me what you want and how you want it. Anything you say is going to please the hell out of me," he said with a crazy sexy smile, "so don't you worry about that. But I don't want to hurt you. And I don't want to make any mistakes here."

"You're so good to me, Shane McCallan. Do you know that? You're the best man I've ever known." The declaration held so much truth, it brought tears to her eyes.

A mix of emotions passed over his expression for a moment before settling on one that took her breath away. "It's easy to be good to someone when you love them the way I love you."

Sara's breath hitched, and a tear fell. "You . . . love me?"

"Aw, darlin'. I'm so in love with you, I can barely think straight." He pressed a long kiss to her lips.

Sara pressed a hand over her heart. "I . . . I . . ." She swallowed hard, determined to be able to say what she felt in her heart in this moment. "I love you, too, Shane. Since you came to check on me in the dressing room that night. Right now, it feels like my chest can't possibly hold it in," she finally managed in a fast whisper.

"Don't cry, Sara," he said with a small smile.

The emotion flowing through her was so big, so intense, she had to let some of it out. "I can't help it. I'm just so happy. I never dared to hope . . ." She wound her arms around him and held him tight. And Shane held her right back. "I love you," she whispered again. "Please make love to me."

Shane let out a groan so low and sexy it was almost a growl. "Just tell me what you want, sweetness. How I can make this good for you?"

Arousal fogged her thoughts, but Sara knew what she wanted. "Can I, um, be on top?"

"Fuck, yes," he said licking his lips. "What else?"

Sara wasn't used to talking so graphically about sex, and she certainly wasn't used to someone's wanting to learn what gave her the most pleasure, but it was just another reason why she felt safe taking this step with Shane. "I want to do so many things with you," she said. "But right now, I really want you inside me."

"Your wish," he said in a rough voice as he worked at the remaining buttons on her shirt. "If you tell me to slow down or stop, I promise to do it immediately." He helped her slip the cotton off her shoulders, then he rolled to the side and kicked off his jeans and boxers.

Holy crap, Shane was gorgeous *everywhere*. His cock stood thick and veined, and another time she was going to revel in learning the contours of him with her tongue. Needing to feel him, she grasped him in her hand and explored the heavy weight of his length from base to tip. A deep groan ripped from his chest that made her need him more urgently. "Mmm, I'm going to enjoy you," she said.

"God, Sara, you are so fucking sexy, I am losing my mind right now." He leaned up and captured her lips in a powerful kiss. "Stand up, sweetness."

Intrigued by the mischievous look on his face, Sara smiled and stood at the side of the bed.

In a flash, Shane sat up and swung his feet to the ground on either side of her legs. He slid down her panties, dragging kisses along her legs until they fell to the floor. Then he wrapped strong arms around her thighs and worshipped her belly and hips with soft, sweet kisses that made her smile.

Shane's mouth dropped to the apex of her thighs. "Just one taste," he said. And then he pushed his tongue into her folds, finding her aroused clit on the first wet swipe.

Sara gasped and nearly screamed in pleasure.

No one had ever done this to her before, but he'd given her so little warning, so little time to get nervous about it, that his amazing tongue had already enslaved her to the wet, fast, flicking sensations before she'd had a chance to think about it at all.

"Should I stop?" he rasped.

The withdrawal of his tongue nearly made her cry. She fisted her hands in his hair and pulled him close. "Don't stop. Please." Sara would've bet every dime she owned that it couldn't get better, but Shane returned with a vengeance, licking and sucking until she couldn't stop moaning. One of his arms continued to hold her thighs closed tight, forcing his tongue to hit the exact right place over and over and over again, while he brought his other hand around to open her just the smallest bit more to his mouth.

A sob of pleasure ripped up Sara's throat. She pulled his hair in an involuntary reaction, and Shane groaned.

The room spun and Sara felt dizzy with mind-blowing and totally unexpected pleasure that spiraled tighter and tighter in her belly.

"Oh, oh, something is, Shane—" The orgasm slammed into her so hard that she saw stars and couldn't make a sound, as if she were frozen in suspended animation. His mouth still pressed to her core, Shane unleashed a groan of satisfaction as his tongue slowed and licked her lazily a few more times.

He leaned back and looked up at her with blazing eyes and wet lips. "I could tongue you all day long," he said, his chest lifting and falling.

"That was the most amazing thing I've ever felt," she said, glad he'd taken the initiative. Had he offered, she almost certainly would've said no. And then she might not have learned the incredible intimacy and indescribable pleasure of having the man she loved pleasure her with such singular abandon. Reaching between them, she grasped his cock, slick at the thick head. "I want you in me, Shane."

He patted her thigh. "Let me get a condom." He crossed to a duffel and, bending over, sorted through an inside pocket. His ass and thighs were corded, lean muscle. He turned with a square packet in his hand.

"Thank you," she said, glancing at the wrapper and grateful she didn't have to have an argument about this. For once. Bruno had hated to use condoms. And though Crystal was on birth control—which was . . . back at her apartment—she suspected Bruno sometimes strayed and had wanted the extra protection. Thank God she'd never caught anything from him.

Shane kissed her hard and deep, and it was an erotic rush to taste the salty-sweet of her own flavor in his mouth. "I'm clean, sweetness. But I will protect you every way I can." He tore open the packet and rolled the condom on. So sexy. Then he stretched out on his back on the bed.

For a moment, she got tied up in admiring the graceful, hard lines of his muscles. And then he held out a hand and helped her onto the bed. She straddled his thighs, and she wanted him—wanted this with him—*bad*. But the moment his cock brushed the inside of her thigh, a stray arrow of panic darted through her, and she froze.

Shane was right there with her. He sat up and stroked her hair off her face, his expression concerned and affectionate. "There's no rush, Sara. There's no expectation. I could ride the high of making you come with my mouth for a week and be perfectly happy. Don't do this for me. Do it for you."

"This is for me. I promise." She leaned down and kissed him, and accidentally rubbed herself against his erection. But there was no panic this time. "You," she said. "You take it all away, Shane. When we're close like this, I feel so safe."

He nodded. "It's amazing to hear you say that."

Looking into his heavy-lidded gaze, Sara reached between them, centered his erection, and sank down. She was so wet, she took the head of him in easily. But then she froze again, like her body was waiting for something bad to happen. Not with Shane. Never with Shane. He was so in tune with her body, he'd brought her the greatest pleasure of her life.

Shane rubbed her cheek with the back of his hand. "You honor me to even give me a chance," he said.

His words loosened the band of fear holding her in place, and she slid down farther, and a little farther, until she was fully seated in his lap, his cock deep inside her. And then something amazing happened. Her brain, her body, and her heart all connected the dots and realized *she* had chosen everything about this sexual experience. The man. The moment. Even the position.

The revelation drained the fear-borne tension from her body and allowed her, for the first time in years, maybe for the first time ever, to give herself over with abandon to the pursuit of ecstasy.

She had to move. Hands on his shoulders, she rode his cock, alternating between fast ups and downs and grinding rocks that dragged her clit against his hard belly. Shane drew up his knees behind her and met her thrust for thrust, moan for moan. Her body felt almost frenzied in its freedom. Nothing forcing her. Nothing restraining her. Nothing controlling her.

Except, in that moment, she craved more of Shane's affectionate touches. One of his hands braced against the bed behind him, and his other wrapped loosely around her hip as if to steady her. Love flooded through her as she realized he was probably keeping his hands off to avoid scaring her. She reached for his arm, and he gave her his hand. Sara brought it to her breast, and said, "I need your touch."

Shane instantly complied, like he'd been desperate to touch her. He cupped her breast and stroked at her nipple, then drew the peaked flesh into his mouth. Pleasure ripped through her as he sucked and flicked, as his hands caressed and gripped with urgency.

"Oh, God," she rasped, as Shane stroked and cradled her while she took him in deep again and again.

"So pretty, Sara. Make me so fucking happy," he said in a low voice. The words made her heart expand in her chest. He groaned and grasped her hips, urging her to slow. "You're so good. I'm going to come too fast," he said, panting.

"It's okay. Come," she said. "I want to see it, feel it."

Shane's eyes flashed hotter still. And then they were racing together toward a steep cliff. With a restrained groan, Shane threw his head back, his orgasm jerking and pulsing inside her. The man's face, always handsome, was exquisite when he came, full of raw, open passion that she'd caused.

Watching him fall apart shoved her body toward her own orgasm. "Oh, my God, I think I'm going to come again," she rasped.

"Fuck, yeah," he said, satisfaction rolling into his eyes. He gripped her hips and rocked her back and forth, creating incredible friction between her clit and his stomach. "Come on me, Sara," he said.

For a long moment, she dangled right on the edge, then she was falling, flying, soaring through space. And when she fell to earth again, Shane caught her in his arms. Even as their chests heaved and their blood raced, Sara's heart filled with peace and love and acceptance. "I love you, Shane."

Still deep within her, he pressed a warm kiss over her heart and looked up, his expression full of adoration and contentment. "That's good, darlin', because you're stuck with me now." He collapsed back on the bed, bringing her down on top of him.

She yelped in surprise and laughed until her eyes watered. "Well, that doesn't sound like such a hardship," she said, grinning. Sara lifted off his lap and allowed him to dispose of the condom, then they fell back in bed together, tangled in one another's arms.

Guilt threatened to wind its way into her little bubble of happiness, but this one time, she refused to let it. She believed in Shane, and he'd saved Charlie. They would bring Jenna home, too. Knowing Shane loved her made Sara that much more hopeful that they would succeed.

What happened after that, Sara didn't know. For so long, she'd been convinced that the only way she could escape Bruno and Church was to leave Baltimore and never look back. But she never expected to find a reason to want to stay.

And not just any old reason. She'd fallen in love with a man who loved her back. A good man. A sweet man. The only man she'd ever want to have.

But once they got Jenna back from Confessions, Sara wasn't sure she could do anything to place her in harm's way again. And that meant leaving. Didn't it?

Sara blew out a long breath, her thoughts whirling.

"You okay?" Shane whispered.

"Yeah," she said.

"We probably have a little time. Wanna sleep some more? It's gonna be a long day."

Between the amazing orgasms, the incredible sex, and conquering of her fear, Sara did feel worn-out. Add the warm comfort of Shane's strong body, and Sara really didn't want to move. "That'd be nice," she said. Even if she couldn't fall asleep, she'd rather lie here with him than do anything else.

Shane tugged the covers back over them. "Then sleep, pretty girl. I'll be right here with you."

The words squeezed Sara's heart with love and loss. Every part of her believed he'd stay by her side, which was miraculous and amazing and more than she'd ever hoped for. But that didn't mean she could stay by his.

If it was in Jenna's best interest—and if Jenna wanted to go—Sara wouldn't talk her out of it a second time. And then Sara would have to be the one to do the leaving behind.

A FEW HOURS of sleep later, Shane talked Sara into a shower together. It had been filled with wet kisses and soft caresses under a stream of warm water. Fucking perfect. Another first for her, she'd told him, streaming a deep sense of male satisfaction through his blood. But as much as he'd enjoyed learning that, he'd find even more pleasure knowing he'd be her last—for everything.

When they were clean and dressed—Sara in clothes Becca had loaned her—Shane guided Sara to the gym so they could touch base with the team and plan for the day. They found everyone there—the whole team, Jeremy, Miguel, Becca, and even Charlie had made it over.

"What's up, everyone?" Shane asked as he pulled up some chairs and gestured for Sara to sit. Murmured greetings rose up all around.

"Busy morning over *here,*" Marz said with a wink.

Shane knew the warning he'd shot from his gaze had been effective when Marz held up his hands. Still laughed, though. Fucker.

Sara sat forward in her chair. "Um, can I say something everyone?" She smiled at all the encouragement she received. "I really need to thank you for what you're going to be doing tonight for me and Jenna. None of you really know me, so it's kinda . . . um . . ." Sara shook her head and glanced to the ceiling. She rubbed her hands on her thighs and took a deep breath. "It really means a lot that you would help us."

Pride roared through Shane at her words, and he rubbed her neck, just a small connection to remind her he was there.

"We're glad to help," Nick said from his seat next to Becca. "Consider yourself and Jenna part of the Hard Ink family." Where he leaned against the wall, Easy crossed his arms and nodded. Agreeing voices rose up around the group.

Charlie sat forward in his chair, a frown on his face. "I'm sorry, but you look familiar to me. Do I know you?"

Sara smiled. "We met in passing."

Becca put a hand on Charlie's knee. "Crystal helped the guys get you out of Confessions, Charlie."

The man's eyes went wide, and he tucked longish strands of blond behind his ears. "I . . ." He nodded. "Thank you. And now your sister's there?"

Sara nodded, her gaze dropping, and Shane put his arm around her. "Not for long."

"Uh," she said, glancing back up again and shrugging. "If you all wouldn't mind calling me by my real name, Sara? Crystal was my name in the club, and I . . ." She shook her head.

Shane met Marz's gaze and saw a deep approval roll through his friend's gaze. One thing was for sure, brave didn't begin to describe this woman.

"All right, then, Sara, everyone," Marz said. "Let me catch you up." Surveying the group, Marz tapped a pen against a legal pad as if ticking off a list. "Overnight surveillance confirms Jenna remains at Confessions and that Bruno is limiting access to himself and someone named Howie."

Sara gasped. "Really? Oh, my God, that's really good news."

"Who's Howie?" Shane asked.

Bright green eyes filled with hope turned his way. "He's a manager at Confessions, but he's always been very protective of me. Howie was good friends with my father years before . . . everything."

Marz nodded. "Good. Also managed to overhear an eight o'clock delivery time for tonight, so we have our when now."

"Speaking of tonight," Nick said, bracing his elbows on his knees. "The Ravens are a go."

"Ike called?" Shane asked.

"Yeah. They don't come cheap, but we've got twenty-eight additional men on our side, so it's worth it," Nick said.

Sara blanched, and Shane laced their fingers together. "How much?" he asked. "Because I have a decent chunk of changed saved."

"Two grand a man plus a twenty-grand surcharge for the fact they have to cancel tonight's drag race in order for all of them to come." Nick threw a long, appreciative glance at Becca, who smiled in return. "Becca agreed to put up the money, so hang on to your savings for now."

Becca had said from the beginning she'd use her father's life insurance for anything the team needed, but gratitude still washed through Shane. They had to be in a hundred grand by now with the Ravens' fee. "Thank you, Becca," Shane said.

Becca nodded. "You're welcome. And you should know that Jeremy offered to put up Hard Ink as collateral until we can get all the money."

Shane gaped. "Jesus, Jeremy, I don't know how to thank you for that. But I promise nothing will happen to Hard Ink."

"Dude, it's okay. I know, and you're welcome," Jer said, like he was uncomfortable with all the attention. Jeremy crossed his ankle over his knee, his foot shaking.

"Wait," Sara said in a tight voice. "It's gonna cost you . . . seventy-six thousand dollars to get their help?"

Shane inhaled to reassure her, but Becca beat him to it. "Don't give it a second thought, Sara. I mean it. These guys helped me and Charlie the same way they're helping you, and it's our father's fault they're in this situation. So it's not a problem."

Sara glanced from Becca to Shane, and he nodded. "Thank you," she said. Shane hugged her against him.

"Something else," Marz said, pulling a sheet of paper from a stack by his keyboard. "I finished the research into the Port Authority registries to see if any businesses or individuals doing business at the marine terminal seemed in any way relevant to our situation." He handed the sheet to Nick, and the other men gathered around. Shane kissed Sara's hand and joined them. "Most are multinational corporations engaged in various sorts of trade. Nothing special. Nothing suspicious. But look at the name at the bottom of the list."

"Seneka Worldwide Security," Nick said. "Why is that familiar?"

"To me, too," Shane said. "Wait, wasn't the founder prior SF?"

Marz smiled and pulled another sheet from the disorganized stacks on his desk. "Ding ding. John Seneka is prior Special Forces. Old school. Served back in the eighties and nineties. Started SWS right after 9/11."

"One of a handful of security contractors employing a lot of SpecOp guys after retirement or discharge, right?" Beckett said. "Actually, SWS is known for being a bit aggressive on the recruitment."

"I didn't get recruited," Easy said, bracing his hands on his hips.

"Me neither," Beckett said, expression dark. Neither had Shane, Nick, or Marz.

"Not surprised to hear it," Marz said with a sigh.

Something niggled at the back of Shane's mind, then finally connected. "Whoa," Shane said, eyes flashing to Marz. "Are you thinking what I'm thinking?"

"Garza," Marz said.

"Goddamn Garza," Shane said, bracing his hands against the desk.

"Holy shit," Nick bit out, sitting forward in his seat. "Did you make a definitive connection?"

"No," Marz said. "Garza's still a freaking ghost. Then again, I can't find much on SWS's personnel at all, except for Seneka himself and a few public-relations types. What I do know is that this company was one of four that the DoD Counter-Narcotics Technology Program Office contracted a few years back for equipment, materiel, and services in support of counternarcotics activities in Afghanistan."

"Some of the same kind of work we were doing," Shane said, his instinct demanding that something useful lay in the middle of all this.

"Exactly," Marz said. "SWS also seems to have been pretty heavily involved in mentoring Afghan officials in drug interdiction and counternarcotics, as well as training the police in counternarcotics."

"So they're right in the thick of it," Beckett said, pacing. "And now they're here in Baltimore, too. Coincidence?"

Marz shook his head. "Need more research to know for sure."

"The photographs offer any help at identifying the boatmen?" Shane asked, glancing at their makeshift most-wanted board.

"The search only found a few of the boatmen," Jeremy said. "Not the leader."

"Figures, right?" Marz asked. "But, I'll keep digging."

Nick nodded. "Good job tracking this down," he said to Marz. "This could be an important lead. Anything else?"

"All I got until we have a location for tonight's delivery," Marz said, yawning.

"Did you stay up all night?" Becca asked.

"Maybe."

Nick pointed at Marz. "Okay, *you*, go to bed for a few hours, or you'll be wasted tonight. I'll take Becca to the bank to get the down payment for Ike."

"Can't sleep," Marz said, shaking his head. "Not until I pick the location up from the surveillance."

Easy stepped to the side of the desk just as Shane was about to do the same. "Just show me how to operate mission control, and I'll do it."

Marz looked up at his friend. "Yeah? Well, the minute you hear, wake me. We'll need to throw together a fast recon. We're not going to have the prep time we did on Wednesday."

"Roger that," Easy said. "Now, what the hell do I do?"

"I'll come with you, Nick," Beckett said. "Between the situation and carrying that much cash, I'd feel better if you had some backup." As the meeting started to break up, Shane returned to Sara's side. The smile she gave him was like coming home again.

"Appreciate it," Nick said. "Okay, let's get anything off-site done this morning, so we're ready to go as soon as we get that location. The Ravens will be here by four."

"And then the shit hits the fan," Shane said. A purchased alliance with a motorcycle gang, a rescue operation, and intercepting a delivery. So, pretty much, a normal Friday night for them now.

Nick nodded, clearly agreeing. "And then the shit hits the fan."

Chapter 22

Sara sat on the edge of the bed, absolutely amazed at what this group of strangers was willing to do for her and Jenna. Part of her mind had wanted to reject what she'd heard them discuss as total fantasy, but then Shane would smile or nod or take her hand in his, and she'd know it was all real.

Still left her feeling like she'd stepped into a fairy tale, though.

Which was why she'd told Shane she'd join him for lunch with some of the guys in a few minutes. She'd just needed to sit in the quiet and wait for the ground to stop moving beneath her feet.

All she knew was, fairy tale or not, sitting in on that meeting gave her real hope that Jenna would be with her again soon. A matter of hours, now.

From her purse on the dresser, a cell phone rang.

Jenna!

Sara gasped, lunged across the room, and tore the phone free. Not recognizing the number, she swiped the button and loudly said hello before she'd even put it to her ear.

"Sara, it's Howie."

Hearing the older man's voice was so unexpected, Sara wasn't sure how to react. He'd always been kind and protective of her, and Marz had overheard that he was helping with Jenna, but Howie was still inside the Church organization. She couldn't help but be suspicious, even as her gut said it was okay. "Howie?"

"You need to listen, honey. I don't have long," he said in a hushed whisper. "You know what's happened?"

"Jenna," she said cautiously, pacing in an almost dazed circle.

"She's bad off, Crystal. And Bruno is not acting right. Erratic, flying off the handle at everyone—"

"What do you mean by 'bad off,' Howie?" God, there were so many ways to read his words. She shivered and hugged herself.

"Horrible seizure when they brought her in. The guys couldn't even watch. Left the room. And I think he must've hit her because she has a black eye. What the hell happened?"

Tears clogged Sara's throat, but she tried to keep a clear head. "Me," she said simply.

"Well, he says he's sending her away tonight, Crystal. If you don't come. And you shouldn't. I don't know what to do."

Sara's mind raced. She needed Shane's help with this. He might know something to suggest to Howie. "Hold on, Howie. I need to check something. Just don't hang up."

"Hurry. They think I'm taking a smoke break out back. I can't be gone long."

"Okay," she said. Sara hit the mute button and tore

out of Shane's room. Racing up the hallway, she called, "Shane? Shane?"

He nearly jumped off a stool at the breakfast bar, his expression shifting from surprise to concerned. "What's wrong?" he asked.

Sara held up the phone and blurted out a fast stream of words. "Howie called me from Confessions. This is the old friend of my father's I told you about before. He called about Jenna. Wants to know how to help. We have to hurry though, he doesn't have much time."

Shane crouched to look in her eyes. "Can we trust him, Sara? Do you?"

Sara's heart beat faster. That was the question, wasn't it? "Yes. I really think so. I'll admit I was suspicious at first, but I've known this man since I was a kid, and I think he's genuinely upset over what's happened."

Marz slid off the barstool and joined them. "Well, let's see what he has to say, but no names, Sara. Don't mention us yet." He dashed to the counter by the phone and returned with a pad of paper and pen.

Sara turned off the mute and turned on the speakerphone. "Howie, are you still there?"

"Yeah, yeah. Thought I'd lost you."

"You're sure Jenna's still there, Howie?"

"Yes. Seen her with my own eyes. But Bruno said if you weren't here by seven, he'd initiate the sale and finalize it when he returned from a meeting."

Sara shook her head, her mind rejecting the very idea. Suddenly, Marz and Shane started whispering back and forth. Sara got the gist, so she just asked the question outright. "Howie, I hate to ask because you've been there for me a lot. But I have to. How do I know Bruno didn't put you up to this call?"

"Truth is, Crystal, you don't. No real way for me to

prove it to you, either. But as a man who held you in his arms as a baby, I'm telling you I'm on your side." Sara nodded at the guys, letting them know she believed him. So many times Howie had covered for her or helped her out over the last four years. For crying out loud, he'd brought her flowers to her high-school graduation and had helped her pick out her father's casket.

"Okay, Howie. I had to ask."

"I know you did, honey. But what can I do?"

Sara's thoughts reeled, but one main idea came to mind. "Well, after Bruno leaves at seven, can you just free her?"

Howie blew out a breath. "I'm the only other person who has access. If I do, he'll know it was me. I may go down for this anyway, but someone else has to be the one to carry her out of that room."

"Well . . . how about this," Sara said, thinking on the fly. "Could you leave a key for me somewhere?" Marz's pencil flew over the pad of paper. Sara read it and nodded. "Like maybe somewhere in the big party room?"

"Uh, oh, Jesus. Yeah. I could maybe duct tape it under the bathroom sink in there. But how will that help you?"

"It just will, Howie. Thank you so much," Sara said, pressing her hand to her mouth.

"This whole thing is just wrong. Who your father was, you girls ought to be treated like princesses around here. I'll keep an eye on her, Crystal. Don't you worry."

Totally impossible, but she appreciated the sentiment and the protectiveness. "Okay," she managed, as her eyes scanned over a note Marz had written. Sara nodded. "One last question, Howie. Do you know where Bruno's meeting's happening tonight?"

"Oh, lordy." Howie's sigh was troubled yet resigned, a sound she'd heard from him many times before when he'd learned about bad things going on around the club. "Parking garage at Wicomico and Ostend," he said in an almost whisper. The line went dead.

"Holy shit," Marz said. "You did great, Sara. And we're in business. I'll call Nick and Beckett and tell them to get their asses—"

"Tell us what?" Nick asked, walking in the door with a briefcase in his hand. Becca and Beckett joined them at the island.

Now that the urgency of the call was over, Sara's body wouldn't stop shaking. And though the news was mostly good—Jenna safe for now, the location of the delivery for the team—adrenaline left her feeling like she was going to cry. Not something she wanted to do in front of all these people. "I'm gonna . . . go," she whispered to Shane, pointing back down the hall. She didn't give him time to stop her. As she retreated, she heard Shane and Marz recount the conversation and the other men's animated responses.

Back in Shane's room, Sara sank onto the edge of Shane's bed. God, Bruno was really serious about selling Jenna. Sara's worst nightmare come true. A light knock against the door. "Um, come in?" she said.

"Hey," Shane said, stepping into the room, a concerned expression on his handsome face "You okay? I'm sorry I didn't come back right away."

She smiled. "I'm okay. Actually, Howie's call was kinda reassuring." And it was true. If she could just forget what happened if they weren't successful.

"Yeah," Shane said, coming closer. He rubbed her arms. "I wish I could spend the day with you, but now that we have this location intel, we need to scout it."

"Oh. Of course."

"Becca will still be here, though. And Jeremy's downstairs in the tattoo shop. Don't hesitate to let either know if you need something. Okay?" He leaned in for a soft, slow kiss.

"Okay. I'll be fine," she said, even though she hated the thought of Shane's leaving. Part of her yearned for the bubble of happiness and love they'd stepped into early this morning. Silly. And selfish. Jenna's return and the team's safety were the most important things here.

"Can I see your phone, please?" he asked. She handed it over and, while she watched, he programmed his number in, then called himself so he'd have her number, too. A buzz sounded from his pocket. "Call me if you need me for anything."

"I will. But if you need to go, go. Don't worry about me."

"Okay," he said, cupping her face and kissing her again. "I won't be long." He smiled as he left, shutting the door behind him.

For a few minutes, Sara stood there, staring at the door. The silence and solitude of the room closed in on her. Maybe there was something she could do, some way she could help. Determined, she left the room in search of something or someone who might need her, so she could avoid going crazy.

Sara found Becca sitting alone at the breakfast bar, a pile of stuffing and fabric in front of her. "Did they leave already?" she asked.

Becca looked up and smiled. "Yeah."

Sara's stomach growled. After skipping dinner last night, the bagel she'd had for breakfast wasn't holding her. "Do you mind if I find something for lunch?"

"Of course not. There's stuff for sandwiches and salads. Cans of soup in the cabinet. Maybe some leftover Chinese." Becca shifted to slide off the stool.

"No, please. I can get it. Do you want something?" she asked, opening the fridge. All the fixings for sandwiches were right in front, so Sara grabbed those and brought them to the island.

"Actually, yeah. I would, thanks." Becca matched two pieces of plush fake brown fur together.

Sara tried to figure out what Becca was doing as she made the sandwiches, asking Becca her preferences as she built them. Finally, she settled a plate with a sandwich and some chips in front of the other woman, careful not to mess up her project. "Something to drink?" Sara asked, grabbing a Sprite.

"I'll have the same, thanks," she said distractedly.

Sara brought the drinks and slid on to the seat next to Becca. "What are you working on?"

"This used to be a teddy bear, but it got dissected."

Sara chuckled. "I'll say. Are you trying to reassemble it?" she asked, wondering if she should offer to help. This was actually something she could be useful for. Sara took a bite of her sandwich and savored the crusty roll, savory ham and cheese, and crunch of the lettuce.

"It was from my dad, so . . ." Becca shrugged and pushed the fabric away as she pulled her plate closer.

"Well, I really love to sew if you want me to take a shot at it," Sara said. It'd be a great distraction, too. Something to do with her hands while the man she loved put himself in harm's way to get ready for saving her sister tonight. Where he'd do it all over again.

Becca's expression brightened. "Really? That would be awesome. What do you sew?"

"I make a lot of our clothes. And occasionally I quilt."

"Wow. That's amazing. I'm not very creative," she said.

As the women ate, they chatted about Becca's job, Charlie and Jenna, and everything that had happened in the past week from Becca's perspective. Sara liked Becca's openness and friendliness, and it made her feel less awkward about being here without Shane. Becca cleaned up their lunch mess and fixed bowls of ice cream, and Sara savored every sweet spoonful. When they were finally done with their leisurely lunch, Becca tidied up while Sara sorted through the parts of the bear.

She could totally put this thing back together. Having something to do made her happy, especially since it was for Becca. "Do you have a sewing kit?" Sara asked.

"A very sad one, yes," Becca said, pointing to the small tin that included two needles, a thimble, and three colors of thread, white, black, and brown.

Sara chuckled. "I can make that work." She reassembled the legs first, then attached them to the body. Turning the torso inside out, she sewed the back seam closed, then turned it right-side out again. "Look, I made you a headless bear," she said.

"Thank you so much, Sara. The poor thing would've been deformed if I'd tried to put it together."

"You're welcome," Sara said, smiling. "If you stuff the body, I'll sew the head back together; and then I'll just need to reattach it." Becca dove into the task of stuffing as Sara looked at the fabric for the head. It hadn't been opened cleanly along the seam, so she'd need to figure out how to hide the tear without puckering the back of the head. She flipped the material around to look at the bear's face. "Oh, his eye's loose." Sara looked closer. "I think this was glued on rather than sewn."

"I'm sure Nick has glue around here somewhere. Or else I'll just run to the craft store when all this is over. The biggest thing is that it's back together again. Thanks to you," she said, wrist deep in the bear's body.

A glint of light caught Sara's eye. She looked at the bear's face again, not certain what it could've been. Holding the material in her hands, she tilted it back and forth.

A little flash from the loose eye. Sara held it up to the light. In the depths of the toy eye, there appeared to be a tiny brighter square that caught the light when you held it just right. The middle of the other eye was darker, flatter. "This is strange," she said, comparing the eyes again.

"What's that?" Becca said, glancing up from stuffing the arm.

"One of these eyes is different. Almost looks like there's something in it."

"What?" Becca said, almost alarmed. "Can I see?" Sara handed it to her, unsure about her reaction, and Becca held it up to the light just as she had moments before. "Oh, my God, Sara. I think you're right. Come with me," she said.

Sara followed Becca down the hall to a closed bedroom door. She knocked. A man's voice welcomed them inside.

"Hey Charlie, up for a chat?" Becca asked.

"Sure," he said, looking up from a laptop as Becca crossed to a chair. Sara hovered in the doorway. A black puppy lying next to Charlie on the bed raised its head, its tail lazily wagging.

"It's okay, Sara," Becca said, waving her into the mostly plain, windowless room.

"I'm really glad to see you doing better, Charlie," Sara said.

"Thanks," he said, peering up at her, almost like he was shy. Charlie's glance shifted to Becca. "What do you need?" he asked, gently swinging his legs off the bed so he didn't hit the dog, who jumped down anyway.

The dog had three legs, Sara noticed, doing a double take. "What happened to him?"

"Her," Becca said with a smile. "Eileen. I'm not sure. I found her that way."

Eileen came over and sniffed Sara's legs, and Sara couldn't resist squatting to give her a pet. The puppy apparently thought that was an invitation to play, though, because she whacked at Sara's hand with her paws and tried to nibble on her fingers. With a last smile at the dog, she rose.

Becca held up the bear. "While you were unconscious, Marz noticed the ID tag on this bear had the number to Dad's Singapore account on it." Charlie's eyes went wide. "So Marz cut it apart, thinking something was hidden inside, but it was empty. Just stuffing. But just now, Sara was putting it back together for me, and she noticed there's something weird about the eye." She handed the bear to Charlie.

Frowning, Charlie looked closely at the eyes. "I don't see anything. But that lamp isn't very bright. Either of you have a flashlight app?"

"I do," Sara said, turning the app on and passing Charlie her phone.

"Thanks," he said. He shined the light in the eyes. First one, then the other. Back and forth several times.

"There's something in the loose eye," Charlie said. "It almost looks like a microchip." *A chip for what*, Sara wondered, stepping closer.

"Like, for a computer? That small?" Becca asked, excitement in her voice.

Charlie nodded. "Smallest chip in the world is two millimeters square. Looks like the Colonel might've given you the key in the form of the bracelet and the lock hidden in here." He rose off the bed wearing a pair of sweatpants and a T-shirt. "Maybe Marz has some tools that I can use to take this apart. Chips this size are fragile. I don't want to break it."

"You might've just unraveled a pretty big mystery," Becca said, squeezing her arm around Sara's shoulders with a smile.

Sara didn't know what to say. The whole thing was crazy, but she was glad to have done something helpful given everything Shane's friends were doing and risking for her.

Charlie led them through the apartment and to the gym. Becca punched in the code, then they headed to the big computer station in the corner. "Where is everyone?" Charlie asked.

"They got a lead on the delivery's location tonight," Becca said. "They'll be back soon."

Setting the bear on the edge of the desk, Charlie searched Marz's station for tools. "Aha," he said, finding a small red toolbox on the floor. While Sara and Becca leaned in as close as they could, Charlie gently separated the back of the eye from the glass. And there, in the center, sat a computer chip no bigger than Sara's pinkie nail.

Charlie held it up with a pair of tweezers and turned it around as he examined it. "What were you trying to tell Becca, Colonel?" he said, almost to himself.

"He wasn't just trying to tell me, Charlie. He sent you the account information, after all," Becca said. Sara glanced at Charlie, wondering why the guy referred to his father that way.

"Hmm," was all Charlie said, looking around. "I wish I had my own equipment. I'd know better how to try to access this." He settled it on a piece of white paper.

"Well, wait 'til Marz gets back," Becca said.

It was like her words conjured him. The door opened, and the whole group of men entered and crossed the gym. Shane was in the middle of the group, looking sexy in a long-sleeved gray shirt and a pair of black jeans. Of course, now Sara knew he looked every bit as sexy without clothes, too.

"We have news," Becca said, almost jumping with glee.

Using the tweezers again, Charlie held up the chip as the men joined them around the desk, Nick going to Becca and Shane taking Sara in his arms.

"Holy shit," Marz said, rushing closer.

"Pretty sure Sara just found what we've been looking for," Charlie said. "In the eye of the bear."

Heat rushed into her cheeks as every pair of eyes in the room turned on her. And then as Shane watched with a wide smile that sent Sara's heart soaring, they all took turns shaking her hand and hugging her. Marz even took her for a few dancing spins, making her laugh and squirm with all the attention. Meanwhile, Becca explained how they'd found the chip.

"Hey, guys?" a voice called, finally breaking up the celebration. It was Jeremy, leaning in the door. "Heads-up. The first of the Ravens are here."

"Well, hell," Marz said. "Guess it's showtime. We'll have to save this prezzie to open later."

As HIS TEAMMATES, Becca, Charlie, and Miguel made for the door to greet the Ravens, Shane hung back with Sara, absolutely overflowing with pride and love. "I leave you alone for a few hours, and you save the world," he said.

Chuckling, she dropped her gaze and shook her head. "I didn't do anything. It was just dumb luck."

Shane tilted her chin upward. No way she was playing this off. "Maybe, but it was dumb luck none of the rest of us have had. I'm serious, Sara, whatever is on that thing is probably going to be huge for us. So, thank you." He pulled her in for a kiss, wishing they could've had the day to lounge in bed and make love and talk about what would happen between them after tonight. She wound her arms around his neck and pressed in close. Shane's body responded immediately, his pulse spiking, his cock hardening. "Mmm, the things I'd like to do to you," he said, pulling away from her lips.

Sara lifted her eyebrows. "That sounds promising."

Shane nearly growled. Sexy, tormenting woman. "Just

you wait." He gave her another quick kiss. "Do you want to come meet everyone or hang inside? Up to you." A sound like thunder rumbled around the building.

"I'll come with you," she said, slipping her hand in his. And, aw, damn. It was a small gesture, but her initiative in showing him affection was proof positive how far they'd come in the past week. Couple more hours, and they'd have Jenna back, then nothing would stand in their way.

As they left the gym, the sound of thunder grew louder, and Shane realized it was the rumble of a shit ton of motorcycles as they entered Hard Ink's parking lot. The sound was almost deafening when they stepped out the door.

Holding Sara close, Shane scanned the lot, almost packed to capacity now. Everywhere he looked, he saw men in cutoff denim jackets with the Raven Riders patch on the back. They hung their helmets on their handlebars and congregated behind Ike and a couple other obvious leaders in the center.

Sara stepped closer to Shane's side, her arm coming around his back, and Shane was only too happy to return the gesture by pulling her close and making it damn clear that she was off-limits. Nick was all but draped around Becca, too, so at least he wasn't alone in the feeling.

Hands were shook, introductions were made, and thanks were given as the two groups made nice.

Time and again, Shane heard one of the Ravens express the sentiment that any enemy of the Churchmen was a friend of theirs, so he didn't have any questions about the loyalty of their new allies. At least, as long as they were paid.

Shane's question had more to do with how twenty-eight guys used to operating loud and visible were going to mesh with the team's general covert approach. Time would tell.

"All right," Nick said to Ike, who they'd learned was a General Board member in the club, and Dare Kenyon, the club's president. Kenyon was tall and lanky, with brown hair nearly to his shoulders. Seemed friendly enough. They all did, so far. "Can we get everyone to come inside so we can get some plans hammered out?"

"Come on, sweetness," Shane said against Sara's ear, earning a smile.

When he'd offered them the space earlier in the day, Jeremy hadn't been lying. This room on the far side of the Hard Ink building was just a big open rectangle unfinished all the way around. Looked like Jeremy had demolished whatever had been in here down to the studs. But at least there was plenty of room for all the men to lean against the wall or sit on one of the sawhorses scattered around. Shane and Sara made their way toward the front with the rest of his team.

It took a few minutes to get everyone in and quieted, but once they did, Nick offered some words of welcome and thanks to Ike, the president, and the club in general. And then Marz took over briefing everyone on the nature of the missions at both locations. At the parking garage near the football stadium, the identification of the players in the trade and possible interception of the cargo—whatever it was. The latter was particularly important to the Ravens. God knew Shane wasn't adverse to interfering with the Churchmen's cash flow, and neither was the rest of the team. At Confessions, though, the mission involved a rescue and was, in Shane's mind, the far more important of the two.

As the conversation turned to Jenna and Confessions, Shane checked in with Sara. "You okay?" he whispered.

"Yeah. Be better when all this is over and Jenna's back." She laid her head against him.

In the planning, the Ravens proved themselves equal

partners in strategizing each of the locations. Within an hour, the men had firmed up the plans and been divided into two teams—a group of twelve for the part inside Confessions, another four on the outside of the club just in case, and the remaining eighteen at the parking garage. The Hard Ink guys would split between the two. Those Ravens heading to Confessions left their jackets stacked in the corner for Jeremy's safekeeping. They wouldn't be able to get in the door with them on.

Back at Hard Ink, Charlie and Jeremy would be running the communications and monitoring the surveillance at the club that they'd just installed at the garage. So at least his teammates would know what was going on at both locations. It was déjà vu of the night they'd rescued Charlie all over again.

After everything was set, the Ravens filed out of the room, and within minutes, the lot outside roared to life.

When just Ike and Dare remained inside with the team, they offered a final recommendation. "You know," Kenyon said to Nick, "Church is going to consider this a full-on assault no matter what you do. So from one man to another, I strongly suggest you consider taking him down once and for all."

"Meaning?" Nick said, eyes thoughtful and intense.

"Church, his Apostles, Confessions. As much of it as you can." Kenyon and Ike traded glances, and Ike nodded, too.

The justice and righteousness of that resonated way down deep in Shane's gut. Tempting as it was, though, the team couldn't give into full-scale vigilantism without becoming just like that which they were fighting against, could they?

Chapter 23

Shane watched as A-Team—the larger team headed for the garage delivery—rolled out of Hard Ink's lot, forming a long stream of bikes following Beckett's SUV and the Ravens' box truck full of barricades to force traffic in the garage where they wanted it to go. With Beckett was Nick and Miguel. The whole team was leaving early to set up the barriers and get well hidden before the Churchmen ever arrived.

The remaining team had a good ninety minutes before they could set out for Confessions. And that gave Shane more than enough time to do something he'd been itching to do. Hand in hand, he led Sara up to his bedroom and closed the door.

And then he pushed Sara up against it, his hips against hers, his hand on the door beside her head. "Sorry, darlin'. I just needed a little time with you before I left."

Sara shook her head, a small, sexy smile on her face. "Don't even think about apologizing for telling me what you want," she said, echoing his words from the previous night.

Shane threw his head back and laughed, but the humor died in his throat as she stole the opportunity to flick her tongue over his Adam's apple and lick up to his jaw.

"You don't play fair," Shane said, bringing his gaze back to hers.

Still smiling, Sara wrapped her arms around Shane's neck and lifted her legs around his waist. She arched a brow.

Groaning, Shane's hands went to Sara's delicious ass, holding her up against the door. "You're killing me, sweetness. I want in you so damn bad." He kissed her deep, plundering her mouth with his tongue. He held back a little, not giving in to the need to ravage her, but Sara's moans and whimpers communicated only pleasure.

"Can you please be inside me right now?" she asked.

He froze long enough to assess her sincerity, and then her jeans and panties were gone. "How?" Shane said, almost frenzied, as he grabbed a condom and pushed his jeans to his knees.

Sara eyed the door. "I'd like to try that," she said, nodding toward where they'd just been standing. "Just please go slow at first?"

"Anything you want, Sara. Always." He rolled on the condom and easily hiked her back up around his waist, her heat already washing over his cock. Gently, he pressed her up against the door. "I love you, Sar. Don't let me hurt you. I'm a little wound up over you right now, but just say the word, and I'll stop."

"Okay," Sara said. "I trust you." And then her center found the head of his cock and she lowered herself down.

"Oh, *fuuck,*" Shane groaned, as her tight, wet heat engulfed him. "Okay?" he managed.

"More than," she said, smiling.

Shane started moving then. Really, he had no choice in the matter. Her body felt too good, he loved her too much, and his veins were flooded with pre-mission adrenaline. The combination had his hips swinging and his hands grinding her ass down for each upward thrust. Sara's gasps were the sexiest fucking thing, so free and full of passion.

"All right, sweetness?" Shane asked.

By way of answering, Sara kissed him. Winding her arms around his neck, she pulled them tight and sucked on his tongue so hard Shane saw stars. The shift in position escalated the wildness of her moans.

All of a sudden, Sara's nails sank into Shane's shoulders and her body tightened around him—her arms, her legs, her sweet pussy. Sara unleashed a strangled moan into their kisses that Shane swallowed greedily. And then her orgasm nearly took Shane to his knees as her body clenched his cock again and again.

Shane's own orgasm barreled down on him like an out-of-control freight train and nailed him in the back, forcing Shane deep, deep, deeper as he spilled himself into Sara's sweet body, and she swallowed *his* moans. When it was over, Shane stumbled backward, carrying Sara until he could sit on the edge of the bed. Under her scant weight, his thighs shook. He pulled away from the kissing and heaved a deep breath.

Tears pooled in Sara's eyes.

Oh, no. Shane's gut crashed to the floor. "Oh, God, sweetness. What's wrong. Did I hurt you?" Shane ran his hands gently over her back. "I was too rough, wasn't I? I'm so fucking so—"

"No," she said in a tight voice. "Not at all," she managed. "Scared for you tonight. Scared for Jenna," she said, the tears flowing now. "I don't want to lose either of you."

Shane's heart restarted again and he heaved another deep breath as he gently swiped his thumbs under her eyes. "You won't, Sara. I'll be home tonight, and I'll have Jenna with me."

Emotions flitted over her beautiful face. Finally, she nodded. "I know, you're right." She grasped his face in her hands and kissed his lips sweetly but firmly. "I believe in you, Shane McCallan."

Kissing her one more time, he helped her off his lap so he could dispose of the condom. And it hit Shane exactly what to do. "Sit with me a minute," he said, patting the mattress beside him. As she did, he pulled up his pants and reached into his pocket, finding Molly's necklace with his fingers. He laid the butterfly in his hand so she could see it. "For the past sixteen years," he said, looking into her eyes, "this necklace has been my most important possession. I never go anywhere without it, and I would never leave it behind without knowing I could have it back again." Grasping Sara's hand, he slowly dropped the pendant and chain into her palm. "So you hold on to this for me. That way, you know I'll have to come back."

Eyes wide, Sara shook her head. "I can't . . ."

He closed her fingers around the necklace. "I want you to have it. And every time your faith threatens to fail, you look at that and know I'll be back. Because I love you."

As Sara threw her arms around him and told him she loved him, too, Shane offered a silent promise to succeed where he'd failed before. Sixteen years ago, he'd lost his own little sister, but tonight, he wouldn't lose Sara's.

FORTY MINUTES LATER, B-Team stood on the floor of Confessions, waiting to be escorted to their party room for Marz's fake bachelor party. It was like the night they'd rescued Charlie—crowded, loud, just bordering on rowdy.

Despite the crowd, Shane felt exposed as hell standing in the bar, and he was glad when Darnell finally found and invited them to follow him beyond the curtain.

Shane, Marz, Easy, and nine of the Ravens made their way back down the hall, laughing, joking, drinking beer. Shane had emphasized they act like regular guys enjoying a night out at a strip club. So far, they were passing with flying colors.

In their private room, the party got under way with food, music, and dancing girls on the small central stage. As the groom, Marz was trapped front and center, and kept up enough antics—like dancing with the girls, loudly joking with the guys, and offering hilarious editorial commentary regarding the porn playing on the big screen—to make sure all attention remained on him.

Shane and Easy leaned against the bar near the door. From which it was a very short trip down the hall, around a small corner, and down the steps into the basement.

A few minutes after they arrived, Jeremy's voice came through Shane's earpiece. "B-Team Leader, this is Eileen," he said, using the joking code name they'd come up with for Charlie's rescue—they avoided real names on the coms as much as possible. "You know who was a half hour late getting to the other location. Just arrived. The other people were already there, and A-Team Leader took pictures of them all."

"Roger," Shane said, glad for the confirmation Bruno was out of the building. Then he looked to Easy. "I'll run to the bathroom, and we'll be set," he said, referring to the key Howie was supposed to have left. Shane slipped inside, secured the door, and crouched to look beneath the sink. Nothing.

He checked every other possible hiding place in the room. Still, nothing.

Caution settled on Shane's shoulders like a warm blanket. He returned to Easy's side. "Dead end," he said in a low voice.

"Shit," Easy said. "Well, there's more than one way to skin a cat. Let's do it."

Nodding, Shane spoke into the coms. "Take down the cameras."

"Doing it now," Jeremy said. "Stand by." Marz's identification of the wireless frequencies that many of the Confessions security cameras operated on gave him the power to interfere with the signal and essentially shut them down. Marz had shown Charlie what to do before they'd left. "Good to go," Jeremy said.

"Now's as good a time as any," Easy said, off coms. "I'd like to get Jenna back sooner than later."

Shane studied the intense expression on the man's face but didn't have time to analyze whether more was going on for Easy than met the eye. Anyway, right now, it wasn't the most important thing.

"Let's move," Shane said.

Out the door. Down a thankfully clear hallway. Shane cleared the corner, waving Easy around. A whole lotta déjà vu washed over Shane as he looked into the dimness of the basement stairwell, but all seemed quiet, so he started his way down, gun at the ready.

Sara had said Jenna would be in the last room on the right. Now that they didn't have the key, they were going to have to be more creative about— The door stood open. Shane pointed, and Easy gave a tight nod. They hustled along the hallway and stopped just shy of the door. Shane indicated for Easy to push it open, and Shane would cover.

Silently counting to three, Easy pushed the door open, Shane swung his gun over the space. Only, the room inside was pitch-black, just like Sara had described. Shane felt along the inside wall for a switch, and finally Easy signaled him that it was *outside* the door. Easy flicked the

switch and eased the door shut behind him so light didn't
bleed into the hall.

It took Shane's eyes a minute to adjust, and not just because the room had gone from darkness to light.

The bed was empty. Jenna wasn't there.

But someone else was.

"Fuck," Shane said, stepping to the center of the room
and crouching next to the body of an older black man
whose shirt was drenched in blood from at least two stab
wounds to the chest. There was no pulse, but the body
was still warm, pliable. This had just happened.

Shane's gaze flashed to Easy's, and the man wore an
absolutely lethal expression. "I want to take this place
down," Easy said, almost growling. For a long moment,
their gazes met and held. Shane looked at the older man
he assumed was Sara's friend, soaked in his own blood
on the floor. He'd probably died helping them. Shane
thought of those nine women disappearing into the boats.
He thought of Charlie and Jenna and the countless others
he knew nothing about.

How many more have to die here?

"B-Team Leader, we have a situation with A-Team,"
Jeremy said, his voice not as calm as before.

"We've got one here, too. The package is missing," Shane
said, wondering how much worse this night could go.

"No, it's not. The package is with . . . you-know-who at
A-Team's location."

"Jesus," Shane said under his breath. *Not again. Not
again. He couldn't lose her again.* "She is their top priority. Their *only* priority, Eileen. Make that clear."

White-hot rage clawing down his spine, Shane looked
at Easy. "Take it down," Shane said. Gun drawn, Shane
walked out into the central hallway and checked the other
basement rooms. All empty. "How much time do you need?"

Easy's smile was nearly sinister as he pulled a pouch

from inside his coat. "I came prepared, dawg. Five minutes to place the materials, then we can remote this motherfucker." He pulled small blocks of the off-white plastic explosive C-4 out and secured them to load-bearing beams, then inserted the blast caps.

"Roger that," Shane said, keeping lookout while Easy did his thing. When they were done downstairs, they returned to the party room and quietly spread the word to the Ravens, who lacked earpieces. *Prepare to haul ass out the front door so they'd mix in with the crowd.*

Jeremy's voice spilled into Shane's earpiece. "Shots fired at Location 1, but A-Team Leader secured the delivery items. Says the package got away, but they are in pursuit."

Shane wanted to destroy something with his bare hands. Whatever had been exchanged via the delivery meant absolutely nothing to him at this moment. Jenna was all that mattered.

"We do this now," Shane growled to Easy, then he stalked over to the wall by the door and pulled the fire alarm. The siren screeched at an ear-shattering decibel level. "Everyone out," Shane said, shooing the dancers out and accounting for all his men before he left the room.

The chaos of the main club was audible over the alarms—running feet, yelling, screams.

"Everyone out," Shane yelled in the main club. "Fire!" He was glad to see no one lingering behind. Customers, dancers, waitresses—everyone bailed. Their group brought up the rear, then they were out in the night air, making a beeline for their cars and bikes as the club's bouncers urged people to the other side of the street.

Having planned to transport Jenna once they rescued her, Shane, Easy, and Marz had parked near the back door. Weaving through scattered groups of people, they wound their way to the road and waited for the bikes to congregate behind them.

When the twelfth Harley joined them, Shane hit the accelerator; and then he looked to Easy.

Watching over his shoulder to make sure the bikers were clear, Easy waited . . . waited . . . then finally pressed a button on a cell phone Shane hadn't seen before. And the world in his rearview mirror exploded with a deafening series of crashes and bright orange fireballs that shook the ground beneath his truck.

But Shane couldn't take any pleasure in the destruction of that godforsaken hellhole. Not yet. Because he still hadn't done his job. He still hadn't saved Jenna.

SARA SAT IN a metal folding chair trying to avoid asking Jeremy for information he didn't have. He'd been honest with her at every step, including the one where Jenna had shown up where she wasn't supposed to be—with Bruno at the garage. And now it appeared Nick and the Ravens with him were chasing them through the streets of Baltimore.

Which meant Shane *couldn't* save her. And the uncertainty and fear were eating Sara up inside and making it hard to sit still.

Just as she inhaled to ask if Jeremy was hearing anything, Sara's cell phone rang. *Shane!* Her gaze dropped to the screen. Instead, it read, "Bruno Ashe." She gasped and showed Becca, and the other woman's face went pale with alarm.

"Bruno's calling Sara," Becca called across the room.

"B-Team Leader, we have another situation," Jeremy said. "Bad guy just called your girl." Jeremy listened and nodded. "He says to answer. Come over here and put him on speaker so Shane can hear."

Sara rushed across the room and swiped the answer button before Bruno hung up. "Bruno?" she answered.

"Oh, if it isn't the lying, scheming bitch I've been

taking care of the past four years while she stabs me in the back."

"I don't . . . what are—"

"I have Jenna, but I'd rather have you. Meet me, and I'll let her go. If you don't, I'll slit her throat and drop her body in the harbor."

Head reeling, Sara asked, "Um, where? Where should we meet?" A few beats of silence passed. "*Where,* Bruno?"

Something roared in the background, like the sound of an engine. "I don't fucking know," he snapped. "I need to think of a place."

Pressing his hand against his earpiece, Jeremy furiously scribbled on a sheet of paper and held it up. Sara nodded.

A screech. The sound of a blaring horn.

What the hell was Bruno doing? "Where, damnit? If you don't have a place, just pick me up where I am." Never before would she have spoken to him that way, but Jenna's life was on the line, and Sara was out of patience.

Bruno almost growled. "Where the hell are you, you little bitch?" Sara read off the address Jeremy had written though she had no idea where that was. "If you aren't there, Crystal, you've just killed your sister. Fifteen minutes. Don't keep me fucking waiting. And don't even think of not coming alone." The line went dead.

"Take over, Charlie," Jeremy said. "Sara, you have to come with me."

Leaning against Becca and trying not to fall apart, Sara looked at Jeremy. "What? Why?"

"It's not far. Shane will be there any minute. He thinks—"

Sara's phone rang again. *Shane.* She picked up right away, walking with Jeremy even as she was confused about what they were doing.

"Sweetness, I need your help." His voice rushed and deadly serious, Shane explained the plan. It boiled down to her as bait. "If there were any other way—"

"I'm glad to help, Shane. If there's something I can do, I want to. I trust you to keep me safe. I'm with Jeremy. We're going right now," she said. The line disconnected.

Outside the gym, she dashed down the steps right on Jeremy's heels. They crossed the lot to a dark green Jeep Wrangler. Soon they were racing through the run-down industrial neighborhood surrounding Hard Ink, but only went about eight blocks when Jeremy parked on the edge of the street along a mostly-fenced-in dirt lot belonging to some sort of supply company, by the battered sign on the fence. Train tracks ran through one section of the fence and into the yard. A row of mostly boarded row houses ran down the opposite side of the street. "What is this place?" she asked.

"A place for this asshole who harassed you to die. Nothing more, nothing less," Jeremy said, reaching across the seat and squeezing her hand.

The rumble of motorcycles sounded out from nearby. Sara twisted in her seat and saw the first of the bikes come into view behind Shane's big truck.

Sara climbed out of the Jeep and ran around the hood just in time to jump into Shane's arms. They held each other for mere moments, when Shane put her down. "Gimme a second," he said, then he turned to the Ravens. "Everyone out of sight. Half of you this way, half of you that," he said, pointing down the street. "You all are the net in case the spider somehow crawls through us. No matter what, he does not leave the radius you establish."

Agreements rang out over the sound of the motors, then all twelve bikes disappeared. Soon thereafter, the sound of their engine noises faded away, too.

"Head out, Jeremy. We got it from here," Shane said. "And thanks." Clearly unhappy to leave, Jeremy nodded, drove down to the next intersection, and turned out of sight.

"Say whatever you have to say to draw him out," Shane said. "It's going to feel like you're alone, Sara. But you won't be. You're totally surrounded. The three of us have sniper training. We'll take him out the moment we have a clear shot, you just stay back from him, so you're not in the cross fire."

"Okay," she said, shaking from the cool of the night and the adrenaline barreling through her body.

Shane kissed her, then retreated to the truck. "This will be over quick, I promise. He doesn't know what he's walking into."

As Shane drove away, a blast of panicky loneliness shot through Sara, but she shoved it away. She *wasn't* alone. She knew it. And this could literally be the only way to get Jenna back. It was worth the risk. Because if Sara knew there was something she could've done to save Jenna but hadn't, nothing else in life would ever make up for the failure.

In the distance, a pair of headlights slowly got bigger. Sara knew it was Bruno. *This . . . this* was the moment Sara had promised her father about. That she would take care of Jenna, no matter what. And she was doing it.

The thought stiffened Sara's resolve and had her taking a few tentative steps away from the fence so Bruno would see her. But then she froze in place, feeling a lot like bullets might very well come whizzing by her head. She hugged herself as Bruno's SUV came to a stop about thirty feet away.

As she made eye-to-eye contact with him through the windshield, Sara's heart tripped into a hard sprint that she felt in her skin and her ears and her throat. She stood there, waiting, not sure what she was supposed to do.

Finally, Bruno flashed his lights and waved her toward him.

Sara took a few steps in his direction, hearing Shane's

voice in her head telling her to keep still. Did Bruno suspect something? Why didn't he just come get her? And what about his end of the bargain to free Jenna?

Two more steps, and Sara froze and shook her head. "I want Jenna first," she yelled.

Bruno frowned and yelled something inside the truck, but she couldn't begin to make out any of it. She put her hand to her ear and shrugged to say she couldn't understand.

Glancing around, Bruno drove closer, then rolled down his window about six inches and leaned his head toward the opening. She couldn't understand the words that left his mouth because just then the side of his head exploded in a spray of blood. Sara was still trying to process that when Bruno slumped forward, then suddenly the truck revved and lurched toward her.

Was he still alive? Had he not died after all? Sara bolted to the right and darted into the open section of the fence where the railroad tracks cut into the yard.

A crash sounded out right behind her, the chain links unleashing a metallic rattle as the truck continued to rev and push into the fence.

Out of nowhere, Shane, Marz, and Easy closed in. Without a word, Shane pushed her behind a stack of railroad ties, then joined the others approaching the truck. Shane and Easy at the ready with their guns, Marz put his hand on the doorknob, then counted to three on his fingers and wrenched it open.

Easy and Shane braced as Bruno slid—as if in slow motion—and fell sideways out of the seat but then hung by his foot as if it were caught. A sickening crunch of bone rent the air, and for a moment, the engine revved louder. The guys jumped back from the truck as it fishtailed in the wet dirt. And then Bruno's body fell free of the Suburban's cab entirely, and the engine calmed to an idle.

Shane reached for the back door, and Sara took off from her hiding place, needing to know, needing to see with her own eyes. Had Bruno been lying all along? Did he not have Jenna with him? Had he sold or killed her after all? A sob tore from her chest, and it felt like she was running through quicksand.

Leaning into the backseat, Shane paused, then turned as if bearing a weight in his arms. Easy appeared right beside him. "Give her to me," he said. "Take care of your girl."

"Jenna! Jenna!" Sara cried, almost tripping into Easy and her sister. She stroked Jenna's face, tears blurring her vision. Unconscious. Bruised. Bloody. And those were just the things she could see. But she was alive, and they were together, and Shane had done exactly what he'd promised.

Jenna's eyes fluttered, and she groaned.

"Let me take her to the truck, Sara, okay?" Easy asked, staring at Jenna's face. "Let's get her home."

"She's alive, Sara. Just passed out. But she's alive," came Shane's raspy voice from behind her.

Sara whirled and threw herself into Shane's arms. "Thank you. Thank you. Oh, my God, thank you. You saved both our lives tonight," she cried.

"No, sweetness," he said, in a strangled tone as he held her more tightly in his arms. "I saved all three of us tonight." The thunder of the motorcycles closed in again. "Come on, let's go," Shane said against her ear. He had a quick conversation with one of the Ravens, who offered to deal with the scene there so the men could get Jenna and Sara to safety. Shane thanked them and guided her to his truck.

"Get in," Marz called from the driver's seat, the engine already started.

Shane opened the back door for her and she climbed

into the middle. Easy held Jenna on his lap like a gentle giant. Sara ran her gaze over Jenna, so damn relieved to see her again, and smiled at Easy as Shane climbed in beside her. He pulled her in tight against his side.

The truck took off into the night. Away from Bruno, away from the crisis, away from the threat of pain and death.

Emotion lodged a knot in Sara's throat, and she tilted her face to Shane's. "I love you so much." A thought came to mind as if someone else had put it there, but Sara knew the truth of it to her very soul. Looking into Shane's eyes, she said, "Molly would've been so proud of you tonight. I know I am."

Shane's breathing hitched, and he blinked toward the roof. He shook his head and met her gaze again. "I can't lose you, Sara. Not after all this. Bruno's dead. Confessions is gone. Nick's team intercepted a huge cache of guns *and* the money that was supposed to buy them from Bruno, which is probably why he lost it. He knew it was over for him. So we crippled Church tonight." Taking her face in his hand, Shane leaned in. "So please don't run. Say you'll stay with me. Say you'll give us a chance. I love you, and things are different now. You don't have to be afraid."

Sara could barely process everything Shane was saying, especially because it was all so mind-bogglingly good. Confessions was . . . gone? Just like Bruno—*that* she'd seen with her own eyes. She shook the thoughts and questions away. There would be time to take apart everything that had happened tonight and look at it piece by piece.

She looked at Jenna, needing to see again that her sister was *really* there beside her. And she was. Of course she was.

Shane had *proven* he could keep her and Jenna safe.

A calmness settled over Sara that she couldn't remember feeling once in the past four years.

Looking back at the man she loved, the man who had saved her in every way she could be saved, she knew.

What couldn't wait a single second more was making her intentions clear to Shane. "I don't want to run. I don't want to hide. I don't want to act, not anymore. I just want to be with you. Wherever you are, Shane, that's where I belong," Sara said.

The truck came to a pause, but Sara barely noticed because Shane smiled and pulled her in for a searing kiss. And though Sara knew everything wasn't settled—not in her life and certainly not in Shane's—she was okay with that because they were in it together.

His eyes blazed in the light of a streetlamp as he looked deep into hers. "That's the best news I've ever heard, darlin'." The truck moved again, the sound of gravel crunching under the tires. "We'll figure everything out. I promise. For now," he said, glancing out the window at Hard Ink, "welcome home."

Acknowledgments

Sometimes a book takes you by surprise, takes you places you didn't expect to go, and forces you into uncomfortable emotional spaces that are rewarding to endure. Shane and Sara's story was like that for me. But I never could've given these characters everything they deserved without the help of a whole lot of people.

First and foremost, I have to thank my good friend, fellow author, and crit partner extraordinaire, Christi Barth, who once again went *way* above and beyond for me and the whole Hard Ink team. Her enthusiastic comments, biting criticism, good-natured ribbing for my sleep-deprived typos, and constant support strengthened this book in more ways than I can count. You deserve more than a T-shirt, Christi! You deserve a medal! Or a spa day!

Best friend and fellow author Lea Nolan also deserves a huge word of thanks. At crucial moments, she helped me plot out the book on a series of Panera paper napkins, now preserved for eternity in the bottom of my laptop case, and talked me down from stress-induced ledges. It's a privilege to get to write with your best friend every day, and I'm so glad that's you, Lea.

So many others stepped in along the way to offer guidance and encouragement, including: Stephanie Dray, my writing partner of awesome; Jennifer L. Armentrout, with whom I can lose a whole morning on the phone and not realize time has passed; crit group friends Joya Fields, Marta Bliese, and Laura Welling, who always cheered me on and offered comments on the early chapters of the manuscript; good friend Carolyn Locke, whose help at a few crucial moments was exactly what I needed; and, finally, my Heroes, the awesomest readers *evah*!

Of course, none of this would be possible without the support of and excellent editorial partnership with Amanda Bergeron, whose belief in me and the Hard Ink team is the stuff of which authors dream! Nor would this have been possible without the incredible support and sacrifice of my husband Brian and daughters Cara and Julia, who let me disappear into the world of Hard Ink with nothing but love and faith that I could do it.

Finally, I offer thanks to the readers, who welcome characters into their hearts and minds and let them tell their stories over and over again! You guys rock!

LK

**Can't get enough of Laura Kaye
and the men of Hard Ink?
Good news, there is so much more to come!**

Summer 2014
HARD TO HOLD ON TO
A Hard Ink Novella

Edward "Easy" Cantrell knows better than most the pain of not being able to save those he loves—which is why he is not going to let Jenna Dean out of his sight. He may have just met her, but Jenna's the first person to make him feel alive since that devastating day in the desert more than a year ago.

Jenna has never met anyone like Easy. She can't describe how he makes her feel—and not just because he saved her life. No, the stirrings inside her stretch *far* beyond gratitude.

As the pair is thrust together and chaos reigns around them, they both know one thing: the things in life most worth having are the hardest to hold on to.

Fall 2014

HARD TO COME BY

Hard Ink Book 3

Derek DiMarzio would do anything for the members of his disgraced Special Forces team—sacrifice his body, help a former teammate with a covert operation to restore their honor, and even go behind enemy lines. He just never expected to want the beautiful woman he found there.

When a sexy stranger asks questions about her brother, Emilie Garza is torn between loyalty to the brother she once idolized and fear of the war-changed man he's become. Derek's easy smile and quiet strength tempt Emilie to open up, igniting the desire between them and leading Derek to crave a woman he shouldn't trust.

As the team's investigation reveals how powerful their enemies are, Derek and Emilie must prove where their loyalties lie before hearts are broken and lives are lost. Because love is too hard to come by to let slip away . . .

*G*ive in to your Impulses!

These unforgettable stories only take a second to buy and give you hours of reading pleasure!

Go to *www.AvonImpulse.com* and see what we have to offer.

Available wherever e-books are sold.

AVONIMPULSE

At Avon Books, we know your passion for romance—once you finish one of our novels, you find yourself wanting more.

May we tempt you with ...

- **Excerpts** from our upcoming releases.

- Entertaining **extras**, including authors' personal photo albums and book lists.

- Behind-the-scenes **scoop** on your favorite characters and series.

- **Sweepstakes** for the chance to win free books, romantic getaways, and other fun prizes.

- Writing **tips** from our authors and editors.

- **Blog** with our authors and find out why they love to write romance.

- **Exclusive content** that's not contained within the pages of our novels.

Join us at
www.avonbooks.com